# CHILD OF A RAINLESS YEAR

TOR BOOKS BY
JANE LINDSKOLD

The Buried Pyramid
Child of a Rainless Year

Through Wolf's Eyes
Wolf's Head, Wolf's Heart
The Dragon of Despair
Wolf Captured

# CHILD OF A RAINLESS YEAR

## JANE LINDSKOLD

A TOM DOHERTY ASSOCIATES BOOK    TOR®    NEW YORK

To Jim—You put color back in my life.

CHILD OF A RAINLESS YEAR

Copyright © 2005 by Jane Lindskold

This book is printed on acid-free paper.

Edited by Teresa Nielsen Hayden

Book design by Heather Saunders

A Tor Book
Published by Tom Doherty Associates, LLC
175 Fifth Avenue
New York, NY 10010

www.tor.com

Tor® is a registered trademark of Tom Doherty Associates, LLC.

Library of Congress Cataloging-in-Publication Data

Lindskold, Jane M.
    Child of a rainless year / Jane Lindskold.—1st ed.
      p. cm.
    "A Tom Doherty Associates book."
    ISBN 0-765-30937-8 (hc)
    EAN 978-0765-30937-2 (hc)
    ISBN 0-765-31513-0 (pbk)
    EAN 978-0765-31513-7 (pbk)
    1. Inheritance and succession—Fiction. 2. Mothers and daughters—Fiction. 3. Missing persons—Fiction. 4. Home ownership—Fiction. 5. New Mexico—Fiction. 6. Adoptees—Fiction. I. Title.

PS3562.I51248C47 2005
813'.54—dc22

2004065941

First Edition: May 2005

Printed in the United States of America

0  9  8  7  6  5  4  3  2  1

# ACKNOWLEDGMENTS

Although it's almost proverbial that writers work alone, there are always those who contribute to the evolving work, sometimes without even knowing they're doing so. *Child of a Rainless Year* benefited greatly from my generous friends.

Paul Dellinger shared with me his memories of reporting and living then and now. Lupé Martinez was of great help in acquiring a couple of obscure texts and in confirming some Spanish phrases. Jeff Boyer very kindly let me use the true story of the cow. Gail Gerstner-Miller generously trusted me with books from her collection of rare works about ghosts. In her professional role as librarian, Gail also helped me hunt up a couple of elusive facts.

When I started telling her about the history of Las Vegas, New Mexico, Bobbi Wolf was the first person to mention liminal space. When my editor, Teresa Nielsen Hayden, made almost the same comment in response to the same stimulus, I decided this was something I'd better investigate. Thanks, too, to Teresa for trusting me, though I gave her the slimmest of propoals. She was also right about which paragraph came first.

In Las Vegas, New Mexico, I met with universal warmth and interest, even from people who didn't know I was researching a book. The tour of the Montezuma Castle was made all the more wonderful by our charming crew of international guides. To those of you who are considering visiting Las Vegas, I say, "Do it!"

My husband, Jim Moore, drove with me to Las Vegas, took pictures for my reference, and listened to me as I exclaimed with delight over seeing things featured in a book he hadn't yet read. He encouraged me to sit and draw (though I have no talent), didn't laugh when I developed a fanatical attraction to anything brightly colored, and, when the book was finally written, served as my first reader.

Yvonne Coats served as a second reader and made several valuable comments.

By the way, if you want to learn more about my writing or to contact me, try my Web site: www.janelindskold.com.

# AUTHOR'S NOTE

Las Vegas, New Mexico, is a real town. Most of the places mentioned in this book, including the Montezuma Castle, are also real. You can go visit them, though I should probably note that as of this writing, tours of the Castle are only available one day a month. If you arrive on any other day, you will be politely turned away, as this is a working college campus.

Most of the historical events recounted in this book are also real. Las Vegas did have dual governments for a long time. The Castle did keep burning down and getting rebuilt. You can read more about these events in the various books I cite in my chapter headings. All of these are real books.

Phineas House, however, does not exist—at least not in this Las Vegas, New Mexico, at this time.

1

Just what colors our attitude toward color? Too much and we risk not being taken seriously; too little and we fear being dull.

—Patricia Lynne Duffy,
*Blue Cats and Chartreuse Kittens*

## COLORING INSIDE THE LINES

Color is the great magic.

I learned that one day as I watched my mother preparing for the most recent of her lovers. She, intent on the mirror over her elegant, gilded vanity, did not see me as I watched her from a mirror set in the border of a picture frame, two reverses making the image right again.

I was some years older than I had been in that rainless year when I had been born—five, maybe six years old. Mother had been very angry with me earlier that day. Then she had forgotten me, as she often did when she was so intensely displeased that even the "my" of her wrath could not ease her pain. Easier to forget.

So, forgotten, I went where I was usually forbidden to go, into Mother's private suite, sneaking in while she was in her bath, hiding in the corner near a full-length framed picture of her, painted to commemorate some past triumph. I turned my back on the room, viewing the chamber only through the mirror set into the picture's frame.

I hid well, for, although now, from the distance of these many years, I can see that I wanted to be found, to have her make me real again even if through the fierce force of her anger, I also feared that anger. Better to be tentatively real in hope, to breathe in the mingled scents of her room, of the perfumes she wore, of the lavender in which the bed linens were packed, of the cedar that lined her closets and clothes chests.

When Mother emerged from the bath she wore a scarlet Japanese kimono trimmed in gold, embroidered with patterns of tigers and phoenixes. Her glossy hair was wrapped in a towel that was a precisely matching shade of scarlet.

Her first task upon entering the room was to bend at the waist and rub the excess water from her shining black hair. She slowly combed the tangles from her hair, never tugging lest one of the long, dark tresses break.

Combed, that dark curtain hung past her waist, and because I knew she was proud of that shining dark fall, I felt proud of it as well. I watched with my breath held as she pulled her hair back and inserted it into a silver clasp, never breaking a single strand.

Hair combed and clipped, Mother seated herself at her vanity and viewed herself in the mirror. She dropped her robe from her shoulders and sat naked to the waist, the breasts that had never nursed me almost as firm and round as those of a girl.

She leaned forward, her gaze intent on her face, on the skin still slightly dewed from her bath. Her gaze was intent, studying those high-cheekboned features critically, looking for any lines, any trace of the sagging that comes with age. There were some, for she was past the first bloom of youth and this dry climate is not kind, even to those who live sheltered from the burning sun.

Yet, although this was a critical review, I could sense Mother's pleasure in what she saw. It was *her* face, after all, and like so many who look at themselves too often in mirrors, she thought that this reverse image, seen rigidly straight on as we are so rarely seen by others, was her truest self.

I was the one who was shocked. This was the first time that I can remember seeing my mother with her features unadorned by cosmetics. This was a different face entirely from the one I knew. Her brows were as pale as my own, her skin—if possible—more sallow. Even her eyes, usually deep blue whereas mine were hazed blue-grey, were not the eyes I knew, their color pale and less vibrant.

I shrank back into my hiding place, watching in the least corner of the mirror as my mother worked the transforming magic of color upon her face; watched as tints from fat, round pots gave her sallow skin smoothness and warmth, watched as her skillful fingers defined some features, diminished others.

Eyebrows were sketched in, dark as the fall of her hair, their tilt mocking and ironic. Tiny brushes pulled from slender vials made her eyelashes longer, painted in subtle lines that made her gaze more compelling. Powders dusted color onto eyelids and along the rise of cheekbones.

I watched, mesmerized, as Mother transformed herself from a pale ghost into the beauty who still commanded legions of admirers. Fear throbbed tight and hard within my chest. No longer did I want to be discovered, for I knew I had stumbled on a mystery greater and more terrible than that of Bluebeard's murdered wives. I had seen the secret magic of color, and how color made lies truth and truth lies.

Even at that young age, I knew I could not be forgiven my discovery.

My mother said there was no rain the year she carried me, the year I was born. Of course, that is impossible. Even here where the climate is dry there is always some rain.

But perhaps what she believed is not so impossible. Overall, my mother was not a simple soul, yet in one crucial way she was. Beneath her intelligence and an education that was far beyond what most women of her day received, Mother was a horribly egotistical woman to whom nothing was real unless it happened directly to her.

So, perhaps, in a way, my mother spoke the simple truth and there was no rain in the year I was born. Perhaps none fell near her, the scattered clouds that are what this desert land knows best shying from the heat of her self-conceit as they shy from the thermal updrafts that well from the baked black lava outcroppings.

She was not a cold woman, my mother. Not in the least. Indeed, the welter of her egotism made her very hot. She felt any slight passionately—any slight to herself, that is. Slights to another, even to those she claimed to love, she seemed indifferent to, yet she was not indifferent, for to be indifferent you must notice.

Mother noticed only rarely, and then in such a personal fashion that the one so noticed would cringe, wishing to have that egotism turned elsewhere, anywhere else, rather than suffer the wails mourning the wrong done to "my"—"my child," "my efforts," "my pain," "my sacrifice," "my . . ." Truly, for her, nothing existed outside of that curtaining veil of self.

To some men, Mother was irresistible. If they thought at all why this was so, they would speak of her charm, her gaiety, her beauty, her intense pleasure in life. If they were honest, and considered beyond this easy answer, they admitted to themselves that they desired to be the one who would succeed in getting beyond that tremendous ego—but of course no man ever succeeded, not even my father, who got beneath so much else.

Other types of men—those who were themselves egotistical, those gifted with that empathy so rare in men, those who had some purpose so great that it carried them outside of themselves—all of these kept from Mother as the rain did during that year she carried me, the year that I was born.

In time, even my father kept from her so that by the day of my birth ours was a household of women: silent women and a host of mirrors. Mirrors hung in picture frames and in stands. They rested within long-handled holders on the tops of polished dressers. They awaited the unwary in unlikely places: hung on the backs of doors usually kept open, beneath the accumulated heap of scarves and hats on the coat-tree by the door, in the kitchen over the stove, even as tiny rounds set into the fabric of elaborate skirts and shawls.

I knew myself through those mirrors as most children know themselves through the stories others tell them. No one in that strange household of silent women was going to waste word or breath on me—child of a passing fancy, child of a rainless year.

I saw myself in those many mirrors: round eyes the color of a heat-hazed sky, fair skin blushed with ash, thick straight hair pale as winter sunlight. I had none of my mother's beauty, none of her vibrancy. For a long time, the only thing that connected me to her was the "my" that prefaced her every mention of me, for I had no name to Mother that did not relate to her. I was "my daughter," "my darling," "my treasure." Later, when I grew older and gave her reason to be displeased, I was "my nuisance," "my burden," "my trial."

When she was truly displeased with me, Mother denied me even that connecting "my." Then I felt stripped of identity, bereft of an increasingly tenuous hold on reality. Sometimes I found myself wondering when Mother would discard me as I had seen so many other treasures—gowns, jewels, lovers—discarded when they failed to please her.

So little respect for myself did I have that this prospect did not trouble me in the least. That I would eventually be discarded seemed right, for in that house we were all her satellites and she the center of gravity about which we revolved.

Mother insisted I be educated. She was very proud of her own education, which was, as I believe I have mentioned, far better than that of most women in that time and place. She intended that I be almost, if not quite, as brilliant as she was herself.

Initially, Mother set herself to be my teacher, but this proved, as even I could have warned her, to be a catastrophic venture. For one thing, I was intractably left-handed, and though Mother tried to break me of this "clumsiness," she failed. I was a lefty, then and forever after.

The failure to learn from Mother's teaching was assigned to me, never to her. Even I accepted this verdict as true, never questioning that Mother's erratic methods might not be suited for a young girl hardly able to see over the edge of the polished mahogany desk where we sat facing each other for some hours each morning.

Next, Mother assigned one of the silent women to be my teacher. This attempt, too, was a failure, for Mother frequently hovered in the vicinity of our makeshift schoolroom. She stayed just out of sight around the corners of doorways, her image relayed flickering and fragmented in the mirrors, so both I and my hapless tutor knew she was there.

By this time I had learned that the silent women did indeed speak— sometimes volubly—but never when Mother could hear them, nor when they knew I was near. Presumably they, like my mother, assumed I was nothing more than an extension of her will. I could have told them they were wrong, but at this time I had no idea that anyone would care to know.

Among themselves, the silent women spoke a language I didn't know, but that sounded familiar. When they did speak in my presence, they spoke English, but without any trace of an accent, certainly without the accent of northern New Mexico.

Intimidated into more usual muteness by my mother's nearness yet forced by duty to speak, the silent woman, my tutor, tried to teach in whispers and by pointing to the pictures on pages. Her voice made no more sound than two leaves brushing together, thus each letter of the alphabet came to my ears as the creak of the floorboards where my mother paced, as the rustle of her skirts.

With this distraction, I learned little of the relationship between the letters of the alphabet and the sounds they represented. I did learn something of their shape and how to draw them with elegant accuracy in the blue-lined copybook.

After the failure of the silent woman came a string of private tutors, each a bright bead on the string of my memory. None lasted more than a few weeks before Mother's impossibly high expectations drove them off. One, a grey-haired woman with a carriage so stiff and upright that I imagined her spine to be made of a metal rod, like those in the dress stand on which Mother aired some of her finer gowns, lasted for nearly a month. She was the first not to begin my lessons by trying to make me write with my right hand. For that alone I would have loved her.

The grey-haired woman raised her voice to Mother before taking her final leave, the shrill harshness of her anger carrying even through the solid wooden door that separated the library from my mother's parlor. There I waited, watching myself in the mirror that backed the parlor door, knowing myself disgraced once again. I could not make out a single word, but this was the first time I heard anybody raise their voice to Mother and so this tutor's departure made a great impression on me.

I saw this former tutor once or twice after that, striding past on the sidewalk outside our house. She looked up at the front parlor window once. I thought she might even have seen me there, cuddled into the window seat, hidden from view to those inside the room by the thick fall of velvet curtain. She gave no nod, no acknowledgment, and that omission hurt me until I realized that the glazed glass turned back the light. If she had seen anything she had seen her own reflection.

The thin grey woman was my last tutor. After that, Mother was forced to send me out to school. She did not choose the public school that served to educate the heterogeneous mass of the town's children, but an elect seminary run by a woman who, so rumor said, was an unfrocked nun.

Our Lady's Seminary for Young Ladies was not a typical school, nor were the students typical students. Even so, it was here that I received my first inkling that my home life might be—to put it mildly—unusual. Here, too, I was first introduced to the ways that I might claim the magic of color for myself.

Before going to the seminary, I had never been given any colored drawing materials—not even those cheap crayons that come five to a box and are sold for pennies. The closest I had come was the dull blue ink found in ball-point pens. As this is the color of nothing in nature, it was not very inspiring. Many years later, I would find there was a reason for this omission, but when as a girl of seven I began at the seminary I had not the faintest idea.

Although the seminary aspired to grandeur, the relative isolation of our town's location kept the staff smaller than one might have expected of such an institution, for the headmistress would only hire those who fit her stringent criteria. Then, too, the headmistress may have preferred having this excuse for a smaller staff, since more of the tuition remained in her own pockets.

For whatever reason, drawing and painting were taught by the same woman who taught us poetry and literature, a delicate woman who reminded me of apple blossoms and the tiny, fragile flowers that grow apparently from nothing after the rains.

This teacher's name was Emily Little. She was a widow with a very young daughter, almost a baby. While her mother gave us our lesson, the baby stayed down in the kitchen with the stereotypically fat and comfortable cook. Sometimes there would be a tapping at the classroom door and Mrs. Little would excuse herself and tell us to mind ourselves for a moment, then go hurrying down the corridor, leaving the classroom door open to assure we would behave. We would hear her footsteps tapping down the polished wood of the hallways and know that some mysterious crisis had transformed our teacher—at least temporarily—into a mother.

By the time my mother enrolled me at the seminary, I was already too old for finger paints—if anything so messy would ever have been permitted in this austere and select establishment. Even so, we were young enough that Mrs. Little did not move us to strict fine arts all at once. She had the natural wisdom of one who knows children are not little adults. She knew that if we were to love art, we must associate it with play—even as those children who are read rhyming verse long after they should have "outgrown" baby books grow to love music and poetry.

Therefore, Mrs. Little did not start us with watercolors or even those bright, garish poster paints so beloved of the classroom. She wanted us to get a feel for drawing without the worry that our medium would soak our paper, yet she wanted us to have something that would allow us to explore our potential. What she gave us was a pad of paper and a box of crayons.

These were not the fat crayons usually given to children in those days, thick, waxy, and yielding very little in the way of color unless one pressed so hard that drawing anything other than bold lines was impossible. What Mrs. Little gave us were the slim crayons about the diameter of a standard yellow pencil, solid but requiring a more delicate touch if one was to use them without snapping them.

As I mentioned before, I had never seen anything that drew in color, and I think I would have been fascinated by a box containing nothing but those most basic colors found in every color box: red, yellow, blue, green, and black. However, wonderful as these might have been to me, they would have been boring to most of my classmates. Mrs. Little knew this, and so for art class each of us was issued a box containing not five, not twelve, not twenty, but twenty-four slim waxy sticks, each wrapped in paper of a shade approximating the crayon's own color when the crayon had been rubbed with moderate pressure across a sheet of white paper.

The other girls in the class cooed with delight when Mrs. Little handed the boxes to one of that week's classroom monitors, then gave a stack of pristine drawing pads to the other.

"Put your names on the box of crayons," Mrs. Little said, "and on the drawing pads. You will be using the same ones all term, so handle them carefully."

We did this. I saw a few of the girls pull out crayons and use them to write their names on the notepad, but, uncertain how crayons worked, I printed with my ballpoint pen. My erratic stream of tutors had managed this much at least. I knew my letters and numbers, and could read and do basic figures as well as most of my classmates—even if I did not surpass my peers as Mother thought I should.

"Now, today," Mrs. Little continued, "I want you to draw me the story of your summer vacation."

A hand shot into the air. Hannah Rakes. A nice girl, but bossy, and full of questions.

"All of it, Teacher?"

"Pick something that you particularly liked."

Another hand. Mary Felicity—always called by both names, never by just one, though she wrote them as two distinct words.

"Teacher, my family went on two trips. Can I draw both of them?"

"You may. You may draw several pictures if you wish." Mrs. Little seemed to anticipate another question coming. "Keep it to, let's say, five in all."

All around me, girls were sliding open the tops of the little rectangular boxes. A row away, Hannah already had a crayon in hand and was making red lines on the first sheet of her drawing pad. I stared, fascinated. Then I heard the rustle of skirts and smelled the vanilla scent that always surrounded Mrs. Little.

"Mira, why aren't you drawing?" she asked, her voice soft and friendly.

I fumbled with the box, and something in the clumsiness with which I opened it told Mrs. Little of my unfamiliarity.

"Is this your first time playing with crayons?" she said.

There was no incredulity or criticism in her voice, so I answered with easy honesty.

"Yes," I admitted.

"They're great," Mrs. Little said, shaking one out and holding it almost like she would a pencil. She stroked a few diagonal lines on one corner of the paper.

Sky blue. I still remember each line. There were three of them, each no more than three inches long. Each a wonder and a revelation.

Mrs. Little took out a green crayon, then made a few vertical lines at the bottom of the page. Already I could see sky and grass, and my fingers were itching to try for myself. Mrs. Little understood my eagerness and slid the green crayon back into the box.

"Have fun," she said, and patted me lightly on the shoulder, before moving down the aisle to talk to the girl who sat behind me.

I heard Mrs. Little say something approving, ask a question, heard the answer, but the sounds seemed very far away, drifting and dreamy, like sounds heard when one is falling asleep—only I was not falling asleep. I felt quivering and alive, desperately and inordinately happy.

Almost as if possessed of their own volition, my fingers slid out the green crayon. I noticed the slightly blunt edge on one side of the tip and immediately understood that the crayons would wear down, lose their sharpness, just as a pencil did. Carefully, as I might have tested my bathwater before getting into the tub, I drew a green line on the page, right next to Mrs. Little's.

It was so faint I could hardly see it. I tried another. Too heavy. For what must have been twenty minutes, I drew blade after blade of grass until I had command of how much pressure it took to make the lines I wanted.

Then I discovered that there were other green crayons in the box, both darker and lighter. I mixed these shades in, thinking of the grass I had seen up close when I had laid on my stomach out in the shadowed shelter of our walled back garden, remembering how it was rarely all one color.

I moved on to the sky. Hatch marks had seemed right for the grass, but didn't for the sky. Glancing around, I saw that Hannah was rubbing her crayon energetically back and forth. I tentatively tried this, experimenting until I had a blue sky creeping down the page to touch the grass.

Blue sky, green grass. Not much of a picture, but it was my very first. Also, given the flat prairie that bordered one edge of our town, it was not terribly unrealistic.

I turned the page and looked at the fresh white sheet with interest and enthusiasm. What would I draw next? The red crayons had been crying out to me ever since I saw Hannah draw what (as I saw when I snooped) proved to be a very boxy house. I didn't want to draw a house, but I thought that I might try a rose bush. We had lots of them in the back garden, and I liked them immensely—even the gently curving thorns were interesting.

My fingers were touching the red crayon when Mrs. Little clapped her hands together in the sign to stop.

"Art period is ending," she said. "Please put away your crayons, close your drawing pads, and pass them forward to the monitors."

There were a few groans of disappointment, and one of them may well have been mine. However, I felt far too happy to really make a fuss. Something had come alive in me that past hour, something that remained alive even when I folded shut my drawing pad and closed the almost untouched box of crayons. I held that happiness to me, and carried it with me as we trooped off to find what the cook had concocted for our midday meal.

My name was on both my drawing pad and the box of crayons, sufficient promise that we would be doing this again.

Our lessons at the seminary focused on basic skills: learning to write a neat hand, adding and subtracting, singing, art, reading, and spelling. None of these touched on the world outside of our classroom.

Sometimes, as when I stared fascinated at a picture of a dog chasing a ball, I revealed myself—as I had on the day I first saw crayons—as having lived in relative isolation. I think Mrs. Little noticed, but I don't think the other children did. I was already enough a stranger—a new girl among the old girls—that I did not stand out as strange for my manner.

I was not the only new girl, but I was among the quietest. The buzzing little horde of girls tried to draw me out with varying degrees of success. Hannah, in her friendly, bossy way was my chief interrogator. Through her questions and through what she did and didn't find odd about my answers, she also became my chief source of information about the world outside of the one I had known.

Hannah liked to ask questions, but even more than listening to my answers she liked to talk. Listening to her chatter about her home, her cat, her dog, her brothers and sisters fascinated me. I had only the vaguest idea of what she was talking about—my mother kept no pets, and I had no siblings. At first, I thought Hannah must live a very exotic life. Then, as I listened to the other girls, I realized the truth.

My life was the strange one, not theirs.

For one, all of the other girls, even those whose parents were divorced, separated, or—in one very interesting case—dead, knew who their fathers were. I was the only one who had no idea who my father was. When Hannah asked me about him, I said he had been gone for as long as I could remember. Hannah decided this meant that he was dead, and being a nice girl also decided that I wouldn't want to talk about such a sad thing. She told the other girls her version of the truth, and so I was saved from questions.

At least from other's questions. From the questions that were now suddenly alive in my imagination I had no relief—and I knew better than to ask anything of my mother.

One of the many things I liked about the seminary was the lack of mirrors. Except for the rectangles over the lavatory sinks, there were none. Even the window glass was clear, its light glaze giving back very little in the way of reflection.

On the whole, I did not mind my lessons, but they did come most to life when color was involved. Even writing on the blackboard was more fun when the chalk was yellow rather than white. When I discovered that chalk came in pink and blue and green as well—these pastel shades as ethereal as I imagined fairy wings to be—I lived and breathed in hope that Mrs. Little would let me write in color.

She was not slow to see that this was a painless way to motivate and reward me. Before long I learned to write a neat hand and behaved myself to perfection in order to win the privilege of writing announcements on the board.

Another privilege was going to fetch something from the supply closet. There I saw pens and colored pencils stacked on the higher shelves. There were bottles of powdered pigment for paint, and stacks of construction paper. After that, I daydreamed about colored inks, and anticipated the day that we, like the bigger girls, would use paints. Already, I guessed how wet tints would blend and flow as crayons, for all their beauty, would not.

But for all that my school days were alive and livened with color, I never mentioned my art classes at home. I had never forgotten seeing my mother give herself a face. A sense that anything to do with color was forbidden knowledge stilled my tongue.

I suspect that for once Mother's obsession with "my" and "me" aided me in my deception regarding colored art materials. She found it so difficult to perceive me as anything other than an extension of herself that she forgot to forbid my exposure to these things until it was far too late.

Her inability to comprehend my life apart from her was so complete that once out of sight I was truly and completely out of mind.

Or, maybe, something else was working in my favor, and I am being unfair to my mother. The only thing I can say is that honestly I am still too close to the matter—even now that decades have passed—to honestly judge.

2

So they come, these childhood memories. They are frag-
mentary and disconnected, life's loose beads with no
straight string running through them.
—Marian Russell,
*Land of Enchantment: Memoirs of Marian Russell*
*Along the Santa Fe Trail*

## INSIDE THE LINES

My mother's name was Colette, but I don't think I ever believed it was her
real name. Its French sound was completely out-of-place in our little
southwestern town, where the names that weren't Spanish were a sort of
American generic.

I thought "Colette" was some self-given name, adopted by my mother—
as she had the style of her face and the shade of her hair—in adulthood.
Later, I saw Mother's birth certificate and learned that Nicolette, for which
Colette is a nickname, was her real name—as real as anything related to
my mother ever was.

But I get ahead of myself . . .

My mother named me "Mira," which all my life people have assumed is
short for "Miranda" or "Mirabel." Until I learned to read and write I always
thought my name was the same word as "mirror." The equation made sense
to me, and even after I learned that "Mira" was a perfectly good Latin word

meaning "wonderful"—really a very nice name for a mother to give her daughter—I persisted in thinking of myself as one among the many mirrors that adorned my mother's house.

Depending where you go in the small town where I spent my first nine years, Spanish is either the primary or secondary language. Overhearing conversations in that language gave my name another dimension: a form of the verb "mirar," meaning "to look at." This only reinforced my peculiar sense of myself as a living mirror.

My mother disappeared the April when I was nine. Will you think me hard and cold if I say that I didn't notice?

Mother often went away for several days at a time, usually when she had a new lover. She remembered to tell me only if she happened to see me while she was making her preparations. When she was gone, the silent women would put my meals on the table and lay out my school uniform for the next day or a dress for weekends. As they usually did these things, I wasn't aware of any great change.

So it was this time. Indeed, I don't think I would have paid Mother's absence any mind at all if Mrs. Little hadn't asked me to wait one day after class.

"Mira," she said, "your preregistration fee for next school year is due this week."

I looked at her, not certain why she was telling me this. I vaguely knew that Our Lady's Seminary was not free like the public schools were, but that was all. Whatever her other sins as a parent, my mother had never made me feel as if any aspect of my care was something that could be reduced to a question of money.

When I said nothing, Mrs. Little went on very, very kindly, "Notices were sent home by regular mail, as were reminder notices. We have heard nothing from your mother, and she usually pays your fees very promptly. The principal thought your mother might have given the check to you, and that perhaps you forgot to hand it in."

I shook my head, then, feeling this was rude answered in a very soft voice, "No, Mrs. Little. Mother hasn't given me anything."

Mrs. Little didn't ask to check my schoolbag the way Mrs. Johnson who had the classroom across the hall would have done.

"I see. Could you take a note to your mother for me? She may have forgotten."

Mrs. Little held out a cream-colored envelope embossed with the school's crest. I put out my hand to take it, then hesitated.

"I can't, Mrs. Little."

"Can't?" Mrs. Little looked rather surprised at my refusal.

I hastened to explain. "Mother isn't home. She went away and hasn't come back."

"When is she due back?"

"I don't know."

Mrs. Little frowned. I knew she would never leave her baby without telling the little girl—a toddler now—when she would be back, even if she was only going to be away for a few hours. However, Mrs. Little said nothing regarding what she felt about my mother's conduct.

"I see," was all she said. "Give this to whomever is looking after you. Someone *is* looking after you, I assume?"

"Yes, ma'am. Several ladies."

"Very well. Give this to one of the ladies and ask her to send a reply with you tomorrow."

"Thank you, Mrs. Little. I will, Mrs. Little." But though I tried to respond with confidence, I had my doubts as to what any of the silent women could do.

My doubts were well merited. That night the woman who had tried to be my tutor came to me when I was finishing my handwriting lessons. She glanced down at the pages full of elegantly curled M's and Q's and smiled the slightest of smiles. Then she held out an envelope very like the one Mrs. Little had given me, only the paper was purest white and the monogram was an elaborate design I knew belonged to my mother.

"Mira," my former tutor said, her voice like the beating of a butterfly's wings. "This is for Mrs. Little. Please give it to her."

I accepted the envelope and tucked it into my schoolbag. When I looked up, I saw my former tutor was biting her lower lip.

"I hope I have done the right thing," she said, the butterfly wings beating faster. "Forgive me, child, if I have not."

She left my room before I could subdue my astonishment enough to ask questions. Later, I saw that note, written in a hand as neat as my own, though the letters were thinner, and the ink so faint that it seemed like the silent woman's own whispery voice.

Dear Mrs. Little,

Greetings. You have written to Mrs. Colette Bogatyr, requesting her reply regarding whether Mira is to remain enrolled at Our Lady's Seminary for Young Ladies. I believe this is what her mother would wish; however, Mira's mother left a month ago and has not returned. We do not know if or when she will return, and although I am empowered to draw money for Mira's welfare, I thought you should know the truth.

The signature was written in a scrawly sort of handwriting that I couldn't read, but I didn't even try—not then. The fact of my mother's disappearance was too much for me to handle.

I was told later that I fainted.

What I remember best about the weeks that followed is the veneer of normalcy that overlaid the transformation of everything I had known.

I continued going to school, and if the girls whispered a bit more when they thought I wouldn't notice, they also made up for their curiosity by treating me with the peculiar delicacy with which they handled the fine china teacups we used at our twice weekly afternoon socials. Mrs. Little was particularly kind, and I don't think it was my imagination that art periods went on just a bit longer than was usual or that they occurred more frequently.

The authorities were now investigating my mother's disappearance. Although they asked me many questions, they didn't expect much in the way of answers from a girl of nine. The silent women did not have it nearly so easy. They were questioned, in groups and apart, and it seemed to me that they looked more fragile every time I encountered them. This fragility was probably their best defense, for no one could believe that these pathetic creatures could have had anything to do with the disappearance of someone as dynamic as my mother.

Eventually, the frequency of the visits by the investigating officers dropped to nil. A short time thereafter the school year ended. That was when I learned that although the investigating officers had failed to find out very much at all regarding my mother's disappearance, they had made some discoveries.

The most important of these—both from my point of view and from the point of view of those who felt that if they couldn't find my mother at least they must make sure I was not left at loose ends—was that Mother had taken action to assure my care if something were to happen to her. A guardian had been appointed—a group of guardians actually. These trustees had found me foster parents, a married couple with no children of their own.

These foster parents were to have complete custody of me, and were to minister to my well-being throughout my minority. I was told a great deal having to do with what would happen to me after I was a legal adult. I understood nothing of it. All I understood was that after having lived my entire life in this one town, practically all of it within the walls of this one house, I was being taken away to a distant place called Idaho.

I didn't protest. One thing life with my mother had taught me was that protest was futile. Therefore, on a day in early June, my belongings and I were packed into a big taxi and driven to the train station. None of the silent women came to see me off, but Mrs. Little did, and Hannah and the Rakes family, and several other people from the school. In fact, there was a fair crowd. My mother's disappearance had been the centerpiece of the town's news for weeks by this point, and my leaving was the last chapter of a dramatic mystery.

I have vague memories of flashbulbs going off, but what I remember most of all was Mrs. Little pressing the strap of a small canvas bag into my hand.

"A going-away gift," she said, and kissed me on the forehead. Then the train was making noises and a deep-voiced man was shouting "All aboard!" with theatrical self-importance, and I was being bundled along narrow corridors and into a window seat.

Then the train shook like some gigantic animal waking out of a drowse, and began to move. I stared out the soot-smudged window and waved at the people waving at me. Sooner than I could have imagined, my birthplace and all I had ever known had vanished from sight.

My foster parents could not come and collect me themselves, but the trustees had made certain I had first-class accommodations all the way to Idaho, and the conductors were friendly and kind.

I still have the sketches I made that trip, clumsy drawings that yet manage to capture the personalities of this changing array of watchful adults. Mrs. Little's gift, of course, had been a bag stuffed with art supplies. There were pencils—and a short knife for sharpening them. There were two pads of paper, fat erasers, and a new box of crayons. Other kind people had given me books and magazines. There was a new doll, a present from the girls in my class. I sat her beside me whenever there was a vacant seat.

Having been solitary most of my life, I wasn't in the least bit lonely, but even if I had been I think the wonder of that train trip would have chased the loneliness away. There, just on the other side of the window, was a world I had only dreamed existed. I couldn't get enough of looking out, feeling confident and safe because everything was framed like in a picture book, interesting, but at arm's length.

Sometimes I tried to capture what I was seeing in my sketchbook, but mostly I stared and stared. The conductors learned I was happy this way, and so rarely bothered me, pleased, I think, to find their charge so easily contented.

One jovial fellow, fat, with a wart on his nose, did ask me "Haven't you ever seen a cow before?" and my quiet "Not this one" made him frown and back away. He recovered quickly enough and made a joke of it that lasted until I switched trains and left him behind. I didn't mind his teasing because it was genuinely good-natured, but the exchange stayed with me for another reason. I think that was the first time I realized I saw things a little differently than did almost everyone else. Where most people saw things as versions of the similar, I saw each thing as unique—belonging to a class, certainly, but still its own thing.

Little enough, you say, but capable of making worlds.

My life with my new foster parents brought home to me, even more than my two years at Our Lady's Seminary had done, how different from normal my life had been.

Before I get into that, though, I should probably say a little about these two people who were effectively my parents from the day I was handed down from the train by the last in a string of pleasant, attentive conductors.

For most of the time I knew them, they went by the names Stanley and Maybelle Fenn, and since that's how I think of them those are the names I'm going to use here. They were in their early thirties when I met them. If I try, I can still see them as they were at the moment I first saw them, standing with their hands clasped, their gazes vague in the way of people who are looking for someone they're not sure they'll recognize.

Stanley Fenn was of about average height and build, wore glasses, and had slightly prominent front teeth. These might have made him look like a rabbit or a beaver if it hadn't been for an aura of steady strength that made the very idea of laughter at his expense impossible. His hair was brown, parted on the side, but slightly combed back. The calmly appraising eyes behind his glasses were dark grey. He wore a muted plaid jacket in earth tones, a white shirt, and dark trousers. His solid tie was a shade of brown that matched a thread in his jacket.

Maybelle was almost as tall as her husband, but plumper. She was just pretty enough to escape being plain, but clearly she'd never been a beauty. Her dark brown eyes were warm, her bosom full and (as I was to learn when she sat me on her lap) very soft. Her medium-length brown hair had golden highlights, and its slight wave was, I would learn later, natural, though she'd shape it on curlers for special occasions. She'd dressed for this trip to the station in a red outfit with navy blue trim, the top double-breasted, the skirt with wide pleats. Her shoes had low heels that my mother would have sniffed at and called "sensible."

I liked both the Fenns right away, so much so that I suddenly felt very, very shy, absolutely certain that they couldn't possibly see me as anything but a burden. I dropped a curtsey as I'd been taught at the seminary, but Maybelle was too warm for that. With a spontaneity that I had never before seen in an adult, she bent and gave me a hug.

"Welcome, Mira! Welcome to Idaho."

Stanley Fenn had gone off and collected my luggage. Now with a grin and a toss of his head he led the way to the family car. It was one of those big, cavernous cars that were so common then. Judging from the shine of its royal blue paint, it was its owner's pride and joy. My bags were put in the trunk, but I was offered a seat up front between the Fenns.

As soon as we were out of the station parking area, Stanley said, "We could take you back to the house right away, but we thought you might like a chance to visit first. Are you interested in having some ice cream?"

The funny thing was, before this trip I probably would have said "No, thank you," very quietly, but I'd learned a little about adults during that long train ride. I'd especially learned to hear when an adult very much needed to give a treat. So I said, "Yes, thank you," and we went off, not just to a lunch counter that served ice cream, but to a full-fledged ice cream parlor, a place that looked like a sweet itself, with pink-and-white-striped wallpaper and Tiffany shades on all the hanging lamps.

Once we were seated, and careful consideration had been addressed to the incredible assortment of flavors and combinations on the menu, Maybelle Fenn gave me a serious look.

"Now, first things first, Mira. We need to settle what you are to call us. We're not your parents, and we don't expect you to call us Dad and Mom—or even Mother and Father. That just wouldn't be right."

I felt immensely relieved to hear this. I had never before met two people who deserved more to be called "Mom and Dad" but with my mother only missing . . . I sat up straight as a thought hit me. I'd always assumed my father was either dead or had walked out on my mother of his own free will. Could it be that he was missing, too? Could Mother be out there somewhere, looking for him?

That last idea seemed ridiculous. Mother had certainly never seemed to miss him, but for a moment my father seemed a little bit more real.

"We were thinking," Stanley said, taking over from Maybelle, "that maybe you could call us Aunt and Uncle."

"Uncle Stanley," I said, testing the words, "and Aunt Maybelle?"

"That would do it," he replied, satisfied.

And it did, but before the year was over he was Uncle Stan and she was Aunt May. The names fit better, and we were all quite pleased: them because it showed them I was getting comfortable with them, me because these new names made them a little more my own.

In all the time I knew them, the Fenns only did one strange thing. Soon after I came to live with them, they sold their house, packed up everything, and moved us to Ohio. This is when they changed their name to "Fenn." Before it had been Flinwick. At this time, my surname was also changed to "Fenn," and whenever anyone asked about my origins, they were told that I was the child of cousins of Uncle Stan. He had a way of saying this that made further questions unlikely, and before long no one asked.

Later, when I thought about it, I realized that the Fenns had been planning this change since before my arrival. They had introduced themselves to me as Maybelle and Stanley, but the few people we had contact with before the move called them "Martha" and "Steven."

Once we moved, however, the Fenns did nothing at all strange. Uncle Stan went to work for an architect for whom he drew blueprints. He also kept—or so I gathered from dinnertime conversations—the architect's more fanciful designs from falling down or coming to pieces.

Aunt May's job was the house and taking care of me. Mine was going to school. I went to a perfectly ordinary school here, rather than the exclusive seminary. This wasn't because the Fenns didn't want to spend the tuition. The public schools in our middle-class neighborhood were where just about everyone went. They offered a good, solid grounding in the basic subjects, with extracurricular offerings in art or music or sports for those who showed the inclination or interest.

Needless to say, I was interested in whatever art classes I could get, but I was getting another education, especially during the first few years following my move to Ohio, an education that almost drowned out my perennial fascination with color. I was learning how the society outside of my mother's house lived, and I was completely fascinated.

For one thing, there was the entire electronic media. When making one of my rare visits to friends' houses, I had listened to radio and seen television, but this exposure had been in passing. Mostly my schoolmate's mothers were eager to chase us outside to play.

Now I lived in a house with several radios. The Fenns encouraged me to tune the one in the family room to programs I liked. There was also a television, but my interest in that was limited. I enjoyed the variety shows, and have many happy memories of evenings spent with the Fenns watching some singing or dancing troupe on the small screen. However, the dramas and adventure stories that fueled the imaginations of so many of my classmates didn't grab my attention. I simply couldn't believe that the black-and-white pictures, everything defined in shades of grey, were real.

Movies were another matter. Those that were in color fascinated me to the point that Uncle Stan laughed and said that I acted like I was drunk after seeing one. Black-and-white films, even those my schoolmates assured me were wonderful, bored me, sometimes even put me to sleep.

But there was so much more . . . Cheap toys from the drugstore. Comic books—I loved those! Ice cream sundaes. Coloring books. I was a kid growing up in a town where the post–World War II security of the fifties hadn't yet been touched by the unrest of the later sixties. My new family was neither rich nor poor, but comfortably middle class. Even when I was denied something, even when I whined and fussed, I knew deep down inside that the Fenns were making the right decisions.

Sometimes, though, especially in the matter of clothing, I longed for something other than the practical playsuits and jumpers Aunt May bought for me. I positively hated stretch pants, and actually preferred skirts to the trouser sets my playmates delighted in.

Back at home in New Mexico, other than my school uniform, my clothing in my mother's house had been styled after the fashions of another time. My skirts had been nearly floor-length, the cuts modified versions of what a grown woman would wear. Everything—even my underwear—had been handmade, tailored to every shift of my growing body by one of the silent women. The fabrics had been expensive and soft. In comparison, the clothing Aunt May and I selected from the Sears catalog or bought at one of the local shops seemed stiff and unforgiving.

I longed for a bit of lace at my collars or for frocks made of velvet, and Aunt May gave in—for special occasions.

"You can't wear party dresses everyday," she said, "especially not the way you're always messing about with paints and crayons—not to mention pastels!"

I didn't push, especially since I knew Aunt May was right. When I got absorbed in whatever I was drawing or painting, I *did* make a mess. Even so, a little rebellious voice inside of me would think, "Mother wore dresses like that everyday—and nicer, too. Her lace never itched. Her velvet didn't go all flat and squashy where she sat. I bet her shoes didn't pinch either."

When things like this made me think about it, I knew my earlier life—so increasingly dreamlike now—had not been at all usual. Life within the walls of my mother's house had been more like growing up in a foreign land—even more than growing up in a small New Mexico town would have been for a girl now solidly ensconced in a small town in Ohio.

As I grew older and learned more, I began to think my mother's clothing had possessed an early Victorian feel: full skirts, scooped necklines, capes and cloaks rather than coats, elaborate hats or even more elaborate hairdressing. Yet, Mother hadn't been wearing old gowns dug out from some musty trunk. Her clothing had been new, the seamstress dummies in the sewing rooms always occupied with some new creation or some older one being refreshed.

It was a puzzle, but as time passed and I became more and more comfortable with my life with the Fenns, my inadvertent comparisons of my life now to what had been and what was faded away until my life before was nothing but a colorful dream. Moreover, I was growing up. Like most girls of that date and time, I had no desire to be thought different by my peers. The strangeness of my early life was something to be put aside in favor of finding my way in the present.

The Fenns were good to me, but they were hardly the unreal, perfect parents presented by television. Uncle Stan could have one too many drinks of an evening, especially when his architect boss had been particularly trying. Then he would become sullen, like a brooding thunderstorm. I learned to go off to my room when he was in one of those moods—not because I was afraid of him, but because I could tell the last thing he needed then was a noisy girl.

Aunt May lavished a great deal of attention on both me and Uncle Stan. Her house was always in perfect order. As I grew older I sensed Aunt May was searching for something. She never said what it was she felt she lacked, but I noticed that she collected churches and religious groups the way some of my classmates' mothers collected recipes.

Officially Aunt May remained a solid, churchgoing Methodist, but the bookshelves in her workroom contained an orderly assortment of myths, legends, anthropological works, religious texts, and self-help books. I am absolutely certain that if Aunt May had been younger when the Flower Child movement began she would have been one of those earnest young people who practiced transcendental meditation and ate only natural foods.

Indeed, one of the few times Aunt May and Uncle Stan had an argument in my hearing was over her attempts to introduce vegetarian meals into our weekly routine. Stanley Fenn was a solidly meat-and-potatoes sort of man, the kind who would eat vegetables reluctantly—mostly because he knew his growing foster daughter needed to eat them and he had to be an example. Aunt May gave up her attempt to adapt the family diet, though I am absolutely sure that when she was alone, as she was so often once I became more and more busy with school, she reverted to what Uncle Stan would have called her "rabbit diet."

But none of this touched me, except to give me a sense of balance. If Uncle Stan could be unhappy but get up and go to work anyhow, then I could do the same. If Aunt May was sometimes restless, well, then, that was a normal part of being human. In any case, I had more than enough to keep me busy.

Somewhere between grammar school and high school, I accepted that my fascination for color, line, shading, and all the rest meant that I really was what I had heard my teachers say practically since my first school term in Ohio. I was "artistic."

I liked knowing that. It gave an explanation to the fascination I had for color, a reason for my preferring to spend my allowance on paints or crayons or colored pencils, rather than whatever toy was the fad of the moment. It put a word to what I was, gave my greatest oddity a place in the usual order—oddly enough, making the abnormal normal.

I wasn't the most social of children, but I wasn't the shyest either. My grades were solidly average, peaking and dropping as my interests did. I joined a few clubs, and when my talent for drawing and painting became generally known, I found myself drafted to help design sets for school plays, or banners and posters for upcoming events.

I was a junior in high school when my art teacher asked a handful of us to contribute a piece to be sent to a countrywide show. I knew she wanted me to give her an oil painting I'd done earlier that year, a complex piece called Homecoming.

Homecoming showed an older woman in all her finery, viewing her reflection in what is obviously a mirror in a high-school public rest room. She is at least forty, but in her reflection she is still the seventeen-year-old prom queen she had been in her days of glory.

I was loading the painting into the family sedan when I balked, almost as if I'd slammed up against a solid wall. I carried Homecoming back inside and returned it to its hook on the wall of the room I proudly called my "studio." Then I took a just-completed collage from my workbench, wrapped it carefully in an old blanket, and loaded it instead.

The collage was a pretty piece, almost a mosaic, worked from fake gemstones glued down in an abstract pattern that nevertheless somehow evoked a rosebush in the fading lushness of late summer bloom. I named it "Last Blush," as I drove over to the school. My teacher was initially disappointed, but she had sense enough not to push—and Last Blush was nothing to be ashamed of. It was painterly in its complexity, recalling Monet or Seurat.

To my great joy, Last Blush won first place in its class, the only piece from our school to do so. It went on to the judged competition for the statewide show and won there, too. So the Fenns and I went from our little town all the way to Columbus so I could accept my prize.

I was terrifically, almost irrationally, excited. It wasn't like I had never gone anywhere before. Thanks to the Fenns, I was actually very well-travelled for a girl of my age and class. Uncle Stan's architect had developed a national, then an international, reputation. Our family vacations had capitalized on this, allowing Uncle Stan to mix business and pleasure. Last year we'd gone to France for a month, then hopped over the channel for two deliriously wonderful weeks in England.

No, what had me so excited was that this trip was *my* trip. The Fenns were my guests, courtesy of my victory. Since some artistic organization had sponsored my prize, we were staying in a really nice hotel, and even had an expense account for meals and travel. Reviewing all the forms and signing my name on various documents was heady stuff for a sixteen-year-old.

The Fenns were excited, too, but I sensed a tension in each of them that I couldn't explain. None of my ever-so-polite questions yielded anything but vague replies, so finally, with the egotism of my age, I decided that they were uncomfortable with this first sign of my coming adulthood, that their pride in me was tinged with regret at the awareness that soon they would lose me. It must be a phase that all parents went through.

We arrived the night before the award ceremony. The next morning, the Fenns suggested that we go to the exhibit early, so we would have a chance to view the other pieces before dressing for the ceremony. I agreed with enthusiasm.

The show was huge. All the pieces that had been runners-up in all the categories, from all the counties of the state of Ohio, were displayed in areas separated by temporary partitions. The blue ribbon winners were displayed prominently within their section, each given a panel of its own.

The exhibition hall wasn't as full as it would get later, but we weren't the only ones who had come to take advantage of the preview. I strolled in feeling like a princess. It only took overhearing an acid-voiced matron who was viewing the oil paintings say to her companion: "I don't see why this one took the ribbon. The one over there is *much* better," to make me very shy about my own accomplishment. Clearly winning and being accorded universal acclaim were not the same thing at all. My egotism went down another peg when I realized there was a Best of Show, and I wasn't it. That honor had gone to a very fine pastel of two girls in a field of corn and poppies.

I couldn't help but wonder whether *Homecoming* would have caught the judge's fancy. Would it have been too fanciful or would they have been taken by the implied story?

Even with my sense of my own self-importance restored to more reasonable levels, I enjoyed looking around. There was a freshness and immediacy to these works that I had never experienced in a museum display. It was as if I could sense the effort that had gone into each piece. Sometimes, I would find myself mesmerized by a picture or sculpture, drawn in not so much by what was there, but by what I sensed had been intended. It was frightening, a little like being on the edge of getting drunk.

Although I felt shy about doing so, I eventually drifted over to where my own piece hung. The collages were off to one edge of the cavernous display area. The category was not entirely to the liking of some of the purists, who said collages and mosaics were more craft than art. These formalists had been outvoted by those who said that Ohio must catch up with trends in modern art.

I was studying each of the competing works, trying hard not to stare at the wonderful sight of *Last Blush* hanging in solitary glory, but for the blue rosette hanging beside it, when I noticed the man studying my piece. His expression was assessing, without any antagonism: purely, thoughtfully critical. There was something else there, too, and I found myself falling back on a half-remembered trick to get a better look at his face.

One of the other collages had made heavy use of fragments of mirror. I moved over to it, shifting my gaze until I found a piece that neatly reflected the stranger. He was tall and lean, brown hair combed neatly over from a left-side part. His clothing was a version of the sports jacket and shirt most of the men in the room were wearing. He also wore a tie, loosely knotted beneath a prominent Adam's apple.

From the critical intensity with which the stranger viewed my work, I guessed he was an art teacher, rather than a parent or family friend of one of the participating artists. I knew my own art teacher would be coming to the award ceremony and showing tonight, partially to share in my glory, partially because she loved art, just a little to see what other art teachers were achieving with their own students.

Then I remembered that I'd seen the man once before, and the memory both soothed and accentuated my own unease. I'd seen him last year at our annual winter pageant. In addition to the usual carols and such, the senior class did a one-act play written by a talented member of their number. It was based on the rather frightening fairy tale, "The Snow Queen," rewritten slightly to give Gerda's journey a more Christmasy feel.

Although a senior was technically in charge, this was the first production where I'd really influenced set design. I'd done a lot of the rough sketches, made the drawings that others had later helped paint. I still remember the joy I felt, how the colors seemed to sing to me, how the glitter we'd liberally applied along the faux roof beams jingled like sleigh bells.

After the close of the final performance, I'd seen this very man standing on the stage, studying the set we'd used for the Snow Queen's palace. I hadn't thought anything of it at the time, but now, seeing him studying *Last Blush*, his posture mirroring what I'd seen then, I wondered. I also felt irrationally afraid. It was like he wasn't so much studying the art as assessing the artist—assessing me.

Swiftly, my heart beating hard, I slipped from the display area and found Aunt May and Uncle Stan. They were chatting with some people Uncle Stan knew through work. Their son had been a runner-up in the pencil drawing category with a marvelously detailed sketch of a barn at harvest time. I liked it at least as much as I did the drawing of a chubby toddler playing with a kitten that had won, though I could understand why the judges had made their choice. It's harder to do subjects that hint at motion than those that don't.

From time to time, I glanced around but I didn't see the man again. Gradually, my heart rate slowed, the irrational sense of panic subsided. That night, walking up on the stage to receive my prize and my share of the polite applause, I thought I glimpsed him standing at the back, but I could have been wrong. I didn't see him again, but I never forgot him.

3

The Tao that can be told is not the eternal Tao.
—Lao Tzu,
*Tao Te Ching*

## INSIDE THE LINES

I finished high school without incident. Then, with the Fenns' blessing, I
enrolled in a prestigious art school in New York City. It took me away from
home, and introduced me to city life. Uncle Stan was doing very well by
then, so he and Aunt May made frequent visits. Sometimes she came on
her own, and the two of us would go exploring together.

Years of disappointments had not dimmed the intensity of whatever private search Aunt May was on. Although neither of us ever said anything
about it, it was tacitly understood that when she visited we would tour
churches and odd bookstores, ethnic neighborhoods, art galleries, and
other places that would be considered downright bohemian in the still-
provincial little town we all thought of as home.

Much of what today is commonly called "the sixties" actually happened
in the early seventies, and so we found a lot worth investigating. In between Aunt May's visits, I would make mental note of places I thought
would interest her, and often check them out in advance. Because of her, I

probably was exposed to a lot more of the counterculture than I would have been otherwise.

I remember when she was going through her Chinese phase. I came back to the apartment I shared with a fluctuating number of other art students to find Aunt May deep in discussion of Lao Tzu and the *Tao Te Ching*. They tried to draw me in, but I shook my head and laughed.

"Too deep for me," I said, and went to wash paint off my right eyebrow.

Despite what the media would have you believe, the majority of us—even the artists—didn't "drop out." We went about our lives much as before, hair a little longer, clothes a little wilder, but otherwise very much the people we had been all our lives before that point. The revolution existed mostly in the media—and in the trickle-down effect as we all came to believe what we were hearing.

Shortly before I finished art school, I passed my twenty-first birthday. I went home for the occasion, and we shared a huge meal that ended with the same sort of chocolate cake and vanilla ice cream that had been served at every birthday since I had come to stay with the Fenns over ten years earlier.

I had just filled everyone's coffee cups and was settling into a comfortable overfed torpor when Uncle Stan's words jolted me to full wakefulness.

"Mira, you're twenty-one now. The time has come for Aunt May and I to discuss with you the terms of your mother's estate."

His voice was very stiff and unwontedly formal, as if he'd been rehearsing how best to say this for weeks. For all I know, he had been. It had been years since any of us had talked about the circumstances that had led up to my coming to live with them. I suspect that the Fenns, like me, preferred the comfortable fiction that we were a family like any other—except that I called them "Aunt" and "Uncle" rather than "Mom" and "Dad."

Uncle Stan reached around behind him and opened one of the drawers of the big sideboard that stood there. He drew out a fat manila folder and set it down in front of him.

"Mira, this folder contains copies of the pertinent documents having to do with the years in which you have been in our custody, including an annual accounting of the money and personal property that—as of today—you will inherit."

I gasped. It may seem incredible, but I had never thought of myself as a potential heiress. I suppose this was because to me my mother was gone, not dead.

"At the time we learned of your mother's disappearance," Uncle Stan continued, "and that you would be coming to live with us, I consulted both a lawyer and an accountant. They helped me set up a trust fund that would cover your care while permitting the bulk of your inheritance to accrue."

He looked at my stunned expression, and answered the question he thought he saw there.

"I regret to say that you are not wealthy," he said, the faintest of rueful smiles touching his lips, "but I hope you will understand that I did not feel it was my place to gamble with your future. I chose safe investments, which, although not exciting, have largely paid every year."

He slid a neatly clipped stack of papers over to me, and I reviewed them, understanding enough to see that he had only told the truth. While I turned through the pages, each one taking me with biannual steps back across the years, Uncle Stan continued.

"This packet"—another stack of papers was slid over to me—"contains an annual summary of those times when money was drawn from your funds. I have the supporting documentation in my files upstairs, should you wish to review them. I would rather like if you would."

Obediently, I inspected the typewritten sheets. Each contained remarkably few entries, and it was several minutes before I realized how to ask the question that had been nagging at me from the moment Uncle Stan had referred to the circumstances of my coming to live with them.

"But, Uncle Stan," I said, hearing a note of protest in my voice, "I don't see anything here for your expenses. There are lawyer's fees, accountant's fees, and a few other things, but nothing for . . ." I hesitated, not knowing how to say it without sounding rude, "my care and feeding. Are you saying my mother just dumped me on you without giving you anything?"

Uncle Stan blinked, unable to find a reply. Aunt May put a hand across the table and touched my arm.

"Mira, dear, it wasn't quite like that. We could have drawn reasonable expenses from the estate. The trustees would have signed off on that. We chose not to do so. You weren't dumped on us. You came to us as the answer to a prayer."

"Prayer?"

Aunt May nodded. "Your mother left instructions for your care should anything happen to her. She named trustees for her estate, and directed them to arrange for your care. Apparently, she had no close relations."

For the first time, other than in dreams, I thought of the silent women, wondering who they had been, what had happened to them. Presumably the big house I vaguely remembered had been sold, and the proceeds from that were among the monies so carefully invested by the trustees.

Aunt May went on. "One of the trustees had become friends of friends of Stan and mine. Our friends knew how much we wanted children and mentioned it by chance to this trustee. Since there remained a question as to your mother's whereabouts, you could not be offered for adoption. The other trustees were prepared to send you to a boarding school. Our friend's friend convinced them to let us act as your guardians instead. The other trustees agreed, as long as we agreed to submit to periodic reviews."

"Reviews?"

She smiled. "Every spring. They kindly notified us in advance, but, especially those first few years, Stan and I were terribly nervous."

I was still shaken by how impersonally my mother had arranged for my care. Trustees! I had been told about them years before, but the word had meant nothing to me then. Hadn't my mother had friends to whom she could entrust her daughter? Perhaps she had not.

"Annual inspections and a half-grown girl," I said, knowing I sounded grumpy, but not able to help myself. "That hardly sounds like the answer to a prayer."

"We hadn't been able to have a child of our own," Aunt May said stubbornly. "Then you came and . . . Really, Mira, it was just like the answer to a prayer."

Her eyes were beading up with tears. Suddenly, kicking myself for my stupidity, I realized how much of that searching I had always sensed in Aunt May had begun with the emptiness of a childless woman who very much wanted children of her own. I was around the table and hugging her before I realized what I was doing. When we all got done being weepy, Uncle Stan resolutely insisted on continuing to present me the contents of the folder.

There was quite a bit, and I was so overwhelmed I hardly heard a word he said. What I did hear, although he never said it, was his plea for me to believe that he and Aunt May had not taken me in and acted as my parents for these past eleven years for money. Indeed, they hadn't taken a penny, not even when I was twelve and broke my wrist when I fell off my bicycle, or when I had braces on my teeth, or for tuition for art school. The only money that had been spent was that which was necessary to maintain the estate, nothing else.

I did hear what Uncle Stan said at the end.

"You can arrange matters to your own satisfaction now, but if you would prefer to have me continue to handle matters, I will do so. The only thing I ask is that you promise to sit down with me once a year and review things. You must take responsibility for your inheritance."

I nodded, my eyes flooding with tears for the second time that evening.

*Inheritance*, I thought, surprised at how sad and abandoned I felt. I *guess that means Mother is really and truly dead.*

✳

After my graduation from art school, I became an art teacher rather than taking the route that might have led to my becoming a professional artist.

When they heard I had accepted a job teaching art at a grammar school in a suburb of Toledo many of my teachers were disappointed. The critical comments came hard and fast—far more ferocious than any that had been applied to my drawing and painting.

"Mira, you have too much talent to be teaching art to little children . . ."

"I know a place that would be happy to have you. It's a technical art studio, true, but they have connections to galleries. . . . You could get paid for doing design while you work on breaking in."

"Don't throw yourself and your gift away. Is there a man? Someone you think will disapprove if you do something so unconventional? He isn't worth it. Marriage is overrated, take it from me."

"Do your parents disapprove? Do they want you to have a 'real' job? I'll speak with them if you'd like."

I turned down all of these kind offers, promised to consider all the good advice, deflected the worst of the critical comments with promises that I didn't plan on abandoning my art. What I didn't tell any of these well-meaning people was that over the last few years I had increasingly felt that, as much as I loved using them, I needed to keep my artistic gifts to myself. I was haunted by my memories of the man who had demonstrated such interest in my *Last Blush*. I knew I didn't want to attract any more like him.

Whoever he was. Whatever he was. I knew nothing about him, but the one thing I was sure of was that he had not been the more usual kind of talent scout. My recent discussion with Uncle Stan about my inheritance had reminded me all over again that my mother had vanished without a trace.

I was more sophisticated in the ways of the world than I had been when Mother had disappeared. Now I began to wonder more seriously what had happened to her. I wondered if she had gotten involved with organized crime or with smugglers. I had no real idea. All I knew was that I didn't want to attract the attention of the kind of people who could make someone vanish without a trace.

Did I hide then? I don't really know, but with hindsight (always 20/20, damn it), it seems like I must have done so. I took a wide variety of jobs involving art, but never again did I show my art in a public place—not even when one of the schools where I was teaching invited me to contribute to a national show.

I moved around, trying big city life, life in other states, finally settling in the town where I'd grown up. I told myself that this was because Aunt May and Uncle Stan needed me close. In reality, I think it was because that little town was the one place where everyone who mattered already knew me, and didn't try to push me out of my comfortable rut.

Did I know it was a rut? I think so, but that doesn't mean I felt useless or unhappy. I did a lot of good as a teacher, a lot more good than I ever would have done as an "artist." I mean, only the most popular artists ever touch more lives than a teacher does.

Maybe it was a dream, not a rut, a dream that this was what my life was and how it was always going to be. It wasn't a bad dream, not at all.

I kept right on dreaming, dreaming in living color, until a single phone call woke me up.

Aunt May and Uncle Stan died in a car crash when I was in my early fifties. I'd been wondering for a year or so if I should at least try to convince Uncle Stan to turn most of the driving over to Aunt May or to me, when I was available. I'd moved back into the area a few years before, and when I wasn't skating between teaching art at three different schools, I had time.

Uncle Stan was seventy-seven, after all, and didn't see as well as he once had. The lenses of the glasses that had framed his eyes for as long as I had known him had gotten progressively thicker, but he stubbornly refused to give up both driving and the freedom it represented.

I wondered if they might still be alive if I'd succeeded in convincing him, and said as much to the police officer who had discovered the wreck out on the shoulder of one of the country roads where Aunt May and Uncle Stan had always enjoyed going for the proverbial Sunday drive.

"I'm not sure, ma'am," he said politely. "All we know is something made the Fenn car swerve. It went off the road, hit a tree."

I felt no relief at this information.

"Drunk driver?" I asked.

"Maybe," the officer said, a defensive note in his voice. "We don't have enough to go on. The Fenns' car showed no sign of impact with another vehicle."

I left the matter there. Clearly he didn't want to pursue it, and what good would it do in any case? What mattered was that the two people who had been my parents for over forty years were gone, taken from me without warning. I tried to convince myself that in some way I was glad. After all, Aunt May and Uncle Stan had been spared the horrible deaths I had seen take so many of my friends' parents. There had been no lingering cancer, no senility, no progressive degeneration.

There might have been a moment of fear or shock, followed by a tremendous impact that their aging bodies could not take. Pain . . . The coroner assured me that death had probably been nearly instantaneous. They had even been spared the pain of being separated from each other. I knew Aunt May had wondered how she would cope without Uncle Stan. She had occasionally talked about it with me as women do, knowing the statistics favor them surviving their husbands. Uncle Stan had never said anything, but he must have feared it, too. He'd have feared leaving May alone, if not for himself.

It really had been a good death, as such things go, but I found little comfort in this. I sat in the living room of the comfortable ranch house into which we had moved when I was thirteen, alone once friends and neighbors had returned to their routine, wondering what I should do.

The accident had come just as the school year was ending. I had intended to take the summer off, travel a bit, do some stuff for my parents around their house. I had my own house on the other side of town, near enough, but far enough to give us all some privacy. Should I keep it or this place? Certainly a spinster didn't need two houses, especially in the same town.

I sat there, unaware that I'd leaned forward to rest my head in my hands until there was a knock at the front door. I came upright with a jerk that caught my neck. Massaging the sore spot I rose and went to the door.

I knew the woman who stood there: Betty Boswell. She and her husband, Alan, were good friends of Aunt May and Uncle Stan. They'd met at some fund-raiser for the church a few years after we'd moved to town. Their eldest son was close to my age, but the Boswells themselves were younger than Aunt May and Uncle Stan by a good six or seven years. They'd been at the reception at the church hall earlier that day, had been among those who had come back to the house after.

"Mrs. Boswell," I said, trying to keep an odd mixture of relief and dismay out of my voice, "did you forget something?"

Betty Boswell smiled. She and Alan were the popular choice to play Mr. and Mrs. Claus most years, but tonight her expression held nothing of its usual easy affability.

"No, but if you aren't too tired, I would very much like to speak with you. Privately," Betty added, lowering her voice. She was usually round and comfortingly amiable, but tonight she reminded me of a rabbit who has heard an owl. "I didn't think anyone had stayed, but . . ."

Frankly mystified, I stepped back to admit her.

"I think there's still some coffee," I said, "and enough sweets to make sure even if I do forget to eat I won't lose any weight."

I ran my hands over my waist and over my hips for emphasis. No one would cast me as Mrs. Claus, but I was far from svelte. Days spent teaching at as many as three separate schools, grabbing lunches and dinners from fast-food restaurants, had not been kind to my figure. I was sturdy rather than plump, and stronger than many women my age. I took comfort in that last—most of the time.

Today, dressed as I was, still in the black dress I had worn to the funeral, I felt myself for what I was: dumpy, middle-aged, plain, and now very, very alone. I had never realized how much that was positive in my own self-image had come from the loving pride I saw in the Fenns' eyes whenever they looked at me. Now that was gone, and I knew how all those fairy-tale princesses who found themselves transformed into unspeakable things must have felt.

I said nothing of this as I led Mrs. Boswell through the living room and into the comfort of the kitchen. Almost without speaking, we took chairs across from each other at the table. The coffee was still acceptably fresh, and neither of us had much appetite for anything, but I set out a tray of pecan cookies just the same.

Betty Boswell seemed to be using the motion of stirring her coffee to focus her thoughts. Now she set the spoon aside, and left the coffee untasted.

"You have already spoken to the executors of your parent's estate," she said.

I nodded. The same lawyer who had helped Uncle Stan set up my trust all those years ago was still alive, though mostly retired. He and the accountant had told me they would deal with the details—and I needn't worry about a bill.

"Liven up the next few weeks," the lawyer had assured me, and I heard in his voice the same note I had learned to recognize on that long-ago train trip. He needed to be kind to me to ease his own pain, and so I gratefully accepted.

"Good," Mrs. Boswell said. "They're good men. Reliable."

"Yes," I said, mystified. "They have already gone over the basics, and say they'll have something together for me next week."

Betty took a deep breath. "You might say that your parents appointed us executors of another sort. At least your Aunt May did—me."

She stopped, frowned at herself, and sighed.

"I'm doing this very badly," she admitted. "Let me start over."

I nodded, rather stunned. What was going on here?

"May and I were good friends," Betty said, "and one day we were talking about keeping diaries. Did you know she kept one?"

I frowned slightly. "I don't think I did. I knew she kept trip journals and such, is that what you mean?"

"No. May kept a diary in the more usual sense—a book in which she wrote down her thoughts and what was happening, and things like that."

"For how long?" I asked, rather astonished.

"I think for most of her life," Betty replied. "She said she'd lost track of how many little blank books she'd filled."

"And she kept them all?"

"All," Betty agreed. "She showed me where. There's a locked box at the back of one of the closets."

I thought I knew where this was going.

"And she wanted them destroyed unread," I said, thinking that's what I would have wanted.

"Actually," Betty said, reaching into her purse and coming out with a ring from which a single small key dangled, "she thought that might be your reaction. What May wanted was for me to make certain that you would read through those diaries—especially the ones since you came to live with her and Stan. I think she thought it might be a comfort to you."

Betty's tone as she said those last words made me think she was guessing at Aunt May's motivation, but I nodded.

"I guess I understand," I said, though what I felt was closer to confusion.

"Would you like me to show you where she kept them?"

I nodded.

Betty got up with a briskness that almost concealed her own discomfort. "They're upstairs."

She led the way to the small room that had once been my studio. After I had moved away, Aunt May had converted it into an all-purpose workroom. Betty opened the closet, bent, and lifted a box filled with fabric remnants.

"Hold this," she said, her voice muffled from the closet's confines. "It's down here."

I stood holding the box, letting my gaze rest on the assortment of color swatches within. Aunt May had taken up quilting about twenty years ago, and this box contained only a portion of her hoard. Idly, knowing I was distracting myself, I made a mental note to find out if her club wanted her supplies.

"Here!" Betty said, emerging, her neatly styled hair a little awry. She dangled a square, grey, fireproof document box from one hand. It was clearly heavy, and I moved to take it from her.

Betty made the trade with me, setting the fabric scraps back in the closet before turning to inspect the document box.

"This key will open it," Betty said, handing me the little key she'd pulled out downstairs. "There's another one about somewhere, but I had the impression May hid it so well that she didn't think you'd find it—or if you did, you would just think it was a lost key."

I nodded. I was doing that a lot this evening, but words seemed to have failed me.

"One more thing," Betty said briskly. "These are her older ones. She showed me where she kept her current one."

She left the room and I followed her, thinking as I did so that Aunt May apparently had not wanted Uncle Stan to know about these journals. Otherwise, once I was grown she could have given up hiding them. What secret was she protecting? Had she a lover? An illegitimate child? Some crime in her past?

Betty turned into the master bedroom, then moved to Aunt May's side of the bed. She hefted the mattress and slid her free hand underneath, bringing it out a moment later holding a slender, fabric-covered journal in an elegantly pretty russet and gold pattern of Japanese chrysanthemums.

"Here," Betty said, a faint note of triumph in her voice. "That's the current one. Now, do you promise me you'll take the time to go through them?"

Her tone had become very serious, and I ducked my head in a wordless promise.

"I will," I said. "Tell me, Betty, did Aunt May tell you anything about what was in them?"

Betty shook her head. "No, she didn't, and I didn't ask. We had a promise between us, the two of us. It came up when Lacey died a few years ago, all so suddenly. Apparently, she'd kept her love letters from before her marriage and her husband found them. Poor fellow took it hard, for some reason. May and I decided that it would have been better if some kind soul had known about them and slipped them away and, well . . ."

She shrugged. "I have a few letters and things. May had these journals. She wanted to make sure they came to you and that you would know without a doubt it was all right for you to read them."

I understood, feeling sad. Now Betty would need to find another confidante. I wondered who it would be. We walked downstairs then, talking too deliberately of other things. Betty promised to look into whether the quilting club would want the supplies, and who might benefit from a gift of clothing.

"Are you staying here tonight?" Betty asked as she was heading out the door.

"No. I'll go home. Too many ghosts here. I'll be back tomorrow though."

"Call me," Betty said. "Especially if you get lonely. Remember, the only ghosts here are memories, and with Stan and May, they'll be good memories."

I smiled weakly. "I know. That's what keeps undoing me."

I left a few minutes later, taking with me the box containing Aunt May's journals. I didn't want to read them just yet, but I felt responsible for them.

It wouldn't do to have her private thoughts sitting around out and available to any of the friends and neighbors I knew would be helping me over the next few days. What if the box was bundled off to some charity by accident? I shivered a little at the thought.

I met with the estate's executors a few days later. After they finished running over what had been done, what still needed to be done, and the like, Mr. Patterson, the lawyer, cleared his throat.

"There's only one thing left, Mira. We found out something rather surprising when we were going through Stan's papers. It seems that your trust from your mother contained one item he chose not to let you know about."

"What?"

I meant this as an expression of surprise, but Mr. Patterson took it as a request for information.

"It seems that your mother owned a house and some property in New Mexico. This came to you along with her other assets."

I blinked, remembering the tall, Victorian house on the tree-lined street.

"It must be a ruin, by now," I said, "if it wasn't sold for taxes long ago."

"Actually not," replied Mr. O'Neill, the accountant. "It seems that although Stan didn't want you to know about the house, he took care to make certain it remained your own. He established an escrow account that covered taxes and repairs. Then, for reasons that I cannot fathom, he chose not to note the existence of this account in the otherwise meticulous documentation of your trust. The annual review of your trust also never mentions this, making me believe that someone at that time must have agreed to this connivance."

Mr. Patterson nodded, "Agreed to it—maybe even suggested it."

"Whatever the reason," Mr. O'Neill said, "the house not only still exists, but remains yours. We have made several phone calls and ascertained that the property is in good condition. A photo was e-mailed to us at our request."

He pushed a glossy printout over to me, and I fumbled for it, not really seeing what was there for a long moment. Then I focused and saw a multi-storied Victorian standing behind a wrought-iron fence. It was painted pale grey with subdued rose-colored trim on the closed shutters.

"It should be white," I said, not aware I was speaking aloud until I did so. "And the shutters should also be white."

"You remember it then?" Mr. O'Neill asked, interested.

"I do," I said. I pointed to one of the windows on the ground floor. "That was the front parlor. The library was directly behind it. My room was on the second floor, around the back, where it overlooked the garden."

I had been sitting in the front parlor the day my last tutor had walked by without seeing me. I had often sat there to do my homework, preferring the comfort of the deep window seat to the formality of a desk.

"I still own it?" I asked, hardly believing it. "Is it still furnished?"

"As far as we can tell," Mr. Patterson said, shuffling papers uncomfortably, "it should be so. There is no record of a sale of the furnishings. Of course, a house vacant for so long . . ."

I nodded.

"Of course. Doubtless there has been some theft. Well, this is certainly interesting. Will the escrow account continue now that Uncle Stan is gone?"

Mr. O'Neill replied, "It should. After all, the estate has been wholly in your name for thirty years now. You will want to notify various parties that you will be administering it instead of Stanley Fenn, that's all."

I noticed that he did not volunteer to take over, nor did Mr. Patterson. I thought there was a reason beyond neither of them particularly wanting to come out of retirement. The appearance of the old house after all these years as part of an estate they had thought they understood had unsettled them both far more than they cared to admit.

Why had Uncle Stan never told me? Had he been kept from the subject by my reluctance to have anything to do with my mother's estate? Had he been afraid I'd run off and live in New Mexico? I didn't know and now I couldn't ask, but between Aunt May's journals with whatever secrets they contained, and this, I was feeling rather like I had never known either of the Fenns at all. It was not a good feeling on top of my grief and bereavement. I wanted to keep them green in memory, just as I had always known them, not to feel them transforming—and in that transformation growing more distant.

4

Almost any Spanish-American will take time to tell you how a resident of Ledoux, near Mora, turned into a frog overnight, that a Frenchman, loaded with gold, lost his way near the same and buried it there; or of the Spanish explorers trapped and starved to death on Starvation Peak just seventeen miles south of Las Vegas; and the miracles of the Hermit of El Porvenir.

—Milton W. Callon,
*Las Vegas, New Mexico . . . The Town That Wouldn't Gamble*

## INSIDE THE LINES

Aunt May and Uncle Stan had been popular members of our community, nor was I without a wealth of friends and acquaintances of my own. In a remarkably short time, I had my parents' personal items cleared from the house. Mr. Patterson and Mr. O'Neill had dealt with the estate—an easy enough task as Uncle Stan had not believed in carrying debt. The house was paid for long ago, and his retirement had been generous enough that they had not been forced to take a reverse mortgage. Had they lived long enough that nursing care or other medical necessity had entered the picture, doubtless it would have been otherwise.

As it was, a month after my parents' deaths, the bulk of the problems were resolved, and I found myself sitting in the kitchen with Betty

Boswell sharing a pitcher of lemonade and a plate of her excellent vanilla wafers.

"Have you decided what you're going to do with this place, Mira?" she asked.

"You mean sell it or not?" I said.

She nodded. "We have a nephew who is thinking of moving into the area, and, well . . ."

"I don't know," I replied honestly. "I have my own house, and it's closer to the schools where I work, but it's not like anything is exactly far in this town. This place is bigger, however, and in good condition—and it would be a wrench to sell it."

"Ah," Betty said. She didn't look at all disappointed, and I made a mental note to see if this nephew really materialized, or if this had just been a polite way to fish for information.

"Actually," I said, "I'm thinking about running away from all of this for a while."

"Oh?" Betty didn't look at all surprised. If anything, she looked pleased. I wondered if she had something she wanted to run away from.

"School's out for another couple of months," I went on, "and I'm not teaching in any of the summer programs. I'd planned on it, but Aunt May and Uncle Stan died right about when I'd have had to start. I just didn't have the energy."

Betty knew this. She'd actually been among those who had advised me to take time off, but she nodded as if this was the first she'd heard of it.

"I was thinking about a long trip," I said. "I don't have any pets right now. My two old guys died this spring, as you know, and I'd been planning on getting a couple kittens or a puppy this summer, when I'd have time to settle them in. Now, though . . ."

I stopped, swallowed hard, and dashed almost irritably at the tears running down my cheeks.

"Betty, I'm tired. Everything here is too full of memories and my life is too empty. I don't have anyone now—I mean, I have friends, lots of friends, good friends, but there isn't anyone I can't leave for a few months. Heck, with e-mail it won't even be like I'm gone. I want to get away. Then when everything doesn't hurt so much, then I can make some decisions."

"Where are you thinking of going?" Betty asked. "Back to Europe?"

I'd been on a Rhine cruise the summer before, me and Aunt May and Uncle Stan.

"No. Too soon. I want to go somewhere I haven't been for a long, long time. I'm thinking of going to New Mexico."

"New Mexico?" Betty tilted her head to one side in thoughtful surprise. "Didn't May tell me that was where you were born?"

"That's right. I haven't been back since I was nine. I was thinking about it the other night, and I realized that I haven't even been much west of the Mississippi. Uncle Stan took us to California a few times, and once to Oregon, but never the Southwest. It's a great place for an art teacher to go—I'm sure I'll come back full of new ideas and projects."

Betty wasn't fooled. "You've lost your parents and now you're looking for your roots, aren't you?"

"Maybe," I admitted. "You know I'm their adopted daughter, but did they ever tell you why I was available for adoption?"

"No, just that you were an answer to their prayers—a girl needing a home when they'd accepted they were unlikely to have children of their own."

I smiled at the familiar words, then sobered.

"My biological mother vanished when I was nine. I never knew who my father was. I still don't know whether either of them are alive. Maybe it's not so much that I'm looking for my roots—Aunt May and Uncle Stan gave me lots of good soil for settling those—I'm looking for an answer or two."

Betty's next words seemed like she was changing the subject.

"Have you read May's journals?"

"I looked at the most recent one," I hedged, "but I think I'll need to start at the beginning. She made some references to things she wrote earlier."

Actually, it was because I couldn't even look at that familiar handwriting without tearing up that I hadn't read further, but I couldn't make myself admit my weakness.

"Take them with you," Betty urged, and I saw she hadn't been changing the subject at all. "If you're looking for answers, maybe May had some of them, and didn't—or couldn't—tell you."

I frowned at her. "Did she tell you that?"

"Not precisely, but once she did say that Stan wanted to focus on the present with you—not on the past. She didn't precisely agree, but as you seemed so happy, she had decided to respect his wishes."

I thought about the house I hadn't known I owned, the escrow account, and slowly nodded. "Yes. I can see that. I'll take the journals with me, then."

"Good," Betty said. "Don't forget, even grandmothers have e-mail these days. Keep in touch."

I smiled at her. "I will."

I decided to drive to New Mexico. Freedom to go where I wished and move at my own pace was only part of the reason. I have a not-so-secret vice. I'm a scrounger.

It's actually not a bad trait for an art teacher these days, when budget cuts have reduced the budget for nonessential electives like art. (Though I do wonder that budget can be found for computers costing thousands of dollars, and in-classroom television monitors, but not for drawing pads and colored pencils.) As I've mentioned, I teach at three different schools, just a few days a week at each one. Even with the savings that gives the system, I'm continually pinched for supplies. We're encouraged to tell the students to bring in their own, but that only goes so far.

So I scrounge. Some of the stuff is fairly usual—milk jugs, cardboard, aluminum cans, newspaper, old magazines. Other is a bit stranger: parts from discarded toys, broken glass, odds and sods of lumber, old clothes. You can find interesting things at Goodwill or the Salvation Army, too. But practicality or potential recyclability isn't the unifying factor in what catches my eye—I Dumpster dive for color.

Plastic is about the best—scraps in brilliant, impossible hues, often twisted into very strange shapes. Fuchsia. Screaming green. Neon orange. Magenta. Fabric can be a good source of odd colors, too, as can the glossy paper used in advertisements.

The current trend in education is toward helping each student feel good about him or herself: validated, empowered, whatever. That means the sort of fussy requirements for perfection that my own art teacher could impose on her better students is not considered acceptable. My own students do a lot of collages, mosaics, papier-mâché figures. I'm also encouraged to assign projects that can serve more than one purpose. Posters or banners to illustrate various issues are always popular with the administration, as is work on stage sets or costumes.

My scrounging loot comes in handy for all of these. I knew I'd just about go crazy on a long trip where I had to leave goodies behind, so, ignoring the probable cost of gasoline, I had the garage give my two-year-old, fire-engine-red pickup truck a thorough going-over, loaded my bags into the back beneath the camper shell, and hit the road. Almost at the last minute, I added in the metal box containing Aunt May's journals.

I didn't look at the journals the first few nights, but somewhere in Kentucky, I discovered that the novel I'd picked up at a thrift shop had good reason for having been consigned to oblivion. It had one of those annoying plots that wouldn't work at all if the heroine weren't both optimistic and dumber than a box of rocks. I chucked it at the wall in annoyance, considered trying the crossword puzzle in the newspaper, then permitted myself to acknowledge the metal box.

Reluctantly, I heaved myself off the bed, my hand fishing in my pocket for the key I'd carried just about everywhere with me since Mrs. Boswell had given it to me. I slipped it in the lock, and for only the second time since I'd been given the box lifted the lid and looked inside.

Now, as before, I was struck not by how many journals there were, but how few. There were only twenty or so volumes, none terribly thick. Nor was Aunt May's handwriting so tiny that she crammed volumes onto each page. Surely if she had been keeping these journals her entire life, as Betty Boswell had seemed to think, then there would be more.

I'd already identified that the journals were stacked so that the first in the sequence was at the bottom of the left stack. Now I took it out. The cover was puffy, lightly quilted, and covered with a pale pink fabric. The years of storage away from light had preserved its attractive sheen. On the front cover the word "Diary" was printed in gold, in a loopy script. A tiny lock clasped the cover shut, but an equally tiny key attached to the cover with a bit of pink yarn opened it. The volume fell open as I pressed on the minute latch.

The entry was dated shortly before I had come to live with the Fenns. I stopped before reading, checked other volumes, but this was indeed the first. I frowned. Had Betty misunderstood? Or had Aunt May deliberately misled her? Or was there another box of journals somewhere? I thought I'd gone through every closet, box, and cabinet, even opening trunks in the attic that were so heavily coated in dust that it was clear they hadn't been opened for decades.

I continued frowning as I stared down at the slightly yellowed page, and the first words resolved my confusion—even as they added to it.

*"For the first time in my life, I have decided to keep a diary. So much is happening now, so much I need to remember as it happens, not confused by time's passage. This is where I will begin."*

I read and reread the words, as if I expected them to change. Then I accepted what I'd known from the start. Even if there had been a journal that started back when Aunt May was a girl, within a volume or two, I would have skipped to this very point—to the point where I entered the story of Aunt May's life. It was an egotistical admission, but true. In the privacy of that motel room with its generic layout and generic furnishings I felt safe admitting it.

Yes. I wanted to know about Aunt May, but even more I wanted—needed—to know about myself. Ever since my twenty-first birthday I had felt a niggling suspicion that Uncle Stan had been holding something back. Learning of my continued ownership of the house in New Mexico had confirmed that suspicion without giving me the least reason why he should have done so. These books might hold the answer.

Even so, I delayed a little more, making coffee in the tiny two-cup pot provided by the motel management, fishing out the bag of dark chocolates I'd bought at a grocery store earlier that day. Then, with a fragrant mug of steaming coffee set on the bedside table and the bag of chocolates near my right hand, I again opened the journal.

## COLORING OUTSIDE THE LINES

For the first time in my life, I have decided to keep a diary. So much is happening now, so much I need to remember as it happens, not confused by time's passage. This is where I will begin.

We are to have a child. Is that the right way to put it? Maybe I should have written this in pencil, but now it is too late. I shall try to be more clear.

We (Stan and I) are being given the opportunity to be foster parents to a little girl. Her name is Mira and she is nine years old. She has fair hair, and a slim, almost fragile figure. It seems that her mother has disappeared, and that no one knows anything at all about her father.

I don't know much of anything about the usual arrangements for foster parenting, but I think this one must be a little odd. For one thing, we will not be able to formally adopt Mira for a good while because her mother is missing, not dead. The whereabouts of her father are unknown. That isn't the oddest part, though.

The odd part starts with some of the conditions to which we must agree.

The first pair are the strangest. We must agree to move our place of residence and change our names. Mira's trustees have agreed to help Stan find a job in some likely place, and as he had been getting rather sick of how his current employers won't acknowledge that he's finished his degree, that's fine.

The name change is a bit odder. However, neither Stan nor I have any living family, so there isn't anyone we will insult by doing this. Since we moved to Idaho for Stan to finish his degree work, we have fallen out of touch with some friends, and those we have made here are not terribly close. That's a hard thing to admit, but I know it's probably all my fault. I couldn't handle all those women with their children and their smug pity of childless me. Stan has been too busy between work and school to really care.

I've often wondered over the course of this last week or so whether Stan and I were permitted to be Mira's foster parents precisely because we have so few ties. Why is that important? What is it about Mira that demands this? I'm afraid to ask for fear they'll take her from us.

There's another condition as well. We are never to—under any circumstances at all—take Mira back to the town from which she came. It's a small place in New Mexico, so I can't imagine why we would do so—except to enable Mira to experience her roots. THEY—these mysterious trustees seem to demand capital letters—THEY apparently don't want her to do this. THEY don't even want us to go to New Mexico to pick her up. We are to meet her at the end of her journey. THEY have indicated that they would prefer that Mira never go to New Mexico at all. I wonder why? Is there more to the disappearance of Mira's mother than we are being told?

The other conditions seem pretty reasonable to me. We are to handle Mira's finances, but THEY will review them. We must submit to an annual inspection of our home. I rather suspect, given how THEY are, that we will be checked out more frequently but less formally—at least for the first couple of years. It's rather creepy when you think about it, but I don't mind. I'm head over heels at the idea of having a little girl of my own to raise. I'm going to try and be good to her, so very good, so what do I have to be afraid of?

Okay. I'm being honest here. I'll write it down. I am afraid. I think Stan is, too, but we're not talking about it. The only thing either of us will admit is that we have our chance to finally be a real family and we don't want to blow it.

## INSIDE THE LINES

The next few entries were pretty normal stuff. How Uncle Stan and Aunt May picked me up at the train station. How I seemed shy, but interested in my environment. What we ate at the ice cream parlor, and again at home.

I matched Aunt May's memories against my own and found they rang true. She really was trying to report, not to project or speculate—at least not more than was reasonable.

I found one comment made a few days after my coming to live with them oddly interesting: "I think Mira must have lived in a home with very well-trained servants. It's not that she's demanding. The little dear tries very hard to be anything but—it's like she's afraid to be noticed. At the same time, she clearly expects to be waited on for small things, like having her clothing put out for her, or food placed on her plate. She is the oddest mixture of independence and passivity that I have ever imagined. But then what do I know about children?"

I had to stop reading after a few entries, though. Aunt May's meticulous accounts of my reactions to my new room and to every aspect of my new life were so full of her eager hope that we would bond that I could hardly bear it. I found myself saying to the empty air: "It's okay, Aunt May. It works out. It really, truly does." Then I started crying, and shut the journal lest my tears mess up the page.

That first entry gave me almost too much to think about as I drove. I had always blindly accepted the existence of my mysterious trustees. I had wondered if the Fenns' moving and changing their names had anything to do with me, but I hadn't wanted to ask. Now I knew. I was reminded of those relocation programs the police and FBI have for witnesses. Was I somehow a witness to something? Or was I being protected from whoever had made my mother disappear?

Either fit with the provision that the Fenns were under no circumstances to take me back to my hometown—and here I was in my bright red pickup truck, making a beeline to that very town. What was I heading into?

Probably nothing. Over forty years had passed since those provisions were made. Doubtless the danger—if there had been a danger—had been more immediate. No trustee had appeared on my twenty-first birthday to renew the restrictions. I was a woman not only grown, but on what people liked to call the wrong side of fifty. Doubtless the risk had been to the vulnerable child.

It struck me then that I was probably far older than my mother had been when she—the reality of it was still hard to accept—had died. My memories of Mother placed her somewhere in her mid-thirties, looking, except for that one time I'd seen her without her makeup, much younger. What would she make of her Mira, her mirror? I was no longer the slender, big-eyed child, but a stocky woman. Only my washed-out coloring remained the same.

Child of a rainless year. I hadn't thought of that for a long time, but as I sped along the highway the epithet came back to me, haunting me, so that I found my gaze scanning the horizon, looking for rain—and as I drove west and then south, finding none.

## OUTSIDE THE LINES

Mira has been with us a full year now, and Stan and I love her as much as we ever could have loved a birth daughter. She has returned our love with such eagerness that I find myself wondering what kind of upbringing did this little girl have?

Mira is not cold, far from it. Indeed, she turns toward affection as a flower does to the sun. No, more like a starving person might a banquet table: eager, but with a certain degree of caution, as if uncertain what her belly would be able to hold.

I find myself wondering what kind of woman her mother was. All we know about her is her name: Colette Bogatyr. It sounds rather French. Strange. I thought just about everyone in New Mexico was either Mexican or cowboys. I guess I don't know very much.

Does our Mira look French? Not particularly, to my eyes, but then what does French look like? All I know is that I was inordinately pleased when a woman in the grocery store told me how much we looked alike. They say that dogs come to look like their owners—or is it owners like their dogs?—in any case, might the same be true of adopted children and their parents?

Maybe because this first year has been such a wonder, I find myself thinking about Colette. Is she still alive somewhere? Will she reappear and take my little girl from me? I am haunted by the thought. Dread threads its way into my dreams.

Stan feels much the same, I am sure, but he won't talk about it. He sticks to the absolute letter of our agreement with the trustees. At first I thought he was lacking in curiosity—so many men are—but then I realized that he, too, loves Mira. He fears that if we violate the provisions set down by the trustees they will take her from us. He will do anything, even step on his own curiosity, to avoid this.

I care . . . but . . . I'm not certain I can go without knowing more. This morning I had to tell Mira I had a headache and so hadn't slept well. The poor dear looked frightened—of me! Is she afraid I'll be angry with her? I try so hard not to ever be, even when she is frustrating.

Sometimes I think her family must have once been very rich. Mira has a liking for fine clothing. I had to explain to her that she couldn't have all her dresses be lace and velvet. We sat down together with the new Sears catalog and worked out compromises. It's really rather funny. Most of the women complain that their daughters are all turning into tomboys. I have a budding lady of the manor.

Whether the family was rich or not, when Colette disappeared there wasn't all that much left. Stan refused to sell the family home, and has paid out of money he inherited from his own father to arrange an escrow account to assure its care. The rest will be kept for Mira. That is how he shows his willingness to keep the faith with our new daughter.

And me? I feel like such a traitor. Far from wishing to faithfully abide, I want to stick my nose in. I want to learn what happened to Colette. Shall I be brutal and honest? Why not! I want to know not because I care a whit about Colette Bogatyr, but because I must assure myself that no one lives who can take darling Mira from us. It's terrible, but I want proof that that woman is dead. DEAD. DEAD. DEAD.

I should hate myself for feeling such things, much less for committing them to paper, but I cannot. I love Mira. Stan loves Mira. I think Mira is coming to love us as well. Stan says the law would probably support our custody of Mira, given how Colette simply abandoned her. I am less certain of that. I can't help but feel that, law or no law, if Colette reappears she will take our child from us, a child she left behind without a word.

I admit it. I want her dead. I'd dance on her grave if I could find it.

## INSIDE THE LINES

I wondered if Aunt May had forgotten how angry she had been in those early journal entries, for the one written on the anniversary of my coming to live with the Fenns was not the only one in which she expressed her fear of and hatred for my absent mother.

The emotions that washed through me as I read these entries were mixed. At first I was astonished that sweet Aunt May could hold such anger. Later, I felt protectively angry on behalf of the vanished Colette. Then, when I remembered the reality of the woman who had borne me, I felt pity for Aunt May. She had been right to fear Colette—had my mother reappeared, there is no way she would have relinquished claim to *her* daughter.

"But she didn't come back," I said to the empty air, hearing my voice reverberate strangely inside my truck cab. "Did you ever feel more secure, Aunt May?"

There wasn't an answer, but somehow, just beyond the edge of hearing, I felt as if there was—and that I simply lacked the ability to hear it.

"There are a lot more journals in the metal box," I said, my voice sounding less strange this time. "I'll keep reading. I guess I'll find out."

I felt comforted, as if a silent listener had nodded approval. Then I noticed the big yellow sign at the edge of the road. I'd just crossed the border into New Mexico.

Crossing the border into New Mexico, especially from the east, isn't much of a transformative experience. I'd followed a whim to see something of Kentucky and Tennessee as I'd traveled—air-conditioning has really taken the teeth out of summer—and so I went south until I reached I-40. By then most of the desire to play tourist was out of my system and I headed pretty much due west.

Somewhere around Oklahoma things started looking more brown than otherwise, and I don't have any fond memories of going through Texas, though at one point I was hungry enough that I almost did stop for that steak dinner all the billboards promise will be free—if you can finish what they put on your plate. I heard at the motel where I did stop that the restaurant puts a lot on your plate. That's how they make good on the deal— pretty much nobody finishes.

Even though the sign welcoming me into New Mexico was bilingual, offering *"bienvenidos"* as well as "welcome" to New Mexico, I didn't see a lot that was much different from Texas, at least not at first. What I saw was empty land, some of it being used to graze cattle, some under cultivation. Now, I was a city girl, but one way or another, I'd seen a good deal of farm country, Midwestern style. New Mexico was nothing like anything I knew.

The best way I can explain it is to tell a story I heard later on. A fellow from New Mexico goes to Kentucky, and while he's driving along a country road he sees a cow having trouble giving birth to a calf. Having been a cowhand himself at some point in his life, he stops and goes to help the cow. His wife takes the car and eventually finds the home of the cow's owner. The cow's owner comes out and together they get the calf safely delivered. Afterward, when they're cleaning up and having something to drink, the cow's owner says, "So you're from New Mexico. I hear that's good cattle country. How many cows do you get to the acre?" The fellow from New Mexico looks at him with all seriousness and says, "You've got it all wrong, sir. It's how many acres to the cow."

That's what I was seeing around me as I drove. In some stretches, once the roads took me into higher altitudes I drove through piñon and juniper territory. I found myself thinking that the fat round trees looked like cattle spread out and grazing. Locals called these growths of piñon and juniper "forests," but then they called anything higher than man-height a "tree," whereas back in Ohio what we called "shrubs" routinely threatened to overwhelm the houses around which they were planted, unless the new growth was regularly pruned.

New Mexico was a different world. When I stopped at a fast-food place and saw that green chile was offered as a condiment, and heard Spanish being spoken by the couple seated in the booth nearest mine, and realized that the dark-haired men laughing together at a table near the window were real live Indians, I felt as displaced as I ever had in Europe. More so maybe, because I was at least supposed to be in the United States—and this was the state where I had been born, and to which I thought I should feel at least some sort of connection. I didn't, though, and that unsettled me even more than Aunt May's journal had done.

Depending on who you talk to, the population of the entire state of New Mexico is given as something over a million and a half—how much over depends on the source. By the standards of the East and Midwest that isn't much, especially in a state large enough to comfortably engulf Ohio, with room to take a solid bite out of the surrounding states. The largest chunk of that population lives in Albuquerque, with Santa Fe to the north, and various cities in the south claiming honors as runners up.

My destination was none of these urban centers. Somewhere west of Santa Rosa I took a road heading north, driving into lands that seemed—by the standards I was used to judging by—nearly unlived in. My destination was a small town that had seen its heyday in the 1880s, when the railroad had come through. Now, according to the reading I had squeezed in before my departure, it went back and forth between staggering along and economic depression.

The town was named Las Vegas, but it couldn't in the least be confused with its glamorous sibling in Nevada. The neon here was restricted to the occasional bar window, the glories of its architecture were definitely rooted in the past. I stopped for gasoline at a very modern gas station, confirmed my directions, and drove to the real estate office that managed my property for me.

I'd called the afternoon before, promising that I'd be in by midday, and now here I was. The building was—as real estate offices so often are—a nicely restored older building, but the sign out front was for one of the national real estate chains. The sun beating through the truck's windshield had made my air-conditioned cab hot enough, but when I stepped out there was a hint of freshness in the air that reminded me that Las Vegas was at over 6,400 feet altitude.

The middle-aged woman working the front desk looked up from some papers she was sorting, and smiled at me as I came in.

"I think you must be Ms. Fenn," she said. "Welcome. I am Maria Morales. How was your trip?"

Her accent was the one I would hear a great deal of during my stay—that of the northern New Mexico Hispanic who had grown up speaking both Spanish and English. It is a distinct accent, almost impossible to describe. At the time it sounded very odd to me, and I accepted that oddness as part and parcel with the general oddness I was finding everywhere in New Mexico. Only after I had been in town a few days would I think to wonder why the accent had sounded odd. Had I really been so isolated from the town around me as to never meet any of the locals? I was beginning to think that my childhood memories—the veracity of which I had dismissed—might hold more truth than I had realized.

"My trip went well," I said, "but how did you know who I was?"

Mrs. Morales smiled and gestured to the window by her desk. My truck—and its license plate—was clearly visible.

"We don't see many cars from Ohio," she said, "and I have been waiting for you. Can I get you something to drink? We have iced tea, sodas, even some coffee that's not too stale. It is unusually hot this season."

"Iced tea," I said. "Unsweetened."

She chuckled. "You have come through the South, I think. Here in northern New Mexico the iced tea will always be left for you to sweeten."

"That's a relief," I said, sharing her laughter. "Sweetened tea tastes like some peculiar species of flat soda."

"To me, too," she agreed.

I noticed a discreet sign indicating a rest room and motioned toward it. "If I might?"

"Of course. I will get the tea. Then I will pull the paperwork for your house."

After using the ladies' room, I followed Mrs. Morales into a side room furnished with a round table, and set about with square-bodied chairs that looked hand-carved. A few pieces of handmade Indian pottery were set in niches on one wall. Framed, limited-edition prints of sunset-tinted mountainscapes hung on the wall. I took my seat, reveling in this break from office superstore furnishings—especially after spending so many nights in the sort of generic motel rooms that had been within my budget.

I hoped the taste shown in the decorating boded well for the care given to my house. As it happens, I was right in this, but I was also seeing what I would learn was a fairly common aspect of New Mexican culture. In even the most pedestrian middle-class homes, you'll often find a taste for art or fine handmade goods. It may not be good taste, but at least it reflects something other than the taste of the buyer for the local home-furnishings warehouse.

"Now," Mrs. Morales said, "here are the records of our custodianship of Phineas House."

I blinked. I hadn't known the house had a name. In Uncle Stan's files, it had simply been referred to by its address.

Suddenly, the stack of file folders reminded me all too acutely of Uncle Stan's methodical records. I was overwhelmed by grief and confusion, as if my twenty-one-year-old self stood side by side with this me of thirty years later. I covered my disorientation by taking a swallow of my iced tea. It wasn't bad, and the caffeine in it seemed to go directly into my tired brain.

By the time we finished reviewing the paperwork, I felt a whole lot better. In contrast, Mrs. Morales seemed increasingly edgy. I wondered at this. Certainly, based on these records, neither she nor her company had anything to worry about. Maintenance had been done systematically, and the house hadn't suffered anything like the vandalism one would expect for a property so long vacant.

"Would you like me to take you over to the house?" Mrs. Morales asked. "The town may have changed a bit since your last visit."

"I'm sure it has," I said. "I haven't been here since I was nine. I'd appreciate a local guide."

"Let me call Domingo Navidad, first," she said. "He's the caretaker. He can lend you a hand with things."

"You mean like getting the power and water turned on?" I asked. "I figured I'd just make a few phone calls from my motel."

"I mean like getting the shutters down and the door open," Mrs. Morales said, phone already to her ear, her expression the glazed one people acquire when they're listening to two things at once. "Even in this dry climate wood can get stubborn."

I nodded. Apparently, Mr. Navidad answered the call, for Mrs. Morales began chattering in a fluid, easy Spanish that was nothing like what I'd learned In school.

"Domingo says he can meet us in an hour or so," Mrs. Morales said. "Would you like to go to lunch first?"

I nodded, though I felt ridiculously impatient at the delay. After all these years, what did another hour mean? Was it that I sensed Mrs. Morales was deliberately stalling, reluctant to go over to the house without Mr. Navidad?

I decided I was being ridiculous. "Lunch sounds wonderful. Can you recommend a motel where I can stay until I move into the house? Someplace not too expensive, but not a roach motel, either."

Unsurprisingly, Mrs. Morales knew a hotel perfect for my needs. Moreover, she fished out a handful of discount coupons for the hotel, then insisted on buying me lunch at a nice if unpretentious place that served both mainstream American and New Mexican food.

"After all," she said, the warmth in her smile free from her earlier tension, "you have been a client for over forty years. We can at least give you lunch."

"I suppose I have been," I agreed. "Okay."

I was prepared to be daring at lunch—after all, this was my first real New Mexican meal—but Mrs. Morales advised me that it was best to order chile on the side until I adjusted to the heat.

"Chile?" I asked. "That's different from what we'd call chile in Ohio, isn't it?"

"I think there you would be talking about chile con carne," Mrs. Morales said. "Here chile is a hot-pepper sauce—different wherever you go, so it's not easy to say how spicy it will be."

"Like salsa," I said.

She smiled, but shook her head. "If you are thinking of what you can get in the grocery store . . . well . . . yes and no. Most salsas, like you would put on chips, also have in them tomatoes and onions and other things. What we call chile is usually just the peppers, cooked with maybe a bit of pork for flavoring, red or green according to the ripeness of the peppers."

"Which is hotter?" I asked.

She gave an eloquent shrug. "It depends on the year and the peppers. If you order 'Christmas' you can try both. Let me do this for you."

I agreed, and was glad for her suggestion. I hadn't considered myself the stereotypical Midwesterner. Both travel and the art world had expanded my horizons far beyond the norm, but when the food arrived I was glad to be able to spoon on just enough chile to suit my taste.

Mrs. Morales seemed eager to tell me anything and everything about Las Vegas.

"You are a teacher?" she said. "You will like it here, then. In addition to the grammar and high schools, we have several institutes of higher learning right here in Las Vegas. There is Highlands University, the Luna Vocational Technical Institute, and a campus of the United World College."

"Then this is a college town?"

Mrs. Morales gave an eloquent shrug, "Not really. Many residents are associated with the schools in one way or another, but ranching is still common. Tourism is important. Many residents work in the arts."

"You should be on the local tourist board," I said.

"I am," she replied with a smile. "Not only because I am in real estate. This town is my home and my family's home, and I would like to see it thrive."

Mrs. Morales saw me glance at the wall clock and rose. "I can pay on the way out. I see you are eager to be going."

A few twists and turns took us from the more modern city into a neighborhood where Victorian-style houses predominated. Some were in excellent condition, newly refurbished and brilliantly painted. Others were lived in, maintained or not according to the resident's needs. A few were flat-out wrecks.

Mrs. Morales directed me to turn down one street after another until we arrived at a curving cul-de-sac, the centerpiece of which was a house I both did and did not remember.

Probably because of memories of this very house, I had always liked Victorian architecture. When I had bought a home of my own, I had even considered a refurbished Victorian, but all the houses I had looked at seemed somehow lacking. Now, staring through my windshield at the towering structure in front of me, I understood why.

The house was built in the Queen Anne style, but in it the excesses of that already excessive style had been taken to extremes. Phineas House had towers and porches, ornately carved balustrades, latticework, and enough gingerbread to make Hansel and Gretel swear off sweets. Every possible style of window seemed to be represented: bay windows and oriel windows jutted outward at various levels; lancet windows stretched tall and narrow; roundel windows marched round and fat. There didn't seem to be a single roof built at the same level as any other, and they were shingled in various shapes of cut slate.

Moreover, quite unlike the photo that had been sent to me, the entire house was painted in a multiplicity of colors—colors that managed to be harmonious even as this crazy quilt of adornment managed to be harmonious. The dominant shade was a warm evergreen that shouted out in contrast to the brilliant blue of the cloudless New Mexico sky, but every other color in the rainbow was represented as well—red, orange, yellow, green, blue, indigo, violet—those and many of the subtle hues that fall between.

"Oh, my," I said softly, getting out of the truck without looking for possible oncoming cars. I couldn't seem to take my eyes off that amazing front facade. "Oh, my."

Mrs. Morales got out of the truck as well. After a long, entranced moment, I became aware of her voice and realized she was talking, but not to me.

I shook myself free of my fascination, and found Mrs. Morales was speaking with a lean Hispanic man whose thick, brown-black hair was just starting to show grey. His sun-browned skin was grooved with enough deep lines that I knew he wasn't young, but he moved with a contained energy that contrasted oddly with the ebullience of the small white dog that danced about his heels. I knew instantly from the mingled expression of pride and apprehension on the man's face that this must be Domingo Navidad, the caretaker of the house.

He seemed to feel no need for introductions.

"What do you think?" he asked when he saw me looking at him. His accent was much like that of Mrs. Morales.

"Amazing," I replied, "and like but yet not like what I remember."

"It was grey," he said bluntly, "with a little dull pink around the doors. It didn't like it, so over time I listened, and this is what it wanted to be."

Now it was Mrs. Morales's turn to look apprehensive, but I had known too many artists to find such talk at all strange. This was no different than how a sculptor might talk about finding the shape of something within a piece of wood or stone.

"I see," I replied. "I agree with the house. It looks better this way."

Both Mrs. Morales and Mr. Navidad relaxed, but they immediately stiffened at my next words.

"I don't remember the yard being so very large," I said. "Weren't there houses on either side?"

"And one around the back," Mrs. Morales agreed. "Old wood, not too well-maintained, and this is a hot, dry climate." She gave an eloquent shrug. "Fire takes them quickly."

"All of them?" I asked astonished, "and this one untouched? And no one bought the land?"

"Not all at once," Mrs. Morales said. "The fires happened over maybe twenty years, and, no, the land didn't sell. This neighborhood is even now not the best, and then it was far less desirable."

"But someone is maintaining the lots," I said, suddenly aware of the summer heat kicking up from the asphalt and moving toward the shade of one of the towering elms.

"I do," replied Mr. Navidad. "Did Mrs. Morales not tell you? The land goes with the house now—the way it once did. The entire makes up a piece shaped rather like a fat half-moon. When some past owner sold the lots, the center was kept, but the back and sides were let go."

I registered this, turning slowly side to side to inspect the property. My first impression had been that Phineas House was the centerpiece of a cul-de-sac. Now I revised it. It *was* the cul-de-sac, the only house that faced the curving street. All the other structures but one faced onto other streets, and the dissenting structure was one I remembered—the carriage house, which even in my childhood had already been adapted to serve as a garage and storage area.

Without my consciously noticing our progress, we had all moved to stand in the shade now, some feet closer to the house.

My gaze had centered again on the front facade, and I had trouble wrenching it free, even though I knew my abstraction must seem rude. My eyes sought among the twists and turns, finding all sorts of carvings among the gingerbread trim. I was sure I saw lions and wolves. A leopard stretched to scratch his claws into a newel post, his long, lean body making a post for the porch rail. Faces peered out of brackets and from the tops of newel posts.

Yet for all these carved eyes, the house seemed blinded. I longed to wrench open the shutters, take down the boarding that protected the doors, but such would need to be done carefully—and probably I should only do it if I planned to take up residence.

I realized the other two were staring at me. I made myself remember what we had been talking about, then voiced a question. "Are you saying that I own the other lots?"

"They were offered at a fire-sale price," Mrs. Morales said. Her tone tried to make a joke of this, but failed. Whereas Mr. Navidad and I were fascinated with Phineas House, she was clearly uncomfortable with it. "Your trustees allocated money to purchase it, feeling the structure would be best preserved that way. Property taxes here are comparatively low, especially for undeveloped lots."

"Wonderful," I said. "The house looks much better this way. I remember it seemed cramped before."

"So I remember, too," Mr. Navidad said.

I looked at him squarely for the first time. "Have you lived in this area long, then?"

He smiled. "I have lived in Las Vegas all my life. My father was a groundskeeper here in the days of your mother. I helped him, then took over from him when he retired. Keeping this house has been my life's work."

"Where do you live?" I asked, startled by his passion.

Mr. Navidad pointed. "The carriage house is there. After the fires, the trustees wanted someone to live near. I agreed to refurbish the upper storage area into an apartment in return for paying no rent."

"A good idea, having someone living on the grounds," I said. Suddenly, that sensation of being two people—this time the woman I was and the child I had been—washed over me. I felt vaguely nauseated. I wanted to believe the feeling had its source in the summer heat or all the driving I had done, or even the unusually spicy meal I had eaten for lunch, but I knew there was something else going on.

"I need to check in to my hotel," I said, now as eager to be away as I had been to arrive. "Mr. Navidad, may I have your phone number? I will call and arrange to tour the grounds—tomorrow, I think. Right now I am very tired."

"By all means," he said. He pulled a business card from his wallet. "Here. My cell phone and my home phone. I do work other than here."

He looked anxious, as if he thought I might choose to fire him for negligence.

"Fine. Fine." I said, stuffing the card into my pocket. "I'll call, maybe tomorrow morning—make an appointment."

I nearly ran to my truck then, and Mrs. Morales scampered to follow. She insisted on staying with me until I had a room at the hotel, then I dropped her at the real estate office. After our earlier easy affability, we were both strangely silent. It was as if there were things we both knew, but couldn't discuss.

Back at the hotel, I unloaded what I needed from the truck, then covered my scavengings with an old blanket. I focused singlemindedly on what must be done before businesses closed for the day—arranging for the electricity and water to be turned on, checking what it would take to get phone service reactivated. I decided to wait on the gas until I was sure whether or not I'd be moving into the house. I certainly wouldn't need heat in summer, and hot water and cooking could wait.

I showered, dined in the hotel restaurant, and went back to my room. I desperately wanted to sleep, but sleep would not come. The television seemed more banal than usual, and although the evening was cooling down nicely, I found I was reluctant to leave the security of my room.

Almost without volition, my hand reached for the volume of Aunt May's journal I had been reading, and I opened it, letting my bookmark fall unheeded to the floor.

## OUTSIDE THE LINES

Since I don't want Stan to find out what I'm doing, I guess I'm going to need to rely on the mail, but who do I write? If I write the local police will they answer?

Probably not. The investigation isn't that old. But what if I told them I am Mira's guardian, and I am interested for her sake?

No. Bad idea. I don't know who reports to the trustees. Stan would be furious if he thought I was doing anything that would risk our keeping Mira. Be honest with yourself, M., you'd be furious, too.

Okay. No police. Not yet, at least. Who then? Newspapers? Good idea. I'll find out what the local papers are. Then write asking for appropriate articles. Yes. That will give me some names, maybe. Someone I can write.

But how do I do this without getting people wondering? Represent myself as family? No. They might already know—must know that Colette had no immediate family. Mira told us there were reporters when she left to come Idaho. Okay. Not family. What then?

Doing research. That's safe. For what? A college paper? Represent myself as a graduate student? Sure. Sociology. Good. I can do that. Would a graduate student use school stationery? Probably not. I can get away with good bond paper. Letters had better be typed. No problem. I can use Stan's typewriter.

"Dear Editor, I am a graduate student in Sociology, doing research into the question of . . ." of . . . women who run away? No. Disappearances? Maybe. Think that one over for a bit. Think about what to say next.

"Someone told me . . ." Too conversational. "I was informed regarding . . ." No, sounds too stiff. "I was told that a woman named Colette Bogatyr disappeared from your town a bit over a year ago. I am interested in any stories you have regarding this disappearance."

Should I offer to pay them for copies? I'd better check with our local paper and find out what their policy is. That's better. My allowance is only going to go so far. I can use some of Stan's paper, but I'll need stamps and envelopes. Should I even give this as a return address? I usually get the mail, but what if Stan's home? He always looks at return addresses, and he'd wonder. Okay. I could have them sent to Betty's, but that would mean telling her or she's going to think I'm having an affair. And if she let something slip!!!

Okay. That means a P.O. box. I don't think they cost much. And going to the library and seeing if they can help me find out the name of the local newspapers. Should I just check Las Vegas? No, better check Santa Fe. That's not too far, really. Maybe even Albuquerque. That's farther, but it's the closest really big city. I mean, Santa Fe may be state capital, but as I recall it's pretty dinky.

It's good to have a plan.

5

The Ideal Queen Anne . . . should be so plastered with ornament as to conceal the theory of its construction; it should be a restless, uncertain, frightful collection of details, giving the effect of a nightmare about to explode.
—Gelette Burgess, quoted in
*Daughters of Painted Ladies* by Elizabeth Pomada

## INSIDE THE LINES

I was still thinking about Aunt May's search when I drove over to Phineas House the next morning. She'd really sweated over the letter she'd sent to the various papers. The journal was filled with rough drafts. Her interests and enthusiasms had been so broad that all the time we'd known each other I'd never really thought about what it must have been like to be the product of only a high school education. Aunt May had never even worked outside of the home. She'd gone from high school to being married—and married for a long time without children.

She'd had to type each letter out individually. There'd been no word processor with which to manufacture multiple copies, and in her fear of seeming ignorant, she'd permitted herself no cross-outs. She'd even had to go out and buy more paper and a new typewriter ribbon because she was afraid Uncle Stan would notice.

She kept saying that the reason she didn't want him to notice was because she thought he'd be angry that she was violating the terms under which they'd agreed to take me in, but I had a feeling it was something more. The fact was, as much as she loved him, this was a time and place when men came home and were waited on—and their wives didn't question this. I had vague memories of how Uncle Stan would come home from work, change out of his suit, then sit and read the paper while Aunt May put the finishing touches on dinner. Afterward, she'd clean up—or I would, when I was a bit older—and he'd go back to his paper, or to watching something on TV.

I felt a bit angry in retrospect. Hadn't Aunt May been working all day, too? Even with those much vaunted "modern labor saving appliances" she was still responsible for an awful lot—and she didn't take many shortcuts when it came to meals.

This didn't put me in the best of moods when I pulled my truck up in front of Phineas House—*my* house—and Domingo Navidad came strolling around the side to meet me, acting for all the world as if he owned the place. As before, his little white dog followed him, bouncing in a rocking rhythm that made the mere process of moving forward a game.

Mr. Navidad was holding a mug of coffee in one hand, and with his free hand he opened the gate in the waist-high wrought-iron fence that bordered the front yard.

The fence was, like the rest of the place, completely and wildly overdone, rioting with vines and leaves. There were creatures hiding in the tangle. I remembered being fascinated with the fence when I was a child, but I hadn't been encouraged to linger out front, so my inspections had been quick glimpses, guaranteed to increase interest rather than otherwise.

I paused now to look at the fence, revelling in making this man wait on my pleasure. The majority of the iron had been painted a glossy black, but details had been highlighted very subtly in dark green and, just occasionally, in gold or cream.

I located a face set in the left panel of the gate. I had particularly liked this detail when I was a child—partly because it seemed so alive and partly because its leering expression scared me that little bit that small children enjoy. Back then the face had been the same flat black as the rest of the iron. Now the eyes had been highlighted with white, so they seemed to be alive and watching me. The face's leer seemed mocking.

"*Lady of the Manor?*" the lips said, moving to show a carnivore's long teeth. "*What right do you have to be so proud?*"

The imagined reprimand made me ashamed of my bad manners, and I tried to make up for my coolness with a smile I knew was a bit too hearty.

"Good morning, Mr. Navidad. I apologize for my lack of greeting. I simply had to stop and look at the fence. You've done a marvelous job maintaining it."

Mr. Navidad smiled and continued holding the gate open for me.

"Sometimes," he said, "I think I get too absorbed in the details, like on this fence. Before you praise me to the heavens for my diligence, there is a confession I must make."

"Confession?"

"It is easier to show," he replied, and motioned me around the right side of the house.

I followed him without a word. The morning was still cool, holding nothing of the heat of the previous afternoon. The heat would come, however. The weather had been the primary topic of conversation that morning in the hotel restaurant. Apparently locals dined there as well as transients. As I took polite shelter behind my newspaper, I had heard frequent mention of the "monsoons." That sounded very tropical to me, and I'd made a mental note to ask what they were talking about.

For now, I enjoyed the relative coolness of the morning, a coolness that increased as we moved into the shade of the trees that surrounded the house. The elms kept a courteous distance from the towering monstrosity, but I knew from experience that their shade was very welcome.

Mr. Navidad led me to a point from which we could see the side of the house clearly, then motioned upward.

"You see," he said, and I did.

The paint job that adorned this side of the house was an illusion—a clever one, but an illusion nonetheless. The wildly ornate designs of the front facade only carried back as far as they could be clearly seen from the street out front. The carved details were still there, but had not been picked out in the same meticulous glory.

It was not that the structure was not well-cared for. Monochrome evergreen paint covered most of the siding. In a few places, mostly railing or window frames, details were painted in lighter shades. The wood beneath was well-protected. The paint was reasonably fresh. There was no peeling or cracking. The house was healthy—but it wasn't alive.

"Oh," I said. "I see."

"It helps," Mr. Navidad said, as if we were picking up in the middle of a longer conversation, "that you own the extra lots to either side and to the back. It makes it easier. Even so, I am embarrassed. I should have done more."

Struggling for a reply, I realized that for Mr. Navidad this *was* a conversation we had had before. He must have been rehearsing how to explain his perceived negligence to me from the moment he heard I was coming to Las Vegas.

"You have done a good job," I said. "I saw the budget you were given when Mrs. Morales reviewed the paperwork with me. It was hardly enough to supply paint and labor for the most routine of cover jobs."

"Maybe in Ohio, yes," he agreed, his gaze sliding from the house to my face and back to the house again. "Here. Well, here sometimes labor can be cheaper—if you know who to talk to, yes?"

I understood he was talking about illegal immigrants and didn't press the question.

"But cheap labor wouldn't be able to design the color scheme for the detail work," I said. "You must have spent hours."

Mr. Navidad smiled and spoke with a quiet honesty that touched my heart. "I did, señora. I took many pictures with a telephoto lens. My nephew is very good with computers and he scanned them into a computer. Then I used what is called a paint program to try different colors. ¡Milagroso! Have you used one of these?"

I nodded. "I've never liked them as much as I do real colors, but for something on this scale . . . It would save a lot of paint."

We stood, staring at the house together. Mr. Navidad's little white dog circled each of the trees, sniffing as enthusiastically as if he hadn't seen them probably every day of his life. I heard a jay scolding the dog, then Mr. Navidad spoke very softly.

"I tried the colors, señora, and sometimes I liked what I saw, but mostly I listened, and let the house tell me what *it* liked. It took more time, yes, but I think it is worth it."

We walked slowly around the house trailed by the little white dog. We didn't say much, but our silence was not uncomfortable. I felt as I had done when I had shared a model with other artists, my concentration intensified by my awareness of another person looking at the same thing.

The back garden that I remembered playing in as a child was still there, its fieldstone walls creating a sanctuary within a larger space. Roses spilled over the walls in cascades of pink, white, and pale yellow.

Once again, Mr. Navidad held a wrought-iron gate open for me, and this time I passed through with a murmur of thanks. I glanced around the walled garden with interest. The green patch that had been my refuge was still there, as were an array of fruit trees neatly pruned to the fit the space or espaliered against sections of the wall. The herb garden was where I remembered it, and so was a flourishing young vegetable patch.

"Yours?" I asked.

Mr. Navidad nodded. "It is a good place. The walls give some shelter from the wind and the little animals. The ground gets watered from run-off—when we have rain."

Something in how he paused before the final phrase reminded me of the conversations I had heard that morning in the hotel restaurant.

"Is this a droughty year, then?"

"Very bad," he agreed. "We are all waiting to see if the monsoons will come. There is much concern."

"Monsoons? I thought those only happened in the tropics."

"It is what we call our seasonal rains. They come in the late summer, less so in the winter. Depending on where you are in the state, most of your rain will come in only two times of the year. It is very serious indeed when the year is rainless."

Rainless. The word rung in my ears as if spoken in my mother's voice, but Mr. Navidad's expression was bland. Did he know the importance of what he had said?

I couldn't ask. It would mean saying too much about things I was still uncertain about myself. And what could I say? "My mother claimed that there was no rain the year I was born"? Even if he had heard some such thing why was it important? There were probably more drought years than wet in this climate.

To cover my discomfort, I led the way out of the walled garden, using the matching gate on the far side of the yard. We finished our slow patrol around the house, and by then I had collected my courage.

"Mr. Navidad, I would like to see the inside of the house. The electric company told me the power should be on by now, but I've brought some flashlights. Would you advise me which door might be best to open?"

His expression was strangely vacant for a moment, almost as if something had distracted him, but he pulled his gaze back to mine.

"I would have said the kitchen door," he replied. "That is the one I use when I go in a few times a year to make certain that the roof is still sound and no pipes have broken—things like that. But I think the House would be happier if you came in through the front door. The kitchen door is not one for a homecoming such as this."

I forced a smile, unsettled by this tendency to personalize the house. I knew that this manner of speech originated in his being a native speaker of Spanish. Spanish pronouns personalize, give genders even to inanimate items. The tendency to speak of things as if they are alive often slips over. Mr. Navidad was too fluent in English to talk like some stage Mexican, *"The house, she is happy to have you, sí, señora,"* but still the Spanish flavor was there. That was all there was to it.

"Very well," I said. "I'll go to my truck and get the flashlights and a few other things I brought along. I don't doubt you have a crowbar we can use to get the boards off the front door."

"I do indeed," he said. "I take them off to make sure moisture has not leaked beneath—when we have much moisture, that is."

"Truly," I replied, "you are the most diligent of caretakers. I'll meet you around front in a few minutes."

Getting the door open was as easy as Mr. Navidad had promised it would be. We stood there in the shade of the porch staring at the double-paneled door.

"Usually," the caretaker offered, "I only open the one side." He motioned toward the right panel. "It is enough and more to admit a man."

I looked at the door. The knobs were shaped like leering gargoyle heads. They were duller than I remembered them being, but doubtless, one of the silent women had kept them polished.

Once again I found myself contrasting the differences between my up-bringing here and in Ohio. In Ohio there had been no servants, only occa-sional "help" before a big party and that, more likely than not, had been someone from the church who would be given a "gift" rather than paid outright.

I never remembered the silent women being paid. For that matter, I had no memory of them ever leaving the house except on a specific errand. Where had they lived? Had they had families? Tantalizing thought . . . Were any of them still alive and in the area? Could I find them and ask about my mother? Who else might I find and question?

"Señora?" Mr. Navidad's voice, politely inquiring, brought me back to myself. "Would you like me to open the door for you?"

I shook myself as his little white dog might have done.

"Sorry. Woolgathering. There are so many memories here."

Without further hesitation, I laid a hand on the knob. It was surprisingly stiff, refusing to turn. I thought it might have rusted in place. Then, belatedly, I remembered the ring of keys Mrs Morales had given me. Blushing, I shook out one labeled "Front door." It was slightly larger and heavier than the others on the ring, and turned the old lock easily.

"You've kept it oiled," I said.

"Graphite powder," Mr. Navidad said, removing a small tube of it from the toolbox he'd brought along. "It works very well. Not all the interior locks may be as easily handled, so I brought this for you."

I thanked him, then, as I turned and pulled the door open I asked, "Aren't you coming with me?"

Mr. Navidad made an apologetic gesture. "If you wish, of course, but when I went back to the carriage house there was a message waiting from my sister Evelina, asking if I might come and help with a window that has been broken. If you don't mind . . ."

He trailed off, and I nodded, feeling a mixture of relief and mild apprehension. There was something creepy about going into a house that had been closed for so long, but on the other hand, this way I could stand and stare as much as I wanted.

"That's fine," I replied. "I have your cell-phone number. If anything crops up, I can reach you."

"Good," Mr. Navidad said. He pulled a scrap of paper from his pocket. "This has my sister's number, just in case the cell phone is not working. I will leave you this toolbox."

"Won't you need it at your sister's?"

"I have another," he said, "and so does Evelina. You may find yourself wanting a screwdriver or something, and this way you will not need to search."

I watched Mr. Navidad go passing through sunlight into shadow and back again, the little white dog bouncing at his heels. Then I turned back toward Phineas House. Bending to lift the toolbox, I balanced one of the more powerful flashlights in my free hand. Then I stepped over the threshold into the house of my childhood.

The hallway was filled with ghosts. Pale shadowy forms moved slightly, as if uncertain whether to stay or vanish soundlessly away. Then my eyes adjusted to the yellowish gleam cast by the flashlight, and I realized that what I was seeing was furniture swathed beneath dust sheets.

I let my breath out with a hard *poof* and played the light around—to get my bearings, I told myself, though I knew perfectly well that at least part of the reason was to reassure myself that there was indeed no one there.

There wasn't, unless you counted the shapeless lumps under white cloths. My mind struggled to equate each lump with a remembered furnishing. There had been a coat tree and one of those elaborate stands that has, in addition to hooks for coats and hats, a large mirror and a chest for boots or other impedimenta. There'd been a long narrow table, perfect for callers to leave their gloves or for stacking letters and packages that were to go out with the mail. That shorter, fatter lump must be the big Chinese urn that had doubled as an umbrella stand—though umbrellas weren't much needed here.

To my left, the foyer opened out into the formal living room. To the right was the door into the front parlor. The door beyond it on the same wall would lead into the library that had also served as my mother's office and sometimes as my classroom. The living room bordered the formal dining room. The kitchens, pantries, laundry, and associated rooms were toward the back of the house.

When I had been a child, there had been an invisible line on the first floor dividing the front and back of the house. I had rarely gone in back of that line. My meals mostly had been eaten upstairs in the suite of rooms on the second floor generally referred to as the nursery. My mother had hers brought to her wherever was most convenient. Therefore, it was with a certain sense of daring that I followed my flashlight beam toward the back of the house. The electric company had suggested I turn on the lights only after I had inspected the fuse box, and I assumed that this would be back here.

"I should have asked Mr. Navidad," I said to myself, hearing my voice swallowed by the swathed furniture, but echoing from where carpets had been rolled up, leaving the hardwood floors bare.

I was immensely bucked up when I found the fuse box down in the basement. Not only that, I found it in good repair. It was an old model, but everything was in place and a penciled chart taped to the inside of the metal cabinet door noted when old fuses had been replaced with new ones. I resolved that I would look into having the fuse box replaced with a more modern circuit-breaker system. After all, who knew how much longer it would even be possible to buy fuses?

The basement was smaller than the rest of the house, extending only under about a quarter of the space. The furnace was here, along with an assortment of the usual odds and ends that migrate to such places. I decided that I could do worse than test the lights here, and after the small ceiling fixture had obediently come on, I ascended to the ground floor with a much lighter heart.

Without the flashlight's wavering beam as illumination, the house looked a great deal less strange. I walked through all the rooms on the ground floor, occasionally replacing a lightbulb from the stash I'd brought with me. Now and then, I peeped under a dust cover, mostly to see if my memories of the furnishing were correct. Everything looked in fine condition, especially considering how long the house had been empty. I didn't even find any traces of mice, a thing I had fully expected.

The second floor was much the same: swathed furnishings, rolled up rugs, and dust. I didn't linger in any one room very long, not even opening the door to my nursery. Instead, I moved on to the third floor, then climbed up into the various cupolas and towers. I even went up into the attic, telling myself I was making certain that the roof was indeed sound, that there had been no water damage. In reality, I was aware of a restless feeling, as if I was searching for something, and had no idea what.

I was coming down from the second floor, wondering what I should do next, when I heard a voice.

"Hello? Señora Fenn?"

"Mr. Navidad?" I realized my pace had picked up, and that I was relieved beyond all reason to hear another human voice.

"Hello," he repeated, stepping over the threshold and looking around the electrically lit entry foyer. From how he was blinking, I realized that bright as the electric lights seemed in contrast to the flashlight, they were dim indeed compared to the sunlit outdoors.

"Did you fix the window?" I asked.

"All finished," he replied with a broad, illustrative gesture. "My nephew—he is the one who broke it practicing baseball pitches—he helped me fix it. Now Evelina has him washing some of the other windows, just so he won't forget them in the future."

"She sounds like a good mother," I said.

"I think she is," Mr. Navidad said contently. "Enrico, he probably does not think so right now."

I laughed. "Children see things differently," I agreed.

"So true. How is the House?"

"Dusty, but as far as I can tell, in wonderful shape."

Mr. Navidad looked pleased. "Evelina sent me back with some chicken enchiladas. If you are interested, perhaps you could come to the carriage house and have some lunch?"

I glanced at my watch and noticed it was already eleven-thirty. I also noticed that my hands were filthy.

"If I can borrow your washroom," I said, "and you don't mind me making your house dusty, I would be delighted."

He smiled. I let him lock up the front door while I beat the worst of the dust out of my jeans and shirt.

"It's gotten hot," I marvelled as we walked along beneath the elms. I realized that I was almost instinctively moving from shady patch to shady patch.

"It is, and it will get hotter still," Mr. Navidad agreed. "Inside, though, it will be cooler. I can warm the enchiladas in the microwave."

Inside the carriage house was comfortably cool. Mr. Navidad showed me where his bathroom was, handing me a clean washcloth and a worn but serviceable towel without my having to ask. When I emerged, somewhat more presentable, he motioned me to a chair at his kitchen table and poured me a glass of iced tea.

"Is Phineas House," I asked, feeling a little uncomfortable about using a name I hadn't known existed until just the day before, "equipped with any form of artificial cooling?"

"No," he said. "I think retro-fitting would be a challenge. The House is built on so many different levels, you see, and has so many odd shapes. It doesn't have central air, but it does have central heat—maybe something could be done with that."

"It stayed pretty cool while I was in there," I said, "but then I guess it would with the windows shuttered."

"Even without that," Mr. Navidad said, "the heat might not be too bad. The central stair acts as a way for heat to drain out, and the trees keep it shaded—as do the porches. People then built with an awareness of the weather, not like today. Today people only build to suit their fancy, without thinking about how the house is oriented on its lot, or where the windows are. Take a look at Phineas House later. Windows placed where the sun will linger are shaded."

"I suppose that makes it cold in the winter, then," I said, trying to remember.

"It's probably not so bad," he said. "Then the leaves are off the trees, awnings can be taken down, and more sun can get in. These old houses worked, not like machinery, but they worked."

All the time we had been talking, Mr. Navidad had been moving easily about his kitchen. The matter-of-fact way he set the table for the two of us, got out some vegetables that looked like they came from the garden patch I'd admired earlier, and put together a quick salad told me that he was not one of those bachelors who subsisted on a diet of canned soup and takeout.

When the enchiladas emerged, smelling heavenly, and he was serving us each a generous portion, the little white dog appeared. He balanced on his back legs and danced a few steps that might have been a waltz—and might just have been some skilled begging.

"Not for you," Mr. Navidad scolded. "Green chile gives you an upset stomach."

He spilled a few kibbles into the dog's bowl, and the dog settled down with a resignation that said that although he didn't get table scraps very often, he hadn't given up hope. Indeed, as soon as the kibbles had been bolted down, he settled by my knee, warm brown eyes under whiskery brows appealing and hopeful.

"What's his name?" I asked.

"Blanco," Mr. Navidad said. "Whitey, in English, but he wouldn't know that, though he is very bilingual in most things."

"Blanco," I repeated. "Easy enough to remember. I had a little Spanish in school."

Mr. Navidad seemed pleased. "That is good. Although New Mexico is officially bilingual—like Blanco there—still there are places where it is good to know a little Spanish."

"I speak it very badly," I said. "I read a bit better."

"Good to have a start. How are the enchiladas?"

"Wonderful," I replied. "Creamy and dense. I can feel myself gaining weight with every bite. When you mentioned they had green chile in them, I thought they might be too spicy for me, but these are just right."

"Ah, Evelina knew you might be having some, and she is a thoughtful woman."

"I hope they aren't too bland for you," I said.

"Not at all. Some things are better not too spicy. Enchiladas are one of those."

We talked food for a bit, then gardening, then dogs, and by the time Mr. Navidad said, "May I offer you some more tea, señora?" I wondered why I had ever resented him.

"I'm Mira," I said. "Please call me that."

"Then if you would call me Domingo," he replied. "I would be pleased."

We smiled at each other, suddenly both a little shy, but happier for having stopped being quite so much employer and employee.

"If I may ask, Mira," Domingo said, refilling my tea glass, then his own. "Do you know what you plan to do with Phineas House?"

"I hardly know," I said. "I hadn't even realized I owned it until recently."

"No?"

I thought he must have heard the story from Mrs. Morales, but his surprise seemed genuine. I sketched the details for him, ending with my decision to come here and see the place for myself. His first words surprised me. I had thought he'd ask what I thought of the place, but instead he looked very sad.

"So you have been orphaned, and so recently. I am very sorry. These adoptive parents of yours sound like good people."

"They were," I said, determined not to embarrass myself by starting to cry, but hearing myself getting choked up nonetheless. "And even though I keep telling myself that they died in about the best way possible—together and with very little pain—you're right, I do feel orphaned."

"I have read," Domingo said, "that no matter how old we are when our last parent dies, still, we feel orphaned. I know it will be so for me."

"Then your parents are still alive?"

"My mother and father both," he assured me. "I was their eldest, and I am not so very old yet."

"I know." I laughed. "You said you remembered me from when we were both children, so I figured we had to be around the same age."

"I am fifty-three," he said.

"I'm fifty-one."

Again, as when we had traded names, there was that sense of shyness, and I found myself talking through it, hearing myself saying things I hadn't realized I wanted to say.

"I think it's that feeling of being orphaned that brought me here, actually," I said. "The Fenns were my adoptive parents. I've never known what happened to my birth mother. I never even knew who my father was."

"No?" Domingo's eyebrows went up, but he looked startled rather than offended. "That is very strange. I knew your mother had vanished. It was all the gossip that year, but I suppose I thought something was found out eventually, something so boring it never made it to my ears."

"No," I said. "Nothing. Nothing at all."

6

He was a little careless with his records, and it has never been fully established whether I was born in 1903 or 1904, but I had euchered Doc out of a birth certificate anyway on the obvious grounds that I was standing in front of him.

> —Milton C. Nahm,
> *Las Vegas and Uncle Joe*

## OUTSIDE THE LINES

News clippings arrived today from the Santa Fe paper! Wouldn't you know they'd come on a Saturday??? Now I'll have to wait to read them until Monday. I don't usually wish for Stan and Mira to get out of here, but today . . .

Just finished reading the clippings. Can't decide if I'm excited or disappointed or what. I felt really weird seeing pictures of Colette. I've hated her for so long in the abstract. Now she's real. Or sort of real. The picture the papers kept printing was taken at some social function—one of those charity balls that're just an excuse for rich people to feel good about spending lots of money dressing up. It was in Santa Fe, not Las Vegas. From what I'm gathering, Las Vegas doesn't have a lot of those kind of things, not anymore anyhow. These days the residents are more likely to get charity than dispense it.

But Colette. She doesn't look anything at all like Mira—of course Mira's just a little girl, but Colette seems to have had very dark hair and even in a b&w newspaper photo she looks like she had vivid coloring. Mira, sweet child she is, but she's kinda washed out. I feel cruel saying that, but I'm not saying I don't think she's darling, just that she looks nothing like her mother. I wonder if that means she looks like her father?

Note to self: Who was Mira's father? Name wasn't given on any of the paperwork we were given. Is that important?

But it isn't right now. Or is it? What if Colette went off to him? Leaving her/their daughter? That's hard to believe. What if he kidnapped her? Why would he leave his daughter? Did he not know about her? There's a romantic image. Colette finding she's pregnant, fleeing some hard-hearted man— husband or lover. Bearing her child. Establishing herself. Man returns for her. She goes quietly rather than risk her child.

I almost like that version of her. I must remind myself I'm making it all up. There's nothing in the evidence to support such a warm, self-sacrificing image of the woman.

Back to the facts. The papers say that Colette's disappearance was reported by a servant. The servant's name isn't given in this story, but I have high hopes for the Las Vegas papers. Back to facts!!!

The disappearance had occurred several days prior to the report. Apparently, questions by the principal of Mira's school forced the servants to come forward. They didn't before. That seems to imply that Colette had gone off without warning before, just not for so long. Interesting. The article refers to Colette as a "socialite," but doesn't list the usual raft of causes those types usually support.

Really, there isn't much, but I find myself thinking about what the articles DON'T say. They don't list her marital status—she's neither listed as a widow or divorced or single. Usually that's just about the first thing they do say about a woman. Bugs the hell out of me usually, but this time it just puzzles me. Don't they know?

The articles—the ones the newspaper sent cover several weeks following the disappearance—also don't mention where Colette's money came from. That's another of those things they usually like to say "wealthy heiress" or "banking scion" or maybe out there it's more like "prominent ranching dynasty." Seems like she might have been as much of a mystery to them as she is to me.

I've made a note of the reporter's name, and if the Las Vegas paper doesn't help more, I'll try writing him directly. Maybe there's something he'll say off the record he won't say on.

———

Las Vegas papers arrived today!!! No one was home to stop me digging into the fat wad of clippings sent, either. No one at the *Optic* seemed to think my interest at all odd. Maybe when something's your local sensation you don't.

I've got a lot more to go on now. For one thing, Colette is referred to as "widowed"—so either that's true or that's the story she gave out. It's a lot more respectable to be a young widow than divorced, that's for sure.

Note to self: Marriage certificate? Long shot, but possible.

Another interesting thing is that the house in which she lived in has a name. It's called Phineas House, and from the way it's referred to in the story it must be one of those places local people know about—the way people around here know about the family that does the gaudy Christmas lights every year, or the Dairy Queen with the big figure of the cow wearing a crown on the roof.

Another big bingo is that they give the name of the servant who reported Colette as missing. Her name is Teresa Sanchez. For all it sounds so exotic to me, it's probably as common a name there as Mary Smith is here. Still, it's a name!

Third, there are interviews with various local people. No one says anything particularly telling one way or another. They're mostly versions of "She was quiet and kept to herself" but in this case a few people come out and say they thought Colette overdid the keeping to herself. One woman— I must find a way of asking Mira about her—seems to have been Mira's tutor for a while. Anyhow, this tutor's name is Hortense Ramsbottom. She was quite waspish on the subject of Colette. Refers to her as an empress with her own little empire within the walls of that house.

Another person quoted is the man who apparently did groundkeeping. His name is Martino Navidad. That surname seemed weird but familiar to me and I looked it up. It means "Christmas"! I guess it's not a weird name for a Spanish person. I understand they sometimes name their children "Jesus" and don't think anything impious about it. There I go again . . .

Okay. What Martino Navidad said that caught my attention was that although he kept the grounds for the house for many years, he was never, ever invited inside, not even into the kitchen. He didn't bring this up to whine or anything, but apparently the reporter asked him if he knew Mira and he said he didn't, explaining he didn't have anything to do with the household.

Maybe that isn't strange. Lots of people don't want muddy-footed gardeners in their houses. It just seemed strange to me, so I'm noting it down here.

Another interesting thing is that this set of clippings contained some other pictures of Colette. They really bear out the grand dame image—and I think they confirm something I've suspected for a while. She must have preferred more elaborate styles of dress. A couple of the pictures—one was a group shot from some gala, another of citizen's at some outdoor fete—gave me a good look at her dresses. Not a one wasn't full-length, and while it isn't easy to tell fabrics from a newspaper photo, I think I now know where Mira gets her taste for silk, lace, and velvet. It's getting so I can't imagine Colette in something as simple and practical as a shirtwaist.

What I find really fascinating is that no one in any of the articles mentions this eccentricity. It's as if they took her strange choice of fashion as a matter of course. Or maybe out West people still dress like that. I wonder how I could find out? I wonder if it's at all important or if I'm just being a woman and too interested in superficial matters.

Oh. And most important! The Las Vegas paper mentions the chief of police by name, and gives the general impression that he had put himself in charge of the investigation. I don't know if that's good or bad or whether I even dare to write him about it. Still, I like having the name. If I do figure out a way to follow up, it will beat writing "Dear Sir . . ."

## INSIDE THE LINES

I remembered seeing a couple of envelopes in the metal box, and now I went and dug out the one containing the newspaper clippings Aunt May had just been referring to. The newsprint had faded and yellowed, cracking in places when I unfolded the various articles. The whole had a slightly sour smell that wasn't precisely unpleasant.

Aunt May's journal entries had mentioned all the salient points, but it was still fascinating to read the yellowing clippings and catch from their faded lines some of the immediacy of the events. Occasionally a line or two was missing, folded into oblivion, but oddly these breaks made the parts that survived all the more real.

I found myself referred to as "the tragically abandoned child." There were several reproductions of what had to have been that year's school photo. Aunt May was right. Side by side with pictures of Colette, I looked very pale and rather insipid. Colette had all the life and vibrancy.

Carefully, I placed the envelope of clippings on the bed. I went into the bathroom and looked at myself in the mirror searching the lines and angles of my face for any resemblance to my mother. I saw none. Of course, I *was* at least twenty pounds heavier. If anything, I looked like Aunt May. This made sense in a way. After all, hers were the mannerisms that had been my subconscious model for most of my life.

I stood staring at my face, looking for something, anything that would connect me to my mother. I found nothing. I began to panic. My heart thudded so fast and hard I could see the fabric of my tee shirt shaking.

I tried to reassure myself. I was probably at least twenty years older now than my mother had been when she—vanished, died . . . The thing to do would be to compare pictures of me from my early thirties with these photos. I could buy one of those programs beauty salons use to show customers potential new looks, then use the computer to shade my hair into black, to tint my eyes, to pluck my brows into that ironic arch Colette favored, even to shave off a few pounds.

That thought drove me into further panic. I was there again, kneeling on the floor in my mother's room, watching her color in her face, seeing it all through the mirror's double reverse. The memory was so acute that I could feel the fabric of my dress against my skin, feel how the pads of my knees were numbing slightly from pressing against the hardwood floor. I remembered how even at the time I'd known I was leaving shiny patches on the velvet, but I was too on edge to care. It was a small violation in contrast to the trespass I had already committed.

A dull *thunk* brought me to myself. I found myself kneeling on the bathroom floor. The "thunk" had been me hitting the tiled floor, but I hadn't felt the impact, only heard it. I sat there, leaning my head against the pedestal base of the sink. I knew the detachment I was feeling was probably shock. I'd been through a lot these last few months, now, here I was, forcing myself to take more.

A sensible, reasonable voice in my head told me that tomorrow I should call Domingo and tell him to board the house back up. Then I should drive over to Mrs. Morales and get her advice on who to use to appraise the place and put it on the market. Her commission would assure that she got me a fair price.

Would the house sell better with furnishings? No. I should sell those separately. There were estate agents who handled that sort of stuff. I'd arrange for one. Domingo could get a commission by being my representative during the inspections and such. And I'd get out of here.

I'd go back to Ohio and adjust to being Mira Fenn again. I'd move into Aunt May and Uncle Stan's house. It was larger than mine, and held so many good memories. The yard was nicely fenced, perfect for a puppy. I'd get a kitten and raise the two together. Then back to teaching art, back to helping young people grow into their best potential.

That's what the sensible voice said, and it soothed me sufficiently that I rose from the bathroom floor, put away the journals and clippings, got myself washed and ready for bed. I slept without dreams.

I woke early and ate in the hotel dining room, listening to the locals discuss the drought. Then I went up to my room and picked up the phone. I punched in Domingo's cell-phone number and heard him answer.

"Good morning."

"Good morning," I replied. "This is Mira Fenn." My next words came from somewhere other than my sensible self. "Can you get the boards down from the windows? I want to see Phineas House in daylight."

"No, problem," he said. "I can get my sister's son to help me. He owes me after the window yesterday."

"I can help, too," I said, wondering where my sensible self had gone. "And since the electricity and water are on, I think I'll move in. I'll call the gas and telephone companies from here before I check out. I can sweep out the front parlor or something and camp there."

"Bueno."

I was surprised to hear Domingo sounded genuinely pleased. My sensible self had thought he would resent this invasion of what had been effectively his property for so long.

"Can I give the gas and phone people your number?" I asked. "You'd be better at answering any questions they might have than I would."

"That would be fine."

"See you in a bit then," I said and rang off.

On the way to Phineas House, I stopped by the real estate office. Luck was with me. Mrs. Morales was in and not busy.

"I've decided to move into Phineas House," I said. My sensible self forced me to add, ". . . at least for now. I need to find what's there and think about what I'm going to do with it."

"That's probably a good idea," Mrs. Morales replied, though something in her tone told me she wouldn't stay there for anything, not if she could afford a comfortable hotel room.

"It's probably in the paperwork somewhere," I went on, "but could you tell me what exactly is the arrangement with Mr. Navidad? He said something about having tenancy in the carriage house in return for being caretaker. Is there a lease or something?"

She shook her head. "Nothing so formal. If you wish the carriage house for yourself, you should simply give Domingo notice. A few weeks, at least, would be polite."

I mirrored her gesture. "Nothing like that. I just wanted to know if the carriage house and property was still mine, or if it had been deeded to him."

"It is yours." Mrs. Morales paused, biting into her upper lip with very good teeth. "Are you planning to let Domingo go? He is a bit of a fool . . . Not mentally impaired or like that, just oddly focused. The way he talks . . . especially about Phineas House. Maybe you have noticed?"

Mrs. Morales's dark gaze was pleading, and I strove to reassure her.

"I have. Domingo Navidad reminds me of many artists I have known, but instead of clay or paint or stone, that house has become his medium. Don't worry. I'm not going to throw him out into the streets."

Mrs. Morales relaxed. "There would be many willing to take him. Both Highlands University and the United World College have offered him positions, but he has refused. I am pleased you will keep him on."

"For now," my sensible self said. "I don't know yet what I'm going to do, but whatever I do, Domingo will have ample warning."

Mrs. Morales sent me on my way with a friendly smile and a copy of a sheet of paper listing good eating and shopping establishments in the area. It was probably nothing more than she gave to every stranger coming through, but I found the gesture warming.

After a stop at a grocery store where I loaded up on a wide variety of pro-

visions, I rechecked the directions Mrs. Morales had given me the day before, then turned the red truck in the direction of the place that once I had
called "home."

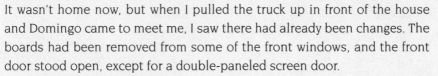

It wasn't home now, but when I pulled the truck up in front of the house
and Domingo came to meet me, I saw there had already been changes. The
boards had been removed from some of the front windows, and the front
door stood open, except for a double-paneled screen door.

"Señora Fenn," Domingo said.

I leaned out the window of my truck and interrupted him.

"Mira."

"Mira, then." He gave a slight smile. "If you wish, you can park your truck
in the carriage house garage. There is room."

I looked rather dubiously at the twisting wrought-iron fence and the
yard. There was no driveway, and certainly the grass under the spreading
elms had never been driven on.

"This is going to sound stupid," I said at last, "but how do I get there?
The car was always brought around front."

Domingo crossed to my truck, Blanco dancing behind him.

"If you will permit, I will come with you and give directions."

"Hop in," I said. "Forgive the litter. I haven't cleaned out the trash from
my drive out here."

"No problem," he said, moving the road atlas to one side and getting
in. Blanco leapt up into his lap and immediately pressed his nose to the
window.

I rolled up my window and switched the air-conditioning on to a higher
setting.

"Go back to the end of the street," Domingo said, "then turn left."

His directions took me to a neat, graveled alley that ran parallel to the
cul-de-sac, though with less of a curve. Like the house and yard, it was well-
maintained. This last wasn't a great surprise, since Domingo himself would
need to use it for his own vehicle.

"This is the gate," Domingo said. "I have equipped it with an electronic
opener and can give you the spare, but for today . . ."

He hopped out, opened the gate, and motioned for me to drive in. The garage door was already open, and a space prepared for my truck. It had even been swept. I felt a little bad about the gravel my tires brought with them. A little, but not too—after all this was my garage.

"Let me help you unload your things," Domingo offered, but I held up a hand.

"Not yet. I need to figure out where I'm going to put them. I brought a tool kit and some groceries, and for now that's all I need."

Domingo insisted on helping me with the groceries, showed me that the kitchen door had already been unboarded, and then left me to myself. Blanco waited a few minutes longer, perhaps hoping that one of the cookies I'd picked up in the grocery store bakery was going to get dropped. When he saw one wasn't, he let himself out the back door. He was clever about it, standing on his back legs and pushing down the lever with his nose, then letting his weight swing the door the rest of the way open.

I started by checking to see if the elderly refrigerator still worked. It was reassuringly cool inside, so I put the perishables in, and stowed a bag of ice in the freezer compartment. Then I stuck the nonperishables in the nearest cabinet. This done, I looked around the kitchen, trying to decide where to start.

"I suppose," I said aloud, "I should see if there are still pots and pans and dishes and things like that. There should be, but . . ."

I went around opening cabinets and peering inside, using my flashlight to probe into the deeper reaches. Again I was caught with a feeling that this place was both home and not. This kitchen was unfamiliar territory to me. I had no idea where anything was kept. I had never sat at the scrubbed wooden table near the garden window doing my homework and talking to my mother. Nor had I covered myself in flour while learning to bake. Those memories belonged to another kitchen, another place.

Even so, time and again as I opened those unfamiliar cabinets, I came across things that were achingly familiar. There was the everyday dishware, the bright Fiesta ware that I had always loved because of its vibrant colors. These were the very same plates from which I had eaten nearly every meal I remembered for my first nine years. I even recognized a hairline crack on the glaze of the shining red plate at the top of the stack. I'd put it there one day when I'd been in a hurry to finish my dinner so I could continue a game that had been interrupted by adult priorities like meals.

In other cabinets I found familiar casseroles and platters, an egg-cup of ruby red glass that had been the only thing which could coax me to eat soft-boiled eggs, the floral flatware, drinking glasses in amber and blue.

Each item held a fragment of memory, yet each piece seemed oddly out of place here where they must have spent most of their time. My memories of them were set on tables, filled with food, or empty and being carried out by one of the silent women.

The pots and pans held fewer memories, but were reassuringly solid: cast iron, thick aluminum, enamelware. No teflon coatings or flimsy light-weight stuff made to be thrown out after a few years' use. Everything in the kitchen cabinets seemed to be for practical, daily use. The good china and silver I faintly remembered must be kept elsewhere.

Slowly it was soaking into me what a tremendous treasure I had in this house and its contents. It was as if I were opening a time capsule—a house that had remained essentially untouched for forty years. The items that weren't outright antiques were probably collectibles. The Fiesta ware was a good example. I'd seen individual pieces selling for about what it would cost me to buy an entire new set of dishes at one of the discount markets.

My scrounger reflexes flared up at the realization. I thought about phoning Betty Boswell and asking her to mail me a box of the reference books I had at home, books I'd accumulated because there were times that my scrounging for art supplies had led me to a real find. Eventually, I'd wanted to know how to identify the next one. With those books, I could do some classifying, set up a shop on one of the Internet auction sites, make a huge killing . . .

Then the impulse died back, quickly as it had risen. As I understood it, estate taxes and the like had been paid back when my mother had been de-clared dead. Property taxes had been dutifully paid every year. I didn't need any money, not immediately at least. I would certainly have major ex-penses if I decided to do anything with the house, but right now I didn't need to—didn't want to—look at the place merely as a repository of things to be looted and sold. I needed to know what was here, yes, but more im-portant, I needed to know what had happened here.

Deliberately, as if making a declaration of some sort, I pulled out three plates of the Fiesta ware—one blue, one red, and one sunshine yellow—and three tall, pressed glass tumblers. I rinsed them, dried them, and made up plates of cookies and fresh fruit. Then I mixed a tall pitcher of iced tea from a powdered mix and bottled water.

Going to the door, I called out above the sounds of nails being pulled and two male voices giving each other orders: "Domingo, why don't you and your nephew come take a break?"

They did, and Blanco got his cookie after all.

**7**

Painting, n. The art of protecting flat surfaces from the weather and exposing them to the critic.
—Ambrose Bierce,
*The Devil's Dictionary*

## INSIDE THE LINES

The mirrors were the worst. Somehow I had forgotten their omnipresence, but as I began taking down the enshrouding dustcovers, I was forced to remember.

After finding the kitchen so overwhelmingly filled with memories, I had decided to take my time getting to those rooms that I had never forgotten: the library, my own nursery, the front parlor—Mother's rooms. The kitchen was plenty large enough for me to use as a base of operations. I could sleep on one of the wide sofas in the formal living room. With this in mind, I uncovered the sofa I remembered as being the most comfortable, then opened the closet in which I vaguely recalled seeing the silent women put away the cleaning equipment.

There was a mirror inside the door, another on the wall in back so my reflection—I had a smudge on my nose—looked back at me, seemingly as startled as I was. Hurriedly, I got out the canister vacuum and trundled it after me down the hall to the living room.

Like the dishes, the vacuum would probably fetch me a tidy price on the Internet, but right then all I cared about was that it started without a fuss. There were attachments for furniture, and I carefully cleaned the sofa cushions as well as the surrounding floor. Time enough later to unroll the carpets.

Then I trotted upstairs to the linen closet. An odor of mothballs and cedar—whoever had last been here hadn't been taking any chances—eddied out as I opened the door. This was no mere multishelved cabinet as in my house in Ohio, but a narrow little room lined in cedar. There were shelves all along one side, and a pull-chain for a light up above.

I pulled it, and the light snapped obediently on. This time I was somewhat more ready for the mirrors, but they surprised me nonetheless. I draped a few pillowcases over them, tired of seeing my dirty, startled features. Then I selected a pair of flat sheets, a few more pillowcases, and a blanket. I had my own pillow with me—something I usually do when travelling by car. I was glad. There were no pillows in the linen closet, and I didn't particularly want to try any of the bedrooms just yet.

When I had transformed a corner of the living room into a sort of bedroom, I returned to the kitchen. It was a brighter, lighter room now that Domingo had taken down the boards over the windows. Unlike the living room, it lacked heavy drapes over the windows. A not too intimidating mirror set over by the sink made me decide that I really needed to wash my face. After I'd done so, I looked around.

"If I'm going to start somewhere, it might as well be here. Otherwise, I'll be eating dirt."

Despite the years the kitchen had been left abandoned but for Domingo's periodic inspections, it was surprisingly—clean wasn't a word I'd usually apply to surfaces covered in dust and spiderwebs, but it was the right word.

Most kitchens—even the best kept—have their slightly grimy spots, the places where grease or moisture has caused dirt to adhere. Not in this room. It looked as though the last thing the silent women had done before going wherever they had gone had been to wash every surface. I had dust to wash away, spiderwebs to brush down, but there was no real need to scrub. Even so, it was a big room—a working kitchen designed to serve the needs of a household that would have included live-in servants as well as the resident family.

By the time I was finished, I had stopped several times for coffee (I'd bought a drip coffeemaker at the grocery store), and even so I was beat. Still, I felt good about what I'd done. This room, at least, was liveable. I'd tested the stove, and like the refrigerator it was old but in good, working condition. I'd had to replace a bunch of lightbulbs, and had made a note to pick up some types I hadn't thought to get.

Even the mirrors set here and there were beginning to bother me less. I was remembering the reflexes of my childhood. How to register motion in the mirrors but not be distracted by it. It was even somewhat helpful. When Domingo came to the back door, I greeted him without turning around.

"Come on in," I said. "I've just made coffee. You're welcome to something cold if you'd prefer. It's astonishing how well the fridge is working."

I saw Domingo start slightly at my greeting, but despite what Mrs. Morales had said, he was no fool. He noticed the absence of dustcovers and the mirrors they had revealed, and drew the correct conclusions.

"I would like coffee," he said. "Sometimes hot is better than cold when one is hot."

"I agree," I said. "I have a few cookies left."

"I would not say no."

"Sit down then. I actually know where everything is—at least in here."

After pouring for both of us, I joined him at the kitchen table, my own coffee in a cup and saucer set I only vaguely remembered. Somewhere must be the mug in which I'd been served cocoa. I remembered it well. It had scenes out of a Currier and Ives print painted on the side—too wintery for a summer day like this.

"My nephew has gone home to his family," Domingo said. "We have finished the ground floor windows, and I would like your permission to do some touch-up painting before moving up to the second floor. Some of the wood was a little—not damaged—but distressed by our handling."

"By all means," I replied. "I have enough to do down here to keep me busy for several days—weeks maybe."

He nodded. "You worked hard today. It looks good."

"Thanks."

"There's still a lot to do, especially if you don't want to be cleaning house into the autumn."

"I don't have 'til autumn. School starts again the end of August."

"School? Are you a student, then?"

I smiled. "Teacher. Grammar school art. Everything from finger painting to sketching and modeling."

"Do you like it? Working with all those small children?"

"Sometimes they get to be a bit much, but most of the time, yeah, I like it."

"Do you have any children?"

"No." I realized I sounded a bit rude and added quickly, "Never met the right man. You?"

Domingo shook his head. "No. Nephews and nieces, plenty of those, but no children. Like you said, I never found the right person."

We'd been sitting companionably enough until then, but suddenly I felt odd—shy, aware of him not as the caretaker of my property or an amiable individual, but as a man. I struggled to find something to say, some way to fill the silence. Surely I could ask about his family. He'd mentioned a sister . . .

But, as I was shaping my incoherent thoughts into a sentence, Domingo rose. He carried his cup, saucer, and cookie plate over to the sink.

"Thank you, Mira. I should be going now."

He was out the door before I could do more than nod. I rose, unwilling to chase after him, but not wanting to end the day on this uncomfortable note. He must have heard me open the screen door, for he turned and gave me a friendly smile.

"I told Enrico to come over at eight so we could start pulling off boards again. Will that be too early?"

"Not at all. I expect I'll be up long before then."

He waved and continued striding off across the lawn. I thought about calling him back, offering to take him to dinner—not a date, just payback for dinner last night. I didn't though. He probably had things he needed to do. My return to the old family home had probably disrupted his routine. After all, I was the one on summer break, not him.

Determinedly, I went back into the kitchen. There would be daylight for hours yet, but I didn't much feel like continuing housework. The walled garden around the back seemed like the perfect refuge. I could sit there with a book until I was tired enough to shower and sleep.

That's what I did. I sat there, the paperback beside me on the wooden bench. I did nothing, just stared without focusing at a profusion of roses. My thoughts drifted through a tangled maze of memory, sorting through things I hadn't considered for years. Eventually, I dug a stub of a pencil out of my pocket and started making a list on the inside back cover of the book.

Mrs. Little
Hannah
School
Police????
Newspaper?
Servants. Teresa Sanchez
Domingo's dad?

I felt exhausted, as if this hour or so of meditation had been more wearing than all the scrubbing, dusting, vacuuming, hauling, sorting, and folding I'd done that day. My head swam as I made my way back into the house, through the kitchen, and into the living room.

I remembered to check that the doors and windows were locked before undressing and sitting on the edge of the sofa. I'd meant to shower before I went to bed, but I couldn't keep my eyes open. I put my head on my pillow, and was in the middle of a thought that the linens smelled rather too strongly of mothballs when I fell asleep.

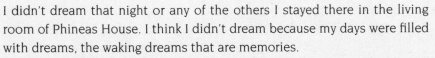

I didn't dream that night or any of the others I stayed there in the living room of Phineas House. I think I didn't dream because my days were filled with dreams, the waking dreams that are memories.

I maintained my resolve not to go into certain rooms, but there was still plenty to keep me busy. I began on the living room, deciding I preferred the mirrors to sleeping surrounded by dust sheets. The front hall followed that, then the formal dining room.

Nor did the incredible luck of my first day-or-so's residence hold. A couple of pipes sprung leaks, doubtless from being asked to carry water for the first time in four decades. The phone service was scratchy, and a new line had to be laid. The old clothes washer and dryer were simply too archaic for me to keep using them. I could practically feel how much power they used. One day I stood outside and watched the new meter the electric company had installed. The little dial whirled around merrily. I made a resolution.

I paid an electrician Mrs. Morales recommended to review the house's wiring. He assured me that after he did a few repairs, I could run modern appliances on the existing wiring, I went on the Internet and ordered a new refrigerator, washer, dryer, and stove. They constituted a major expense, but one that I easily balanced by surfing the Internet one evening until I found a site specializing in "antique" appliances.

It's really becoming truer every day that if you have something, there's someone out there who will buy it. In this case, the sums I got for the old appliances more than covered my purchases—and the electrician's fee, too. Even though I experienced a twinge of sadness at seeing the old appliances go, I also felt a whole lot safer when I no longer needed to fear that one of them would cause a short and bring the whole towering Victorian monstrosity down in flames.

So it went. The residents of houses on neighboring streets started dropping by. I kept my entertaining to the back garden, making the excuse that the house wasn't yet safe for visitors. Since most of them were living in similar houses—in a few cases, were restoring houses that hadn't been as well cared for as Phineas House—my excuse was easily accepted.

Yet, despite the friendliness of the neighbors, despite Domingo's presence on the periphery of my days, I was becoming a hermit. The house and the memories it held claimed me and seized hold of all my attention. I was living half in the present, half in my childhood, trying to understand what once I had taken so much for granted.

Caught within waking dreams, I woke one day, my mind full of thoughts of finally getting into the front parlor, and how I just might move my sleeping quarters from the living room into one of the upstairs bedrooms, when I glanced at the calendar and realized that it was August. It had been August for several days now.

August. I needed to be back to work in a few weeks. I'd done nothing for my lesson plans for the fall term. Of course, the first few weeks weren't all that demanding. Half the time elective courses were canceled for one special assembly or another. I usually found myself moderating lunchrooms or helping the office to unsnarl the annual maze of new student problems.

I sat up on the sofa and met my gaze in the nearest mirror.

"But I don't want to go," I said. "I've hardly started here."

"Then don't," I answered myself. "Stay. Tell the administrators you need some sort of compassionate leave. You did just lose your parents a few months ago—and you're not hurting for money. The House will give you more if you need it."

"But my house. Aunt May and Uncle Stan's house."

"This is your house."

"My friends."

"Can visit you. New Mexico isn't the end of the world. They can fly into Albuquerque and drive to Las Vegas. It's only one hundred and twenty or so miles. Or if they don't want to do that, they can catch a puddle-jumper or shuttle into Santa Fe. That's even closer, about sixty-five miles. You could even pick them up yourself."

I stared at my reflection, seeing it as nothing but patches of color, listening to my internal debate. One thing was true. I didn't really want to go back. For all I had been living like a hermit, I hadn't felt in the least lonely. When I wanted conversation, there was Domingo or one of the neighbors. Now that I had an Internet connection, I was even keeping up with the daily lives of my Ohio friends.

Yes, I had two houses back there that would eventually need my attention, but I didn't like to think of Phineas House boarded up again. Like Domingo, I had started thinking of it as a person, with feelings and preferences, and I imagined how it would feel to find its eyes boarded shut again just when it was getting the dust out of its passages.

Moving slowly, I went into the kitchen. I'd set up my laptop there at one end of the kitchen table. While I drank my morning coffee, I drafted half-a-dozen e-mails. I sent them before I could think any further, but when I went upstairs to shower, I noticed that my feet felt light upon the stairs.

I made some resolutions while I showered. If I was going to take time off, then I needed to do more than house cleaning. I needed to pursue what had brought me back—the question of what had happened to my mother forty-some years before.

I thought of some of the lists Aunt May had made. I'd save myself time and trouble if I looked into her journals, saw how far she'd taken her quest. Some of the things that had been so hard for her to do would be easy for me now. More and more newspapers were scanning in their morgues, putting the information online. Moreover, I was here in Las Vegas. I could find out if the police chief was still alive, any of the reporters. If they were they would be older now—sixty or seventy at the least. They'd probably be happy to talk about a long-ago mystery with the person it had most deeply affected.

Unlike Aunt May, I had no need to fear those mysterious trustees, those men who had placed such peculiar conditions on my adoption. Why hadn't they wanted the Fenns to have any contact with my earlier life? Was it indeed, as Aunt May had suspected, some sort of protective custody? There were similarities to witness protection programs: the move, the changing of names.

When I'd dealt with Aunt May and Uncle Stan's final paperwork, I'd come across the decrees they'd signed when they had legally changed their names. His full name had been Steven Stanley Flinwick. I suspected he might have already gone by Stan, since Aunt May referred to him that way, even in her journals. Hers had been Martha Ann. Maybelle had suited her better. May's Beauty. Her birthday had been in May. I liked to think Uncle Stan might have chosen it for her.

I jerked my wandering thoughts back to practicalities as the water began to get a little chilly. I made another mental note: replace hot-water heater. I wondered if anyone out there collected old water heaters. Probably not, but it never hurt to check.

Getting a leave of absence from my job was made easier in that I wasn't asking for a sabbatical, where I'd get paid, just leave. I'd been working for the school system long enough that periodic raises meant that some bean counter was probably celebrating the sudden fat in the budget.

No matter. I'd dotted all the i's, crossed the t's. My job would be waiting for me next year.

I'd also arranged for someone to mow the lawns at the two houses I now owned back in Ohio. Betty Boswell had said she'd keep an eye open for someone who might want to housesit. I put the word out among my own friends as well.

Domingo Navidad expressed pleasure when I said I'd decided I needed to stay a year in Las Vegas in order to decide what to do with Phineas House. Doubtless his pleasure was intensified by the fact that I made clear I had no designs on his carriage-house apartment, and that I wanted to invest in having the house fully painted.

"You've done a wonderful job," I assured him, "but the escrow account didn't allow for you to hire the hands you'd need to finish the exterior. Can you write me a budget for what you think you'd need?"

He agreed with enthusiasm, and the price he came back with—and swore he would keep to—made me fairly sure he planned on giving work to some people of questionable citizenship. I decided not to worry about it. Domingo had a contractor's license. We'd decided that he could handle hiring and firing without involving me if I hired him in that capacity for the painting, rather than having him direct the work in his role as caretaker.

I had no doubt he'd do a good job. I had the evidence all around me as proof.

Over the past couple of days we had worked our way around the uncomfortable awareness of each other that had followed our discussion of our mutual lack of marital partners. We met many mornings for coffee and some sort of breakfast cake, usually sitting out in the walled confines of the back garden. Domingo came and went there freely now, tending his garden. When he brought me roses or cut flowers there was nothing romantic about it, just the lovely end result of pruning.

I stopped working on the downstairs long enough to transform one of the front bedrooms on the second floor into a room for myself. It was across the landing from the rooms that had been my mother's and had ostensibly been the best guest room. However, the only overnight guests I recalled had been my mother's lovers. As I had my doubts that any of them had actually spent a night in the spacious chamber, I felt quite comfortable taking it over for myself.

The furniture was in good condition, all but the mattress of the queen-sized bed, in which the foam padding and satin fabric had dried and deteriorated so that lying on the bed felt like lying on old crackers. I didn't think I could find a buyer for the mattress even on the Internet, so I junked it and bought myself a nice new one.

I found linens to fit in the cedar closet, gave them a good laundering to get rid of the smell of mothballs. Up in the attic, I found a couple of big steamer trunks that had been used to store quilts and other heavy bedding. Las Vegas nights could grow chilly, even in summer, and I picked out a pretty star pattern patchwork quilt done in a riot of yellows and greens with touches of pale pink. I had no memory of ever seeing it before, and that pleased me.

The furniture in the room was heavy cherry, a good wood that responded well to oil soap and polish. The rugs rolled against the wall were simply patterned orientals in neutral tans, blues, and pale golds, perfect for a guest room. I aired and vacuumed them, and found their muted colors glowed.

I was pleased with this place I'd made for myself, but in the process of setting it up, in going up and down, up and down from the attic searching for this accessory or that, I had felt a puzzle growing in my mind.

There, in a side wing, toward the back of the house where they overlooked the gardens, were my own rooms. Mother's had been on the front left (as you faced the street) of the second floor. These rooms I still had not entered, as I had not entered the front parlor or the library. However, by now I was sure I had opened every other door and at least peeked inside. I found more spare bedrooms, an office that clearly had not been used for even longer than the rest of the house, even an infirmary of sorts.

One of the towers proved to have been furnished as a sitting room, pleasantly situated so that you seemed to be nesting among the tossing boughs of the elms. Another showed traces of having been used as an artist's studio, though, as with that second office, my impression was that it had been a long time since it had been so used. There was a music room, the piano horribly out of tune, over half the strings on the impressive harp broken. There were numerous instruments stored in cabinets or closets: violins and violas in flaking leather cases, two matching silver flutes and piccolos, a brass trumpet, a French horn, and even a pair of maracas painted with parrots.

In short, I found everything and more than that for which I was searching. Where were the servants' quarters? Where had the silent women slept? I remembered them as omnipresent, whether putting me to bed at night or bringing me my breakfast in the morning. True, I had never known them well. Mother had discouraged familiarity with the servants, even with the one who was intended to serve as my tutor.

Did they go home at night? It seemed that I should have had some memory of this, some sense of the guard being changed, but all I remembered was them always being there, answering the ring of the bell or my mother's imperious summons.

I'd hoped to find something of theirs left behind in what must have been a fairly hasty evacuation. A book with a name written on the flyleaf, a notebook, a letter case—something that would give me an idea where I might find one or more of these women. They might have an idea what had happened to my mother, an idea they might be willing to share with her daughter.

Mother might have commanded them to silence, and I remembered Mother well enough to know that her commands would have been respected even after—maybe even *especially* after—she had apparently disappeared, but surely they would break that silence now, over forty years later, when the interrogator was Colette's own daughter.

But I found no trace of them, not even in the kitchen, pantries, and other workrooms that I remembered being their domain. There were no scribbled notes in recipe books, no partial grocery lists. They had cleared away every trace of themselves, perhaps while they settled the house beneath its dust sheets, preparing it for its long nap.

I had one name, Teresa Sanchez, a name Aunt May had found in the newspaper articles about my mother's disappearance. I decided to ask

Domingo about it, and did so one morning over coffee and a particularly good pecan roll his sister, Evelina, mother of Enrico, had sent over.

We were in the back garden, and Domingo was already dressed for painting in off-white overalls that held the rainbow in tiny teardrop splatters. I had resolved to finally start on the front parlor that day, but the pleasant weather was making me reconsider. Maybe I would ask permission to join the painting crew. The buckets with their liquid color practically sang to me whenever I went outside.

"Domingo, you mentioned that you helped your father when he was groundskeeper here."

"That's right. As soon as I was large enough not to be a nuisance, and, I suspect, rather before." Domingo laughed, probably at some memory of his own ineptitude.

"Were you friendly with any of the women who worked in the house?"

"Oh, no. We were outdoor workers. That was made plain from the start. I don't think I ever went farther than the kitchen door until I was given care of the place when my father retired."

"Did your father?"

"Go inside?"

"Yes. I mean, that's not the point. Did he make friends with any of the women who worked here?"

Domingo shrugged. "I don't know. He has never mentioned it."

I sighed, then cut myself another hunk of pecan roll. One thing about my steady physical labor around Phineas House. I wasn't much worried about gaining weight.

"I told you I wanted to learn what happened to my mother. I thought one of the servants might know something she didn't want to tell the police."

Domingo might have a foolish attachment to Phineas House, but he was no fool when it came to anticipating what I was thinking.

"And you think they might not have wanted to tell the police?"

"My mother was a formidable woman," I replied. "I think if she told someone something and said it shouldn't be told to anyone, that secret would be kept—even from the police."

"But now . . ." Domingo nodded. "I will ask my father. I was going to visit him and my mother tonight in any case. He's interested in the progress on the House."

"Tell him to come over if he wants," I said. "I'll give him a tour of what I've done."

"I will tell him," Domingo said.

The morning was showing promise of turning into a lovely day. Suddenly, I could not face another round of moving furniture, dusting, polishing, of the vacuum howling in my ears.

"Can you use another hand with the painting?"

Domingo grinned. "I have been making a bet with myself on how long you would wait to ask—artist that you are. Come. I have just the place for you to start."

What Domingo had reserved for me were leopards. There were three of them, bordering a lancet window on the ground floor that looked in upon the formal dining room. One leopard crouched at the top of the window, its tail hanging down, apparently without regard for the leopard stretching up from below with every intention of giving it a good swat. The upper leopard's disregard could be understood, for its attention was fixed on the leopard beneath the windowsill, its long body elongating in a crouch so lifelike that it seemed impossible that it would not be completed.

"Wonderful!" I said. Then I frowned. "But I don't remember it at all."

"But, Mira," Domingo said, "then there were houses on either side. These were framed by comparatively narrow side yards—I don't think anyone but my father and myself ever came here, and then just to tend the roses that climbed the wall."

"I remember them," I said, "a glorious pale yellow. They only bloomed once a year. The rest of the time they were just a nice, dark green—unless bare in winter."

"That's right," Domingo said, pleased. "Old roses. After the fire, I transplanted what I could save to one of the back walls. You will see them flower again in the spring."

I returned my attention to the leopards. The area surrounding them had already been painted the dark green used elsewhere for the window frames. The leopards themselves had been primed, but waited for an exterior cover.

"Looks like this is ready to go."

"All you need to do is select your colors," Domingo agreed. "Come this way."

I did, and a short time later returned carrying brushes, rags, and a tin of golden-yellow paint. Enrico, Domingo's nephew, followed with the stepladder I would need to reach the upper portions of the frame. I thanked the boy absently, my mind already taken up with the challenge before me. Brush went into paint, and I lost myself to the demands of color.

Hours later, when Enrico returned to tell me the crew was breaking for lunch, it was probably a good thing I was standing on the ground, for I was so lost that I would have fallen off the stepladder if I'd been up there.

But the leopards were done, and they were magnificent. It must have been the relative dryness of the New Mexico weather, but the base coat of golden-yellow paint had dried almost as soon as I had it just the way I wanted it. I'd returned to the paint cans and poured a little brown into the yellow, blending it until I had what I needed for the touch of shadowing that would give dimension to the three figures.

I'd brought along a couple other shades of brown for the spots, a dip of red for the tongues in the open, playfully snarling mouths, a dab of white for the fangs and extended claws. What color to make the eyes had been a dilemma. Contrary to popular belief, the great cats don't usually have green eyes. Most often their eyes are gold, similar in shade to their coats. I debated, and decided that here myth served better than reality. I'd been dabbing the last eye green and adding a white sparkle when Enrico had come for me.

The overall effect of my paint job was an extravaganza more usual on a carousel than on the side of a house. I couldn't have been more delighted. The boy—he was about ten—grinned at me in equally enthusiastic appreciation.

"Wow!" he said. "Those are wonderful. Will you do the others, too?"

"Others?" I asked.

Enrico indicated the other three lancet windows that served the dining room. All were adorned with variations on the great-cat motif. There were lions, tigers, tassel-eared lynxes, ocelots, cougars, and other wild cats.

"I think I might," I said. Then I felt the aches in my body from the long time I'd spent up on the stepladder. "But not today. I still have work to do inside."

"The inside of the house is looking nice," Enrico said, shyly. "I looked in the front door and some of the windows. When I was little, and would come to help Tio Domingo I thought the house was haunted because of all the white things. It is better now."

"I think so, too," I agreed.

Behind me, the soughing of the wind in the eaves sounded like the house's own whispered agreement.

The fact is that Vegas is a small town and you are likely to run into the "characters" in a hamlet more frequently than you would in a metropolis. The small town "centrics" permit those of their citizenry who are farther off the beam to run around without let or hindrance.
—Milton C. Nahm,
*Las Vegas and Uncle Joe*

## INSIDE THE LINES

Although I was now splitting my time between painting the great cats, and working on the front parlor, I did not give up my intention to pay some serious attention to my search for my mother.

Domingo's father had not known anything about the women who had worked in Phineas House in my mother's day. Like me, he had recalled them as always being there. No, they had not lived in the carriage house, nor had there been another building on the grounds. I began to think that at least one of the rooms I had dismissed as an unused guest room must have been servant's quarters, and that any sign of its former inhabitants had been tidied away with the same meticulous attention that had left the kitchen free of grease and dirt.

Although this seemed to be a dead end, I still had several names. I was disappointed to learn that the chief of police who had put himself in charge of the investigation into my mother's death, had himself died since.

"Forty years, Mira," I said to my reflection one evening as I was scrubbing off the day's accumulated grime. "See if you can find out who else was on the force then. See if any of them were close to the chief and would have assisted him."

I bit into my thumbnail, uncertain how to do this. Then it occurred to me that the newspaper morgues might help. In a small town like this—like the one I'd grown up in—it was more usual for assisting officers to get some sort of credit. Thinking about the newspaper gave me insight into another avenue I might explore—the newspaper's own reporters. As with the police chief, the older ones might be dead, but the younger ones could still be around.

There was another reason I liked the idea of talking to a reporter. It seemed much less likely that a reporter would have been feeding information to the mysterious trustees. After all, a reporter made his living and reputation by publicly sharing information. Sitting on the details of a hot story would be a lot less attractive.

With these resolutions in mind—and with the need to purchase more furniture polish, soap, glass cleaner, and half-a-dozen other items as good reason for leaving Phineas House, I told Domingo I was going shopping, and would probably be gone for a bit. The map Mrs. Morales had given me showed the location of the Carnegie Library. There I figured I could fill in the rest.

The library did have the *Las Vegas Optic* on file, and I picked a corner and delved into facsimiles of old newspapers. Intent as I was on my quest, I had to keep dragging myself back on course. There were so many fascinating bits of trivia, windows into a time and place about which I was coming to realize just how little I knew.

On the other hand, I had only been nine when my mother had vanished. How much would I have known—or if known—cared about local events? I'd barely cared when J.F.K. had been assassinated a couple years later. I knew it was a big deal, but mostly I enjoyed the holiday from school as a chance to play with friends and indulge in an orgy of painting.

My research paid off by giving me several names, both of police officers whose names seemed to show up on a regular basis in association with the police chief, and of a reporter who, after the first hue and cry of my mother's disappearance had ended, seemed to be doing the majority of the follow-up reporting.

I had vague memories of the reporter at least. He'd been youngish, slim and wiry, with brushed-back brown hair. His left jacket pocket had always contained a small tin stocked with brightly colored hard candy. When I remembered him I again tasted a particular raspberry flavor and felt the lumpy texture of the candy in my mouth, the slight ooze of the soft center when I broke through the outer shell.

Unlike many of those who had asked me questions over those troubling days, Mr. O'Reilly seemed genuinely to listen to my answers. He'd also been the one who had interviewed Mrs. Ramsbottom, my former tutor, and recorded her scathing assessments of Colette for posterity.

My heart beat rather erratically when I cross-referenced his name the local telephone directory and found it listed: Chilton O'Reilly. I wrote down the number and stared at it. Unlike Domingo, I didn't have a cell phone, so I couldn't follow my immediate impulse to make the call. By the time I got home and unloaded my supplies, I was so nervous that my hand shook when I picked up the phone and punched in the numbers.

"Hello?"

The voice was young and strong, and my heart sank within me. A son. The name probably belonged to a son.

"May I speak with Chilton O'Reilly?"

"Speaking."

"I was actually hoping to speak with Chilton O'Reilly, who reported for the *Optic*," I said, hearing myself sound very tentative. I added for clarification, "Could you help me locate him?"

*Please, please, please, don't let him be dead*, I prayed silently to who knows who.

"That would be my grandfather," Chilton the Younger said. "One moment."

My heart rose back to its normal place within me, but I remained nervous. After what seemed like an eternity, a voice very like that of the younger man, but with a more polished diction, said, "Yes. This is Chilton O'Reilly."

"Mr. O'Reilly," I said. "This is Mira Fenn, that is, when you knew me I was Mira Bogatyr."

There was deep sigh from the other end of the line, as if breath that had been held these forty years had finally been released.

"Good to hear from you again, Ms. Fenn." He spoke the modern neutral abbreviation as if it came hard to his lips. "What may I do for you?"

"I was wondering if we might meet. I'm trying to learn what I can about when my mother disappeared."

"She never returned, then?"

"No."

I felt that blunt monosyllable had given away far more than I had intended, and heard that knowledge in Mr. O'Reilly's reply.

"Why don't you come over to my house? I have some files here, I think, and it would be more private than a restaurant. I assume your return isn't widely known?"

I knew my voice must sound puzzled when I replied, "I haven't exactly hidden it."

"But no one from the paper has come by to interview you?"

"No, no one."

"Well, it's a very old story, and I don't suppose anyone there even remembers it now. Where are you residing?"

"Phineas House."

"I see."

"When would be convenient for you, Mr. O'Reilly?"

"Can you come by tomorrow midmorning? I would like time to pull the files and refresh my memory."

Somehow, I didn't believe he needed to refresh his memory at all, but I couldn't disagree that it might take time to locate files from a story forty years gone.

"That sounds great," I said. "Can you give me directions?"

He did, and we rang off with mutual assertions that it would be interesting to see each other again after so long.

The next morning, I spent a couple hours working on the tigers around the window. Their stripes were intricately carved, and I found they took even more attention than had the rosettes on the leopards' coats. As requested, young Enrico stirred me from my painter's trance in time for me to shower and dress for my appointment.

New Mexico throve on informality, but I decided that this visit merited dressing up. Mr. O'Reilly had sounded just a bit old-fashioned. I chose a watered-silk skirt in blues and purples that swept my ankles and made stockings unnecessary, a pale blue blouse, and a contrasting rope of glass beads that I had strung from various scrounging finds. I finished the ensemble with comfortable sandals, and a pair of fused glass earrings. It was an outfit I liked a great deal, and in which I was psychologically as well as physically comfortable.

So girded and armed for battle, I mounted my red pickup, waved to my painting crew, and drove to Chilton O'Reilly's house.

His neighborhood was not as old as mine, but it showed signs of long occupancy. The tile numbers for his house were hung on an adobe curtain wall spilling over with silverlace, a vine in which clusters of minute white flowers mingled with dark green leaves. The gate in the wall curved gracefully, and the flagstone walkway echoed that curve. The house itself was Territorial style, a blending of the Spanish adobe with the columned porches brought in by later settlers. It was an attractive house, but not in the least ostentatious.

In the lines of the man who opened the door when I rang the bell I could just recognize the young reporter of my memory. He was still wiry, but thin rather than lean. His posture was slightly stooped. His hair was a duller brown touched with grey, but he wore it in a similar fashion. The eyes behind glasses that I did not remember remained lively, but the color had paled from a medium brown to something closer to grey.

We stood for a moment while our memories adjusted themselves to reality. Then Mr. O'Reilly stepped back and opened the door wider to admit me.

"Ms. Fenn," he said, and without the distortion of the telephone I was paradoxically more aware of the changes in its timber, even as I heard its similarities to the voice I remembered.

"Please," I said, stepping over the threshold and into a cool, shadowed entry hall. "Call me Mira."

"Then you must call me Chilton," he said.

"It's an interesting name," I said.

"I have always thought so," he agreed, leading me back through the house. "I liked how it looked on bylines. My son seems to agree. He passed it on to his son. That was who you spoke with, by the way. My grandson, Chiltie."

"Chiltie?"

Mr. O'Reilly was leading me into the kitchen.

"He goes by Chilton, just as I do. His father is Chilt. It gets confusing, especially since my grandson came to live here, so my wife and I have permission to call him Chiltie—just as long as we don't do it in front of any of his friends. Chiltie's going to Highlands University. The arrangement works for everyone. My wife and I have been rattling around in this sprawling place. Chiltie has a section pretty much to himself, and having him here adds some liveliness. Meanwhile, his family is spared paying for a dorm room, and Chiltie doesn't have to commute from Albuquerque."

He took a deep breath, then continued right on talking, "Can I offer you anything? I just made coffee, but there's tea, lemonade, sodas . . ."

"Coffee would be great," I said. As always after a painting session I felt unaccountably drowsy.

"Two coffees, then." Chilton poured. After we'd done the usual routine of "Milk? Sugar? Sweetener?" he said, "I thought we'd go into my office. It's reasonably tidy."

"Are you still working as a reporter?" I asked.

"On and off," he said. "Not full time. Maggie—that's my wife—asked me to retire to part time so we could travel. We're comfortable enough. This house is bought and paid for, bought it when real estate was bottomed out. After I retired, we rapidly found we got along a whole lot better if we had some outside interests. She teaches a few courses up at the university, and I cover a few stories. We're just back from Greece. That's why I didn't know if your return had been covered."

"I see."

Chilton's office was a pleasant, cluttered, book-lined room, in which I could detect the evidence of some hasty housekeeping—probably in my honor. His desk sported both a very modern desktop computer, and a type-writer. From the faint film of dust on the typewriter keys, I could tell which got more use.

I was offered a seat in a chair I was willing to bet had been buried under one of the stacks of books now resting on the floor. Chilton moved auto-matically for the chair behind his desk, then stopped.

"Go ahead," I said. "You won't make me feel like I'm being grilled by the principal."

"Principal?" he said, settling into his chair. "So you're a teacher?"

"Art teacher," I said. "Grammar school, in Ohio." I heard my own words with a certain amount of surprise. Not long ago I would have said "back home in Ohio." "I've taken a leave of absence to deal with things here."

"Things? You mean finding your mother?"

"That and Phineas House. You see, until about three months ago, I didn't even know I still owned it."

Chilton's eyebrows rose in eloquent inquiry, and I hastened to explain. When I finished giving him all the details, up to and including Aunt May and Uncle Stan's deaths, and how I'd learned then I still owned the house,

I nearly went on to tell him about Aunt May's journals. I didn't though. Those were between her and me.

"So," I concluded, "I decided that if I was going to be in town anyhow, I might as well see if I could learn anything more about my mother."

"Even if you find her," Chilton said, "she won't replace the mother you just lost. You know that, don't you?"

I nodded, and heard myself talking. There was something about this man that encouraged confidences. I bet he'd been a great reporter.

"I certainly don't think my mother—Colette—could replace Aunt May. I'm not even sure why I want to find her. Maybe I just want a chance to ask her why she left me. Maybe I want to give her a chance to justify herself. Maybe I want a chance to yell at her for what she did. I don't know."

Chilton steepled his fingers and looked at me over the top. "You do realize that even if you find out what happened to her, you may not find *her*. She vanished over forty years ago. She was in her midthirties then. It's possible she's still alive—she'd be seventy something—but it's easily possible she's dead. I'm ten years younger, and I've buried a fair number of my contemporaries."

"I know," I said, and tried to sound mature and well-balanced. "I just have to try."

"Fine. Let me see what I can do to help you. What do you know?"

"What I remember—which isn't much—and what I read in the papers."

"Which isn't much," Chilton repeated. "Right. The *Las Vegas Optic* hasn't always been known for the rectitude of its reporting. Fact is, the man who founded the paper didn't care much if a story matched the facts. However, when we were covering the story of Colette Bogatyr's disappearance, we pretty much decided to err on the side of what we were sure about."

"Good editor?" I asked.

"That, and a story that got stranger the more deeply we looked into it."

"Tell me?"

Chilton stared down at the files on his desk, but I didn't think he was really seeing the typescript sheets, nor the newspaper clippings, nor even the sheaf of handwritten notes. I think he was seeing a time when he had been young and optimistic, eager to be the reporter who solved a case that had baffled the police, and so make his reputation.

And here he was, still in Las Vegas, a town that despite some pretty fine pretensions had never amounted to much of anything. Had he ever left? Did those intervening years contain laurels won elsewhere? I didn't ask. I didn't dare alienate this man.

"Well," Chilton began, "you know better than I do that the trail your mother left was already cold before the law got onto it—a month gone she was, and the time might have been longer if one of the maids hadn't felt something should be said. That she chose to say it to your schoolteacher, rather than the law, seemed strange to me when I first heard it, but it doesn't anymore.

"You see by the time she disappeared, your mother already had a bit of a reputation about the town. For one thing, no one could quite remember just when she came to town. Folks argued about it, some saying she'd been in residence in Phineas House only for about ten years, others swearing that she had been born there. One thing everyone agreed about. No one ever remembered seeing her in her teens or early twenties. I got a whiff of some sort of scandal, but never could get farther than that.

"Then there was the way Colette Bogatyr dressed—those elaborate, sweeping, somehow old-fashioned gowns she wore even for a trip out shopping. Some of the men thought Colette was living out of her mother's trunks, putting a good face on poverty. The women knew differently. They knew good tailoring. The ones who knew even more said that the styles weren't *quite* right, that they didn't match anything you'd find in Godey's or the other fashion catalogs from a couple generations back. They said your mother made her own style, and even the most waspish admitted it suited her far better than modern fashions would have done.

"Another mystery associated with your mother was Phineas House itself. In a town where some of the residents can trace their families back to the founding of the town in 1835, there's usually someone who brags, 'My grandfather tells when . . . ' Funny thing. No one remembered when Phineas House was built. It just always seems to have been there."

I interrupted, "But it's Queen Anne style. I know Americans are used to thinking of Victorians as old, and they are, compared to lots of what's around, but Queen Anne is a late fashion, comparatively speaking: late eighteen, early nineteen hundreds."

"I know," Chilton said. "I'm just telling you what folks said. I even checked the property registration one time. Some documents weren't there to find—you know about Las Vegas's having two governments early on?"

I didn't, but I didn't really want a history lesson right now, so I nodded.

Chilton didn't press me. "Well, as far as I could tell, the property has been in the family for several generations. Colette's father inherited it from his father, and apparently it was in the family before that. It's quite possible that the current Queen Anne was built over older construction."

"That's completely possible," I said, thinking of the odd layout of the inside of the house, how spaces didn't always seem to fit into each other. "I think that was often done when fancier exteriors became the fashion. Even Sears sold kits for adding gingerbread trim to gussy up the average farmhouse."

Chilton realized we'd strayed off topic. "Anyhow, none of this has much to do with anything, except that Colette Bogatyr was already a lady of mystery when she capped every tale ever told about her by disappearing."

I decided the reporter was being a bit too polite, sparing me the worst side of the gossip. If I was to learn anything, well, I had to press the issue.

"Seems to me that my mother must have had a reputation for something else," I said boldly. "I remember her boyfriends. That had to have raised eyebrows, even if she was a widow, maybe even more so, since she had a daughter to raise."

Chilton didn't say anything, but he did slide open his top desk drawer and take out a battered tin I instantly recognized.

"Piece of candy?" he asked. "It's getting harder to find this stuff, so I lay in a supply at Christmastime."

I smiled and took a lumpy, sugar raspberry. It tasted just like I remembered.

"More coffee?" Chilton asked.

I shook my head. Chilton crunched a bit of brightly colored candy ribbon between his teeth, letting his eyes drift half-shut, as if he might see the past that way.

"There was talk, yes," he said, "but less than you might imagine. Throughout its history, Las Vegas has been one of the rougher frontier towns. Billy the Kid wasn't an unknown visitor. Neither were Jesse James and a host of lesser known outlaws. It's said that Doc Holliday tried to set up a practice here, but even rough and tumble Las Vegas didn't welcome him. Even during those interludes when the town has tried hard to become respectable, there have been those who don't forget that one of the first structures taller than one story to be built here was a windmill that for a long time was the town's favorite hanging tree.

"Maybe if your mother had been slatternly there would have been more animosity toward her. Maybe, she would have awakened resentment if she had worn the finest Parisian fashions or flaunted her wealth or famous friends. Fact is, she did none of that. I've already mentioned how Mrs. Bogatyr's clothing excited curiosity, but not envy. It was like that about the rest of her—she was just so eccentric that even the worst prudes didn't harp about reforming her. Probably if anyone commented about anything it was that for all she said she was a widow, she still used her maiden name."

"I think I see," I said.

I voiced a thought I hadn't even realized I had formulated until Chilton had started talking about my eccentric mother's relationship to the rest of Las Vegas society.

"So it wasn't because my mother was some sort of public embarrassment that she wasn't found?"

"Oh, no. An honest effort was made to find her," Chilton said. "If that's what you mean."

"I think it is," I admitted. "I'd read about how the chief of police put himself in charge of the investigation. Two reasons he could have done that: if he wanted to make the best effort to find her—or if he didn't."

"Rest assured on that point," Chilton said. "Chief Garcia did his best to find Colette Bogatyr. How completely he failed remained a matter of frustration to him to the day he died."

"He's dead then," I said.

"Five years ago," Chilton replied. "At the ripe age of ninety-five. After he retired, we'd still meet and chat, and sometimes he'd mention that case."

"You were friends then?"

"Pretty much. Sometimes we found ourselves on opposite sides of a story, especially where local politics were involved, but we were both advocates of Las Vegas, believers that she had a future, if only she could stop fighting herself."

I thought of the town I'd driven through on my way to Chilton's house of the bits of history I'd heard from Domingo over our morning coffee breaks. It didn't seem that Las Vegas had much of a future, just a past full of disappointments.

That morning Las Vegas's history didn't seem pertinent to my search, so I didn't ask any of the obvious questions. Later, I'd learn I had been wrong about this, but only later.

"Seems to me that you must know a great deal about what was done. Could you tell me?"

Chilton nodded, and glanced without really seeing down at the notes spread on his desk.

"As you may have seen in the newspaper articles, Colette Bogatyr was last seen driving out of town to the northwest, in the direction of the towns of Llano and Montezuma. Now, she owned a car, but witnesses swear that she wasn't driving that car, but a neat little one-horse, two-seater carriage she kept for tooling around the countryside. It was one of those things, like her manner of dress, that Colette had done for so long that everyone took it for granted.

"Witnesses all agreed that she was alone. A couple said she seemed tense or anxious, didn't pass the time of day as she usually would. Most didn't volunteer anything of the sort. Last person who reported seeing her was a small-time farmer along the road northwest. After that, nothing."

I had indeed read most of this in Aunt May's newspaper clippings, then again in the library. I envisioned the map of the area, pinpointing various locations.

"That's it?"

"That's it. The police questioned everyone along what they figured her route would have been. They learned a few things that didn't make it into the papers. One was that Mrs. Bogatyr often drove that particular route, and that when she did, she was almost always alone. Sometimes she had a companion with her, but never more than one."

I frowned. "Could she have had someone with her that day, hunkered down toward the floorboards or something?"

"Not likely. The carriage was a light gig, meant for elegant driving, not for hauling."

"Was the carriage or horse ever found?"

"Not either. The police did their best to find wheel tracks, but that time of year—late April—there's often enough rain to make the roads hard to read. Also, back in the late fifties, the locals out that way still used wagons or burros. The tracks of your mother's gig were just one set among many."

"I see. Chilton, what's out that way that she could have been going to visit?"

"I asked myself that. So did Chief Garcia. There were quite a few families living out that way, and then there was the Montezuma Castle itself. At that point it was being used as a seminary for training Mexican priests. Police officers were sent out to all those places, but no one except a few people who happened to be outside working in their yards would admit to having seen Mrs. Bogatyr. A certain reporter replicated the police's efforts, but he didn't have any better luck."

Chilton grinned ruefully and scratched behind his left ear. "I had dreams of breaking the story by talking to the one farmer or housewife or seminarian the police overlooked. I even skulked around, sneaking into stables and sheds, hoping to find the missing rig or the horse that had pulled it, but the fact was Chief Garcia's men did a good job. I didn't learn anything because there was nothing there to learn."

"So my mother simply vanished into thin air somewhere between Las Vegas and the town of Montezuma."

"Probably nothing so dramatic," Chilton said. "She could have been overtaken by a vehicle. A truck hauling a trailer could have picked up both her and her gig. No one would have noticed the like along that road. Fact is, trucks are as common as cars. Trailers aren't a whole lot more rare. The train ran a lot more frequently in those days. It's possible that she got aboard.

"Thing is, we thought of that, too. Both freight and passenger trains were checked and double-checked, and not a damn thing useful came out of all that work. Trucks were harder to check out, but an effort was made there, too. Just about everyone in the area who had a rig that could have handled both horse and carriage found themselves getting called on by the police. No traces of horse, carriage, or woman were found."

He held the candy tin out to me by way of commiseration. I took out something flat and multilayered that tasted faintly of cocoa.

"Mira, maybe if the police had known sooner something could have been learned, but a trail a month old is a pretty dead trail—even today when the police can use computerized databases and a bunch of fancy forensics to help. Then, hell . . . The horse could have been sold weeks before. We're close enough to the Colorado border that it could have been gotten out of state. It might even have been slaughtered and fed to the dogs. Personally, I doubt that. It was a nice animal, a four-year-old blood bay mare with a white blaze. Good for riding or driving."

"I remember her," I said, startled to realize I did. "Her name was Shooting Star. I named her, because of how her blaze splashed into the white on her muzzle. She was a good horse, incredibly steady for her years. Mother would sometimes let me be put up on her. I'd ride up and down the street, proud as a princess. I'd forgotten all of that until you mentioned it."

Chilton nodded. "Your mother didn't keep the mare at Phineas House, but the house next door hadn't converted its stable into a garage. Those poor people came in for a real grilling, but nothing could be proved against them."

I remembered that fire had taken that house, along with all those bordering Phineas House.

"Were they still there when the fire came?"

Chilton looked momentarily confused. "You mean the fire that took that house out? No. They'd moved a long time before. Fact is, once you were gone and Phineas House was all shuttered up, property values tumbled in that area. They'd been sliding before, but a house that big, all closed up, didn't do anything to encourage prospective buyers."

I nodded, vaguely relieved. I hadn't really known any of the neighbors. If Mother had socialized with them, I hadn't been included. Even so, I was glad they hadn't been hurt—even while feeling guilty at my pleasure in Phineas House's expanded yard.

"So they didn't find Shooting Star," I said, bringing us back to the subject, "and I guess they didn't find the carriage either."

"Not a trace. That would have been even easier to dispose of—and it probably was destroyed, since it would have been easier to trace. Thing is, out on the ranches, folks burned trash—what trash they didn't pitch into a convenient ravine. Maybe a modern forensics team could learn something from the remnants of a bonfire, but not then."

"Was there a bonfire worth looking at?"

Chilton shook his head. "Not really. I'm just saying that even if the police—or an ambitious and nosy reporter—had come across something, all there would have been were ashes and maybe a few bits of metal."

"Sounds like the police really did try," I said. "You, too. Tell me. When did people stop looking?"

"It wasn't all at once," Chilton said, "or even like the search was ever formally called off. It's possible the file is still stuck in the back of some cabinet somewhere, though I honestly doubt it."

I doubted it too.

"Mira, how serious are you about trying to find your mother?"

"Fairly," I said, "though I don't really know where to begin. I hoped you might have something for me."

"But all I've given you are more dead ends." Chilton said what I hadn't. "Look. Let me offer you some help. I won't deny that I'd be helping myself, too, if that makes you feel better."

"Go on."

"When you came in, I asked if anyone had done a story about your return to town. You said no one had. Let me write that story. Late summer is a slow time for the paper, usually. I'm sure I can get permission to run a human interest piece on you—maybe even a couple. You say you're staying in Phineas House."

"That's right. I'm having Domingo Navidad help me fix it up. I haven't thought much more about that."

"Great! I could do a piece on your return, another on the resurgence of interest in the old Victorians—and mention you again."

"And what good would that do?"

"I'll say that you're interested in learning what you can about your mother—not just about her disappearance, but about her as a person. I can play the pathos of it—a grown woman, trying to learn something about the mother she barely remembers. Maybe someone will come forth."

"And maybe someone will run," I said.

"That would be information in itself," Chilton said. "I still have connections with local law enforcement. If anyone is reported missing, I can ask to be told."

I remembered the trustees and the care they had taken that my whereabouts be kept secret, Aunt May's wondering if my mother might have been involved with organized crime, or something.

"Will saying I'm looking for information about my mother be safe?"

Chilton shrugged. "I can't see it as being any more dangerous than your poking around, looking up semi-retired reporters."

"I remembered you," I protested. "I liked you."

"The key word there," Chilton said seriously, "is 'liked.' You remember a man from forty years ago. A lot can change in forty years."

I nodded somberly, suddenly chilled by the risk I might have run. Still, I thought that where Chilton O'Reilly was concerned, my memory hadn't played me false.

"Okay, Chilton. I'll go for it. Find out if the *Optic* will run the story, then. I'll give you a tour and an interview."

"Done."

We shook hands across the desk, made arrangements to meet again, this time at Phineas House, and shortly thereafter, I took my leave.

Sacrificial altars of carved stone and fired clay were the hallmark of priestesses, and among their uses they may have served as mortars to grind the chunks of colored ore into powder; these magical colors themselves then became body or textile paint.

— Jeannine Davis-Kimball, Ph.D., with Mona Behar,
*Warrior Women*

## OUTSIDE THE LINES

I wrote that reporter, the one from the *Las Vegas Optic*, but he hasn't replied. I guess reporters have more to do than assist fictional college students. Or maybe he saw through my deception. I tried to get everything right. Went over my spelling, and tried to use some jargon. Maybe I got something wrong.

Anyhow, I'll try one more time. Letters do get lost in the mail. Maybe the reporter is too busy right now. Maybe he's not able to reply until the story is older.

Maybe I just need to leave this whole thing alone. Mira's trustees wouldn't have taken her from Las Vegas if they really thought Colette would be coming back. I mean, there were servants there. Couldn't they have just hired a nanny or governess, and left Mira with her familiar school and friends?

Funny. Mira doesn't mention friends very often. She doesn't mention school often, either. A Mrs. Little comes up sometimes, but it's like Mira's working hard on leaving the past behind her. Shouldn't I be willing to do the same?

But Mira has so much to concentrate on. I . . . I FEEL STIFLED. I started out hating Colette. Now. Honest, M. I envy her. Envy. Great dark green envy . . .

What a life she had. Those clothes. The paper said she'd been seen in her horse-drawn carriage when she vanished. Says it matter-of-factly, too. There's mentions of interviews with her servants, her groundskeeper. The one photo of the house there—too blurred to show detail, but so big and imposing. My first thought when I looked at it: "I sure wouldn't like to be the one who keeps that clean." Then I realized. She didn't. She told other people to do it. She never had to pick up the newspapers Stan leaves by his chair every day. I mean, does he think there's a newspaper fairy who picks them up? If I watch another man—mine included—act like he's done a huge thing by picking up his plate and sticking it on the sideboard . . .

Betty told me Alan thought it was great when he gave her a new electric iron for her birthday. Said how much easier it would be for her to get his collars right. I'd have strangled him with the "extra special, new, deluxe in-sulated cord" I swear. I think Betty wanted to but she didn't.

Yesterday I found myself looking at that damn cookbook my mother gave me before we got married. "Meals that Please HIM." "Tempting Tasties for the Most Finicky Kid." "Hearty He-Man Hot Sandwiches." Tips on mak-ing a great impression on HIS boss, HIS family. The closest it came to any-thing for the bride were hints for SLIMMING. I went out, got an entire box of iced chocolate cream-filled cupcakes, and ate every one.

I bet Colette didn't worry about her waistline. Well. Maybe that. Those dresses didn't look too forgiving. But I bet she didn't worry about pleasing HIM. Whoever HE was. Mira gets really, really quiet when the subject of fa-thers comes up. Once she mentioned how one of her mother's beaus used to bring her taffy. Something about how she said that . . . I bet Colette had more than one beau. And I bet she didn't worry about pleasing them. I bet she expected them to please HER.

My fingers are cramping—stupid thing to write. Note to self. Get in Stan's files and find that copy of Mira's birth certificate. What is her fa-ther's name?

Stan's files!!! Why HIS!! Why is everything important, official HIS? I am such an idiot!

## INSIDE THE LINES

I sat staring at this entry, wondering how I could have missed Aunt May's unhappiness. Had she perhaps come to terms with things by the time I was adjusted enough to my new life to notice? I started leafing back through that journal, reading the entries that I'd skipped earlier because they dealt with something other than my mother and me.

Maybe because I'd been doing so much housecleaning, the details seemed very real. The dusting, laundry, "hoovering," the cooking, eternal cooking. Later I found an entry noting she'd decided I might as well learn to wash up after dinner: that "Mira had better get used to the idea there are no servants *here*." Subsequent entries noted how often Aunt May went down and had to wash some pot over again, or get the spots off of glassware. Apparently, Uncle Stan—a man I had always thought of as easygoing—could be a domestic tyrant. The knowledge made me uncomfortable.

I found some comfort in other of Aunt May's entries. At least Uncle Stan didn't think appliances were appropriate Christmas or birthday presents. He bought her jewelry or books. He always took her to dinner, and sometimes to lunch as well. They went out to movies and the occasional play. There were hints that they had a good sex life.

Even so, Aunt May had felt imprisoned by the expectations imposed on her gender and her social class—that tier of the middle class that cares so much about what other people think. I began to see her interest in religions and odd customs as the huge rebellion it must have seemed to her.

"Poor woman," I said aloud, as I put the journal back in its place in the metal box. "Aunt May, wherever you are, thanks for letting me stretch my wings. I don't think I ever realized how much you had to work against."

It seemed to me that there was a rippling smile in the air. When I turned out the bedside light and settled in to sleep, I felt a relief from the sorrow that had dogged me, almost unknowing, without relief, from the day the phone rang and I learned that my true mother was dead.

Chilton O'Reilly had been right. News was slow this time of year, and the *Optic* was more than happy to run a couple of stories about me. We decided to start with the "return home" one, so early the following week, Chilton came over to Phineas House.

I was in the kitchen setting up a pot of coffee when one of the painters called down from his scaffold, through the open window, "Señora Mira, a car has stopped. *Uno viejo está aquí.*"

"Thanks," I called back. As I went to open the front door, I made a mental note that Chilton and I might want to discuss anything sensitive somewhere away from an open window. But then, what sensitive matter might we discuss? I pretended I didn't know, but the question came to my lips almost as soon as we'd exchanged our greetings.

"Tell me, Chilton," I said, "why didn't you answer my mother's letter?"

"Your mother? Mrs. Bogatyr never wrote me."

"Not Colette," I said, "my adopted mother, Maybelle Fenn. Apparently, she wrote you about a year after I came to live with her, asking for details about Colette Bogatyr's disappearance."

Mr. O'Reilly looked surprised. "I never got her letter. Did she write care of the *Optic*?"

"I imagine so. That's the only address she would have had. She notes that she wrote at least twice. As far as I can tell, she never got an answer."

"Are you sure she wrote me, not another reporter, or the editor?"

I nodded. Aunt May had made carbons of her letters. I'd found them in a large envelope wedged into the metal document box alongside the journals.

Chilton looked sincerely embarrassed. "Mira, I don't remember receiving either of those letters, and I'm sure I would have remembered hearing from the woman who was taking care of you."

Now it was my turn to look embarrassed. "Actually, Chilton, Aunt May didn't mention that. She represented herself as a sociology student doing work on why women abandon their families."

Chilton's expression became quizzical. "Now, why would she do that?"

Even as I shaped an answer I thought would work, I found myself thinking, *Because in a way that is what she was interested in. She loved Uncle Stan and me, but there was a part of her that wanted to abandon it all and have a life of her own.*

Aloud I said, "Because she thought no one would tell her anything if they knew who she was. Apparently, the trustees for my mother—that is Colette Bogatyr's estate—were pretty cryptic about the circumstances surrounding her disappearance."

Chilton coughed a dry laugh. "They had to be, didn't they? They didn't have much to tell, and who would want to admit that? But, Mira, believe me, I never heard from Maybelle Fenn—or from a sociology student either. I'd remember that, too. I would have been thrilled to be part of a research project of any kind. I was young, eager, and very determined to make a difference."

He looked sad, then, as if wondering if anything he'd done had mattered in the least.

"I wish I knew where those letters went," I said, but I didn't push the matter further. To do so would be to come straight out and call Chilton O'Reilly a liar—that, or accuse him of being part of a conspiracy to conceal what did happen to my mother. I didn't think he was a liar, and if he was—or had been—part of a conspiracy, I didn't think accusing him of such would do any good. It might well do harm, because then he'd know I had reason to suspect there *was* a conspiracy, and if he was part of it . . .

I shook my head as if I could clear the confusing tangle of thoughts that way.

"I've made coffee," I said, "and there's iced tea, orange juice, and some pop."

"Coffee would be great," he said, and followed me back into the kitchen.

Once we'd poured and doctored, I suggested we sit in the living room.

"I've put a lot of time into getting it cleaned," I said, "and I'd enjoy showing it off."

He agreed, but I noticed him glancing toward the closed door of my mother's library/office as we went past. Interesting. Had he been in there at some point?

We seated ourselves, me on the sofa that until recently had served as my bed, Chilton on a high-backed chair. I'd placed a coaster on the table nearby, and as he rested his coffee cup on it, he smiled at what else was there.

"My favorite candy," he said. "That's not easy to find this time of year."

I grinned back. "I lucked into some at one of the general stores. I can't swear it's not stale, but the bottle was sealed."

He took a piece, and nodded his approval.

"Good," he said, his words slightly distorted by the candy tucked in the corner of his cheek. "Now, I prefer to take notes as I do an interview, but I'd also like to run a tape. That way I can double check my notes if necessary."

"No problem," I said. "What do you want to know?"

He started by asking a bunch of questions for which he already knew at least some of the answers. I guessed he was making sure he had his facts straight. Then he moved into other things: my art, my teaching career, my impressions of Las Vegas now as compared to what I remembered.

The process took a while, and I warmed our coffee a couple of times before we were done.

"That's far more than I'll ever be able to use," Chilton admitted as he folded his notebook closed and pushed the Stop button on the tape recorder. "However, I prefer to have rather more than less. This way, if there's a followup story, I'll already have some of what I'll need. Now, one more favor. Can I have a quick walk through the house—and maybe around the outside? It'll let me better plan what to do with the photographer when we do the other piece."

I rose, nodding. "That would be fine, but I haven't gotten to even half the rooms. I'd rather we restricted ourselves to the ones I have done. Certainly, you're not going to be able to run more than one or two pictures in any case."

"True enough," he agreed, but I had the impression he was disappointed. I didn't let that change my mind. The way he had looked at the door of my mother's office had made me uneasy.

I began the tour with the room in which we stood, took him through the dining room and kitchen, down into the cellar, then up to the room in which I was currently sleeping. I made a point of showing off details like the cedar-lined linen closet and the elegant—if outdated—fixtures in the bathrooms. When he asked to see a room that hadn't yet been cleaned up—for contrast, so he claimed, I showed him the music room.

I hustled him outside before I had to flat-out refuse to show him the library or front parlor—the latter still a work in progress. We walked slowly around the house, looking up at the intricate carvings adorning the facade. Domingo came down from his ladder, and took over the tour, proud as if he'd done the original construction himself. If a few of the workmen made a point of keeping out of the reporter's way, none of us were so impolite as to comment.

At last, Chilton departed, leaving me feeling an odd combination of jazzed and exhausted. Domingo seemed to sense my mood.

"Have you had something to eat?"

"Not since breakfast," I admitted.

"And that was a sweet roll," he said.

"I'll go in and make myself a sandwich," I said, glancing at his watch and noticing that it was well past one.

"Better," Domingo said. "Tomás went out for burritos earlier, and there is half of one—beef and bean—hardly touched. Take that. It's in my refrigerator."

I wanted to refuse, suspecting I was stealing his dinner, but the fact was a cold sandwich sounded completely unappealing, and I didn't have the energy to make something more complex. I accepted his offer, and took the Styrofoam box back to my own kitchen. As part of my orgy of appliance buying, I'd gotten a nice microwave at a very good discount. Soon, the burrito, and a good-sized portion of Spanish rice and refritos were steaming on a brilliant green Fiesta ware plate.

As I ate, my energy returned, and along with it a sense of resolution. I needed to stop putting off going into my mother's rooms—and into the library as well. Doubtless the police had been through both with great care, but there might be something in which Colette's daughter would recognize significance where a stranger would not.

I nodded sharply to affirm my decision, and fragments of my reflection nodded with me from mirrors and polished pot bottoms. Determined not to delay, I set my plate in the sink, unwashed, mentally promising to take care of it later.

I went to my room, changed into my housekeeping clothes, and stood, indecisive on the upper landing. What first? I decided on the library. I'd been allowed in there. It had even been my schoolroom for a time. I didn't think I'd feel quite so much like I was trespassing.

The door was locked, but I had the key. It turned without difficulty. Aware that my heart was beating ridiculously fast, I stepped over the threshold into the dark-paneled confines.

The closed space smelled of old books, dust, paper, and, oddly, given how long it had been since any cleaning had been done in there, furniture polish.

I was right in my guess that the police had been in here—not that the place had been torn up or anything. It was actually very tidy, but the tidiness was the wrong sort of tidiness. It wasn't Mother's sort of tidiness. There was another clue as well.

Wherever possible, mirrors had been turned to face the wall. I imagined some dutiful sergeant sent into the library to methodically go over correspondence, old bills, any record or bit of written material that might give some indication of who my mother's associates were, who were the people with whom she was in communication.

He'd sit there at the desk, an older man, responsible, but not very energetic, going through file folders and stacks of unanswered letter. He'd feel a bit voyeuristic about the job, and every time he looked up, he'd see his own reflection in a half-dozen or so mirrors, his expression guilty and hangdog. Finally, he'd push back from the desk, get to his feet, and, moving with deliberation around the room, start turning the mirrors over so they faced the wall.

Where he couldn't turn them over, he'd find something to cover them. One was covered with a crocheted lace doily, another with a knitted afghan, a third with a shapeless garment that—after some investigation—I realized was a man's cardigan, probably the sergeant's own. I wondered why he'd never retrieved it.

The image was so vivid that I found myself wondering if it was something I had actually seen. Had I been lurking in some corner of the room? Perhaps I'd been in the front parlor, peeking through a partially opened door, using the mirrors to expand my range of vision as I had learned to do from spying on my mother.

I had no memory of doing this, but then my memories of those days immediately following the realization that my mother had disappeared were all very vague for me. Likely I'd been in shock. I know I'd entertained a strange notion that I, too, would vanish now that my mother was gone—not through anything as immediate and real as kidnapping, but by fading away, melting as a snow angel does, retaining the form of the person who pressed it into the drift, the edges blurring until all that is there is a hole, and then even that is gone.

When I shook myself from my reverie, I realized that the library differed from all the other rooms in the house that I had inspected in one marked and complete way. It was the only room that hadn't been completely tidied, the furniture shrouded in dust sheets. The elaborate oriental carpet remained in place under the desk, covering the polished hardwood floor, its patterns in turn covered by a chokingly thick layer of dust. Doubtless, the police had ordered that this room remain untouched while they continued their investigation, and no one had thought to have someone care for it when the house had finally been closed.

"First step," I said aloud. "Get the vacuum in here. Otherwise I won't be able to do anything because I'll be too busy sneezing."

I put a fresh bag in the vacuum, and gave a good cleaning to what I could easily reach of the floor, curtains, and edges of bookshelves. Occasionally, pieces of paper caught in the draft of my activity drifted to the floor, distributing even more dust as they fell. This caught the sunlight coming through the windows. One of the upper window panels was crafted of multicolored stained glass and the dust caught in its light glittered in a fashion that reminded me of Tinkerbell and her fairy dust.

"Clap if you believe in fairies!" I said, and did so, the sound of my palms hitting together distant and muted over the roar of the vacuum cleaner.

Again I felt that odd tug of being caught between the reality of my adult self and my younger self. The sensation was not so much one of memory, but of reawakening to a part of me that I had forgotten existed. How much had I made myself forget in my shock? I was beginning to believe that I'd forgotten quite a bit, that in my fear that my mother's disappearance would mean my own dissolution I had started to reinvent myself even before I had come to live with Aunt May and Uncle Stan.

I remembered how much effort I had put into absorbing the view outside the window of the train, how I'd concentrated on each and every cow, chicken, house, barn, flower, car, tree, as if each and every thing I took into myself made me real in a way that had nothing to do with being my mother's "Mira."

The thought was not a comfortable one, and so I concentrated on getting up the dust, sucking it into a dark, fluffy world within the cylindrical bag. I imagined the layers building, stratified with various subtle shades of grey and brown: book dust (greyish white, tinged with yellow), floor dust (darker grey, mingled with brown and bits of carpet thread), curtain dust (grey with a strong undertone of maroon shed from the velvet curtains). Shed a little light on it, and draw your own conclusions.

Couldn't forensic scientists do that these days? They'd progressed a long way from Sherlock Holmes and his different types of cigarette ash. What might they learn from the relics in my vacuum bag? I fought back a hysterical impulse to take it down to the police station and announce portentously: "Here are your clues. Do with them what you will!"

I didn't though. What I did was put the vacuum away, wash my hands and face, tie a damp cloth over my nose and mouth, and feeling like some strange bandito, return to the library. This time I took a seat at the desk. I sat in my mother's chair for the first time in all my memories. I half-expected to find my gaze just level with the top of the desk, as it would have been if as a child I had had such temerity.

I didn't though. Instead, I looked down at the neat stacks of paper, most of which were weighted down with glass paperweights. One was held down under a heavy—by today's standards—pop can. Again I saw my mythical sergeant. He had liked orange pop, judging from the evidence of this can and the two in the small trash can. I set all three carefully aside. If no one wanted to buy them over the Internet, I bet I could incorporate them into a Warholesque collage that would garner good notice in a trendy gallery.

For lack of any better order, I started with the papers that had been under the pop can. They proved to be bills: telephone service, electrical and gas service, city services. To each one was clipped a personal check, written in my mother's hand, and duly canceled. I wondered if my mother had done this matching herself, or if the methodical sergeant had done so.

Eagerly, I checked to see if one of the stacks contained monthly bank statements.

"Bingo!"

They were arranged in reverse order by date. I unclipped the stack and worked through them. Almost immediately, a pattern appeared, but it wasn't a pattern I particularly wanted to see. My mother had regularly written checks, but every single one was to a local business: utilities, grocery, a gasoline station/garage, a couple of department stores. There was one written every month to Martino Navidad, Domingo's father. Others were written less regularly to people I recalled as the family doctor, dentist, veterinarian. Twice a year, one was written to Our Lady's Seminary for Young Ladies. Tuition seemed ridiculously low by today's standards, but when I compared it to what Mother was paying for other services, I realized she had invested a tidy sum in my education.

As I worked my way back through the years, I couldn't find a single check written to someone outside of Las Vegas. I vaguely recalled that it wasn't as easy to use nonlocal checks back then, but this seemed to indicate that Mother had done much of her business in cash. Could she have had a credit card? I glanced at the various piles of paper, but didn't see any statements for credit cards, not even those issued by local businesses or gas stations.

Interesting, but perhaps not unusual forty and more years ago. I'd have to do some investigating, if I decided that it mattered. I noticed one other thing. Although all the checks were signed by my mother, some of them, especially those to local groceries and related establishments, often had the amount filled out in a different hand. The writing was thin and spidery, with a sense of something tentative to it, and I was sure that it belonged to one or more of the silent women. Then I noticed that each of these checks had a receipt stapled to it. Mother had trusted, but only so far.

However, this got me thinking. How had the silent women themselves been paid? I didn't find a single check made out to any of them, nor to a maid or temporary service of any kind. Mother must have paid them in cash. Why? She had paid Martino Navidad with a check. She had paid other local businesses with checks. Why not them? Had they requested cash? Had they been illegals? Had Mother had some strange reason for not wanting any record to exist of their being in her employ?

I stared down at the stacks of paper, feeling rather less enlightened than I had when I had entered the library. The light spilling through the window behind the desk was dimming, and I decided I had had enough. I wanted a shower and clean clothes. My stomach growled, reminding me that Domingo's half-burrito had been eaten and digested quite a while back.

Before leaving the library, I checked the window locks before pulling the curtains shut. Then I locked the door behind me. I had rather liked Chilton O'Reilly, but I couldn't forget his interest in that closed door. If he was interested, who else might be? I'd better play it safe.

I carried the orange pop cans into the kitchen, and set them in the sink. After I'd run water into them to loosen any antique particles of sweetened syrup that might remain, I squinted at the sink. Something wasn't quite right. Then I remembered leaving the dishes from my late lunch to wash later.

Now they rested, shining clean, in the dish rack to one side of the sink. Momentarily, I was startled, then I understood.

Domingo or Enrico must have come in while I was running the vacuum and decided to perform a small act of kindness. I smiled, thinking how nice it was to have friends rather than servants. I wondered how many friends my mother had had. Perhaps tomorrow, as I went through some of the still unexamined papers in the library, I'd begin to get some sort of idea.

10

This visible, physical world in which we live is interpene-
trated by more than one unseen world, just as perfect
and complete in itself as the material planet, which is
the only one most human beings are conscious of. All
around us is the great crowd of witnesses, themselves,
except on rare occasions, invisible.

—M. Oldfield Howey,
*The Horse in Magic and Myth*

## INSIDE THE LINES

I started the next day with the lions around the dining room window. After
the intricacies of the leopards and tigers, I had thought the relative monochrome of the lions would be a relief. Once I had the base coat of tawny
golden-brown down and was mixing in a bit more brown for shadowing and
highlights, I realized I was bored.

Impulsively, I gave the male lions (there were two) dark manes, making
them shaggier than even the carving suggested. I couldn't do much with
the females, so I decided to go ahead and continue the green-eyed theme
I'd started with the leopards. One of the females had a cub near her flank.
Following a vague remembrance that baby lions had spots, I gave him
some, making sure he didn't look like a misplaced leopard.

Once this was drying, I reluctantly put my paintbrushes to soak and went
inside. Since I planned to continue searching my mother's office, taking a

shower seemed counterproductive. I'd been in New Mexico long enough, listened to enough discussions about the hoped for monsoon rains, that I was becoming preternaturally aware of the scarcity of water. Las Vegas wasn't the driest part of the state by far, but even so, to one with my Ohio upbringing, it seemed as if the average annual rainfall couldn't be enough for one season, much less an entire year.

"Child of a rainless year." The phrase had hovered in the peripheries of my imagination for my entire life, but only now was I coming to understand just what a rainless year might mean.

So I skipped the shower, settling for dabbing off the worst of the paint with thinner, and on-point applications of soap and water. I changed out of my painting overalls into an old skirt and blouse, and taking my sandwich and iced tea with me, unlocked the library door.

Pulling back the curtains gave me more than enough light. Opening the window allowed drifts of the house painters' conversation to come my way. Most of it was in Spanish, so I understood only a little, but I found it restful, like listening to classical music, the *vox humana* simply another instrument in the orchestral whole.

My first self-assigned task was to find if Mother had another checking account, one that she used for out-of-state purchases, and possibly to pay a few bills she didn't choose to pay with the other. I knew I was reaching, but my mother had been so odd in so many ways. Why not in this as well?

This led only to my eating a fair amount of dust along with my sandwich. I put my lunch plate in the sink, refilled my glass, and went back to the library. I'd found bank statements from several accounts, and for the next hour or so I reviewed these.

End result: Deposits were regularly made into several savings accounts. Money from these was either withdrawn or transferred into the checking account; occasionally, there were transfers between savings accounts. More money was withdrawn as cash than was spent as checks. I guessed some of this went to pay the silent women, and perhaps others who preferred there not be a record of their earnings.

That gave me an idea, and I went searching through the stacks and file drawers until I found my mother's tax returns. Just looking at them gave me the funny, queasy, semipanicked feeling that tax forms always do. Go figure. I never have cheated on my taxes, never will, but there's something about those forms that scream "Guilty until proven otherwise—and even then we'll come after you."

My mother paid a local accountant to prepare her forms, so these were typewritten and easy to read. From them I did get some new information. Mother's income came from several sources: real estate, trust funds, at least one annuity, and repeated onetime sales of various commodities; works of art, a coin collection, a stamp collection, a Stradivarius violin, an antique automobile.

For a moment I entertained the idea that my mother might have been—like me—a scrounger with an eye for the hidden value of things, but the image was too difficult to maintain. What did stay with me was the fact that my mother had apparently never worked a day in her life—or at least in the fifteen or so years of tax returns I had reviewed. I found myself thinking of the resentment revealed in Aunt May's journals, of how Uncle Stan had gone off to work for his various architects week after week until he retired—and even then he'd gone back to help out when his former employers were in a crunch. I thought how hard I myself had worked since graduating from college, about the commutes between various schools, about the continued wrangling for funds and supplies, and I wondered who Colette Bogatyr had been that she had won the right to be a dilettante.

*You could have lived that life,* said a little voice in my head. *Look what you've found since you've come here. Stan Fenn was honest with you, showed you what you'd inherited the minute you became an adult.*

I stuck my tongue out at that inner nag, pushed back from the desk, and surrendered the hunt for the day. I'd learned a lot more about how my mother managed to live her life, but when it came to where she might have gone that day or who might have had reason to make her vanish, I felt I was further than ever from finding my way.

"Follow the money." "Who stands to gain?" Those were two of the oft-repeated mantras in the mystery stories I loved to read. I'd tried that. The money came in and went out, but there was no pattern in how it did so. Even when Colette sold some commodity, the money didn't go rushing out without explanation. It simply went into one of the savings accounts, and was used along with the rest. I detected no pattern of panic, no need for quick cash.

I supposed that the regular cash withdrawals might indicate Colette Bogatyr was being blackmailed, but it also might simply indicate that she preferred to do most of her business in cash. It's hard to remember now that credit and ATM cards are omnipresent, accepted by everything from grocery stores to fast-food restaurants, that not long ago most transactions were made in cash.

"Most murder victims know their killers." The same might be true of kidnappers. Judging from milk cartons and those slips that come in the ad circulars every week, it probably was the case. So, if Mother had been made to disappear, rather than doing so voluntarily, she probably knew her kidnapper.

I stared at the heaps of paper. There wasn't a lot of personal correspondence there. I'd skimmed a stack of bread-and-butter notes when the tax forms had become too much for me, but they'd mostly been from local businesses or causes:

"Dear Mrs. Bogatyr,

Thank you for attending our annual (fill in the blank) fund-raiser. Your presence was greatly appreciated . . ."

There'd been notes from both the Democrats and the Republicans, so Mother hadn't taken sides there. There were notes from Protestant churches, the Jewish synagogue, and, of course, the Catholic Church. They'd been signed by Anglos and Hispanics, from just about every possible cause imaginable. Apparently, they'd been happy to take her money, if not her alliance. I did a quick spot comparison against the checkbook register, and found records to confirm that she had contributed, if not always generously, to all these causes.

That job gave me one of the few heartwarming moments in the whole business. Colette clearly cared about people more than politics, for her larger checks were written to organizations fighting hunger, or poverty, or working to provide clothing or whatever to the less fortunate.

When I went out to the kitchen, I found my lunch dishes neatly washed again. I smiled as I put them in the cabinet, wondering if Martino Navidad, groundkeeper, had ever found a bonus in his check at a hard time, if the kindness I'd received from his son and grandson were flowers from seeds planted by my strange, seemingly distant, mother.

I don't know why I expected to find something in the library that the police had missed. Although I didn't find anything that gave me a hint into why my mother had disappeared or where she might have gone, my time hadn't been wasted. I had a more complex image of the woman, and while I couldn't say I understood Colette Bogatyr, at least I wasn't locked into a child's view of her formidable mother.

Chilton's first article, the one on my "homecoming" to Las Vegas appeared in the *Optic* right around the time I was finishing my search of the office. It was a typical enough article of its type, but I found myself reading it with undue fascination, as if Chilton's words about me could reveal myself to me. It was an unsettling feeling. When I found myself reading the article for the fourth or fifth time, I buried the newspaper section under a heap of other reading material.

The article did bring results in the form of several phone calls. A couple were from people who claimed to have known me when I was a child. A few were crank calls—mostly from people who wanted to be paid an unspecified amount of money to tell me what had happened to my mother. One was from a real estate agent wanting to know if I was interested in selling the house. Only one was of real interest.

I recognized her voice even though over forty years had passed since we had last spoken.

"Mira? Mira Bogatyr, I mean, Fenn?"

"Hannah? Is that you?"

The voice was more mature now, but the breathy timbre, like the speaker sucked in air to carry her through each rushed statement, was still there.

The voice now sounded terribly pleased. "That's right. Hannah. Hannah Rakes then, Hannah Schaeffer now. I'm so pleased you remember me. I saw the article in the *Optic* and couldn't believe it was you."

I forced a chuckle, knowing how different my stocky self was from that pale, attenuated child. "Well, a lot of years have passed."

A self-deprecating chuckle echoed my own. "Haven't they just? I didn't mean that. I meant I couldn't believe you'd come back here, after all that time. I'd wondered where you'd gotten to. I was devastated when you left, you know. You were my best friend in all the world. I felt dreadfully abandoned."

"Well, here I am," I replied somewhat awkwardly. Once I would have dismissed Hannah's statement as mere hyperbole, but I'd been a teacher long enough to know that the outspoken children were sometimes as or more lonely than the quiet ones. I might well have been Hannah's best friend. She certainly had been mine—really my only friend.

I hastened to take up the conversational thread. "I'm so pleased you're still here in Las Vegas, Hannah. Any chance we can get together?"

"Actually, I'm not," Hannah said, "not in Las Vegas, I mean. My mother read me the article over the phone, then I checked it out online. I live in Albuquerque now. I do nursing and rehab at Lovelace. My mother is still in Las Vegas, though, so I get there fairly regularly. I have plans to be there over the weekend. Any chance you can free up for lunch?"

"Lunch, dinner, whatever fits your schedule," I said, surprised at my eagerness. "Won't your mother mind?"

"Not a bit. She was the one who suggested I look you up."

"And how's she doing?" I asked. I had fond memories of Mrs. Rakes, memories having to do with freshly baked cookies, jelly glass tumblers of milk, and sleeve-polished apples eaten around the kitchen table to the accompaniment of the chatter of Hannah and her siblings.

"Pretty well for someone of her age . . ." Hannah began. After she ran down after a five minute outline of her mother's age, including certain details I guessed nurses talk about without embarrassment, we made a date for lunch the following Saturday.

Talking to Hannah had made me suddenly eager to finally open up my "nursery" and revisit the child I had been. I mounted to the second floor, my feet thumping up the stairs in rapid accompaniment to the memory of Hannah's voice in my ears.

At the top of the stairs, I turned toward the back of the house. My rooms overlooked the walled garden Domingo now tended even more lovingly than his father had. Since my return, I'd looked up at those windows, but even when the shutters had been opened, they remained secluded behind long curtains, giving nothing away.

As I had now found was fairly usual, the door to the room was locked, but the key was there on my ring. The lock turned with a minimal amount of stiffness, and I pushed open the door, automatically reaching up for the light switch.

I didn't find it, not until I adjusted and slid my hand down. I turned on the light and one bulb in the overhead fixture flickered dimly to life. I'd come prepared for this, and a few minutes labor with stepladder, flashlight, and fresh bulbs brought the room into view.

The layout was much as I remembered it. Nor did I suffer the usual "everything seemed smaller than I remembered," for the scale of Phineas House was so much larger than the house in Ohio that I was still startled to find how much room had been at our disposal. I had entered via my playroom and study. As with most of the house, the furniture had been shrouded under dust sheets, the rugs rolled up and set neatly along the walls.

Sighing in anticipation of yet another long bout of dusting and vacuuming, I crossed to the window and opened the curtains. Once again, I looked down into the back garden. For a moment my mind struggled to return the plantings to their remembered layout, then the garden of memory vanished, leaving me with the more attractive present.

I walked briskly through the suite. My bathroom was through one door, my bedroom through another. The bathroom was spared the shrouding dust sheets, but the bedroom looked rather eerie. My bed had been a four-poster, and the canopy had been removed and stored away, leaving the slats exposed. Seen this way, they reminded me of a skeleton, and I turned away with a shiver.

Another round of curtain opening brought ample natural light into the bedroom. I removed dust sheets, heaping them on the floor in a big pile, and opened the drawers to highboys and lowboys. All were empty, which was rather odd. I distinctly recalled how one of the first things Aunt May and I had done was buy clothing for me. I'd assumed that was because my belongings had been left behind. Now I checked the closet and found the same bareness.

Had the silent women taken my clothing with them when they'd left? Did those lace-trimmed velvet dresses I recalled so fondly end their lives as Sunday best for a slew of other little girls? I told myself I didn't really mind, but somewhere inside I did. I'd been looking forward to some physical reminder of myself. Now I found everything was gone.

The playroom was somewhat better. I found a couple of chewed-end pencils in the back of a desk drawer, a bag of cat's-eye marbles forgotten on a closet shelf. Most of my favorite toys had been sent with me, so I didn't expect to find them, but apparently the things I had not chosen to take— old school papers, a handful of knickknacks, had been tidied away. I wondered why these two rooms had been so carefully cleaned free from personal items when the other rooms I had looked into had not.

I wondered, but I did not expect an answer. When I went down into the kitchen, I found the beginnings of one.

She was standing over by the sink, polishing hard-water spots from the chrome faucet. Slim but not slender, with straight pale brown hair pulled back from intent, regular features, she wore a white apron over a pale-blue, collared blouse. The hand in which she held the washrag was encased in a yellow plastic glove. She looked about thirty.

I stood motionless in the doorway, unable to move, much less speak. Who was this? Some relative of Domingo's? She didn't look much like him or Enrico, but she did look somehow familiar.

Then I realized why. I was looking at one of the silent women. I must have drawn in my breath or made some other sound, for she looked up from her polishing. Our eyes met. Hers were light blue, a different shade from the blue of her shirt. I saw that distinctly.

Just as distinctly, I saw her vanish.

I stood there for a long moment, then I walked slowly over to where the woman had been standing.

There were no water spots on the faucet and the washrag was dropped in a damp heap on the bottom of the sink. I lifted it, shook it out, hung between the paired sinks to dry.

That dampness was the first clue that what I had seen was real. Ever since I had come to New Mexico, I had delighted in how quickly things dried. I could wash my face in the morning, and an hour or so later the heavy terry cloth would hardly be damp.

The second proof was that I'd found the cloth lying in the sink. Even if Domingo or one of the workmen had come in without my permission—and I doubted they would have since they all preferred to use the facilities in the carriage house—they would have wrung out the cloth and hung it to dry.

Third proof was the absence of water spots. I was a fair housekeeper, but no perfectionist. Even if I had been, the sheer amount of work to be done around the house would have daunted me. Five minutes spent polishing the sink chrome could be better spent folding dust sheets or washing a window or painting a bit of the outdoor trim.

No. I had never left the chrome so gleaming and bright. Someone else had done it. And I'd seen that someone with my own eyes. Was the house haunted? If so, these were admirable ghosts. No rattling of chains for them. They preferred clean dishes and polished fixtures.

I remembered the story of "The Shoemaker and the Elves." Aunt May had read it to me when I was small. I think she'd meant it as a hint, because every so often she'd remind me to tidy my room by saying "No elves here, my little shoemaker." We'd both agreed that it would have been nicer if there were. Later, I'd read other tales of brownies and pixies, house spirits that cleaned and did chores.

The strange thing was that some stories were like that of the Shoemaker and the Elves. If you thanked the house spirit or gave it a gift, it grew insulted and left. In others, you had better leave out some sort of gift for them—a bowl of milk seemed typical. That kept them happy and working hard.

Was what I had seen a brownie of some sort? She surely hadn't looked like one. From what I remembered from fairy tales those were short and squat or deformed in some way. The woman who had been polishing my faucet had looked as normal as any woman I might pass in the grocery store.

I stood staring at the polished sink, trying to figure out what to do. If the silent women had returned, I didn't want them to leave. My reasons had to do with more than the pleasure of having my dishes washed and my sink cleaned. They belonged to the "before"—to the time when Colette had ruled Phineas House. If I could gain their trust somehow . . . I knew they could talk. I had so many questions, but would they have answers?

Somehow I had to make contact with the silent woman—the silent women, for now that I had seen one, I was sure that the others were present as well. There had been several. The one I had seen in the kitchen had done a lot of cleaning, but there had been cooks, seamstresses, even "Teresa Sanchez," the one who had tried to be my tutor.

What had happened to make them come back? I was certain they had not been here when I had reopened the house. Was it the cleaning? Were they responding to echoes of their former activities? Was it simply having someone living here again? Were they house spirits like the elves and brownies in my fairy-tale books or were they ghosts or something else entirely?

I didn't know. I didn't know how to go about finding out. What I did know with absolute certainty was that I did not want to drive them away.

"So what will it be, Mira?" I asked myself flippantly. "A saucer of milk? New clothes? Nothing at all?"

I had a strong suspicion that Colette had given the silent women nothing. I had found no record of payment. If a bowl of milk had been sufficient . . .

I shook my head as if I could physically banish an ugly thought. I remembered the silent women. I remembered their whispers. I remembered the terror of the woman who had tried so hard to be my tutor. If somehow they were bound to this place, if somehow my coming back had forced them to come back, well, they had no idea what they were getting into. For all they knew, they were in service to another Colette.

I had thought I knew nothing about the silent women, but now I realized

I did. They could be unhappy. Knowing that, I had to make a choice. Be Co-lette or be Mira—and if being Mira meant that, as with the Shoemaker, my elves would go dancing away, well then, Aunt May had taught me how to do just fine without elves.

"Thank you," I said to the air. "I only just now realized who has been pick-ing up after me. I appreciate it."

There was no answer. No neatly clad woman shimmered into sight then or while I made my dinner. Nor did I see any flicker of motion in any of the many scattered mirrors. I avoided the temptation of leaving my dirty dishes in the sink as a test. After I had eaten I went out to sit in the garden for a while. Domingo seemed to be away, but Blanco bounced over and I tossed a stick for him to chase while I watched the coming of night suck the color from the roses.

When I went inside, there was no sense of anyone but me being in the house, but when I went up to bed that night, I found the quilt turned down. There was a sprig of Spanish lavender—the tiny dark purple blossoms still unwilted—resting on my freshly plumped pillow.

The next several days were very odd. I didn't catch another glimpse of any of the silent women, but I knew they were there. My bed—which I usually made simply by pulling the quilt up over the sheets underneath—was made to perfection. The fixtures in the bathroom and kitchen were flaw-lessly polished. A button I popped off my painting coverall was sewed back on.

Most dramatic was finding the entirety of my nursery and my mother's li-brary put into perfect order. None of the missing clothing reappeared in the nursery, but the dust sheets I'd left heaped on the floor were neatly folded, the woodwork polished, and the floors dusted. The same happened in the library. The neat stacks of sorted paperwork were left in place, but the room was dust free.

One morning, coming back from a run to the hardware and grocery stores, Domingo met me outside the carriage house. He took a couple plas-tic bags from the back of my truck, then looked at what remained rather strangely.

"You must have been gone for quite a while, Mira."

"I left early," I agreed, looping bags on my fingers. "I wanted to be back in time to paint before it got too sunny on that side of the House."

Domingo walked beside me to Phineas House. "I think I told you that I wouldn't be here this morning."

"That's right," I replied. "You said you were taking the crew to help you with an emergency job."

"That is so, but before I went to meet them, I remembered I had left a tool kit over by the house where I'd been tightening a shutter. I went over there and—I could have sworn I heard a vacuum cleaner running inside. I thought you were up and being industrious."

"Not me." I denied cheerfully. "You must have heard something from another house. Sound can carry strangely in this area, what with people leaving windows open."

"That must be it," Domingo agreed, but I could tell he wasn't happy. He helped me put the bags on the kitchen table, then hurried away to meet his crew.

I thought about saying something to the silent women, just in case they were listening, then I shrugged. I wanted to lure them back, and reprimanding them wasn't going to help. So I just cut myself a slice of the breakfast cake I'd brought back, donned my painting gear, and went outside.

As usual when I was painting, I found myself getting lost in the process. I'd finished the series of wild-cat windows and was now doing some routine work along the porch railings. Domingo's crew had already laid down the base coat, and I was putting on the contrast. I lost myself in the rise and fall of my brush, the pleasure of seeing the two colors coming together so perfectly, until the rumbling of my stomach and the feel of the sun burning the back of my neck where I'd tucked my hair up under a painter's cap reminded me that a good amount of time had passed.

Young Enrico was getting ready to go back to school now, but we'd cut a deal that he'd continue being paid for doing small jobs around the house after school—and after his homework was done. One of these was cleaning paintbrushes, a job I hate almost enough to make me eschew jobs that use a brush any larger than about two inches.

Leaving the brushes to soak, I put away my other gear, rinsed off in the shower, and went down to make a sandwich. This consumed, I grabbed a bottle of cold water from the fridge and headed upstairs toward a job I'd known I was going to tackle today—and that I'd avoided thinking about in case I found an excuse not to do it.

Keys in hand, I made my way to the door of my mother's suite. As I searched for the correct key my hand shook so severely that the entire ring rattled. All over again I was a little girl, doing the forbidden, invading my mother's territory without her permission. It took all my will to put the key in the lock and turn it. By the time I had opened the door and reached for the light switch I felt as drained as if I'd run a couple of miles.

Pushing the switch into the on position was almost more than I could manage, but I did it, flooding the room with light from six or seven small candelabra style bulbs in the elaborate fixture that hung in the center of the room. There were at least as many bulbs that had burned out, but with the daylight coming in from the hall there was plenty to see by. I stepped over the threshold and into the room that had been Mother's private parlor.

The layout of her suite was not unlike that of the nursery: two rooms and a full bath. The parlor was closest to the front of the house, the bedroom in back of it, the bathroom behind that. It was a tidy arrangement, and contained a great deal more space than many New York apartments I'd seen. The only thing it lacked, in fact, were kitchen facilities, and, as there was a dumbwaiter in the bedroom, even those needs could be considered served.

The parlor was furnished in elegant comfort: a small writing desk, a few bookshelves, a sofa, some chairs, scattered tables—one of which my mother had frequently used when she took meals in her room. I remembered sitting there across from her when she chose to have me with her.

Like the library, the parlor was swathed in dust sheets, and I didn't look forward to uncovering everything and dealing with the dust. Rather than doing so now, I checked the chandelier bulbs and made a note of the size and wattage I would need. These were the small stemmed sort, and I had none in my hoard.

From the parlor I passed into the bedroom to again be confronted with dust sheets. Even so, I recognized some shapes. The bed, of course, the various dressers, the vanity, the big portrait. The bathroom had been spared the dust sheets, and I stood for a long while staring rather stupidly at the huge claw-footed tub. There was a separate shower in another corner, a toilet politely tucked behind a low wall that I vaguely recalled being topped with a planter containing orchids.

In each room I opened curtains, methodically noted what lights had blown out, replaced what I could, and tried not to run out in a panic. The tactic worked—at least some.

"Where to start?" I said aloud. "The bedroom. Mother entertained in her parlor—in her bedroom, too, I guess, but I think if she had anything special to hide she would have hidden it in her bedroom. Fewer excuses for anyone to go in there."

I was rather surprised to realize I was hunting for something hidden. I even wondered if one of the silent women had whispered a suggestion in my ear, but that was ridiculous. Of course I had to be looking for something hidden. If it had not been hidden, if it was apparent, then the police would have found it. I had read through both Chilton O'Reilly and Aunt May's accounts of the investigation, and the police really had seemed to want to find the missing Colette Bogatyr.

I'd never asked the silent women for anything before, but I decided I would now. I started by removing the dust covers from the furniture, talking aloud all the while.

"I'd really much rather search than clean, but there's no way I can do much searching with this place such a mess. I need to put in some laundry and get dinner going. If I could have a little help up here . . ."

I let the words trail off, suddenly feeling completely foolish. Even so, I finished stripping off the dust covers in both the bedroom and the parlor. I carried them downstairs and added a few to a load of laundry. Then I went to the bathroom I had been using, and, after rinsing off yet again, I gathered the rest of my laundry and took it downstairs. There I determinedly did chores I really did need to do, including answering some e-mail from friends back East. All the while I wondered what—if anything—was going on upstairs.

Of one thing I felt fairly certain. The silent women were very good at what they did, but they could not do it without tools. There was a utility closet upstairs, well stocked with everything, but if they needed the vacuum . . .

I took my laundry outside to hang—I've always preferred the smell of sheets hung out of doors. When I did so, I shut the kitchen door very firmly behind me and tried not to listen.

This was easier than you might imagine. Afternoon was merging into that wonderful lazy time that isn't quite evening but that has left the business of the afternoon behind. After I hung the laundry, I wandered the garden, looking at the flowers and enjoying the soft brilliance of their conversation.

Then I circled the house, feeling a great deal of pride in the expanded paint job. A neighbor saw me and came over to chat. A bird feeder needed to be filled. Only after that was done did I venture back inside.

I went up the stairs two at a time, eagerness now overwhelming my earlier dread. Would my experiment have worked?

It had. Neither the parlor nor the bedroom were what anyone could have called "clean," but the nose-tickling welter of dust was gone.

"Thank you," I said, not feeling in the least foolish about speaking to what was still—to all appearances—empty air. I had unqualified evidence that someone—or someones—was there and willing to help me. "I really do appreciate it. I have dinner on now, but afterward, I'll come up and start going through things."

It turned out that I didn't. Domingo dropped over, wanting to chat about the day he'd spent with my borrowed crew fixing a section of porch that had chosen this inopportune time to collapse. It had been quite a job, and I think he needed to wind down. I certainly did.

When I went upstairs that night, I was aware of the rooms across the hall, cleaner now, and awaiting my inspection. If I'd been a kid of twenty, I suppose I would have torn over there immediately, but I wasn't. My bones were tired from a morning painting and a highly stressful afternoon. Whatever Mother had left—if she had left anything that had not already been found—had waited for forty years. It could wait another night.

11

Does color hold a power that makes us want to remove its brighter and bolder forms from such serious settings as boardrooms and lecture halls? And, if so, just what power does color have?

—Patricia Lynne Duffy,
*Blue Cats and Chartreuse Kittens*

## INSIDE THE LINES

Turned out it had to wait more than another night. The next morning Domingo and his crew were back on the job, working on a Saturday to make up for the time they'd taken off. I was needed to offer my opinions on what colors a certain rather bizarre frieze of bat-winged dragons should be painted.

I'd gotten as serious as Domingo about this, but unlike him, I didn't need to dummy up models on a computer paint program. A handful of paint color sample slips combined with a good long stare at the design element in question and I started seeing the way the painting should be done. "Seeing" isn't quite the right word for it, but I don't have another. "Hearing" almost comes closer, but if I was hearing the description, it wasn't linear. It was almost more like looking at a frame of a well-drawn comic strip, narration and action coming at you all at once, but here, of course, if there was any dialogue it was between me and Phineas House.

These weren't simple descriptions, either. Nothing like, "Do the body in metallic blue and the wings in that pea green." No, I'd get an entire image, right down to the highlights and shadows. I'd know if it would take an undercoat to get the right color or a wash to manage the shadows.

The first couple of times I saw how a segment of the house should look, it scared me. But I couldn't escape the feeling that to do it any other way would be a disaster, so I took notes. It was a laborious process, and Domingo drifted over about halfway. I don't remember when he took over the writing so I could concentrate.

After a while, I stopped thinking about what was going on. I convinced myself that it wasn't all that different from when I was working on a painting or mosaic. I'd envisioned those before starting, too, done my rough sketches and then refined them.

Eventually, the workmen simply accepted me for an extraordinarily difficult to please client, but since I was paying well and regularly, and Domingo was perfection as a foreman, no one complained. They went about scraping old paint, sanding wood smooth, puttying, priming, and, in the case of the most skilled, doing detail work. I had told them I didn't mind if they played music, and most of the painting was done to an ebullient mariachi soundtrack.

Domingo, though—I had the feeling that he actually had a sense of what I was doing. A couple of times he even muttered the color before I said it out loud, but he always waited for my narration before making any notes. I remembered how he had spoken of the house being "unhappy" in its white-on-white paint, and wondered if he'd seen it adorned in its new colors.

When we finished the design for the last dragon, I headed inside to grab a cup of coffee and go upstairs. The calendar was hung near the coffeepot, and as I wiped up drips I saw what I'd written neatly on today's square: "Lunch. Hannah. Maria's Cafe."

I glanced at the clock. As was usual when I was involved with Phineas House, I'd lost track of time. It was past eleven now. I had time to dab off the inevitable spots of paint and change into a clean clothes. I chose a pretty aqua broomstick skirt with golden-brown highlights, and a coordinating blouse. My necklace was strung from some of my finds—rather like a charm bracelet in the round. I'd made the earrings from leftovers. In Ohio I'd looked exotic and bohemian. In New Mexico, I fit in just fine.

Nervous about the impression I should make on this woman I hadn't seen in so long, I fussed over my hair longer than I should have. Happily,

Las Vegas wasn't very large, and I'd been in town long enough to know my way around most of the typical traffic bottlenecks.

Casting a forlorn glance in the direction of my mother's bedroom door, I ran up the stairs to my room.

"I'll be back," I promised. "Just a few hours more."

Just as time had changed me, it had done its work on Hannah. The image I'd carried fixed in my mind was of a girl of my own height, a bit heavier in build, with straight brown hair worn in pigtails, one of which was usually a little askew. The woman who rose from a booth toward the back of the cafe was quite different.

I was the taller now, she the slimmer. However, there was a lot of strength in her as I discovered when we shook hands, then impulsively embraced. Obviously, being a nurse is not a job for the weak. Hannah's brown hair was cut in a neat, short style that read "easy care" while escaping being in the least dowdy. Her gaze was warm, and I knew instinctively that she was the type of caregiver who heard a lot of confidences.

That made me feel good, because on the ride over I'd resolved to do some confiding.

"Mira, Mira, Mira," Hannah said as she slid herself back into the booth. "You look good."

"Thanks. You, too."

The waitress came over and took our drink orders, then left us to peruse the menus. While we did so, we continued the catching up we'd begun on the phone. Hannah, it turned out, had been married once, right out of college, divorced soon after, and had remarried.

"We're both in medicine, which everyone will tell you is exactly the wrong thing to do," she said, "but it works for us. We know exactly what the other is talking about, and about erratic schedules. His folks and sister live in Albuquerque, and take over more than their fair share of running the kids to soccer practices and things. It sounds like hell, but actually it works."

"Your family," I said, "I mean when we were kids—always seemed in constant motion. I remember how it fascinated me when I'd come to visit."

Hannah grinned. "Constant motion is right. I was the youngest and felt like the duck on the end of a long string—and just like when you play crack the whip, the one at the end flies the farthest. I think that was one reason I liked you. You had this quiet to you."

"I don't think I ever spoke three sentences in a row," I said with a rueful laugh.

"No," Hannah disagreed. "That's not what I meant. I didn't know the term then, but today they'd call it being centered. All the rest of us were running here and there, and you'd just watch out of those calm eyes and I'd know you were soaking it all up. Somehow, having you there made it all more real."

The waitress brought our food. Enchiladas and a salad for me, and an incredibly stacked club sandwich cut into fours for Hannah. Hannah picked up one corner of her sandwich and studied me while taking a bite.

"You still have some of that," she said when she finished chewing. "It must come from being an artist. That's what the paper said you were—an art teacher, right?"

"That's right, but I wouldn't call myself an artist."

"Well, unless you've changed since we were kids, I would. I remember how incredibly quickly you learned to draw and paint. One class you're handling a crayon like you've never seen one, three weeks later you're doing pictures with shading and dimension. It was like magic."

I grinned. "I didn't think anyone but Mrs. Little had noticed me and the crayons."

"I did. I was dreadfully snoopy in those days. Only way to keep ahead of all those older brothers and sisters. Still am." Her expression held a friendly challenge. "So, what brought you back to Las Vegas? I know the basics—we talked about them on the phone. I mean, what has brought you back to stay?"

"I'm not staying," I said automatically, though I wasn't sure I was speaking the truth.

"Really? My mother told me that you're putting a lot of work into the old house."

I must have looked surprised, because Hannah went on.

"You haven't started mingling yet, but when you do, you'll know soon enough. Las Vegas is a small town. It has its groups and factions and all the rest, but you know that old saw about six degrees of separation?"

"You mean that everyone is no more than six people away from knowing everyone else?"

"Right. Well, in Las Vegas, you'd better narrow that to two or three. My mother plays bridge with one of your neighbors a street over. She actually swings by Phineas House on her way to their biweekly games. Initially, she didn't connect the lady from Ohio with my childhood friend, but the newspaper article made her remember. Until then, she hadn't even been sure it was the same house. That neighborhood has changed a lot in forty years—and I never came to play there. You always went to our house."

"My mother," I said, a trace more heavily than I had intended, "did not encourage any guests other than her own."

I determinedly ate a forkful of enchiladas, then went on.

"Hannah, I remember your mother pretty well. I bet that ever since she made the connection she's been, well, remembering about my mother."

"Gossiping, you mean?" Hannah said. She bit her pickle wedge in half, but didn't seem the least offended. "You're remembering her right. She always did love to speculate on what other people were up to, and your mother, well, she was a colorful figure."

"The thing is," I said, finding this hard to say, despite my earlier resolve, "I don't really remember my mother all that well. I was only nine when Mother vanished. My memories are all of a towering figure in sweeping skirts. I have no adult perspective in which to view her . . . and I want one, even a gossipy one."

Hannah nodded and finished the pickle. "I can see that. You've just lost the woman who was your real mother, and now you're confronted with the property of the woman who bore you. In the one case, you're so close to grief you don't even know how much it's pressing you down. In the other, you don't know what to feel."

"That's clearer than I could ever put it," I said.

"I talk a lot," Hannah said, "but I listen, too. You do a lot of listening when you're a nurse, and you're close to death and dying—or fear of death and dying—every day. Even those who specialize in obstetrics or pediatrics can't get away from it."

"Well, whatever the reason, you understand better than I do why I need to know about my mother—about Colette. The newspapers cover her disappearance, and a bit of back story but there's nothing to tell me what she was like."

"Like?" Hannah frowned. "My memories are a child's, too, and what my mother has said is largely hearsay, and, quite honestly, somewhat malicious."

"Even so. I'd like to hear it."

Hannah went after another corner of her sandwich with a thoughtful silence that pretty much demanded I finish some of my enchiladas. When she spoke, she lowered her voice.

"Mira, I'm going to start with the worst thing I heard. If I don't, then I know you'll sense I'm holding back. I'd rather work up to it, but . . ."

My stomach twisted, but I managed a smile. "Go ahead. I swear I won't go storming out of here in a huff."

"Okay." Hannah drew in a deep breath. "My mother said that talk was that your mother was insane—mentally unstable. The gossip was she had been brought to Las Vegas and spent time in the state mental hospital—you know that's here, don't you?"

"I didn't, actually, but go on."

Hannah studied me for a moment, apparently decided that I meant what I said, and continued, "Well, my mother said that your mother had trouble with her parents. My mother hints that this problem was pretty serious. I think she doesn't know the details. Anyhow, Colette's family couldn't deal with her and finally had her institutionalized. The treatment was successful—at least to a point. Afterward, Colette was permitted something like what we'd call 'residential placement' today."

"You mean she could live 'off-campus.'"

"Basically, but my mother said that she'd heard that Colette had to stay near enough to the State Hospital so that if she started to slide again, they could get her into treatment again."

I thought about this. Could those mysterious "trustees" have been my mother's as well as mine? I shook my head, refusing to believe the theory, even if it did explain a lot.

"Phineas House does not seem like your typical residential placement," I said. "If I understand correctly, it's been in the family for generations—and there was certainly no one there looking after her. She ran the place."

"I believe you," Hannah said. "I'm just reporting nasty gossip."

"Right."

The waitress came by, and by silent consent Hannah and I each ordered dessert and coffee. When it came, we lingered over it as Hannah went on.

"Anyhow, the theory that your mother was mentally unstable covered all the bases very neatly. It explained why she dressed as she did, some of her odd habits, and her . . ."

Hannah pinked lightly and swallowed a mouthful of double-chocolate cake.

"Apparent promiscuity?" I said. "I remember my mother's boyfriends."

Hannah relaxed. "That's right."

"Anything in your mother's cornucopia about my father?"

"Now that's an odd one," Hannah admitted. "Best as Mother recalls, your mother went away for about a year. When she came back, she came back with an infant—with you. That's also when she started using 'Mrs.' and gave out that she had been widowed, but interestingly, she kept her maiden name—and went on with her habits. Apparently, there was a lot of gossip, but nothing definite. The charitable said she must have been married and after her husband's death returned to familiar grounds."

"I can guess," I said, whacking the hard lump of my ice cream with the bowl of my spoon, "what the uncharitable said."

"And that's about all I know," Hannah concluded.

"That's all about Colette the woman," I said. "What about the girl? I haven't found anything yet about where she went to school, her parents, all that—and, no, she never talked about any of that to me."

"I can ask," Hannah said, "but Mother has never said anything specific, none of that 'Now I know Maria who went to school with her and she said that . . . ' I do think Colette was local, but maybe she was educated at home."

Hannah's expression filled with compassion. "When we were kids, I thought your father had died. I figured your mother was odd because she was weighed down with sorrow."

"Maybe so," I said. "If so, I never saw it, and a constantly changing string of boyfriends is hardly the way to mourn."

"I don't know," Hannah said. "They say that widowers who were happiest in a first marriage are the most likely to remarry. Maybe it's the same with widows—only most women outlive their spouses and don't exactly find a ripe crop of new prospects waiting around. Your mother was young and beautiful. It would have been different for her."

Hannah's tone became dreamy as she went on, "That string of boyfriends could have been part of her endless search for a man who could live up to her memories of the man she had lost."

"And she dumped each one," I said, putting my white china coffee mug on the table with a thump, "as he failed to measure up? I suppose."

"Well," Hannah said. "It's a nice alternative to my mother's version."

"True." I rubbed my temples, feeling exhausted. "I just wish I knew more. Being here has been good for me. I'm actually adjusting to the idea that Aunt May and Uncle Stan won't be there in Ohio when I go back—for a while

I realized that's how my subconscious was trying to jolly me along. Work on Phineas House has been absorbing, but I don't know what to do next."

"Let it go," Hannah suggested. "Come up to Albuquerque next week on my day off. We'll run the kids to a game or something, catch up, go to the zoo . . ."

"Maybe," I said, but both of us knew my tone meant "probably not." "When do you come back to see your mother?"

"I usually make it here about twice a month," Hannah said. "She has a friend who drives her down to Albuquerque on one of the off weeks."

"Maybe next time you can come over and see Phineas House," I said. "I'll give you the tour."

"I'd like that."

We exchanged e-mail addresses, and I insisted on settling the bill. When we went our separate ways in the parking lot, I felt good. Meeting with Hannah all these years later could have been disastrous, but it had actually been fun. She was nicer than I remembered, and I wondered if some of my mother's elitism had made me see Hannah and her family as rather "below stairs."

I also had the possibility that Colette had been in the State Hospital to check out—but I only would if nothing else panned out. I didn't know much about my mother, but of one thing I felt certain, for all her self-absorption, she had been coolly, even terrifyingly, sane.

But maybe my thinking so was simply proof that I was becoming as crazy as she had been.

When I got back to the house, I stopped to chat for a moment with Domingo and admire the advancing work on the dragon frieze.

"Want to have a hand?" he asked.

For a moment I was tempted, but I shook my head resolutely.

"Maybe tomorrow. Today I have to get some things done inside."

"I'll save it for you," Domingo said, "when we have the base coat on."

"Thanks."

"By the way," he called after me, "you look very nice."

I waved a hand in acknowledgment, but I was pleased.

Inside, I changed out of my blouse and skirt, and into a pair of my collection of increasingly disreputable jeans and tee shirts. I'd never been one of those slovenly artists—the influence of both of my mothers, I guess—and I made a mental note that I needed to go shopping.

Right now, Phineas House was folding itself around my mind. Even though some of the windows were open, I hardly heard the workmen's music or the occasional street noise. There was nothing but that room across the landing. My fingers found the key on its ring as surely as if I'd opened the door dozens of times before.

I was unsurprised to find the suite elegantly tidy, smelling warmly of wood polish and wax. The curtains had been cleaned of dust and tied back, but the blinds were drawn, retaining privacy. Today's painting was going on over on another side of the house, so I felt no reservations about pulling up the blinds and letting in the afternoon light. I slid open a few windows, enjoying the fresh air.

"Clean windows, too," I said aloud. "I'm impressed. I wonder if you ever sleep?"

I went into my mother's bedroom, and again opened windows. I found that the bed—where yesterday the mattress had been naked beneath the dust sheet—had been made up. I peeked beneath the thick quilted bedspread—gold tissue embroidered with white swans—and found only a mattress pad.

"I see," I said. "Not anticipating company, just putting something between the mattress and dust. That's a good idea. I hadn't thought about it, but then it's dustier here than in Ohio."

Carpets that yesterday had been rolled were now spread out in their accustomed places. I stood in the center of the largest and forced myself to look where Colette's portrait hung. As I expected, the enshrouding dust cover was gone, the frame with its glinting mirror inclusions clean and polished. Yet ornate as was its setting, Colette's image dominated it all, even as her personality had dominated her surroundings in life.

She stood tall and regal, one hand resting gracefully on the edge of a table. The painter had chosen a three-quarter angle that showed Colette's arrogant head on that long, slender neck in profile, the shining dark hair up in an elaborate arrangement in which jeweled pins glinted. Her gown was shown in full, the flaring skirts in-cut to reveal shimmering inner layers. She looked like a young queen from a book of fairy stories.

I didn't recognize where the picture had been painted, and while she looked a bit younger than I remembered, the difference was not great.

Could this picture have been painted during that mysterious year when she had been absent? If so, she certainly hadn't been pregnant at the time. The pinched waist beneath her swelling bosom showed no sign of thickening.

I forced myself to confront that image, to compare it without hesitation to my own as it was captured in a hundred versions in as many bits of mirror. The comparison was not kind. I was older, greyer, stouter, and shorter, but for the first time in my entire life I saw a similarity. There was something in my bearing that was like Colette's—not the arrogance, but something of the same unflinching pride in how I held myself. There was in both of our postures that which said: "Here I am, as I am."

It was a startling revelation, especially since to that point I had seen nothing alike between us—indeed, I had seen much more alike between myself and Aunt May. Still, if there was something I had to have inherited from Colette, this was not a bad thing at all. I smiled, and turned to inspect the room.

Bed, several dressers, built in closets, vanity. There was a blanket chest at the foot of the bed, and I started my search there. I found nothing but several blankets of varying weight, each woven of the finest lamb's wool, soft as the hues that whispered to me from interstices between the weave.

Next I turned to the closets, but I found that unlike the closet in my former nursery these were filled with clothing, the floor beneath the hanging skirts arrayed with neat lines of shoes.

I balked. Colette's favorite perfume—something like Chanel Number 5, but with a muskier, sexier bite—eddied from the ranks of elaborate dresses. I staggered back from it as I had not from the portrait, overwhelmed once again with fear, with the sense that I was a trespasser here.

Holding onto the edge of the closet door I steadied myself, forcing myself to breathe deeply, to accept this stale scent for what it was—a bygone breath, dissipating even now by the fresh air from the open windows.

"She's not in there, Mira," I said aloud. "She hasn't set foot in the house in over forty years. Get a grip on yourself."

I managed not to run, but neither did I delve deeper into those clothing-crowded closets. Later. There would be enough time later.

Guessing that the dressers would be as filled as the closet had proven to be, I cast around. My dilemma was not too few choices, but too many. Here there was no evidence of methodical searching by the police. Doubtless they had made a cursory check, probably focusing on whether Mother had taken a change of clothing or luggage with her when she had vanished.

I really had to see if I could get a look at the police records.

For now, though, I had a sense that if I started going through closets I'd become mired in minutiae. What I was looking for might be hidden within the folds of a skirt, the dip of a sculptured bodice, but my feeling was that Mother would not have hidden anything important where it might be found—say by a servant doing mending or alterations, or laying out that evening's formal wear.

I paused, wondering if the silent women, well, counted as people that way. I decided to act as if they did. Mother had been careful enough with those blank checks she'd sent out for local purchases that the silent women must have merited being watched.

Or something. My thoughts were swimming as I tried to make sense of things that wouldn't add up in a sensible fashion. I didn't want to go through the closets. Fine. I wouldn't. I cast around, looking for a new target. My gaze rested on where the vanity stood by itself on one side of the room, uncrowded, an altar to the perpetuation of beauty—or perhaps to the perpetuation of illusion.

Compared to the closets and dressers the vanity was a contained challenge. I crossed over to it with something like eagerness, for once finding comfort in the repetition of my familiar image in the mirrors that faced me.

Like the rest of the bedroom set, the vanity was painted antique white, elegantly accented in gold. The table was kidney shaped, and held seven drawers: three on each side, a broad one in the center. Bracketed to the vanity's back were triple mirrors, angled so the one seated there could apply her cosmetics to the greatest effect. Bulbs to provide even lighting were set around the edges, but I didn't bother to activate them. My interest here was exploration, not adornment.

I sat myself on the elegant little bench seat. It wasn't a comfortable fit. Mother had been much trimmer behind than I was. Still, I soon forgot my discomfort as I focused on my search.

I started with the center drawer and found there, as I vaguely recalled I would, the smaller cosmetics: tubes of lipstick, eyeliner, and mascara all arranged in neat order, lighter colors to the left, darker to the right.

The top drawer on the right-hand side yielded a variety of hairbrushes and combs, as well as a hand mirror, doubtless for those times Mother needed to see the back of her head. The drawers below were filled with more hair-related items: nets, pins, clips, even a couple of shower caps, never removed from their packaging. There were spare brushes, old combs with a few teeth missing. Oddities that had probably been tried and found, for some reason now lost to time, wanting.

The one thing I expected to find but didn't was hair coloring. Later, I found a store of it in the bathroom cabinet under the sink. It was, for the time, professional grade stuff, and I wondered if one of the silent women had been trained to act as a beautician. The idea seemed very likely.

The left-hand drawers were devoted to cosmetics: eye shadow, eyeliner, eyebrow pencils, foundation, powder, rouge, nail polish, more lipstick, lip liner, gloss, mascara, and exotic items I couldn't identify. Mother had more cosmetics than many a well-stocked store, all of very good quality. She must have had the stuff shipped from New York or California.

I opened a tube here, a case there, and found that, natural deterioration aside, some of it was in fairly good condition. Most of it had been transformed by time into pure junk, oils separating from coloring compounds, pastes drying and cracking so they looked like highly colorful renditions of drought-stricken riverbeds.

My scrounger self was making a mental note that the cases and bottles might fetch something, even while my artist heart was weeping at so much lovely color gone to ruin. I wondered if I could do something with it, and the odd idea of painting a second portrait of Colette, a counterpoint to the one that now dominated this room, came to mind with almost frightening force.

I was fingering through the drawers, estimating volume and coverage and wondering if I could somehow salvage something from all the pretty, perfumed trash, when I realized that the bottom drawer on the right side was shallower than it should be.

Pushing back the bench and kneeling on the floor, I slid out the drawer. It came easily enough, the tracks unswollen as they almost certainly would have been in a more humid climate. Gingerly, I tipped the accumulated mess of old combs and brushes onto the carpet. With them came a heavy piece of stiffish white fabric folded up around the edges.

"A drawer liner," I said aloud. "Meant to make it easy to lift out the lot without making a mess. I'll know next time."

The bottom of the now empty drawer was apparently seamless. Feeling like a bit of a fool, I tapped and heard not quite hollowness, but certainly not the dull thud a solid bottom would have given. I have a good eye for detail and discrepancy, and it didn't take me long to find the place where I could press down and release the hidden catch. The false bottom lifted up on hidden hinges, revealing a compartment about four inches deep and as long and wide as the drawer.

"No wonder it didn't sound hollow," I said. "It's completely full, but what of?"

The compartment was filled with tubular objects, each ranging from roughly eight to twelve inches long. The diameters varied too, from narrow enough I could span them with thumb and forefinger, to fat tubes thick enough for a gerbil to set up housekeeping. Inside they were made of wood, of metal, of glass. No two were alike, though all had similarities. Each rested neatly in a velvet-lined trough clearly fashioned to hold it alone.

I stared blankly for a moment, then registered what I was seeing.

"Kaleidoscopes!" I said in astonishment. "It's a hoard of kaleidoscopes! I hope I haven't broken any of them."

One by one I lifted the kaleidoscopes from their places in the holding tray and held them to the fading sunlight coming in the window. Each was unique, each extraordinarily beautiful. The mandala views within were enough and more to match the external adornment.

I don't know how long I sat there on the floor, looking through each kaleidoscope in turn, then beginning again with the first. I couldn't seem to get enough of the gem-colored scenes. There were the simple, classic mandalas; there were elaborate snowflake patterns. Multicolored patterns contrasted with rare, nearly monochrome arrangements, these all the more beautiful in that they relied upon subtle differences in shading for their effects.

Eventually, the failing sunlight made me aware how much time had passed. I set the kaleidoscope I had been holding—a triangular one made of stained glass with an elaborate handblown sphere set in a bracket on the end—into its holder, got to my feet, and stretched.

After the brilliant colors in the kaleidoscopes, the white and gold of my mother's bedroom furnishings seemed pale and insubstantial. I crossed to the wall and switched on the lights, noting again where bulbs needed to be replaced. The electric light was not as satisfying as the sunlight had been, but it was ample to see by.

Going back over to the vanity, I thoughtfully stared down at the hoard I had discovered, wondering what to do with it. I knew something about kaleidoscopes. Each one of these was worth a tidy sum. Something other than their value awakened my curiosity. The artistic renaissance of the kaleidoscope was only about twenty, maybe thirty years old. Before that the elegant optical playthings that had so delighted the Victorians had declined to cheap, if charming, toys made mostly of cardboard, their inner mirrors a bit of bent metal as often as not.

This hoard was at least forty years old. That almost certainly meant they were antiques, their value enormously higher than that of contemporary pieces. But that was not reason enough for my mother to have hidden them in this way. She had left her jewelry in the open—even the better pieces had been tucked away in a velvet bag in her lingerie drawer. I knew this, because it had come to me with the rest of her estate.

Why would she leave jewelry out and hide these kaleidoscopes? And what should I do with them now?

Frowning, I decided that the place in which the kaleidoscopes had remained safe this long would do a bit longer. As I was lowering the false bottom on the drawer into place and resetting the liner and the concealing junk, I remembered I hadn't checked the left-hand drawer.

Knowing what I now did, I made a much neater job this time. I found the liner could be removed without taking the drawer out of the vanity. With this out of the way, I found the release and opened the false bottom panel. At first I thought I'd found more of the same, for again I was confronted with neat rows of kaleidoscopes, each in its tailor-made velvet bed.

Then two things caught my attention simultaneously. One kaleidoscope was missing from the first row. Then I realized that all the pieces in that first row were not kaleidoscopes but their close cousin, the teleidoscope.

I took out the one from the niche next to the empty one and held it to my eye to confirm my realization. Instantly, I was treated to a mandala in which the bedspread's gold and white were fragmented into a perfectly symmetrical mandala. I moved my head, and the view shifted with me, picking up glints of silver from the wall mirrors, a dash of the green from the foliage outside the window—for unlike the kaleidoscope, which relies on the images in the object chamber at one end to make its images, the teleidoscope transforms the world around the viewer by means of a convex lens set at one end.

I lowered the teleidoscope, pulling myself away from the enchanting images with difficulty. I had to resist an urge to leave this room with its dominating pale hues and see what the teleidoscope would do with the richer colors elsewhere in the house. I did resist, and instead sat staring at the teleidoscope, my earlier puzzlement returning.

There was no doubt that the instrument in my hand was a beautiful thing. The case was wood, the rich hues ranging from dark honey to nearly black. The woodworker had turned it on a lathe, giving it an almost femininely seductive curve. The whole had been polished so satiny smooth that my work-roughened fingertips could hardly believe anything was there. The lens at the end was actually a perfect crystal sphere set into the wood without seam or join.

The exteriors of the others varied somewhat, but not as much as with the kaleidoscopes. Here wood, enamel, inlay, or other less fragile materials seemed to be preferred over the stained glass that had been common in the kaleidoscope casings. Yet there was no reason why the exterior casing of a teleidoscope shouldn't be as varied as that of a kaleidoscope. It was the arrangement of mirrors within, the set of the eyepiece, the arrangement of the lens that effected the image.

So why had my mother preferred these relatively hardy teleidoscopes? Why had she hidden the collection in this way? Why had she hidden it at all? And why was one teleidoscope missing?

I started to put the teleidoscope I had been using away, but stopped at the last minute. Instead, I set it carefully on the vanity top, then hid the others away. After drawing the blinds and shutting off the lights, I left my mother's room, taking the teleidoscope with me. Once outside, I locked both the bedroom and the upper parlor doors. Then I went into the room I was using as a bedchamber and slid the teleidoscope into an odd sock. I hid the bundle at the back of my sock drawer.

I did this methodically, not even thinking whether or not I felt stupid about it, but that night, after I'd eaten and chatted a bit with Domingo, and gone back up to my room, I didn't read in Aunt May's journals as I usually would. Instead I lay on my bed, turning the crystal at the end of the length of polished wood here and there, watching the colors transform into wonderful symmetrical patterns that followed me into my dreams.

12

In the Middle Ages, color was used in *heraldry* . . . *Color* helped carry the message of the design: White = faith and purity; Gold = honor; Red = courage and zeal; Blue = purity and sincerity; Green = youth and fertility; Black = grief and penitence; Orange = strength and endurance; Purple = royalty and high birth
—Betty Edwards,
*Drawing on the Right Side of the Brain*

That an argent field meant purity, that field of gules meant royalty or even martial ancestors, that a saltire meant the capture of a city, or a lion rampant noble and enviable qualities, I utterly deny.
—A. C. Fox-Davies,
*The Complete Guide to Heraldry*

## INSIDE THE LINES

Until the day I discovered Colette's secret hoard, I had faithfully read forward in Aunt May's journals. Mostly, I had read of frustration—how her efforts to learn something from police and reporters had met with silence, how she had tried and failed to learn who my father might have been, how pushed beyond patience, she had even tried to find Colette's own birth certificate.

All of this had met with no success—or so she thought at the time—and given that the search had now stretched over a year, Aunt May had good reason to give up in frustration. Then came the announcement that a much loved cousin was dying in faraway Arizona, and with that announcement came temptation.

## OUTSIDE THE LINES

Breast cancer, her mother writes. They've taken both breasts away, and all sorts of glands and muscles, but it seems the cancer persists. I can't believe it. Linda and I played together as kids. Death is something that happens to old people, not to a woman who isn't even forty-five.

But it's going to happen.

I've been moping around for a week now, and yesterday Stan told me he wants me to go out to Arizona and see Linda. He doesn't spell it out, Stan doesn't, but he knows I need to see her to make this real. And, yes, I need it to be real. Otherwise, there's going to be a phone call and a funeral someday, and I'm going to break down and hate myself for lost chances.

So I agreed to go, and while I was looking at the map something came at me. Arizona borders on New Mexico. The drive to Las Vegas would be a long one, but . . . I could make excuses to Linda and her mother. Stan wouldn't know where I was. Long distance costing what it does, he isn't going to call me every night or anything like that.

I could rent a car, but I've checked. Trains run that way. I could catch one from Tucson, get to Las Vegas. Stay a day or so, ask some questions. No one would know. How could they? It's been over two years since we adopted Mira . . .

*Two days later.*

I asked some questions at a travel agent while I was doing the shopping. A round-trip ticket from Tucson to Las Vegas wasn't all that outrageous. I made a deposit. Tonight Stan came home with my airplane tickets to Arizona. He'd gone to get them on his lunch break. Different travel agent, of course. He's being so kind, I almost hate myself for breaking our promise, but this is something I have to do.

## INSIDE THE LINES

And almost as soon as Aunt May had made this decision, her doorbell rang. With that cascading chime, not only did her plans change, so did the journal. Up to that point, I'd been reading it with a certain detachment, but with the first two paragraphs something odd happened. I felt pulled inside, and read without awareness of the words, seeing the scene before me with all the vividness of life.

## OUTSIDE THE LINES

Dear Mira: I've been writing this journal to you all along. Today was the first time I realized it. I felt a fierce temptation to go back and tear out those earlier pages, but I've decided to leave them in. It's best that if you ever read this—as I plan that you will—that you don't have any illusions about what set me on what I did, and maybe even more importantly, what I'm planning on doing, though more than good sense tells me I should not.

You've read what comes before this. If you haven't, go back and do so. Now you can go on with everything straight.

Yesterday I put a deposit on a train ticket from Tucson, Arizona, to Las Vegas, New Mexico. Midday today, around ten o'clock, when I'd stopped to have a cup of coffee and a sweet roll and glance over the newspaper, the front doorbell rang.

I was surprised, but not too much. Salesmen are something of a fact of life, and they're just about the only people who use the front door. Friends come around to the kitchen.

Finishing my coffee, I went to the door, but I didn't find a salesman standing there. I found a man I recognized, and if I tell you my heart leapt into my throat, well, you'll just have to believe me.

He was about my age, short, plump, and fair-haired. As every time I've seen him, he was impeccably dressed in one of those suits that you know is expensive, even if it doesn't look all that different than every other suit you've ever seen. I know him as Michael Hart, and he's one of the trustees of Mira's estate—the youngest of the three, I think.

I opened the door to him immediately.

"Mrs. Fenn?" he said politely. "May I come in?"

I couldn't quite make myself talk yet, so I nodded and motioned him in. I thought he'd sit in the living room like he has always done before, but he moved past me into the kitchen and sat across from where I'd left my coffee cup. Somehow this made him a little less frightening, but I was still plenty nervous as I went in after him. I offered him coffee. He accepted, then added about half the contents of the sugar bowl. He got right to business.

"Mrs. Fenn," he said. "It has come to my attention that you are planning to make a trip to Las Vegas, New Mexico—in direct violation of the agreement we made when you and Mr. Fenn took in Mira Bogatyr."

I nodded. I didn't see any sense in lying, and I wasn't about to ask Mr. Hart how he knew. It occurred to me that I'd been stupid using a travel agent here in town. There aren't that many. I should have made the arrangements once I was in Tucson.

This flitted through my mind, even as I listened to his next words.

"It also has come to my attention that you have sent various letters to Las Vegas, letters inquiring after the fate of Colette Bogatyr."

I didn't even nod this time, just stared, and as I waited for him to continue his accusations something in me grew white hot.

"I know the terms under which we took Mira in," I said, and my voice shook, but it wasn't because I was afraid. I was furious. "If you're going to take her because I've broken them, well . . ."

I trailed off, not certain what I was threatening, but knowing that if my impulsiveness had lost me my daughter, I was going slit my wrists—if Stan didn't do it for me. Mr. Hart seemed to understand my desperation.

"Mrs. Fenn," he said, "why were you trying to locate Colette Bogatyr?"

"I want to know what happened to Colette. It's like I've already said. If something happens and Mira is taken from us . . . I don't know what I'd do.

I wanted to find out if anything had been learned about what happened to her. I wanted reassurance that she wouldn't come and take my little girl."

The smallest hint of compassion mingled into Mr. Hart's professional severity.

"Do you swear that is all?"

"What else could there be?"

"Mira has an inheritance coming to her. Perhaps you are interested in securing that. This would be difficult to do if her mother returned."

I was so shocked at being taken for a gold digger that I didn't say a word, and my silence apparently made a better answer than any words could have done.

"I see," Mr. Hart said. "If I assure you that Colette Bogatyr is not likely to return and take your daughter from you, will you stop your prying? I am pleased with how the child is thriving in your care, and so am reluctant to have her removed from your home. My colleagues might feel otherwise."

"Can you really swear Colette won't be coming back?" I said. "Is she dead then?"

Mr. Hart's expression became vague and I don't think he even saw where he was for a moment, so intent was he on an inner vision of some sort.

"She may be or she may not be, but though Queen of Mirrors she certainly is, and Mistress of Thresholds as well, she knows less than she could wish of color and of light. That is why she had a daughter."

I heard the titles, but shaken by the oddness of those words all I said was, "What?"

Mr. Hart shook his head, as a dog might shake water from its coat. "Trust me. Colette Bogatyr will not return to take your daughter from you. If you wish to keep Mira safe, let her grow here in this quiet place, let her find her strengths in her own time. That is the best thing you can do for her. Now. Do I have your word you will not go to Las Vegas, New Mexico, and that you will cease writing letters to those involved with the disappearance?"

What else could I do? I swore.

"Do not tell anyone of my visit. My leniency would be misinterpreted, and not only would you lose Mira, you would lose one who thinks well of how you care for her."

Mr. Hart rose from my kitchen table, and I walked him to the door. As he was about to leave, he handed me an envelope.

"Your deposit," he said, and without a further word of parting, he went down the walk. I glanced down at the envelope in my hand, and when I looked up again, he was gone.

Mira came home today with her folders stuffed with drawings from her art class. To this point, I had looked at them mostly to see how her skills were developing. Now for the first time I saw the riot of color she used. Not even a simple daisy was drawn in the white and yellow more usual for a child of her age. It was white and a dozen shades of yellow, from deep gold to the lightest lemon, petal edges touched with green, and given depth with shadow.

Color. Somehow my Mira has more than an artist's eye. Something in her ability to use color is key to her relationship with Colette. There's more here, too. Mr. Hart seemed to think I was interested in getting control of Mira's inheritance. I thought at the time he meant the money and property. Now I wonder. Could this "inheritance" be some ability? Maybe her artistic ability. I keep thinking about what Mr. Hart said: "She knows less than she could wish of color and of light. That is why she had a daughter."

Weird, but no stranger than anything else to do with Colette.

I have promised I will not do any more research regarding Colette's life in Las Vegas, but can I find out what those strange titles might mean? They sounded like something from a fairy tale, but I have heard that fairy tales often are watered-down versions of older stories, stories that have their roots in truth. Maybe there is some tiny country or Masonic lodge or something where these titles belong.

It seems like a safe enough thing to do, and not even Stan will find anything odd in a new mother who suddenly becomes obsessed with storybooks.

---

## INSIDE THE LINES

And so began Aunt May's search for the meaning behind those words, a search that I had seen the traces of in her interest in every religion, philosophy, and occult tradition of which she could learn. I had thought her interest a curiosity, an odd hobby, later even an attempt to compensate for the limitations inherent in the life of a suburban housewife.

Now I knew it for what it was, a quest as noble as that on which any of Arthur's knights ever rode out, more noble even, for while they sought the Grail for the honor it would bring to their king's house and to themselves, Aunt May sought knowledge so that she might use it to arm herself—and her daughter—against a danger she could not understand but knew nonetheless was there.

That night, reading her words, and knowing the end of that quest as Aunt May herself never could have done, I bent my head and wept over the handwritten pages, my tears the rain that never fell in the year that I was born.

Maybe it was because what I read in Aunt May's journal forced me to confront what was going on more directly than I had before, but the next morning I realized I was awakening more than the silent women. Something was coming alive, something that had . . . I struggled to find a word that would explain what I myself only nebulously understood. Slept? Been suspended? Been held in abeyance? Slept seemed easiest, but in that ease I recognized the danger of oversimplification.

Something that had slept, then, for forty years, ever since Colette had vanished.

I'd like to say that what was awakening was the House, but just as the term "slept" was a dangerous oversimplification, so was this. It was more like what the House stood for was coming alive. No. That wasn't quite right either. It had to do with the nature of the House itself.

Can something be alive and yet not? Aware and yet unaware? If so, that was the nature of the House.

The House was not a person but a place, a living place. There are long traditions of sacred sites, of places sanctified due to some nearly forgotten event—or perhaps the original event has mythologized almost beyond recognition of what originally happened. Myth might tell of how a god of war came to earth riding upon a flaming horse. The original event might have been an iron meteor falling to the ground.

There are other occult traditions that touch on the idea of living places. In the lingo of the New Age they're called "ley lines" or "alpha vortexes."

There are those who claim to sense "vibrations" or "emanations," from the living earth. These terms are all right, but still limited in their ability to express what's really going on.

It's like a tone-deaf person trying to sing Handel's *Messiah* a capella, or an artist trying to draw a rose with one red crayon. Semblance is there, but not substance, not dimension. If you know the *Messiah* or have seen a rose, you'll recognize what is being attempted, but going the other way around and trying to discover the original from these distorted representations is harder—if not completely impossible.

But nonetheless I knew. I knew that this house I had inherited from my mother was not just a house—even as it was indisputably and inarguably a house. All the things I had been doing since my arrival in New Mexico—the cleaning and dusting, ordering Domingo and his crew to complete the exterior painting, even the finding of Colette's hoard—were playing their part in this awakening, but these weren't the only things.

It was as if the research I had been doing into my past and into Colette's past, the reading I had been doing in Aunt May's journals and the transformation this had worked on my settled images of my childhood and of the people who had raised me, had reshaped my mind. I felt as if I was being reworked, made into the key that would unlock the puzzle that was Phineas House.

If this was the case, I was no linear shape of metal, but something more fluid and irregular, more like the final amoebalike shape that completes a jigsaw puzzle, transforming it so that everything seen before as little individual, unrelated scraps of color becomes a whole.

I was not the only one aware of the awakening of whatever potential it was that Phineas House held. Domingo Navidad may have been aware before I was, for Domingo had ever been the House's acolyte. Perhaps the relationship had begun when as a boy he had assisted his father about the grounds. Children's minds are more plastic than those of adults, and, if the evidence of the presence of the silent women can be taken as anything, the House was awake and alive then.

Perhaps when the House was being pushed back into sleep it reached out and touched Domingo, wrapping a tendril into his awareness, and through him maintaining a touch on the waking world. When this thought first occurred to me, the image was gentle, a green-hazed climbing vine setting a gentle hold on a support. Later, when I knew more, I came to think that what the House had done was crueler—more akin to the setting of sharp-hooked thorns that roses employ when they climb, digging into whatever is soft and yielding in their surroundings.

But this later image had no part of my initial reaction when I realized that of all the people I knew there was one, at least, who would not think I was insane, as Colette had been thought insane. I think Aunt May not only would have believed, she would have welcomed Phineas House as an answer to many of the puzzles whose edges she had discerned in her research, but whose inner logic remained frustratingly incomplete.

## OUTSIDE THE LINES

Mirrors. I decided to start there, not only because the title "Queen of Mirrors" is a lot more promising than "Mistress of Thresholds," but also because I remembered a strange comment that Mira made when she first came to live with us.

"There's only five mirrors in the whole house," Mira said, plopping into a chair in the kitchen. "One in each bathroom, one in your bedroom, one in mine, and one in the front hall."

I remember laughing. "Do we need more? Just how often do we need to look at ourselves?"

Mira didn't answer, but there was a thoughtfulness in her expression that stayed with me.

Very well. Mirrors. Well, the first one that came to mind was the one in Snow White, the one the Wicked Stepmother uses to spy on the young princess. I checked, and it's in the original *Grimm's Fairy Tales*, not just in the Disney movie.

I read the story through, end to end, thinking about it, not just reading it. It's a strange and nasty story really—about envy and vanity. I think those are two of the deadly sins—or is the one pride, not vanity? At the end, strangely, I found myself feeling pity for the old queen. True, she was willing to commit murder, but her tools were poison. Being forced to dance until dead in red-hot iron shoes . . . Brr . . .

And I couldn't help but think that Snow White was a bit of a twit, for all her goodness and beauty. I mean, the old queen tries to kill Snow White repeatedly, and the dwarves keep warning Snow White, and *still* she eats a slice from the apple!

But I'm getting away from mirrors. It seems to me that there must be more than this example.

I've read so many fairy tales that my mind is alive with princess and princesses, wise fools and foolish wise men. I dream about them at night. Strangely, many of them bear Colette's face.

I've learned more about mirrors. One thing is for sure. They're definitely considered magical. In several stories they're used to create illusions, usually of a great pool of water or a flashing fire.

Mirrors are magical in myths as well. Perseus defeats the Medusa using the mirror-bright reflection in a shield. Narcissus fades away because he is obsessed with his own reflection. It seems it is dangerous to look at oneself too closely. At least it was for Medusa and Narcissus.

And it seems that spying on others through mirrors wasn't restricted to the old queen. Sometimes a pool of water is substituted for a mirror, just like for Narcissus. I bet if I was to search around for other references I'd find that pools of water came first, then mirrors, and that our gypsy crystal ball is a relative latecomer.

Mirrors and water seem to be closely related. Mermaids are often depicted with a hand mirror and comb, combing out their long golden hair as they lure sailors to their doom. I bet at first they didn't bother with the hand mirror, just looked down into the water.

I came across a passing reference in some scholar's turgid opening to a collection to seven mirrors used in cabalism. That's some sort of Jewish magic, I think. But that's all I know. I'll have to look further.

The more I look, the more I see. I feel like Alice in Looking-Glass Land!

---

## INSIDE THE LINES

Domingo and I had acknowledged our shared perception of the House as somehow alive for quite a while before we actually discussed it openly. That awareness had been implicit in his earliest statements to me about Phineas House. Only later, as my own perceptions began to unfold and broaden, did I accept that Domingo was speaking more than artistically.

It's important to understand that when an artist says he (I'm going to say "he" here because I'm talking about Domingo) "sees" a shape or image, whether in a lump of stone or a heap of wet clay or even in a blank canvas, he means what he says. He's not speaking figuratively. It's there. The artist simply tries to bring it into a shape that will enable others to share the vision.

That's why artists are so often disappointed with their own work. That's why some artists make multiple renditions of the same theme. They're reaching for that illusive transformation.

So I never made the mistake of thinking Domingo was talking figuratively about Phineas House "wanting" certain things. Where I made my initial error was in thinking that the House was a passive lump of wood, stone, odd bits of metal, all coated in a rather monochrome paint job. I didn't realize that not only did it "want" that garish paint job, it needed it if it was to reach something like its full potential.

But I'm getting ahead of myself.

Domingo and I first discussed the House's role in what we were doing one morning in late August.

Those promised monsoon rains had not materialized as they should have some time in late July. The monsoons and how much rain they generate varies throughout the southwest, but the basic pattern is that clouds back up against the mountains and the initial rains start there. Evaporation cycles build more and better clouds, and soon the rains fall pretty much daily.

They're regular, too, Domingo reminded me. Rain often falls hard and steady for a half hour or so sometime in the late afternoon, then the skies clear back to their usual blue, all but for drifting clouds that herald the next-day's storm.

I had this all by hearsay, though. Like most children, when I was young I'd operated on a different sense of time. Rain happened, was a nuisance or a delight depending on my mood, but was not something to be measured and calculated. Since my arrival in New Mexico, my life in Ohio had been warring with my awareness that the local drought wasn't a good thing. I couldn't get enough of the bright, clear days, but as I watch Domingo hand-carry water to his garden, saw the Gallinas River (which runs through town) dwindle to a narrow damp thread, I knew something wasn't right.

"At least," I said to Domingo one morning when we were having our now traditional sweet rolls and coffee together, out in the back garden, "the lack of rain is letting us get the painting done. We haven't lost a day, and the place is looking astonishingly good."

Domingo nodded, but his expression was unwontedly solemn. Usually where matters regarding Phineas House's adornment were concerned, he all but glowed with quiet contentment.

"I hope," he said, "that the House itself is not contributing to the drought. It so wishes the painting to be done—and selfishness is a very hot thing and heat chases away the clouds."

I felt uncomfortably certain he was right. Child of a rainless year. I thought of Colette and her perfect centeredness, and wondered.

Instead of voicing this, I asked, "Why do you think it is so important to the House that it be painted? It has been a long time without this paint. In fact, it may never have been this colorful in all its history. I remember it as greyish white. We haven't found anything like this level of color when we've scraped."

Domingo looked at me, his gaze very clear but slightly vague, as if he were listening. Then he said, "I think the need for color has something to do with you, Mira. I don't know why, but it was shortly before your coming that the impulse to repaint became very strong. Before that I had restrained myself to trim and such, but the work on the front began that winter."

"Before I even knew I was coming," I said. "Before Aunt May and Uncle Stan had their accident. It couldn't be."

But I felt uncomfortably that Domingo might well be right. Did that mean the House had known Aunt May and Uncle Stan were going to die? That was ridiculous. A house couldn't know. But I felt that uncomfortable sensation again, and wasn't at all sure.

"The House," Domingo said, "wants something. I don't know what it is. Of one thing, though, I am certain. It does not want to go back to being a dull house with boarded windows. It wants to be open and . . ."

"Alive?" I suggested when he trailed off.

Domingo gave another of his eloquent shrugs. "And whatever it is becoming now. For your mother it was a house filled with mirrors. For you it is becoming a house of many colors."

"And still filled with mirrors," I said, for I had never taken them down. They belonged as much as did the carvings around the windows and the silent women.

"So it is," Domingo said. "But I have no idea why."

Thinking of what I was reading in Aunt May's journal, I had a slight idea, but I didn't say anything then.

I admit. After reading Aunt May's first section on mirrors, I skimmed ahead, looking for more on the same topic. I couldn't forget how important mirrors had been to Colette—as important to her, it seemed, as color was to me. Aunt May didn't find anything immediately, but when she did, it was pure gold.

## OUTSIDE THE LINES

I went over to Mr. Gillhoff's new-and-used bookstore today after dropping Stan's suits and my blue wool dress at the cleaner. I know I could hand-wash the dress, but it has so many pleats! I just couldn't face the pressing.

Mr. Gillhoff is getting used to seeing me come in. If it's not something for me, I'm looking for something for Mira or Stan. So he's pretty friendly.

"I'm looking for a book that will tell me the ways that stories relate to each other," I said, feeling rather flustered. "What I mean is why the same stories get told over and over again—like in fairy tales. I think there must be some root they all spring from."

"Maybe so, maybe not," Mr. Gillhoff replied, but he didn't laugh at me, or worse, look completely lost like the librarian at my local branch had when I'd tried to ask the same thing.

"Maybe so, maybe not?" I repeated. "I realize I didn't ask very well, but . . ."

Mr. Gillhoff shook his head and peered at me over the tops of his half-glasses.

"Forgive me, Mrs. Fenn," he said. "My answer was to the latter half of your comment. I meant that maybe stories do all come from one root. However, maybe they grow from something more general—a common impulse to explain the inexplicable. What you want is a book on comparative mythology and legend lore. The classic work of that type is, of course, Sir James Frazer's *The Golden Bough*."

I stared at him. "Is it difficult to understand?" I asked, adding apologetically. "I only finished high school."

"In parts," Mr. Gillhoff said, "but it's fascinating reading, just the same. Frazer doesn't concentrate on fairy tales, of course."

"That's fine," I said, thinking that though Colette did rather seem like an evil witch queen from a fairy tale—at least as I envisioned her—that couldn't really be the case. "Mythology and legends. That sounds promising."

"And magic," Mr. Gillhoff said, almost as an afterthought. "Frazer considered magic an important part of the entire picture because it was how 'primitive' people tried to control their environment."

"Oh," I said, wondering if Stan would mind having a book on magic in the house, then thinking he probably wouldn't. Then I had another thought. "Is the book very expensive?"

"Not at all," Mr. Gillhoff assured me. "Frazer's work has been in print a long time, through many editions. I can sell you a used copy of the abridged edition—that's as much as you'll want at first, I think, for a few dollars."

He went to find me a copy while I browsed, and when he came back, he had two other volumes with him. They were quite thick.

"I ordered these for a customer who later decided he didn't want them. They might interest you. They're essentially a dictionary listing symbols, images, and people from myth and legend. None of the entries are very long, but they might help you get through Frazer—give you something to cross-reference when he refers to someone you've never heard of."

I looked, knowing already that I wanted those books, but dreading what they would cost.

"How much?" I asked.

The figure he named was much lower than I had envisioned.

"I'm willing to sell them to you at the publisher's discounted price," Mr. Gillhoff explained. "You're saving me sending them back and waiting for a refund."

I didn't quite believe him. I knew kindness when I heard it, but I accepted his price anyhow. I wanted those books, and I could just stretch my allowance to meet the price, especially if I went without a few of my usual indulgences.

I dove into the Frazer as soon as I got home, and instantly found myself overwhelmed. Who was Adonis? What was this about a priesthood of Diana? Hadn't Diana been a Roman goddess—one of the virgin ones? Wouldn't she have had priestesses? I turned to the mythology dictionary with something like relief and when next I looked up, an hour had passed in browsing.

Hurrying into the kitchen, I propped the book on the counter while I cut vegetables for dinner. This time I was more efficient. I turned directly to "Mirror," and to my delight found a long entry.

In its own way, it was nearly as cryptic as Frazer. Single words indicating things mirrors were apparently symbols of or associated with were listed, among them a few I thought might apply to Colette. "Courtesan" and "vanity" leapt out at me. I saw that my guess had been right, that mirrors did have a long tradition of being associated with divination. There was a final listing of more specific important mirrors, important to magic.

I wondered if Colette had mirrors she used for magic. I wondered if that was what Mr. Hart had meant when he called her the Queen of Mirrors.

I wondered, too, if I was crazy to even think such a thing.

## 13

What I was thinking about was the Pecos, certainly an enchanting and enchanted place. Where else could one
come across a man by the name of Mr. Merlin, living on
the banks of a stream called the Holy Ghost. And where
else in this sophisticated world could you find a Mr. Merlin wholly and completely unaware of this conjoining of
fact and fable, of pagan and Christianity?

—Milton C. Nahm,
*Las Vegas and Uncle Joe*

## INSIDE THE LINES

You can imagine how I nearly went crazy myself skimming through, looking
for entries that said more, but as far as I could tell, there were none. Aunt
May had discovered the joy of research for its own sake, and her hungry
mind was devouring stories and building connections. No doubt about it.
The world lost a great researcher when Aunt May was locked away into the
bland expectations of suburbia.

I didn't mind the tangents. Actually, her enthusiasm was a delight, and I
had a feeling that there were more jewels for me amid the scrawled paragraphs, maybe even the gem I sought, but I was too impatient to wait.

I thought about racing off to the local library and seeing what I could
find. There was a university in town as well. I felt certain they had some sort

of program through which I could do research or borrow books. I might have to pay a fee, but unlike Aunt May, who had to wait on an allowance, I had my own money.

Then I had a thought. I checked the time, decided it was too late to call, and settled for drafting an e-mail to Betty Boswell.

"Dear Betty," it began, "I was wondering if you'd take the spare key and go over to my parents' house. There are a couple of books of Aunt May's that I'd like to have here. I don't know the exact titles, but one is a dictionary of mythology and the like. Also, if she has any books on mirrors and on the symbolism of color, that would be great.

"Could you send them to me? I'll reimburse you for the postage, of course."

I sent it before I could regret the notion. If I got too impatient, there still were libraries and local bookstores. Indeed, New Mexico was a New Age haven, and I could probably find anything I wanted in Santa Fe.

But I wanted Aunt May's copies if at all possible. Her books would bring her closer.

And who knew what she might have written in the margins!

Was it in defiance of the influence Phineas House was asserting over me that after nearly two full months of residence, I finally began to explore the town that was becoming my new home? Or was it the desire of the House that I do so and in this way gain some sort of understanding of the deep and twisted complexities that surrounded the House—and with understanding, more deeply bind myself into those same complexities?

This I do not know, even at this late date, nor do I ever expect to do so. Whatever the reason—defiance or domination—I began to learn about the strange history of Las Vegas, New Mexico. As I learned I also began to suspect the role Phineas House had played in those events—or if not the House itself, the forces of which the House was somehow a part.

As I have said before, for all that my birth certificate states that I was born in Las Vegas, my knowledge of that town was minimal. My earliest world was Phineas House itself. Later this expanded to include the seminary and the homes of a few school friends. I remember little else.

The real estate agent, Mrs. Morales, had told me a little of the town's history. I had gathered a bit more from my neighbors, most of whom were amateur historians by virtue of their interest in restoring old homes. Now I decided to set this fragmented information into a pattern, and who better to ask for help than Domingo? He had lived in Las Vegas all his life, apparently contentedly. Chilton O'Reilly might have some interesting tales. But I began with Domingo.

"What does 'Las Vegas' mean, anyhow?" I asked one morning. "I keep having to tell my friends that I'm not on the gambling strip in Nevada."

"It means 'the Meadows,'" Domingo said, the twinkle in his eyes telling me that I was not the first resident of the town to have this problem. "Called so, I think, because in the earliest days when this was a land grant given by the Spanish government to the family of Luis María C. de Baca, all that was here were meadows, good for nothing much but grazing—though by all accounts they were very good for that."

I'd heard a little about the Baca land grant, and knew that even now, a hundred and eighty or so years later, it was a sore point with some of Hispanic residents of Las Vegas, especially those of Spanish descent. Judging from his tone Domingo did not seem to be among these.

"'The Meadows,'" I said, trying it out. "I guess I can see it. I must say, though, that the mountains stand out just as much."

"They do," Domingo agreed. "Some years ago a publicity campaign for Las Vegas—trying to bring in residents and businesses, you understand— used the slogan 'Where the Mountains Meet the Plains.' It did okay, but nothing like Santa Fe calling itself 'The City Different' or Albuquerque's nickname, 'the Duke City.'"

"I like it," I protested. "It speaks to the heart."

Domingo smiled. "You have an artist's heart, Mira, and you like contrasts very much. But 'Las Vegas' is not the town's full name."

"No?"

"No. She is Nuestra Señora de Los Dolores de Las Vegas."

"Our Lady of the Sorrows of Las Vegas?"

"Yes. The Virgin Mary has many mysteries. They are celebrated in the rosary. It is as 'Our Lady of Sorrows,' though, that most Catholics love her best, because her sorrows mean she will understand our own."

"Oh." I felt a little uncomfortable with this Catholic mysticism. Aunt May had been religiously eclectic in her views, but those views were private. Publicly, we were a tidy little Protestant family, trotting off to our nondescript but good-hearted little church each week.

I hadn't thought about whether Domingo was religious or not, or, to be honest, whether he had a religion other than his devotion to Phineas House. This easy familiarity with Roman Catholicism was unsettling—because it separated me from the only person to whom I felt at all close, the person who shared a private mystery with me. I decided to shift the subject.

"So," I said, "if I was going to play tourist, what should I see?"

Domingo gave this serious consideration. "There is always the plaza. Have you been there?"

"Not really. I've been through, but never to look around."

"Well, in a Spanish town, the plaza is always the heart, and this is still true today. Of course, Las Vegas is odd in this as so many other things. Did you know that for much of its history Las Vegas was two towns, not one?"

"Two? No offense, Domingo, but there's hardly enough population for one town, much less two side by side. I thought that only happened where urban sprawl had filled in the gaps."

Domingo's smile was sad. "It can happen where hatred and resentment rule as well. Las Vegas was, as I have said, a town that originally developed as many towns do—because here there was water and elsewhere there was not. With the development of the Santa Fe Trail, and, later, the founding of Fort Union, the town began to thrive.

"Then in 1879 the railroad came, and this changed everything. For various reasons I cannot recall right now, the railroad chose to run its line a mile from what was then the heart of town. Almost immediately, a second town—a boomtown—grew up near the railroad. From the start, the old town and the new were rivals, each fiercely resenting the other."

"Money will do that," I said.

"New money meeting old," Domingo agreed, "but there was more. The old money was mostly Spanish. The new money was Anglo—and New Mexico had not been a part of the United States for very long."

"Was it a state yet?"

"Oh, no, not for a long time yet. That would come in 1912, but the United States took over governance of New Mexico from Mexico in 1846. Interestingly, Las Vegas was the first place in the territory where the announcement of United States' rule was made. General Kearney, who did this, did his best to reassure the local population that they would be well-treated, but . . ."

Domingo gave one of his eloquent shrugs.

"I know enough American history to guess what happened," I said. "As long as there was nothing of great value—other than trade that was already locked down—the locals were pretty much left to go on as they had, but when the railroad came, and there was new money to be had . . ."

"Exactly," Domingo said. "Now, you must understand, I am American, but even so, the first language I learned to speak was Spanish. Old memories run long here. When the train came to Las Vegas in 1879—on July 4th, incidentally—thirty years had passed since the Americans had taken over, but there were still many who thought of themselves as Spanish. Spain had ruled here, too, within many of their lifetimes. They were *dons* and *doñas*—lords and ladies—and they did not at all like the sudden influx of rough men who called them 'Mexicans,' 'greasers,' and other things less kind."

"So two towns grew up from this?"

"That's right. East and West Las Vegas, or sometimes called the Old Town and the New Town. Each was proud, each thinking itself right. Side by side, two towns, two governments, two school systems, angry twins glowering at each other over old grudges. When the local economy finished its long collapse in the early 1920s, the money was gone and the only currency left was resentment."

"You know a lot about this," I said, mildly surprised to find my handyman such a historian.

"All of us who love Las Vegas know these events and occasions," Domingo said simply. "We are still trying to figure out why we cannot recover. Santa Fe is a mere sixty-five miles away and thriving. Being the seat of the state government helps, but that cannot be the only reason. Taos, in the mountains to the north is isolated, yet it continues to grow and thrive—even to take over some of the trendiness that Santa Fe has lost. Albuquerque is a great ugly city, but vital. Here in Las Vegas, we shrivel and fade, no matter how hard we try. It is an eternal puzzle."

I felt odd and shivery, almost as I had when we stood together outside the closed doors of Phineas House. Domingo had shown me something important here, but I lacked the key to understand it. Giving myself a quick shake, I turned to him.

"So, can you tell me what I should look for in the Plaza? Or is there a tourist center where I can go and get maps and things?"

"Both," Domingo said, with a shy and yet courtly smile. "Or I can escort you. As you said, I know a lot about local history. I would very much enjoy sharing it with a native come home again."

My cheeks grew hot, and I felt a sudden prickling under my collar, but I ignored this.

"If you can spare the time."

"Well, I already have the crew coming to paint today," Domingo said, looking less pleased than he had a moment before. "However, we are coming up on Labor Day weekend. I am sure they would not mind an extra day off—and if there are those who need to work, I can find them some. Can you wait until Friday?"

Today was Wednesday.

"I can," I agreed. "It will give me a chance to do some research. It seems there's a lot more to Las Vegas than I realized."

Domingo smiled. "I will tell you some books to read. I can even loan you some."

I nodded, uncertain whether he was seeing this venture as a date, a duty, or an opportunity to lecture. Later, when I found the stack of books on my kitchen table, beside them was a very nice bouquet of roses, fancy ones, wrapped in florist paper, not cut from our mutual garden. They were mostly yellow, with one red glowing at the heart.

Then I thought I knew.

The water heater stopped heating Wednesday afternoon, and dealing with plumbers and the like made the days between my conversation with Domingo and our planned outing speed by.

Betty Boswell had e-mailed to say that she had found a bunch of books she thought would interest me, and that she had mailed them that same afternoon. However, appalled by the cost of shipping, she'd sent them the cheapest—and slowest way.

I resigned myself to waiting, though I could well have afforded the more expensive rate. I'd sold an old toaster online for an amazingly good price, especially since I was quite definitely afraid to use it. The chrome might have dazzled, but the wiring screamed "fire hazard."

Friday morning I took a hot shower with a new appreciation for the pleasure, then went downstairs to meet Domingo. He poked his head around a door frame and asked if I wanted to start our touring immediately after breakfast, and I agreed.

Torn between feeling like I was going on a first date, and a purely practical awareness that we were probably going to spend much of the day walking, I had fussed over what to wear the night before. I settled on my lightweight hiking boots, a nice pair of jeans, and a short-sleeved, hand-painted silk blouse in swirling shades of dark amber and honey that reminded me somewhat of the images in one of Colette's kaleidoscopes. I added amber earrings, and a matching bracelet I'd bought for a song on one of my European trips with Aunt May and Uncle Stan.

When I hurried down the stairs to put on the coffee, I felt festive and happy. My own reflection in one of the mirrors rather surprised me. Yes, I was still a somewhat stocky, fifty-something woman, but there was a sparkle in my rainy-day eyes and a hint of rose in my pale cheeks. Even my hair seemed to have more shine.

"New Mexico agrees with you, Mira," I said, and avoided my own blush in the myriad mirrors in the kitchen as I made the coffee.

Domingo and I had fallen in to an unspoken routine for our breakfast meetings, alternating who would bring the sweets. The leftovers (if any, we both had a sweet tooth) would usually be put out for the painting crew's midmorning break. Sometimes Domingo would bring a pound of coffee beans from a specialty roaster he knew. It was very relaxed, very casual, and there was no reason for my heart to flutter so as I stepped through the screened door out into the yard.

Domingo was already there, standing beside the wrought-iron table and chairs where we always met. The patio set was painted ivory white, but with his usual flare Domingo had picked out the flower shapes worked into the iron with pastel hints, each soft as the faint hint of color that heralds the sunrise. Domingo was tossing a stick for Blanco, and his back was to me.

Selfishly, I took a moment to study him. He was not overly tall—perhaps five ten—but so lean and muscular that he seemed taller. His features were angular, his cheekbones high, but there was a contrasting broadness that hinted at some Indian blood in his family tree. This was not uncommon in the older Hispanic families in New Mexico. Neither the Spanish nor the French shared the English prejudice against mixing with the local inhabitants—and the first exploratory expeditions had been entirely male. Even the later ones, ostensibly meant for colonization, had been largely male.

There probably are no old Spanish families without a trace of Indian blood, and there's a reason why many of the resident Indians have Spanish surnames.

But that was neither here nor there. I wasn't examining an anthropological specimen. I was enjoying a good look at a man who seemed to be interested in me as more than a friend with whom to share morning coffee—though the wealth of yellow roses surrounding the single red seemed to say Domingo didn't want to relinquish our friendship.

Or maybe I was simply reading too much into a polite gesture. I decided to take care that I didn't assume too much—or say too little either. With this in mind, I began descending the stair, the tray with the coffee carafe and two mugs, one red, one shining green, balanced carefully in my hands.

Domingo must have heard my feet on the stair, or maybe the increased intensity in Blanco's bounding after the stick gave something away. In any case, Domingo turned and came to take the tray from me, the gesture neither servile nor indicating that he thought I'd slip and fall on my nose if he didn't come to the rescue.

*Yellow roses*, I thought. *Why do I see roses?*

"Good morning," I said. "You look ready for our expedition."

He did, too. The usual paint-stained coveralls he wore had been replaced by dark blue, crisply creased jeans and a tan western shirt with touches of embroidery on the yoke. Like me, he had chosen hiking boots, a promise of a long day ahead.

"And you look very nice," he said. "I like the blouse. Is it silk?"

I nodded, busying myself with pouring the coffee to cover a sudden awareness that I was blushing again. It was Domingo's turn to bring breakfast, and he now opened a bakery box to reveal a very solid-looking pecan ring. The buttery pastry broke apart easily, but didn't crumble.

"Wonderful," I said after a bite, "but assured to put ten pounds on you just from looking at it."

Domingo smiled. "We will do a great deal of walking today, so eat without fear. I thought we would start down at the Plaza. The Labor Day festivities will not get too busy until the weekend proper. We can enjoy looking around."

"Sounds good," I said, then continued with what I hoped was the right degree of casualness. "I wanted to thank you for the roses. They were beautiful."

Even as a I spoke the words, I felt a rush of apprehension. What if the roses were one of Phineas House's odd manifestations, like the silent women? What would Domingo think? Had I just made a fool of myself?

But Domingo's smile only widened. "I am glad you liked them, Mira. I was walking past a store and saw them in the window, and thought of you."

Thinking of the symbolism of that red rose amid the yellow, I wanted to ask, "Did you see roses or that arrangement?" "What made you think of me?" I decided to keep my mouth shut, and reached for another piece of pecan ring to seal my resolve.

Shortly after we left, taking Domingo's truck and Blanco. The little white dog sat happily in the backseat, snuffling out the rear cab window that Domingo had left slightly ajar. The front cab had been meticulously cleaned out, a gesture to our outing. Domingo and I parked side by side in the carriage house garage. I knew full well he didn't keep it this clean all the time.

We drove down to the Plaza and parked in one of the spaces marked along the edge. The Plaza seemed a small place to have once been a city's heart, just an irregularly shaped island of Siberian elms with an understory of various shrubs surrounded by paved roads. A gazebo painted white with brilliant blue trim dominated one end. At the other end, a tall pylon of petrified wood displayed a bronze plaque on which there was a reproduction of General Kearney's speech when he formally assumed control of New Mexico for the United States. It seemed impossible that this quiet green could have been the site of such a historic occasion.

Shop fronts ringed the Plaza, many of them empty, but a few caught my eye and invited later browsing. Perhaps the most famous building among those ringing the Plaza was the Plaza Hotel, but its flat, greyish brown brick facade appealed to me far less than did the beautifully restored cream and periwinkle blue facade of Plaza Antiques.

We walked over so I could get a better look, and while I admired the wide store window and the balcony that stretched the full length of the building's front, Domingo told me that this building had been in place since the days of the Santa Fe Trail.

"It is called the Wesche-Dodd Building," he said, "built, I think, in 1870. In some ways, it says everything about Las Vegas."

"What do you mean?"

"It is built on the original site of the first Our Lady of Sorrows Church," he explained. "When the church was moved, a mercantile establishment was built on the site. The city of our Lady of Sorrows of the Meadows chose to be a city of business, instead of one dedicated to spiritual values."

"I guess they had to do something with the space," I said.

Domingo shrugged. "They did, but Albuquerque has kept her church on the Plaza in Old Town. Santa Fe has the great cathedral very close to the Plaza, so that the bell tower is easily seen. It seems to me that Las Vegas changed its focus when the church was moved, but maybe that is just my fancy."

The Art Stones gallery across the Plaza from the hotel was less spectacularly painted than Plaza Antiques, but it made up for this with the colorful array of items displayed in its windows, among them—no exaggeration—a full-sized horse painted in every color of the rainbow. Unlike the antique store, the emphasis here was on new art, the array of painting, jewelry, and handmade clothing enlivened with a wide assortment of gems and minerals.

Domingo was a good guide, spicing details that I could have learned from any tourist guidebook with anecdotes about things that had happened to his family and friends. In turn, I found myself talking about things I had done with Aunt May and Uncle Stan, about childhood triumphs and failures. Oddly, this awakened no sense of either sorrow or homesickness, just the nicest tang of bittersweet nostalgia.

*It was good for you to get away, Mira*, I thought, but my thought was spoken in Aunt May's voice.

We had finished our touring of the Plaza and associated areas and were heading back toward Domingo's truck when I noticed the woman. Despite her long, dark red hair, she was clearly Hispanic. She was sitting on the edge of a platform I didn't remember having seen during our first pass through the area, gently swinging her long, lithe legs, and smoking a cigarette. She was very beautiful in a wild, almost unkempt fashion, her beribboned blouse unlaced to show off the rounded tops of her full breasts, her multitiered skirts riding up to her knees with each swing of her legs.

*She must be dressed for some part of the Labor Day weekend festivities*, I thought. *That looks like one of the traditional Spanish outfits they still wear for the dances. She'd better take care, or she's going to catch a bit of ribbon or lace on that platform.*

The red-haired woman waved casually—though I thought more likely to Domingo than to me.

"A friend of yours is waving," I said to him, feeling an odd prick of jealousy. Domingo might never have been married, but I didn't believe he'd never had lovers.

"Where?" he asked, turning slightly to look back across the Plaza.

"There," I said, indicating the platform with an inclination of my head, "on the . . ."

I stopped in midsentence. The platform and the red-haired woman were both gone, vanished as if they had never been there.

"Never mind," I said. "I must not have eaten enough at breakfast—or had too much coffee. I'm hallucinating."

Domingo didn't question my sanity, but instead asked almost shyly, "Well, then, may I take you to lunch, Mira? The restaurant in the Plaza Hotel is famous locally, and you would probably enjoy the dining room. It has been completely restored to something of its former grandeur."

"I think I'd like that," I said, sneaking a glance where I had seen the red-haired woman. "I read about the Plaza Hotel in some of the books you loaned me. Weren't the tin-work ceilings covered for a long time, and only recently restored?"

"Not so recently as when those books were written," Domingo agreed, "but even so."

We made our way to the hotel, and had a fine lunch in the lovely dining room, but even as I admired the detail and listened to Domingo's enthusiastic descriptions, I couldn't stop thinking about the red-haired woman.

Had it been one of the silent women on holiday? I knew they could leave Phineas House, so that seemed possible, but somehow I couldn't imagine that wild and sensuous creature running the vacuum or washing my dishes. Did the city have its own silent women or was I seeing ghosts? Did that mean the silent women were ghosts? If so, why did they haunt my House?

Only after I realized that I was becoming so absorbed in my thoughts that I was being rude to Domingo did I make myself stop thinking about what I'd seen. I resolved that once the holiday weekend was over and I could come down here alone again, I would come back, and see if the red-haired woman also came back.

"I thought we had walked enough this morning," Domingo said, "and that perhaps a bit of driving would be a rest. Would you like to see the Glorieta battlefields?"

I agreed. My readings had mentioned the battle, and I was interested in seeing where it had happened.

"It's hard for me to believe," I said after a spell of admiring the increas-ingly rocky landscape, "that something that happened here—basically in the middle of nowhere—could have been a turning point in the Civil War. I always thought the fighting didn't happen much except down through the south and, oh, maybe as far north as Pennsylvania. I never realized that any battles took place west of the Mississippi, much less one so important."

Domingo nodded, his gaze intent on the curving road. We were heading away from the plains now, into the mountains. Were we to continue on, we would end up in Santa Fe.

"That's the usual Eastern view," he agreed without malice. "What I think is strange is that the battle played a decisive element in the Union's even-tual victory—but that the Union lost the battle."

"That's right," I agreed. "The Confederates won, but the Union succeeded in destroying their supply train. That severely crippled them, and they never managed to make the push up into Colorado that would have given them access to the gold fields."

"And the money the Confederates so desperately needed to win the war," Domingo finished. "Yes. I've always seen the Battle of Glorieta as yet another example of how Las Vegas twists reasonable expectations. Noth-ing that happens here ever seems to come out as it should."

I thought about that as we drove back toward town. I hadn't finished all the histories Domingo had given me, but I sensed the truth in what he said. I also found it odd and unsettling how often the disasters were linked to water, and not just the lack of water one would expect in a desert, but to floods, hailstorms, even hot springs.

Hot springs reminded me of something I'd wanted to ask.

"Domingo, do you think we could tour the campus of the United World College?"

"Montezuma's Castle?" Domingo chuckled. "You anticipate my surprise, Mira. I was going to ask you if you'd like to go there with me tomorrow. I had arranged to take you on a tour when the campus would have emptied out for the long weekend."

"Domingo, do you read minds?"

"Not at all, Mira. But the Castle is one of the famous landmarks of the area. I thought you would like to see it from more than a distance." He turned his head and gave me a grin that was distinctly boyish. My heart did a stupid flip-flop. "Since you have stolen my surprise, I shall at least reserve my stories about the place until we are there."

I grinned back, enjoying his enthusiasm. Suddenly, I was reluctant to have the day end.

"Domingo, do you have enough gas for us to get to Santa Fe? Let me take you to dinner. You can show me around a bit there."

"It's going to be crowded," he warned. "Labor Day weekend is when Fiesta starts. They burned Zozobra yesterday, but still there will be crowds."

"Burned Zozobra?"

"Old Man Gloom," Domingo said, his words leaving me as confused as before, but after a pause he went on, shifting to what I thought of as his tour guide voice. "It is a tradition, though not a very old one. It began in the 1920s with a couple of artists. They felt the Santa Fe Fiesta was too religious, so they made a big figure, shaped rather like a man, and burned him in a bonfire. Then it was just a celebration held for a few friends in somebody's backyard. These days the figure is very elaborate, and constructed so it moans when it burns. The burning of Zozobra has become so popular that they had to move the burning from Friday to Thursday to cut down on the crowds."

I found myself thinking that it was a reflection of New Mexico's long cultural heritage that an annual tradition more than eighty years old was thought of as "not a very old one." But then, in a region where some of the pueblos had customs that were old when Shakespeare was considered a daring new playwright, the attitude made sense.

"A fiesta meant to burn away gloom is exactly what I need," I said. "I've been locking myself away in Phineas House lately. I want to see people dressed up in brightly colored fiesta clothing, and walls painted with gaudy murals and all the rest. What do you say?"

In answer Domingo pulled away from the lane he'd been about to exit onto.

"Let's do it," he said.

14

Perhaps there was an old Indian curse on the place. Certainly the Santa Fe eyed the books that always seemed to be in the red.

—F. Stanley,
*The Montezuma (New Mexico) Story*

## INSIDE THE LINES

We got a later start the next morning, but as we hadn't made it back to Las Vegas until after midnight, this was only reasonable. I'd lost track of the places we'd been, the galleries we'd seen, the interesting people we'd talked with. Domingo seemed to know someone just about everywhere, and from just about every level of society. We'd visited with hotel clerks and bartenders, with the owners of posh galleries, and with popular musicians.

Many of them lived in Las Vegas, since they were unable to afford the increasingly high price of Santa Fe real estate. When they learned I had been born in Las Vegas, even if I had grown up elsewhere, I instantly became a neighbor rather than an outsider.

On our drive back, I asked Domingo about this friendliness.

"It doesn't seem to go with what you told me about two towns and old rivalries," I explained a bit apologetically.

"Those are inside rivalries," he explained, "and these days they find their greatest outlet in street gangs. When you are outside Las Vegas, though, especially in cities like Santa Fe that increasingly do not belong to traditional New Mexico, but to some tourist dream of the state, then we are all one against the others."

"Makes sense," I said. "I suppose it's the same everywhere—us against the world."

"It is the same and not the same," Domingo replied. "Here we face an old dilemma. How much must we give up of our traditional ways in order to thrive in the modern world? New Mexico is a poor state with a low population, yet we are rich in heritage. Do we sacrifice that heritage for the benefit of our children? What must we give up to attract teachers and doctors? Perhaps transforming towns like Santa Fe and Taos into caricatures of their true selves is the answer."

"The other day it sounded like you envied Santa Fe and Taos their popularity and tourist dollars," I commented.

"I am a Las Vegan," Domingo said simply, "divided even against myself."

That morning I recalled this conversation as we drove from Las Vegas proper out to where the Montezuma Castle was living its latest incarnation as a campus of the United World College. This was the road along which Colette had disappeared, but although I enjoyed the assortment of houses that lined the road, I didn't think many of them had been there as long as forty years. Construction styles were dominated by modern one-story ranch houses, and though I glimpsed dogs, cats, horses, and in a couple of cases sheep and chickens, my guess was that the residents worked elsewhere.

I forgot even Colette upon my first sight of the Castle. It sat on a hill overlooking the river valley below, a sprawling, impossibly elegant structure whose warm reddish brick and stone walls were accented by silvery white roofs and window borders. Other buildings were visible lower down the slope, but although some of them were quite large, none challenged the Castle's domination of the scene.

Once I would have thought the construction of the Montezuma Castle fanciful, even ornate, but that would have been before I had come to live in Phineas House. Now the Castle's asymmetrical assortment of towers, gables, and cupolas looked right—if a little subdued.

"It's huge," I said.

"It has over two hundred and fifty rooms," Domingo replied. "Including a grand foyer, reception rooms, a small campus store, and a spectacular dining hall."

"You sound as proud as if you built the place yourself," I said teasingly.

"I did in a way," Domingo said. "Caretaking Phineas House hasn't been my only job, as you know. I worked at the Castle during the renovation project. One of the contracting firms was based in Las Vegas and hired locals whenever possible. I learned a great deal about preservation techniques I've used since on the House—though sometimes I wonder if she minds."

I filed that last statement away without comment. Domingo often referred to the House as "she." At first I had taken this as a literal translation of the Spanish language's giving genders to nouns. "Casa" is, of course, feminine. However, the longer I had known Domingo—and even more important, the longer I had known Phineas House—the more I wondered just how literal he was being.

Even though I hadn't said anything, Domingo apparently regretted his statement, because he cleared his throat and started to rattle off his promised tourist spiel.

"The Castle in its current form is a relative newcomer. It was built in 1886 to replace a nearly identical hotel that had burnt to the ground the year before. However, the area has been in use since prehistoric times because of the hot springs.

"Local legend says that the hot springs were sacred to the Indians, both tribes from the pueblos and from the plains. I've even heard it said that rival groups would schedule their visits in advance, so that they would not meet and risk bloodshed at a sacred site. I don't know if it's true, but I think it makes sense. Another old story says that the emperor Montezuma of Mexico was trained here for kingship, and it was from here the eagle came to carry him to found his empire."

Big eagle, I thought, but I decided it would be rude to share the joke. Mythology is too darn close to religion for me to risk joking about it before I knew Domingo better.

"When Las Vegas was founded," Domingo went on, "the hot springs immediately became a popular place for family picnics. Also, travellers on the Santa Fe Trail, mountain men, and trappers all appreciated a place where they could camp and get a free hot bath."

I laughed. "I imagine they would, after weeks on the road. I've boiled water over a fire, and it takes forever to heat even a little."

Domingo nodded. Then, still talking he pulled the truck into a parking lot. Blanco bounced out after us and began casting around for a stick.

"There was one problem with this new popularity, though. Eventually, someone thought about using the springs to make money. Two Anglos learned that the hot springs were not included in the Las Vegas land grant and asked the Mexican government for a grant. This was given, on the condition that the men become Mexican citizens. They had no problem with this, and soon after the first fees for use of the springs were collected. This is also the first time a scientific study of the springs was made. A doctor noted that the temperature of the main spring was one hundred thirty degrees. A more practical member of the same expedition noted that eggs and venison could be boiled to edibility in about twenty minutes."

We got out of the truck and started walking slowly toward a building neatly labeled Old Stone Hotel. The weather was incredibly pleasant. I was beginning to understand why the locals considered autumn the best season in New Mexico—even if the state wasn't getting the rain that was so desperately needed.

Domingo bent and accepted the stick Blanco had brought to him, but he kept talking. Such a stream of words was so unlike Domingo that I had a feeling he was trying to tell me something without directly doing so. Feeling an odd sense of urgency, I made myself concentrate on what he was saying.

"However, despite collecting fees, the new grant owners didn't do very well in their venture. In the mid-1840s, the U.S. Army, which was based at Fort Union to the northeast, took over the hot springs. They built a hospital there for the treatment of wounded and ill soldiers. This prospered until 1862 when for various reasons—including, I think, the distance of the hot springs from the fort—the hospital was closed. The land was sold to the first of many to attempt to set up a hotel that would exploit the proximity of the hot springs."

I looked at him sharply. "You don't sound happy about this. Wouldn't having a hotel be a service to the ill people who came to visit the springs? I'm sure they were glad not to have to drive the six miles back to Las Vegas in bumpy wagons."

"I suppose it could be seen that way," Domingo said, "but six miles is not so far, and I think the area must have been lovely when wild."

I had the feeling he wasn't telling me everything, but, again, I let it pass. A nice intimacy was growing between us, but even a person's closest friends don't like being accused of prevaricating. Was I also being cautious because I was fancying him as a possible romance? I can't say I wasn't.

We'd reached the Old Stone Hotel by now, and Domingo went inside and found the administrator standing the weekend watch. It wasn't the usual weekend for tours, but she made an exception for Domingo.

"We keep trying to hire him," she said to me with a laugh. "He can think of this as a bribe. All I ask is you stay on the normal tour route. Oh, and leave Blanco with me."

We agreed to her conditions without hesitation. After we chatted for a moment—it seemed that though the woman in charge was clearly not local, she knew Domingo's mother through some shared charity work—we excused ourselves and headed back outside.

Domingo frowned slightly. "Where was I?"

"You were telling me the history of the hot springs," I prompted. "I'm confused. The building we just left is labeled 'Old Stone Hotel,' and you said the Castle began its life as a hotel. Were there a bunch of them?"

"Not quite," Domingo said. "A series. Let me see if I can remember how it went."

I had no doubt that he could, but politely walked beside him in silence as he organized his thoughts.

"I don't recall all the dates perfectly," Domingo said, "but I think it was in the late 1870s that a man from Boston bought the first hotel—it was called the Adobe Hotel—and the surrounding property. Immediately, he began building a larger, finer hotel. He called it the Hot Springs Hotel, but people insisted on calling it the Stone Hotel because it was made from local stone."

"And probably," I added deadpan, "because they were used to calling the Adobe Hotel after what it was made from. It would be natural to note the contrast."

Domingo grinned at me, and went on with his lecture. "Now, you remember I told you how the railroad came to Las Vegas in 1879. Well, the Stone Hotel immediately caught the eye of some railroad officials. They set up the Las Vegas Hot Spring Company, and through this bought the Stone Hotel and the surrounding land from their owner—but everyone knew the real buyer was the railroad.

"As with the man who had bought the Adobe Hotel, these new owners were not happy with the existing building. They had big dreams. They wanted to build a resort that would be served by a spur run off the main rail line. The Stone Hotel was not big enough for these dreams, so they built the first of the Montezuma Hotels. It opened in 1882, and was absolutely enormous. It had two hundred and seventy rooms, including ballrooms, parlors, and a veranda for taking the air. Although built of wood . . ."

"Tempting the locals to call it the Wood Hotel," I quipped.

Domingo flashed another grin and went on. "Although built of wood, it boasted modern firefighting equipment, and claimed to be fireproof. Three years after it opened, a gas main clogged and fire broke out. Only then was it discovered that there was insufficient water pressure to make the various plugs function. When I was a boy, my grandfather still told stories about the night of the fire. Furniture was thrown out of windows—and ruined in the attempt of being saved. Firefighters gave up the battle and got drunk on the hotel's excellent wine cellar. Apparently, someone even sat on a hillside playing an accordion as accompaniment to the party."

"A bonfire," I said, "an early incarnation of that Zozobra you were telling me about yesterday in Santa Fe."

Domingo's face went very still. Then he shook his head.

"No, it cannot be. Old Man Gloom is burned at the turning of summer into autumn. This fire was in the winter, in January."

"I was joking, Domingo," I said, alarmed by his intensity.

He blinked at me, shaking himself from that strange stillness. "Shall I tell you more?"

I was feeling rather creeped out. If we'd come in separate vehicles, I might have remembered an appointment elsewhere, but I'd come in Domingo's truck. Moreover, I'd asked him to bring me here. There was no escape.

"Go on," I said. "Was that fire why they moved the hotel up the hill?"

We'd started up an apparently endless flight of concrete steps at this point, and I was wordlessly damning the higher location—no matter how magnificent the new setting might be.

"That's right," Domingo said, taking the stairs without effort. "The company hired a different firm of architects this time, and they decided that the higher location was being wasted. This was called Reservoir Hill then. In addition to offering grand views, it also allowed for better water pressure. This hotel was even more elaborate than the first—I can show you photos of the first if you wish—and, as with the first hotel, the builders also boasted it was fireproof. However . . ."

"Oh, no!" I said, instantly dismayed.

"That's right," Domingo said. "Only four months after it was completed, the new Montezuma Hotel caught fire. It turned out the hotel's internal hoses were too short to reach the tower where the fire started. By the time water could be gotten there, again, the hotel was a complete loss."

"And they built it again," I said in disbelief. "Was it such a moneymaker then?"

"They built it again," Domingo agreed. "The third Montezuma Hotel—which was built from the same plans as its predecessor—was christened the Phoenix Hotel."

"For the bird that arises new and refreshed from its ashes," I said.

"Yes. But the locals were stubborn—or else the new name was too much a reminder of old disasters. Within a few months, no one was calling it anything but the Montezuma Hotel."

"And that name persists today," I said.

"Though people tend to refer to it as Montezuma's Castle," Domingo said, "because compared to local architecture it rather looks like one, and because, after all, it is no longer a hotel."

We'd reached the top of the stair by now, and I stopped to admire the Castle up close—and to catch my breath. Now that we were even with the building, I found the place more overwhelming. Distance had obscured its size. Gingerbread and trim such as adorned the House would have looked foolish here, like a boy putting on his sister's prom dress as a prank. Idly, I recalled that while "casa" is feminine, "hotel" is masculine.

"What happened with this last hotel?" I asked. "Was it a success?"

"It didn't burn, if that's what you mean," Domingo said. "However, the resort did not thrive. The Grand Canyon was becoming the tourist spot of choice. The Phoenix Hotel opened in 1886 to much fanfare and publicity. It closed in 1893 after losing money for several years in a row. Some estimates say it was losing as much as forty thousand dollars a year—and that was the value of the 1890s dollar."

"But the hotel wasn't wrecked," I said, "and no vandals burned it—so it must not have stood empty all that time."

"No," Domingo agreed, "it did not. Since it was closed as a hotel, the building has been a sanitorium, a YMCA, a Baptist College, a social club, a summer resort, a film-company headquarters, and a Catholic seminary. It even served as a training camp for a famous boxer in the early nineteen hundreds. In between, it often stood empty. I remember coming up here and sneaking in through a broken window to explore. My friends did this more often than I did, and several of them even lived here as members of a 'Chicano power' group when they were students at Highlands University."

"But you didn't?" I asked.

"No." Domingo shook his head. "The Castle interests me, I will not deny that, but I could not live here."

There was something in the way he said "could not" that rang warning bells, reminding me of how he had spoken of his worry that the House might not like him learning conservation techniques by working here. It occurred to me that the way Domingo spoke of Phineas House was how someone might speak of a demanding parent—or lover.

I felt obscurely jealous.

"Shall we walk around the outside, then go in, Mira?" Domingo asked.

"Sounds good," I said, and fibbing valiantly. "I can't wait to see what's inside."

If from the outside, the Montezuma Castle was overwhelming in its size and stony solidity, once on the inside, it overwhelmed the senses with not only the present beauty but a sense of past hopes and dreams.

In the entry foyer, now the King Hussein Welcome Hall, the registration desk had been preserved, along with the hundreds of tiny cubbyholes that once held room keys. The shining painted door to the hotel safe remained, though the safe was no longer in use. The enormous terra-cotta brick fireplace balanced against the honey-glow of polished woodwork everywhere.

The dining hall, though converted to the needs of a functional college, still was framed by elaborate stained glass windows, their jewel tones in vibrant argument with the two lime-green and yellow, six hundred pound, handmade glass fixtures hanging from the ceiling in the room's center. The intricacies of the modern glass sculpture fascinated me, but even as I admired them, they reminded me of Medusa on a particularly bad bad-hair day.

Although I had originally looked forward to this tour, I found I wasn't eager to probe the building's secrets. The Castle tingled against my senses as bright colors normally did, teasing me with an added intensity that shouldn't have been there given the structure's muted hues. I resisted an urge to flee, reminding myself over and over again that I had been the one to ask Domingo for this tour.

Domingo's tour was idiosyncratic to say the least. He told me how the new elevator shaft had been drilled and how the old one was now used as a cable conduit. He told me about ceilings lowered just a few inches to permit wires to be run without being visible, and about the challenges involved in putting in sprinkler systems without ruining the elaborate ornamental patterns that adorned the ceilings of some rooms.

"And, of course, given the history of fires in this building's various incarnations," I said, "no one was going to skimp on fireproofing—even if it did mean drilling through ornamental work."

"Better a small hole," Domingo said, "than a large fire."

The Castle possessed a liberal scattering of stained-glass windows, many meticulously restored with glass that perfectly matched those panes that had survived vandalism and ill use. Even amid my tension, their colors made my heart sing. I soothed myself with the way they took the clear brilliance of the New Mexico sunshine and transformed it into almost solid color.

*Like a kaleidoscope*, I thought, and wished I'd thought to bring one of the teleidoscopes along. It would be fun to see the detail here replicated into shifting mandalas.

Domingo explained that parts of the Castle were still sealed off, awaiting need, and, quite honestly, reducing the cost of the tremendously expensive restoration. Millions had already been spent—ironic, considering the original hotel had cost something like $750,000.

"All that could be done to restore the structure and preserve it from further decay was done," Domingo said, as if he were reassuring me, "but the expense of cosmetic work in areas that were not needed for classrooms or offices was a necessary savings."

"What parts did you work on?" I asked.

"Bits of everything," he said, "but perhaps I am proudest of the work done on window frames and doors. Wherever possible, the original wood was restored and reused. However, the doors had not held up as well, and replicas were made. We took great care that the replicas match the originals. There are no cheap hollow-core doors here, no aluminum window sashes."

Again, I had the sense that he was telling me something important. I tried to find out more.

"I suppose that the need for wood was because it will shrink and expand with the changes in the weather, not like metal."

"That is so," Domingo said. "Metal is fine in many types of construction, but not always against wood. A wooden house with wooden fixtures swells and contracts with the weather—almost as if it is breathing."

I felt I was close to something there, but I couldn't quite grasp it—and I was afraid to ask more. There was an unwritten rule here—I knew that much. Domingo might hint, but he could not tell me what he knew or suspected.

Or perhaps I was reading too much into his words. Maybe they were nothing more than what any devoted conservationist might say when faced with the damage modern construction techniques can cause in an old house. Hadn't Domingo explained to me how the steel trusses put up in the late thirties to support the vast expanse of the dining room floor had ended up damaging the very structure they were meant to hold? Hadn't I myself seen how a metal screw or nail used to mend a piece of antique furniture would eventually split and ruin the wood?

"I'm amazed at how well the Castle adapted to use as a school building—and the care that was taken to do the work," I said. "Wouldn't it have been easier to wreck the place and start over?"

"Easier . . . maybe," Domingo said, "but remember, the Castle is not just a beloved local landmark. It was named one of 'America's Treasures' by the White House Millennium Council in 1998. It was the first property west of the Mississippi to be so honored. More than local protest would have been raised if it had been destroyed."

"And," I said, thinking out loud, "preservation of such a building is right in keeping with the mission statement of the United World College. I don't mean they're dedicated to architecture, but they are to preservation—of cultures, of peaceful interaction. Saving a lovely old building and showing that old ways can blend with new needs is almost a metaphor for what they're doing."

"I think they would like that you see this, Mira," Domingo said. "I think some of the administrators may have taken criticism for spending so much money on a building when there are so many other problems in the world that need to be solved. It is not spoken of, of course, but whenever a vast sum is expended on one thing, there are always those who think it should have been spent on another."

"Like the story in the Bible," I said, "about Mary Magdalene and Judas arguing over how she should have sold the ointment she rubbed on Jesus's feet to raise money for the poor. Sometimes we need beauty and grandeur to inspire us to be the best we can be—to remind us of what humans are capable of when they turn their minds to something beyond the purely practical. We have the capacity for art, for beauty. I think we should use it."

Domingo reached out and squeezed my hand, a brief touch, quickly retracted, hardly different from what Hannah might do, but I felt his warmth against my skin when he dropped his hand away.

"Mira, you must have been an inspiration to all those children in Ohio. I hope that you will not stop teaching—wherever you choose to stay."

He coughed then, and turned to lead the way up a wonderfully curving staircase that went into one of the towers. I followed, light footed and with a fluttering heart, feeling ridiculously pleased.

*Careful, Mira. Spanish people touch a lot more than Anglos do. He may not have meant anything more than what he said. Don't start having a midlife crisis now, and getting all goofy over a man just because you're newly orphaned and out of place.*

But my sensible self couldn't convince my heart. I was getting far too fond of Domingo Navidad to pretend his words—and the hint that he cared whether I stayed or went—didn't matter.

We did a lot more touring that long weekend. After I swore I could handle more walking, Domingo took me to the Hermit's Cave, where, in the latter eighteen hundreds, resided an Italian mystic who the locals claimed could heal at a touch. I liked the story, which seemed to belong to the misty reaches of the Middle Ages in Europe, rather than to almost modern times, but I liked it even better when Domingo told me how the Hermit always denied doing anything magical, saying that all he did was use medical techniques he had learned in his travels.

Eventually, the Hermit left the Las Vegas area—maybe because of the strain of being regarded as a living saint. Sadly, soon after he took up his new residence, he was murdered. The killer was never found.

We went to the campus of Highlands University and walked among the fine solidity of its building. Highlands began as a branch of something called the "Normal" University system. Domingo admitted he had no idea what this meant, but that old books frequently referred to the Normal University as one of the highlights of Las Vegas. Domingo proudly told me that today Highlands is increasingly important to education in northern New Mexico.

As contrast to the Normal, we drove by and looked at the exterior of the State Hospital. There Domingo told me both about how the early insane asylum had developed from the charity of a single Spanish don, and about the doctor who stripped down to their skeletons the corpses of those indigent patients who died without family or friends to care about what happened to their bodies.

I found myself wondering if Colette had really been a resident of that formidable institution, and was happy that it was a holiday, so I wasn't tempted to go in and ask.

From Domingo's tales I realized anew how violent this region had been. Today it is rather thrilling to read about the presence of outlaws and vigilantes, but for the farmers and shopkeepers who were their victims they were rarely heroes.

Although we were gone for long spans each day, I doubt Phineas House felt neglected. After a few restaurant meals, Domingo and I found ourselves drifting back to that property where we dwelt both together and apart. One day I cooked chicken on the grill. Another Domingo made some of the best burritos I'd ever had. It was very companionable, but for that one hand-clasp and those enigmatic roses, Domingo behaved with perfect friendliness, and I reluctantly decided he probably wasn't interested in me at all. It was Evelina, his sister, who called and invited me to join them at the family cookout on Labor Day itself.

*Maybe he's gay*, I thought. *He's never been married. Maybe his heart was irrevocably broken by someone. I wish I knew Evelina better and could ask a few questions. I'd hate to make a fool of myself though.*

And Evelina, busy with coordinating a cookout for what seemed like at least half her neighborhood, was hardly available for intimate chats. I tried to take comfort in the fact that Domingo didn't seem interested in any of the many attractive women who chatted with him over the course of the afternoon, but then he didn't treat me any differently either.

I tossed sticks for Blanco, played catch with Enrico, and made small talk with the other guests. It would have been a good party, but for my nagging sense that I was missing at least one subtext to the weekend—and my sensible self telling me that in this, at least, I was simply fooling myself.

## 15

It is feared that the soul, projected out of the person in
the shape of his reflection in the mirror, may be carried
off by the ghost of the departed.

> —Sir James G. Frazer,
> *The Golden Bough*

## INSIDE THE LINES

After the emotional ups and downs of the weekend, the arrival of Tuesday
and the return of the painting crew was a distinct relief. I went out and
painted some griffins that were guarding the exterior of a dormered window outside the music room. I listened to the painters' anecdotes about
their adventures over the weekend, and was pleased to find my command
of colloquial Spanish had gotten a whole lot better.

Indeed, I had to restrain myself from teasing a young fellow after he told
a rather ribald story—one he certainly would not have told if he'd known I
understood. I'd read the same anecdote almost word for word in a book.
Happily, one of his fellows called him on it, and I had the pleasure of listening to the young man's attempts to defend himself.

Moreover, I had the pleasure of feeling like one of the crew. They weren't
gossiping about me behind my back or grumbling about my odd demands
for precise colors and detail. They were simply enjoying doing a challeng-
ing job right.

It was a good time, but when the mail arrived late morning, bringing with it the box from Betty Boswell, I was glad to clamber down from my ladder and see what she had sent along from Aunt May's library.

Betty had chosen eight books, one volume of which was the abridged *Golden Bough* Aunt May had mentioned. Two others must be the dictionary set she had been sold by the sympathetic bookseller. The other five were familiar to me in that I remembered seeing them on Aunt May's bookshelf, but as I'd never shared her interest in comparative religions—beyond the field trips we'd taken together—I hadn't done more than dip into them.

Now I picked up the Frazer and started browsing. Once I got a feel for his writing style, it was surprisingly absorbing stuff. I carried the book with me into the kitchen and read about priest-kings, dying gods, and fertility rituals while I munched on a sandwich.

Frazer didn't have a whole lot on mirrors, but what he did have gave me a new perspective. He discussed reflections in the same section that he did shadows. Essentially, he didn't define a great deal of difference between the two: Both were copies of the self, both were thought by primitive peoples to be vulnerable to magical attack.

I thought how, as with the tale of Snow White's stepmother and her magical mirror, these ideas had continued down to the present day. Peter Pan met Wendy because he lost his shadow. Hadn't she sewn it back onto his foot? And wasn't there a Mary Poppins story where Jane and Michael's shadows come to life and take the children to some party? I was sure there was. The story ended with all those whose shadows had gone out without them coming sleepwalking to look for them—they felt the loss, as, well, as if their own souls had gone from them.

How did this fit in with my mother's obsession with mirrors? Frazer claimed that mirrors and reflecting pools were to be avoided, lest one's soul be taken away. Colette had surrounded herself with mirrors, doted upon her own reflection.

Mildly frustrated, I selected another book from the collection: Robert Graves's *The White Goddess*. Skimming, I gathered that the author was attempting an even more ambitious effort at comparative religion than Frazer had. Graves's goal was to find connections for the present day back to an ancient Moon Goddess, something that he saw as a lost feminine principle.

Hope fluttered in my heart as I flipped back to the index, for Colette was most certainly a very feminine female. However, Graves disappointed me. I only found one reference to mirrors. This proved to be part of a discussion of mermaids, which in turn seemed to be part of a discussion of Muses.

Graves seemed not to know what to do with the mirror in question. In one sentence he dismissed it as a possible artist error—a substitution for, of all things, a quince! In the same sentence, with only a semicolon's pause to note his shift, he says that the mirror probably stood for "know thyself" and was a part of some ancient mysteries. By the end of the paragraph, again without any explanation other than his own fluid connectivity, Graves states that the mirror was an emblem for vanity.

Remembering Colette at her makeup table, that aptly named "vanity," I could almost believe this last, but in the end I found Graves too facile for me, and put the volume aside.

Graves had mentioned several names that were not familiar to me, so next I reached for the dictionary. The entries were terse, even cryptic, but tantalizing. I hunted up the entry for mirrors, and found it satisfactorily substantial. Skimming over the brief list of words associated with mirrors, I found hints of both Graves and Frazer. Doubtless, were I better read in the area, I would have recognized the contributions of other eminent scholars. Toward the very end of the entry were subcategories related to specific mirrors. One of these entries seemed oddly familiar, but I couldn't place why. Aunt May had said something about this section, but this was something else . . .

It was a reference to seven mirrors that in the cabalistic tradition were tied to specific types of divination. Unlike the references in Frazer and Graves, these were very solid, practical mirrors. The dictionary's brief listing included what metals each mirror was to be made of, the planets each was associated with, and noted that each was meant to be used on a specific day of the week in order to divine answers to specific types of questions.

I'd been looking at the books in the first-floor front parlor, and now I rested the thick volume in my lap, trying to figure out why this seemed not precisely familiar—I was sure I had never encountered anything like this before—but somehow connected to something I'd seen, and recently, too. Then it hit me, and I got to my feet so quickly that I nearly dropped the dictionary. Instead I tucked it under my arm and rushed up the stairs to Colette's room.

Now that I knew how it was done, I managed to get the secret compartment holding the kaleidoscopes open quickly, without spilling the contents all over the floor. Examining the neat rows of kaleidoscopes I found what I had remembered. Seven of the kaleidoscopes were inscribed with emblems I vaguely associated with various planets. There was the round circle with the dot in the center that stood for the Sun. There was the circle with the arrow coming off it at an angle that today is more commonly used to mean "male," but started as the sign for the planet Mars. There was its mate, the circle with the cross below that stands for both "female" and "Venus."

I'd have to look the others up, but I was sure about these. I lifted out the kaleidoscope marked with the Sun sign, and checked its characteristics against those listed in the dictionary. The outer casing was of hand-beaten gold, the shining, ruddy warmth of the metal still showing tiny hammer marks. I put the eyepiece to my eye, and was delighted by mandalas of gold-dust intermixed with minute rubies and multifaceted golden topaz.

The next kaleidoscope in line bore the characteristic crescent shape that even small children know is the mark of the Moon. This casing was dull grey, but when I rubbed my finger against the metal, the tarnish came away, revealing the gleaming metallic white of pure silver. The silver within the object chamber at the kaleidoscope's end had fared better than the casing, probably because the object chamber was sealed away from the outer air. Flakes of metal shown silver-white, mingling in patterns with the bluish white opacity of moonstones and the pale pastels of irregular pearls.

Mars came next, out of order in how we post-Galileans arrange the solar system, but making perfect sense in the ancient order of things. After the Moon, anyone can see that Mars and Venus are our closest neighbors.

The casing for this kaleidoscope was also dull grey, but no amount of rubbing brightened it, for the metal in question was the war god's favorite metal: iron. In a damper climate, the metal might have shown rust, but New Mexico's dryness had preserved the iron's dull solidity. The images I viewed through the kaleidoscope's eyepiece were anything but dull. Here the red planet was given his due, his warrior's booty. Rubies glittered against bloodstones, jasper, agate, garnets, and even against chips of ruddy sandstone.

I only looked briefly through this eyepiece, because according to the dictionary, the day on which the Mars mirror was used was Tuesday, when the kaleidoscope might be consulted as to enemies and lawsuits, neither of which I thought I had—and if I did, I didn't really want to know.

My own superstitious reluctance to look made me hesitate, considering whether I'd spent too many hours reading books whose authors seemed to at least half-believe in their subject matter. Wasn't I a practical woman? I was a schoolteacher, for heaven's sake! Then I looked around the room where I sat, remembered where I was, remembered, too, how this room had come to be so spotlessly clean. If I could accept the silent women, then there was a lot more I needed to accept.

Even so, I put the iron-cased kaleidoscope back in its holder and reached for the next one. Here the formula called for a mirror of crystal encasing mercury. The kaleidoscope maker had invoked this by making the case from slabs of smokey quartz crystal, the rock nearly transparent in some places, in others heavily veined with darker lines. This was the first of the lot not constructed in the "traditional" round-barrel shape usually associated with kaleidoscopes. Instead, the casing was a rough triangle, the seams joined with a metal solder.

I studied the case, thinking about what I knew regarding how kaleidoscopes are made. It had been that knowledge as much as the planetary emblems on each case that had made me think of these devices when I'd read the entry about the seven cabalistic divining mirrors.

You see, the working heart of every kaleidoscope is a reflective surface— essentially, a mirror. In a cheap child's toy, this might simply be a folded piece of metal with a polished inner surface. In the more elaborate kaleidoscopes, high-grade mirrors are used, at least two for each reflecting system. Two-and three-mirror kaleidoscopes are the most common, but more mirrors can be used, as long as the reflecting chamber is properly aligned. The shape of the mandala the viewer will see is affected not only by the number, color, and quality of the mirrors used, but also by the angle at which the mirrors are placed.

The casing exists for no other reason than to hold the mirrors in place. I'd demonstrated this to my students in a summer "Art and Science" course, showing them how a simple kaleidoscope could be made with mirrors, duct tape, and a small plastic container to serve as an object chamber. These makeshifts were neither pretty, nor particularly durable, and my students always agreed it was worth the trouble to make a casing.

In my classes, we usually used premade cylinders, everything from potato chip cans to cardboard tubes to PVC piping. However, as the kaleidoscope in my hand showed, a triangle encasing the mirrors could work as well or better. At arts-and-crafts shows, I've seen casings with six or eight sides; I've seen cases created from stained glass, polished wood, and precious metals. The Victorians, who were the first to enjoy kaleidoscopes after Sir David Brewster invented them in 1813, loved elaborate exteriors for their "elegant philosophical toys." In the intervening years during which the kaleidoscope was relegated to a role as a cheap children's toy, these elaborate exteriors were neglected, but I doubt they ever will be again.

But no matter how elaborate, the casing isn't the kaleidoscope. If the mirrors are the heart, and the eyepiece, well, the eyes, then the object chamber is the guts. The object chamber is the container that holds the objects that tumble and twist, ready to be transformed into an infinity of mandalas when the kaleidoscope is turned. As with other aspects of Professor Brewster's creation, object chambers have evolved over time. Some use stained-glass wheels. Others are brackets meant to hold interchangeable spheres—often your standard cat's-eye marble. Still others hold viscous liquids in which various objects are suspended. The patterns of these last never remain constant, but are in constant motion.

When I looked into the Mercury kaleidoscope, I saw that this object chamber held liquids. The heavy, silvery one was almost certainly real quicksilver. The others might have been colored oils. They shifted and slipped about each other, carrying with them drifts of glitter and infinitesimal emeralds. Tomorrow, if I wished, I could consult this one on matters relating to finance.

I set the Mercury kaleidoscope back in its place, then lifted the next, the one dedicated to Jupiter. The tin casing had resisted tarnish better than had the silver. Moreover, the artist had followed a Spanish tradition and pierced the surface in intricate patterns. Usually, pierced tin is used to decorate lamp shades and candelabra, to let the light can shine through. This artist had instead put a thin layer of gold foil beneath the tin. It created a fine illusion, giving back the lamplight in irregular little stars.

Examining the interior of Jupiter's kaleidoscope, I felt fairly certain that the mirrors used for the reflective chamber were tin, just as the cabalistic spell had demanded. They gave back the light more reluctantly than did the silver or gold, but with a muted steadiness. Jupiter's object chamber was dominated by white and azure. I saw tiny lightning bolts intermixed with the gems and bits of glass, and wondered if I augured for success with this, if they would form some sort of recognizable pattern.

There were two kaleidoscopes left. Venus's copper sheath had greened, but as with Mars's iron, Saturn's dull lead stubbornly refused to be affected by the passage of time. Again, the items in each object chamber were coordinated to the colors and symbols related to the appropriate planets, the kaleidoscopic patterns brilliant and enigmatic.

As I set Saturn's kaleidoscope back in its place in the drawer, I wondered how one actually used these to divine. The dictionary's entry had been complete, as far as it went, but offered no directions as to how these divining tools were to be used. Did I just gaze into them as a carnival gypsy did into her crystal ball, or did I need to say magic words or wave my hands or something?

In my reading, I had come across a reference to the need to smear oil on the divining tool in question—though that one had been a polished shield, rather than a mirror. Did I need to do something similar here? The kaleidoscopes were sealed systems, but maybe the elaborate casings played a role in the effectiveness of these divining scopes that they did not in a normal kaleidoscope.

And how did the teleidoscopes fit into my evolving theory that Colette had employed these as divining objects? Unlike the kaleidoscopes, teleidoscopes lacked an object chamber. Effectively, the world served as the object chamber for a teleidoscope. The type of lens set at the end—Colette's all seemed to be spheres—affected how those external scenes were transmitted to the mirrors, but that was all.

I opened the drawer containing the teleidoscopes and studied their casings. They did differ from each other, but there was no tidy planetary symbol to tell me what each might be used for. I considered what the different names Brewster had given his creations meant—for although the word "kaleidoscope" has entered our general language, coming to mean any repeating image, or even any broad view, the word did not exist before Brewster coined it for his invention.

Brewster derived "kaleidoscope" from three Greek words meaning "to see a beautiful form." "Teleidoscope" in turn meant "distant-form viewing." Thus, the kaleidoscope seemed to be intended to be employed to see beauty, to create art. The teleidoscope's purpose didn't seem much different from a telescope, a "far-seer." I guess Brewster must have been less impressed with the teleidoscope than with the kaleidoscope, or maybe any word he could invent that would mean "to see the world busted up into fragments and rearranged into interesting patterns" would simply have been too much of a tongue twister.

I studied the teleidoscopes in the drawer, hoping to note some sign or symbol that would give me a hint as to their use. Some of the cases were intricate, and there might indeed be magical symbols in their workings, but I couldn't tell if there were. I'd have to do more reading in Aunt May's books, mark pages that gave symbols, and do some comparing. Then there were kaleidoscopes other than those I had mentally dubbed the Cabalistic Seven. Were these also "magical," or had Colette simply collected them because of their undoubted loveliness?

I didn't believe it. Were Colette simply collecting them as decorative objects, she would have had them out on display. What now seemed certain to me was that, like the wicked queen in Snow White, my mother had been using mirrors for scrying—or for spying.

Did all the mirrors in the House serve this purpose, or just these carefully designed kaleidoscopes? And why had Colette chosen to use kaleidoscopes rather than simple mirrors for her divining? What use was there to a fragmented and repeated image?

Each time I found something that seemed an answer, it also seemed I also found more questions—questions so complicated that they all but invalidated my original question. "Why mirrors?" led to kaleidoscopes. "What use are these kaleidoscopes?" led to "Why kaleidoscopes at all?"

Sitting there at my mother's vanity, methodically restoring the false bottoms to the drawers, I thought about my original questions. It seemed to me that both Aunt May and I had started with the same ones, "What happened to Colette Bogatyr? Is she alive or dead?"

Trying to understand Colette, and thus the reasons she had disappeared, had led Aunt May into a search for Colette's background—and the warning from Mr. Hart that asking such questions was dangerous indeed. So Aunt May had turned to trying to find out the source of those enigmatic titles Mr. Hart had let slip—or perhaps had deliberately dangled as bait or distraction.

Following Aunt May's lead and my own memories of Colette had brought me to mirrors, and through researching mirrors I had discovered some undoubtedly fascinating things, but none of what I had learned seemed to offer an immediate answer to my initial questions. Where had Colette driven on that day forty-odd years ago? Why hadn't she come back? Was she still alive?

To these I added one more, "Why had Colette taken a teleidoscope with her that day?"—for I was absolutely certain that she had done so. If, like the kaleidoscopes, the teleidoscopes were used for some sort of scrying, then it followed that Colette had been looking for something—some "distant object." What had she been looking for—and had it found her first?

I slid the drawers shut, locked them, and left the room, locking the doors to the suite. Frowning, I walked across to the room I had taken for my own, and dug the teleidoscope out from under the socks. I held it to my eye and looked around, but though the fragmented patterns were undoubtedly as lovely as anything a kaleidoscope could produce, they showed me nothing I did not expect. I slid the teleidoscope back into its protective concealment, and went downstairs.

The silent women hadn't gotten to the point where they cooked meals, and I was hungry.

Wednesday morning the phone rang just as I was bringing in the coffee mugs from breakfast.

"Hello?"

"Mira, this is Chilton O'Reilly. I've finished the background work, and I was wondering how you felt about going ahead with the feature story on area Victorians."

Actually, I felt a lot less enthusiastic about it than I had when he'd first proposed it, but I couldn't say so without too much explanation.

"Sounds good," I said. "By the way, one of my childhood friends got in touch with me after the last piece. We've been out to lunch."

"Great!" Chilton said. "Listen, can I bring a photographer by on Friday? If things go well, we can do a big feature in the Sunday paper. If we get delayed, there will be room later in the week."

"Friday morning will work," I said. "I haven't gotten a lot more done inside, but the outside is progressing nicely."

"We'd really like some inside shots, too," Chilton said. "After all, people can see the exteriors just by driving by."

"I'm sure we can handle that," I said. "I have the living room in shape, and I know my neighbors would like to get involved. Many of them have put a lot of work into their homes, and furnished them beautifully. Let me give you a few phone numbers."

I did so, rattling them off from a list I had near the phone. "You understand," I concluded, "that the last thing I'd like to do is alienate my neighbors. We're getting along very well."

"Of course," Chilton said. "I'll call these folks and see what we can work out. September is often a slow season here, and I think the paper's going to give us a good spread."

We set that Chilton and his photographer would come by Friday morning around ten. After I'd hung up, I walked outside to let Domingo know. Some of his crew did not like to be photographed, and given the good work they'd done for me, I did my best to honor their wishes.

Looking at the exterior of the House with the upcoming photography session in mind, I couldn't help but be pleased with the result of our labors. Yes, the exterior might be called gaudy, but it was gaudy in the way an old-style carousel had been gaudy. Colorful, but never garish. In Ohio, the color scheme might not have worked, but against the impossible blueness of a New Mexico sky, Phineas House looked just fine.

"It looks good," I said to Domingo. "I like it better than I do the Castle. That was elegant. This is, well, splendid. I want you to get the credit, tomorrow. I hope you won't mind."

Domingo frowned. "The credit belongs to the House. I have only followed what she wants."

"I don't think she'll mind," I said, "and you must admit that wouldn't make for a good newspaper story—or rather it would, but not the right kind of story."

Domingo might be a bit fey, but he was not a fool, no matter what people thought. He smiled now, then nodded.

"Yes. I agree, but let us take the credit together. After all, you have supported this project, and selected many of the colors."

"Fine," I agreed. "Anything I can help with? I may go run some errands later, but the weather is so nice I don't feel like going anywhere now."

"We have found some more wildcats," Domingo said promptly. "They're along one of the oriel windows on the third floor. I had two of the crew put scaffolding there because we needed to work on some of the shingles. That's done now, but I've left the scaffolding in place."

"Great," I said. "I'll be out as soon as I get my coveralls on."

I spent the rest of the morning and most of the afternoon in a happy dream state, painting a collection of leopards and lynxes that looked as if they could have been right out of Dionysus's entourage. Midafternoon, the wind gusted up, bringing a few spits of rain, not enough to be considered a break in the drought, but certainly hopeful.

"Do the monsoons ever come in so late?" I asked hopefully.

"Not usually," Domingo said, "but we are hardly into September yet, and there is often some rain during the State Fair."

"Is that held around here?" I asked.

"No. In Albuquerque," Domingo said. "Enrico is quite excited. A project his class did is going to be shown in the school art show, and he and his sisters had something to do with the San Miguel County display in the Bolack Building. He has something planned for the 4-H display as well."

None of this made any sense to me, but I could tell Domingo was pleased.

"So you're going?"

"Certainly," he said. "I plan to enter tomatoes, squash, and maybe some beans in the Bolack Building show. Those have cash prizes, and stay on display the entire two weeks of the fair. I'm also considering entering some of the old rose varieties in the flower show, but I never decide with roses until the last moment. The competition can be fierce, and the long drive is hard on the blossoms."

"Maybe I can help," I suggested. "You'll have to tell me what to do."

"I accept," Domingo said promptly, "though you don't know what you've just gotten yourself into."

Since the rain, light as it was, made further painting unlikely that day, I decided to keep my resolution to go into town. I hadn't forgotten that strange, red-haired woman I had glimpsed down on the Plaza, and figured I'd go looking for her.

I'd thought a lot about what I'd seen, and had come to the conclusion that the woman had probably been sitting on a folding table set up near the gazebo. What had happened was that when I'd turned to talk to Domingo, someone had come along to claim the table. She'd probably hopped off her perch, picked up an end of the table, and gone. She might not even have realized the confusion she would create.

On the other hand, remembering the wildness I'd sensed about her, she may very well have known what she was doing, and had enjoyed giving the "gringa" a turn. However, I wouldn't be comfortable until I took a look for myself.

Parking wasn't that hard to find. I deliberately picked a spot across the Plaza from where I'd seen the woman, so I could retrace my steps. I did this, marvelling how little activity there was. I mean, I knew school was back in session and the tourists gone home, but surely this late in the afternoon there would be some activity.

I walked slowly, feeling a hitch in one calf from where I'd been balancing on the scaffold while painting. I bent to massage out a knot, and when I stood straight again and walked a few steps, I saw the platform.

Immediately, I dismissed my theory that what I'd seen had been a folding table. It was too big, too solid. It also had an extension of some sort that after a moment I recognized as a windmill in not the best condition.

When my gaze lowered from examining the windmill, I saw the woman. As before, she was seated on the platform base dressed in a colorful skirt, its tiers adorned with contrasting ribbons. Her off-the-shoulder blouse was snowy white and, as before, low enough to display an ample bosom. She was smoking a cigarette, and as I drew closer I saw it was hand-rolled. The odor was tobacco, though, not anything else.

Looking at the woman, I felt an odd mixture of jealousy and admiration. There was something so free and easy about her, a blatant sexuality that I myself had never been able to express—although certainly I'd felt the urges. I knew every man who saw her couldn't help but be moved. Yet, though I envied her, it was admiration without resentment. I admired her as you would a beautiful flower: a California poppy or a particularly vibrant hibiscus.

As so many times in my life, I felt as if I'd been constructed from squares: awkward and graceless, female without being in the least feminine. This woman went beyond femininity and gave lie even to my claim of being female. I had the equipment, but I didn't know how to tap into its power. Even my love of clothing and jewelry seemed more like an extension of my art, a thing unconnected to my inner self. Colette had known how to use the same tools to become a beauty. More than once I'd wondered if my lifelong love/hate relationship with her, my fear and desire of being her "mirror" had made me deny myself things I could have had.

I struggled with a desire to run from this strange woman. She watched me coming, full lips twisted in a smile that was ironical without being in the least unkind. I had the unsettled feeling that she knew my thoughts, but neither of us were going to mention this—it would be one of those open secrets.

"Hi," I said, suddenly feeling amazingly awkward. I'd felt a connection to this woman, but it was based on believing her some sort of hallucination. What was I going to say now that she was here in front of me, "How did you vanish last Friday?"

She grinned at me the way cats grin, and again I had the feeling that she knew exactly what I was thinking.

"*Buenas tardes*," she said with lazy formality. "How are you?"

"Fine," I replied automatically, then caught myself. "Actually, I'm confused as hell. I saw you here Friday. Then I didn't—not you, not this windmill. Now you're here again. You and nobody else. I don't suppose you'd care to explain, would you?"

She grinned again, and I half expected her to stretch like a cat. She reminded me irresistibly of one, a sleek queen dozing on a windowsill, or maybe one of my leopards.

"I might," she said, "but first I'd like you to come with me. I don't really much like sitting here."

She motioned toward a bar with a toss of her head. "We can go over there, have a drink. What do you say?"

What I wanted to say was that I didn't remember the bar either, but I kept quiet. I kept remembering the silent women, how my bed was made for me every day, how the interior of Phineas House was spotless, how the chrome sparkled. I'd forced myself to accept that—and not only because it was damn convenient. The silent women belonged to the tapestry of my childhood. This woman might have, too, if I'd been out much—and perhaps she belonged somehow to Colette's life. Maybe they'd been rivals over some man. I could imagine that. There were similarities, though Colette had never had this sulky sensuality.

"Sure," I said, shaking myself from the whirl of my thoughts. "I could use a beer."

"Come on, then," she said. "By the way, I'm Pablita Sandoval. People call me 'Paula Angel.' You can just call me Paula."

"I'm Mira," I said. "Mira Fenn."

"Or Mira Bogatyr," Paula said. "Colette's daughter, come home again."

And before I could ask her how she knew, if from Chilton's article or some other way, Paula had hopped down from the windmill's base, shaken her skirts into order, and started leading the way to the bar. I hurried to keep up, afraid that, as before, she'd vanish, leaving me with more questions than ever.

16

In 1866, the hanging of Pablita Sandoval for murdering her lover created quite a sensation, according to information gleaned by W. J. Lucas in the 1920's, although the name was changed to Paula Angel in later published versions.
—Lynn Perrigo,
*Gateway to Glorieta*: A History of Las Vegas, New Mexico

## INSIDE THE LINES

The bar looked like a setting from a Western: bat-wing doors, a long wooden bar backed with a mirror, polished brass spittoons, and tables scattered around almost at random. The floor was thickly covered with sawdust. There was a man playing an upright piano to one side, a bartender polishing the bartop with a rag on the other.

Four men in western clothing so carefully adhering to the fashions of a bygone day that it qualified as costuming, were playing poker well away from where the mirror might give their hands away. Other than these, the place was empty. I guessed it was too early in the day for a regular crowd. I wondered if the poker players were waiters, killing time until the evening crowd showed.

Paula gave the bartender a casual wave and called, "Two of the usual" as she led us to a table where the music from the piano pretty much guaranteed our privacy. The bartender followed us over almost immediately, a tray with two frothy mugs of beer balanced on one hand. He set the mugs down and left without waiting for payment. I figured we'd be running a tab, and tried to remember how much money I'd brought with me.

"So, *amiga*," Paula said, blowing the foam off the top of her beer, "why did you come looking for me?"

"I told you," I said. "I saw you, on Friday, you were there, then you weren't . . ."

I trailed off, feeling really stupid. Then I recovered my determination, and forged on. "And today, I'm sure you weren't in the Plaza, then you were—and nobody else."

"And you want to know what's going on?" Paula said.

"That's right."

"You are, Mira."

I stared at Paula Angel. Her eyes were the rich brown of chocolate syrup, and the corners crinkled as she smiled at my confusion.

"Me?"

"You, Mira. I think you suspected this all along, didn't you? You just wanted to hear it from someone else."

I pressed my splayed fingers to my forehead, as if I could physically force my thoughts into order. There was some truth in what Paula had just said. When Paula had done her appear/disappear act that first time, I'd been irresistibly reminded of the silent women. I'd wondered if Paula were one of them or something else. Although a part of me wanted to continue to deny, to resist that the oddness I associated with Phineas House could spill out into the rest of the city, I wanted answers more than I wanted to hold on to whatever sense of normalcy remained to me.

And before you fault me for being a coward, or lacking a sense of adventure, let me tell you, reading about it is a lot different from having it happen to you.

"Me," I repeated, letting the word roll around my mouth. "You seem to know a lot more about this than I do. Any chance you can explain?"

"Explain why you could see me when your friend, Domingo, could not."

"That would be a good start."

Paula Angel smiled, picked up her heavy glass beer mug and took a couple more swallows. She had to balance the mug between two hands to do this.

"To make you understand this," Paula began, "I'm going to have to tell you something about me."

*Isn't that always the case?* I thought. *People love to talk about themselves.*

Paula gave me that sly look that made me wonder if somehow she could read my mind—or if she was just a really good judge of character.

She didn't say anything else, so I said, "Go on."

"Well, for one thing," Paula said, "I'm dead."

I'd been raising my beer mug, now I set it down with a solid thump.

"You're what?"

"I'm dead," she replied matter-of-factly. "I was executed. Hanged. You can find my story in a bunch of books. There's even a poem about me."

I nodded very slowly, as if my head might go flying off my shoulders if I didn't take care.

"I think you'd better tell me about it," I said.

Paula grinned wickedly. "I thought you'd see it that way. Very well. Like I told you, I was hanged, hanged for murdering a man. That wasn't terribly fair. There was a dance. He was feeling me up. I didn't like it much. Pulled out my knife and warned him off. When he didn't listen, I stabbed him. Did a better job than I expected. Cut something vital. He died pretty fast.

"This happened at a fiesta, so there were lots of witnesses to what I did, but not so many who supported my claim that I was justified in what I did—a man doesn't go after a girl that way right out in the open, you know what I mean?"

I nodded again, managed to get a swallow from the beer mug I held up in trembling hands.

"Well, one thing led to another and the trial wasn't fair at all," Paula went on. "Not that many people liked the bastard I knifed, but all the lawyers and judges and law officers were men, and men don't like if a woman stands up for herself. That's what men are supposed to do for them. So the *hijos de putas* sentenced me to hang. They put a rope up over the limb of a tree and put me in a wagon, and drove the wagon underneath the tree."

Paula's tone was flat and even, but there was a tension underlying the words that made my skin creep.

"I was sitting on a bench in the wagon and they put the rope around my neck. When they got the noose just right, the driver whipped up the horses and the wagon was pulled out from under me. I was supposed to drop and have my neck snapped.

"Didn't work that way. I was young and strong, and though that rope cut into my neck, it didn't break it. They hadn't tied my hands tightly enough, and I'd worked them free while they were fussing with getting the noose just right. When I realized I wasn't dead, I reached up over my head, grabbed the rope and started hauling myself up along it. I figured to get up onto that tree limb and see what I could do after.

"Now, a funny thing happened then. There'd been a crowd gathered around. There always is for a hanging. They'd been eager to see me die. The men wanted to see me die because I'd killed a man. The women wanted to see me hang because I was young and pretty, and they didn't like me around their men. They'd all wanted to see me dead, and if that rope had snapped my neck then and there, well, they'd have thought no more of it than they would have about wringing a chicken's neck for the stew pot.

"But now, seeing me struggle to win against that rope, the feeling in the crowd changed. They started cheering for me, willing me to win. That was better sport than they'd bargained for, and their cheers gave me heart and soul, they did, because I figured if I could get to the top, they'd demand that I be given my life.

"But the sheriff didn't feel this way at all. To be fair to him, at another time, he might have been watching with all the rest, but something big had happened in Las Vegas not that long before. The United States of America had taken over the New Mexico Territory from Mexico, and the sheriff was eager to show his new bosses that he was their man.

"He ran forward and grabbed me by the legs, dragging me down with all his weight, trying to make me strangle if he couldn't break my neck. The crowd wasn't having anything of it. It was between me and the rope now, and they saw the sheriff as butting in where he wasn't wanted. They pulled him off me, and I pulled my way up the rope and somehow got my leg over the tree branch, and just lay there panting.

"I listened to what was being said below me, though, you can bet that. Most of the crowd was saying that I'd been hanged and hadn't died, so that meant I should be set free. The sheriff, though, he insisted on calling the judge. The judge brought with him some of those Anglo lawmen. He also brought a copy of the sentence. They looked this over while the crowd grumbled, and I let some of the kinder folks get me down from the tree and help me get that rope off my neck.

"Then the judge spoke. 'The sentence,' he said, prissy as a maiden aunt, 'was that the criminal be hanged by the neck until dead. Justice has not been satisfied.'"

Paula Angel had been speaking faster and faster as her story unrolled, and I'd been leaning forward as if I might lose the thread of the tale if I didn't. Now she stopped.

"And?" I said, feeling my breath catch.

"And," she said, "they pulled me from the crowd and tied my hands again, and hanged me from that tree. My neck still wouldn't break, but I strangled good and proper."

"Oh, God," I whispered weakly.

"I didn't much feel like God cared," Paula said, "and maybe that's why I'm still here. I haven't forgiven the old bastard for letting me hope, and then letting me hang."

"I'm not sure I could either," I said. "So I didn't somehow bring you here?"

Paula looked at me for moment, rather puzzled. Then she grinned.

"No, *amiga*. When I said that you were the reason you could see me when others couldn't, I didn't mean you were the cause of my damnation. I meant what I said. The reason you can see me has its roots in you—not in me. You didn't create me. I'd be here anyhow."

"But why can I see you?"

"Because there are people who can see ghosts or spirits, people for whom the borders between states just aren't as firm as they are for most people." Paula looked pensive. "Mira, I'm no wise woman, no *bruja* or *curandera*. In life I was a pretty girl, maybe a little wild. I enjoyed living and loving, and died twice for doing so. In death, well, mostly I've been angry, but I've been around long enough that I've seen things, and I've been curious enough to wonder about them. If you can take a hanged woman for what she is, I can tell you a few things, but don't get angry with me when I don't know everything."

I reached out a hand and patted Paula's where it rested on the tabletop. It felt warm and smooth and young.

"Tell me what you can," I said. "You know more than I do."

Paula motioned for the bartender, and he brought over a couple more beers. I nodded my thanks and reached for my purse.

"It's on the house," the bartender said, but oddly, I heard it as "on the House," and shivered just a bit.

Paula noticed my reaction, but she didn't comment. She sipped at her beer, obviously organizing her thoughts. I schooled myself to patience. In some ways, Paula was much older than I was—had to be if she'd been around since the mid-eighteen hundreds—but I had the feeling that in some way she was much younger than I was, and I remembered how hard it could be to explain things you knew intuitively.

"I knew your mother," Paula began. "Colette, that is, not the woman who raised you. Colette was incredible. She'd been born here, at Phineas House, of a family that had owned the House for generations, but by the time Colette was born, the Bogatyr family had lost touch with what had once bound them to Phineas House, the House to them—maybe been made to lose touch would be a better way to put it."

"I don't understand," I said.

"Neither do I, entirely," Paula admitted. "There's a history to Phineas House. It has been there a long time, and not by accident either. The people who built it were called witches by those who lived nearby, but as they never did any harm and often did good, well, they were suffered to live. Later, when they became stronger, people were glad to have them around. At least that's what I think it must have been. This has not been a kind land, you know, and anything that might give an edge would be welcome."

"I suppose," I said. "I'd never realized I came from such an old Spanish family."

"Oh, very old," Paula said, "but not necessarily Spanish, not Indian either. Your people are defined not merely by bloodline but by what they can do."

"And that is?"

"Have a beer with ghosts, for one thing," Paula said. "Now, let me tell this my way."

"Very well," I agreed, but I'd be lying if I didn't admit to feeling very strange about what I'd just learned.

"Colette was a throwback to older times," Paula said. "I watched her when she was a little girl, noticed her because she noticed me. Not many people did, not even those who came here looking for ghosts. Like I said, I'm just a little famous.

"Now, Colette's parents weren't comfortable with their strange daughter. They were solid, upright people. They still owned Phineas House, but they had sold much of the property around it, they and their own parents. No matter what money they got for this, their fortunes declined. When Colette was born, though, something that was dormant in the House began waking up with her. It responded to her, and the solid, unimaginative people who were Colette's parents, and who had been trying hard to live down some of the earlier stories about their family, they didn't like this."

I thought about the silent women, about the sense of will and awareness I had sensed in the House, and thought I understood how Colette's parents—my grandparents—must have felt.

Paula went on, "Phineas House didn't like Collette's parents. It started doing little things to make them uncomfortable. Colette's parents were too practical to blame a house—so they blamed Colette. They punished her, locked her away in her room but this only made matters worse. The House could concentrate—if that's the word to use for a House that has no mind, only will—on Colette, and Colette, who had both mind and will bonded with the House.

"Her father was the one who punished her most often, and together Colette and Phineas House set out to put him out of the way. She was just a child then. I don't know what was done, but Colette's father was found one morning at the bottom of the main staircase. His neck was broken."

I was appalled. "An accident, surely. That's an old house."

"An accident, probably," Paula said, moving her bare shoulders in a fluid fashion that could not be called a shrug. "But Colette did not think so. She was young, yet, and very strange. The next time she behaved in a fashion her mother did not like, and punishment was threatened, Colette bragged that she had caused her father's fall—she threatened, too, that her mother should take care unless she wanted something to happen to her.

"Now, the mother was not of the line that owned Phineas House. That had been the father's line. Moreover, after the custom of the day, her family was all too eager to send a male relative to advise and protect her. Colette's uncle had no patience with his niece. He told his sister that her daughter was unruly and spoiled. Once I heard Colette tell one of her lovers as they rode in her carriage about the Plaza that her uncle had beaten her."

I thought I knew what was coming. "Did he fall as well?"

Paula smiled a lazy smile. I could tell she had no love for domineering men. No wonder, given her history.

"He fell, but was not killed. Again Colette claimed the fall was her doing—this, though she was locked in her nursery at the time. The uncle used this claim to have Colette committed for insanity. Conveniently, the State Hospital was right here in Las Vegas, and, like most public institutions, eager for donations."

"So it was true, what Hannah told me," I said. "My mother was committed."

"But was she crazy?" Paula said shrewdly. "You have lived in that house. You know it is more than boards and nails."

"Yes," I admitted. "I do. But how did Colette get out?"

"After Colette was committed, the uncle tried to sell Phineas House, but he learned he could not do this. The mother had inherited her husband's personal property, but Phineas House and its earnings belonged to Colette. The best they could do was take what they could and leave. This they did."

"Leaving Colette?"

"Leaving Colette. Can you blame them? This was a child who claimed to have done murder—and threatened to do it again. You knew the woman she became. She was not a loving child either."

I didn't know what to think. It was hard imagining my mother as a little girl of any type, much less one who would brag that she had killed her father.

Paula was merciful, and did not press me to speak.

"Colette's story after that is only partially known to me. The State Hospital is not a place I care to go. It is . . . unsettled. I next saw her a few months after her twenty-first birthday. Many things had happened in the ensuing years. Her mother had died in an influenza epidemic. Trustees associated with her father's estate ordered a review of Colette's situation. The doctors they hired ruled the young woman was functionally sane, a bit delusional, but certainly not in need of institutionalizing. However, they recommended Colette remain near some facility where she could undergo periodic reviews.

"This suited Colette fine, as it got her out of the hospital. She had no desire to move away from Phineas House, so saying that she'd stop in at the State Hospital from time to time was no skin off her back. Far as I know, she never went back, though. Instead, Colette reopened the House and took up residence. The money that had been left in trust for her was sufficient for her to maintain Phineas House, and to travel some. I don't know where she went, or what she did, but each time she came back she seemed a bit wealthier.

"That was a good thing, because as time went on Colette got odder and odder, too, dressing as if from an earlier time, and all that . . . People are more patient with strangeness when the odd person is either very rich or very poor. Eventually, when Colette was in her late twenties she committed what in any but a confirmed eccentric would have been an outrage. She bore a daughter—you—without bothering with a husband. Few people knew this, and fewer cared. Colette put about that she had been widowed, and as she was a local eccentric, people believed her. In a way, her disappearance proved a fitting capstone to her odd life."

Paula Angel drained the last of her beer in what was without doubt the equivalent of a terminal punctuation mark.

I thought about all the questions I had, and chose the one that seemed most important.

"Do you know who my father was?"

Paula shook her head. "Colette had lots of boyfriends, both before and after you were born. Could have been any of them."

"Oh." I sat in silence for a long while, then said, "Paula, that's a lot to absorb all at once. Tell me, can I meet with you again?"

Paula gave one of those feline grins. "Sure, why not? I'm not going anywhere. I don't know a lot more, though. Mostly I watched Colette because she was interesting, and because she was one of the few people who could interact with me. It gets dull being dead, and even someone who does nothing more than incline her head in a regal nod breaks up the boredom."

"I want to keep talking to you," I said, "but I can't think straight. There's too much to take in."

"Yeah," Paula said, stretching. "It's quite a story, almost as good as mine."

"Yours," I said, "is far sadder."

Paula seemed pleased to be given precedence. "I'll take you back to where you can find your car. If you want to chat, just come down here. I seem to find myself here a lot—around that damned windmill. Wasn't there I was hanged, but I guess we're akin somehow."

I refused to think about this. It was a little too unsettlingly like the relationship between my mother and Phineas House. Instead, I accepted Paula's escort back to the Plaza. She sort of faded me in or faded herself out. As I walked to where I'd parked my truck, I noticed that the bar where we'd gone to talk wasn't there. Somehow, I wasn't surprised.

After I pulled my red pickup truck into my space in the carriage house, I got out and stood staring at Phineas House. My visit with Paula Angel had taken longer than I thought and darkness was falling, but the outside security lights I'd had the electrician install soon after my arrival illuminated segments of the wildly colored exterior.

I stood there, almost frozen, considering the tales I'd been told by a ghost. I'd known there was something strange about the House, but was it capable of murder—or conspiring at murder? I'd thought that whatever spirit—if spirit was even the right word—that inhabited the House was benign. Paula's story made me wonder if it was otherwise, if the welcome I'd met since my arrival had been offered for ulterior motives.

Then again, was there any reason I should believe what Paula had told me? Was the fact that she was a ghost any reason for her to be honest? It didn't take much to realize, based on her own account of herself, that she'd probably not been from the highest social class nor too careful around men. Women who were—especially at the time Paula had been alive—didn't tend to find themselves in dark corners at wild parties.

But why shouldn't I believe her? She'd spoken of Colette with a certain odd affection, as someone who acknowledged her existence. What reason would Paula have for lying to me? If I found out, she'd lose someone else who could break up the monotony of her deathless existence.

I stood there for a long while, staring at the House, almost mesmerized by its color, brighter where the lights hit, attenuating into shadow by gradual stages until it was hard to decide where the color ended and the shadow began. My gaze flickered back and forth, hunting for the certain border, as if where there was neither color nor shadow I'd find an answer.

The sound of a door opening behind me broke me from my trance.

"Mira?" Domingo's voice spoke from the square of light that spilled out from the interior of the carriage house. "Mira? Is that you?"

"It's me," I said, so softly I could hardly hear my own voice. I repeated it more loudly. "It's me."

Domingo stepped out into the garage. His jeans and work shirt looked as if they had been pulled on in haste, and he cradled a gun of some sort in one hand. He continued to hold it as he came to join me.

"I heard the truck come in, then nothing, not even the garage door closing," he explained, his tone almost apologetic. "I thought you might be ill."

"I'm sorry," I said. Blanco had come out with Domingo and was sniffing around my ankles. I wondered if the little dog smelled the scents of the bar where I'd sat drinking with Paula. Did sawdust cling to the soles of my shoes? "I was thinking about things I learned tonight. I guess I got lost in my thoughts."

Domingo said nothing, but his silence was a listening one, one that invited confidences. I went on.

"Did you know that my mother claimed to have killed her father? That she later claimed to have tried to kill her uncle? Did you know that she spent time in the state mental hospital?"

"When I was a boy," Domingo said, "and Colette vanished, some people called her 'the crazy lady,' but I thought they only meant her odd ways. I never heard the rest, not even after I became caretaker here."

"I suppose time and money could make even a juicy story like that one die away," I said, "and Mother did give a lot of money to local charities. She was a minor at the time of her father's death, too. I wonder if juvenile records were sealed then, like they are now?"

I heard a quiet thump as Domingo put the gun down on the hood of his truck, then felt his arm slip around my shoulders.

"Who told you this, Mira? Did you go to the hospital?"

"My school friend Hannah told me a little, but she didn't know if it was just malicious gossip. I heard the rest from someone named Pablita Sandoval. She told me to call her 'Paula Angel.'"

Domingo's grip around my shoulder momentarily tightened. "Someone who calls herself 'Paula Angel' may not be someone to trust. Here in Las Vegas, that is a name from *cuentos*, from stories."

"From histories, I think," I said. "She told me who she was—and when she lived. She is the woman I saw last Friday in the Plaza, the woman you did not see."

"And you went looking for her again today?"

"I did. She seemed very real. She was there. We went and talked in a bar, a bar that isn't there now. Paula had been acquainted with my mother. It seems my gift for seeing ghosts may be inherited."

Maybe Domingo didn't push me away and call me a liar because his traditional culture hasn't rejected stories of ghosts and spirits. Maybe his reaction was rooted in the fact that he was Domingo, who had lived near Phineas House and served it since he was a child. Perhaps he could feel that I was on the edge of breaking down, and he did not wish to be the one to push me over.

For whatever reason, Domingo didn't say the things most people would have. Instead, he asked, "And you believe what Paula Angel said?"

"I think I do," I said. "I might even be able to get Colette's records, if the hospital has kept them for so long. I don't know whether she killed her father, but the woman I knew would have been capable of making such a claim. She was the most coolly confident person I have ever met—and she enjoyed inspiring fear."

"How," Domingo phrased his question very carefully, "did she claim to have done it?"

"Paula didn't say. My grandfather . . ." I swallowed hard, for this was the first time I had spoken aloud the intimate connection to myself. "My grandfather broke his neck in a fall down the front staircase. Colette claimed responsibility."

"Did she say she pushed him?"

"She was supposed to be locked in her room at the time, being punished for some infraction. I suppose she could have gotten out. Children are more clever about this than their parents like to admit. However . . ." That lump was back in my throat, but I forced myself to speak around it. "Paula told me something else. She told me that my mother was a throwback to those of her ancestors who built Phineas House—people she called 'witches' and '*brujos*.' The House was somehow connected to their . . ."

I couldn't say "magic," and so concluded rather lamely, "To their abilities." Then, "Why am I telling you this?"

"I think because this is not the type of story you could not tell," Domingo said, "and because you know I know Phineas House and might believe you just a little."

"And do you?"

"I know the House is not just a thing of wood and paint and nails, but I wonder, maybe it is because I have cared for it for so long, but I wonder, is it evil?"

"If Colette used it to kill . . ." I said, shaping the words carefully, thinking frantically, *Why did I confide in Domingo of all people? He was the House's caretaker long before I formalized the agreement. How could I have forgotten that?*

Domingo's next words were not precisely reassuring. "I have a gun, several guns, and I know how to use them very well. If I take a gun and shoot someone, is the gun evil?"

I forced a laugh. "'Guns don't kill people. People kill people.' Is that what you're getting at?"

"Maybe a little," Domingo said. "But more. Was Colette a kind mother to you?"

"No. I told you. She liked having people fear her. I was no different than anyone else in this."

"So if she was like that as a child, and if she had some sort of association with Phineas House, then if she used it to do harm to someone she hated—and children can hate with such simple purity—then the House is no more evil than if she had found her father's gun in a drawer and used that."

"So she was evil," I said, anger tightening my voice. This was my mother we were talking about, after all, never mind how she had treated me.

"Evil? Maybe. Maybe insane. Maybe merely a child with a child's urges and too much power." Domingo's voice was very calm, very level. His arm was still around my shoulders, but I could feel he wondered if he should take it away. "I did not hear this story Paula Angel told, but if Colette was a throwback, then maybe her parents were not comfortable with her. It is often the case when a child is different."

There was something in that last sentence that caught my heart. All of us feel one way or another that we're different. Certainly I had, especially in my youngest years, before the Fenns took me in and ensconced me in comfortable normalcy. I had the feeling that Domingo had always been viewed as a little different. I remember how Mrs. Morales at the real estate agency had spoken of him, "a bit of a fool." Did everyone see him that way? Some thinking him a touch retarded, an idiot savant. I'd been comfortable with him because I'd known too many artists, but not everyone would have been.

"Yes," I said. "I can see that. Colette was different. Paula made sure I knew that. Maybe she didn't start out so detached and self-centered, but how her parents treated her could have started her that way, and all those years in a mental institution, surrounded by people who viewed the world askew . . . That could have finished it."

"I think, too," Domingo said, "that being taken from Phineas House would have been very hard for her. It isn't . . . human . . . maybe isn't even intelligent . . . I don't know what I'm trying to say, except that it can make one feel welcome, and for a child to be torn from what might have been her only friend and ally . . ."

I nodded. "Yes. She was young enough that a favorite toy or doll would have seemed as real as most adults, and Phineas House could respond in its fashion."

I had brought my gaze back into the immediate area that Domingo and I shared, watching, if I watched anything, Blanco's circling about the garage and driveway, reading smells with ceaseless fascination. My real anchor had been the arm around my shoulders and the soft voice in my ear. Now I raised my gaze again to the House's painted facade, and bit my lip, forcing myself to repress a shudder.

"Domingo, I'm afraid to go in there. What if the House is still my mother's ally? What if the reason I was drawn here was on her business? I'm afraid. Afraid that some board will rise and trip me in the night or that the tap water will scald me or . . . I think I'll sleep at a motel tonight. There're certain to be vacancies."

"Stay here," Domingo said. "I have a spare room. It is even clean. One of the workmen was staying with me until he earned enough to take a room at a boarding house."

I thought about it. If I left, even to go as far as a hotel, I wondered if I would have the courage to come back. I knew the temptation would be there come morning to keep running. I knew I couldn't make myself go into the House tonight, but come morning it might be easier.

"Thanks," I said. "I'll take you up on that offer."

17

The house of every one is to him his castle and fortress,
as well for his defense against injury and violence as for
his repose.

—Sir Edward Coke,
*Semayne's Case*

## INSIDE THE LINES

The next morning, I returned to Phineas House. I think I knew that I would
as soon as I agreed to stay at Domingo's rather than a motel—and, equally,
I knew that if I had stayed at a motel, I would have turned the truck for Ohio
and what passed for sanity the next morning.

I'd decided, and in deciding, decided more than merely whether or not I
was going to go into a certain structure again. I'd decided to face—and
possibly to embrace—whatever heritage that house represented. It was a
heady, frightening, and somehow wonderful decision.

I think Domingo saw my decision in my eyes when I came out from his
spare room after putting back on my clothing from the day before—I'd
washed my face and such, but had figured I could shower in my own house.
The night before, Domingo had loaned me a tee-shirt to serve as a night-
shirt (I didn't bother to explain I usually slept nude) and his robe so I could
slip out to the bathroom in relative decency during the night.

There'd been a curious intimacy hanging the spare toothbrush Domingo had given me next to his own, to using his soap, and a worn washcloth that was twin to the one already on the rack. Somehow, it felt even more intimate than if, overwhelmed by nerves and strangeness we'd tumbled into bed together. That would have been sex. This was a confirmation of friendship, of shared secrets, a promise to protect.

I could see that Domingo felt that new intimacy, too, but with the larger problem of Phineas House and all it represented, he didn't have to talk about it. Instead, he poured me a cup of coffee and slid a plate with a blueberry turnover on it toward the seat at the other side of his small kitchen table.

"So. You're going back into the House," he said. "Want me to come with you?"

"Not this time," I said. "I need to make sure . . . I mean, if it's going to be my home as well as my house, I can't be afraid of it. Right?"

Domingo didn't try to dissuade me. When I had needed a strong arm about my shoulder, he'd been quick to offer, but he also seemed to understand that too much protecting can make the other person incapable of action.

"Just remember what I said last night. Don't blame the House for how it may have been used."

"I won't," I said, though I knew it wouldn't be easy.

I was already making mental excuses why I shouldn't use the front stair, but stick with the servant's staircase in the back. Intellectually, I'd realized that at least one person must have died in a house that old, but it was another thing entirely to know exactly where someone had died—and that they had died by violence.

I had worked my way through one cup of coffee and was almost done with my turnover when Domingo asked, "Mira, do you know anything about your family? From what . . ." He hesitated, but pushed on, "Paula Angel told you they have been in this area for a long time. Were they Spanish?"

"I don't think so," I said, "or if so, not precisely so. I read in one of the books you loaned me that the early settlers were not solely Spanish."

"Not in the least," Domingo agreed, "though many of my relatives who would like to view themselves as pure Spanish don't like what our own records show. The Spanish crown was quite happy to hire mercenaries of many groups. Indeed, the very C. de Baca to whom the Baca land grant was given was probably of Basque descent, not Spanish."

"Isn't that just about the same?" I asked.

Domingo gave a lazy grin, "The Spanish might like to think so, but the Basques think differently. They have their own distinct language—a language that may be the oldest in the world. Some of their customs are unique as well. They were great sailors, and many of the Spanish ships probably had Basques among their crews."

"Do you think my ancestors might have been Basques then?" I asked, surprised and curious.

"No, though it is indeed possible. I just mentioned them because it is one example of many where the Spanish colonists were not all so Spanish."

"I don't look very Spanish," I said, thinking of my all too familiar reflection. "Too fair, too thick. I used to wonder if I were German, perhaps, or Irish, for all my mother's first name is French and her surname is Russian."

"But you mentioned that Colette's mother was not of Phineas House's line," Domingo said. "Perhaps she was of French descent."

"Quite possible," I said. "I'm really going to need to look at records. Paula Angel indicated that Colette was born in Phineas House. That should be a start. Perhaps other members of her family were also born there."

"Let me do the research," Domingo said. "I know people, both at the archives and the various libraries. I also read Spanish as well as I do English."

"And I read it not nearly as well as I do English," I said. "But why do you want to do this?"

"Because, Mira, you came here looking for your mother. You cannot find her, nor can her vanishing be traced in any of the usual ways. Paula Angel's story has opened that which is, shall we say, unusual. It cannot be ignored."

"But what about the painting?" I said, grasping at straws, though, in all truth, I did not want to spend hours going through archive documents looking for the names of ancestors I wasn't sure I wanted to know.

"Tomás can be foreman today," Domingo said. "Most of the painting is moving along very well. The crew will work well, even without me. They are quite pleased that their work is going to be shown in the newspaper."

"Lord!" I said slapping myself on my forehead in astonishment. "I'd forgotten about that. I feel like I've lived a dozen lives since we made that appointment."

"In a way, you have," Domingo said. "So, will you accept my offer?"

"I will," I agreed. "And I'll raise your archives by one family library. Last time I was in there, I was mostly looking for paperwork directly related to Colette and her disappearance. It's time I looked into whatever else is there."

"*Bueno*," Domingo said.

We looked at each other, and I wondered if either of us had the courage to say more about friendship, about intimacy. We might have, but the arrival of the painting crew put an end to that. I walked downstairs, hoping I didn't look as unshowered and unkempt as I suddenly felt, and Domingo came with me. None of the crew exchanged even a sly look.

As I walked back to the House I felt thoroughly sad that I was now so old and so unattractive that I could be found alone in a man's house early in the morning and not even raise an eyebrow.

Phineas House felt no different when I walked in through the kitchen door, and that was difference enough to make me stop. I'd learned so much since, dear lord, was it only since yesterday afternoon? Late afternoon at that. My interior landscape had changed. I guess I figured the exterior should too.

"And you should be used to changes by now, Mira, my dear," I said out loud to myself. "That's about all you've had since May."

And *even before*, I finished silently, not trusting those words to the listening House. *Alice through the Looking Glass—but in my case it was out of Wonderland and into Reality. Now it looks like I'm heading back to Wonderland.*

Odd as the thought was, it cheered me. I ran up the front stairs defiantly, probably right over the place where my maternal grandfather had tumbled to his death. Showering refreshed my spirits. I went into the kitchen, poured myself a tall glass of cold water, and carried it with me into the library.

I'd always talked to myself, and had always thought that the habit was probably a result of being an only child—and one who had been fairly solitary for the first years of her life. Now, as I looked around the book-lined room and heard myself saying, "Lord, there's a lot of stuff here. Where should I start?" I wondered. Did I really talk to myself or had I developed the habit because in the peculiar entity of Phineas House, there had always been someone to listen?

It was an interesting and captivating insight, but when nothing extraordinary happened—none of the silent women came gliding in to offer guidance, no books pushed themselves off the shelves to drop significantly onto the floor—I started scanning the titles on the shelves. For the sake of method, I began at the far right side of the desk, and worked my way around, using a convenient three step ladder I'd found tucked at the end of a row of shelves when necessary.

The first group of books focused on history, not just of this area, but worldwide. The breadth of interest expressed would have done a college library proud: just about every time period and nation was represented. The depth of coverage wasn't very good: this was a history survey, not a seminar. History merged almost imperceptibly into philosophy and theology, the two shelved together as if whoever had arranged these books hadn't seen much difference between them. Then came books on languages: dictionaries and primers, as well as linguistic studies. There was a selection of poetry, with the emphasis on narrative epics, but almost no novels.

I couldn't resist browsing at first, but as the collection moved into science and mathematics, my interest waned. It wasn't that I didn't like these subjects—it's amazing how often art overlaps science—but I was becoming overwhelmed by the sheer amount of information. Even just scanning the titles began to become too much. I started scanning for categories, looking for where topics shifted. The organization was idiosyncratic—Dewey of the Decimal system or whoever put the Library of Congress's catalog together would have had fits—but there was an internal logic I could almost follow.

For that reason, when I found a large Bible shelved separately from the rest of the books dealing with religion—even away from other translations of the Bible—I felt my heart skip a beat. This might well be what I was looking for.

I pulled the fat, leather-bound volume down from the shelf, sat on the stepladder, and opened the volume to the front. As I had half-expected there was a family tree printed there, and someone had filled in many of the names and dates. At the very bottom was one word, written in what I recognized as my mother's handwriting, followed by one date: "Mira" then the year of my birth.

I traced up to where my parents were listed, thinking that at last I was going to learn who my father was. However, Colette had remained coy. "Nicolette Bogatyr" born in 1928 was listed as my mother, but where my father should be listed, the line was blank.

Frustrated, I traced up to Colette's parents, my grandparents. Both names were given here. My grandfather was Nikolai Bogatyr. His wife was Chantal Lowell. Colette had been their only child.

The same could not be said for the next generation back. Nikolai had been the middle of three children. His older sister, Pinca, had died when she was in her early twenties. His younger brother, Urbano, had survived both his siblings. I noticed that Colette's handwriting had entered the year of Urbano's death, but that another—possibly Nikolai's, possibly someone else's—had entered the names and dates of birth.

Tracing up from Nikolai and Chantal, I noticed something interesting. Nikolai's parents had been Pinca Jefferson and Ivan Bogatyr. Pinca's mother's maiden name matched that of the couple above. It seemed wrong, somehow, then I realized why.

The family tree was not that of the Bogatyr family line, as might be expected in Colette Bogatyr's family Bible. It was tracing some other sort of inheritance line. After a moment, I thought I had it. What this family tree traced was not simply the descendants of one Aldo Pincas—the man whose name was at the top of this list—what was important was the line that led down to Colette, and to me.

Had the listing all been written in my mother's handwriting, I would have thought it just another example of Colette's egotism, but the handwriting shifted several times. After studying the chart for a moment I thought I knew what it was tracing. I thought that what I was seeing was the line indicating who had inherited Phineas House.

There was a basic similarity between Aldo Pincas's surname and the name by which the House was still known. I had been told that the name of the house was Phineas House. It is not a far leap from "Phineas" to "Pincas," especially with the irregularities of spelling common in the older records. However, just to double check, I went and looked up "Phineas" in a book of names sitting in the linguistics section of the library. "Pincas" was given as a variant. Both were apparently derived from a Hebrew word meaning "oracle."

Another thing that had initially kept me from seeing what the chart was tracing was the fact that both my mother and I were only children. However, her father had not been, yet his siblings' lines weren't detailed. All that was given were birth and death dates, no indication whether Great-uncle Urbano had married or fathered children. Nothing.

Pinca, Nikolai's sister, might have died too young to have children, but brother Urbano probably had a family. The further back I went, the same pattern showed. Siblings to the House heir were listed, but after that it was as if they had ceased to be of interest to the person keeping the chart. Neither issue nor marriage was listed.

There was another thing that made me think that something to do with the Pincas line—and thus Phineas House—was the key to this chart. Aldo's eldest son, Amerigo, was the chosen member of his generation. However, Amerigo's second child, his daughter Isabela, was the one who came in for the detailed listing.

Isabela married one Wallace Jefferson. They had two children. The eldest, a girl, was given a name clearly derived from her mother's maiden name: Pinca. Pinca's own first child, my great-aunt, had also been named Pinca. It seemed to me that remembering the connection to the line of Aldo Pincas was essential.

I have a good eye for color, and that's probably why I noticed the next anomaly, a discoloration on the page near Great-aunt Pinca's entry. The paper alongside her name was both lighter and darker at points, indications of very careful erasure, erasure that had left at least a little smudge. So there had been further information about her. Likely, then before her early death, Great-aunt Pinca had been married, maybe even had a child, but someone had erased that information.

Why? What harm could it do?

I remembered what Paula Angel had told me, about how the ability to use Phineas House had seemed to skip a few generations—so that when it manifested again in my mother, her parents didn't know how to deal with it. What if the true story was slightly different? What if the talent or ability or whatever you called it *had* manifested in my grandparent's generation—and it had manifested in Great-aunt Pinca. Then Pinca had died, and the right of inheritance, but not the ability to use the House, had passed to Nikolai.

Might that be a better reason for Grandfather Nikolai's unreasoning attitude toward his daughter—not fear of a witchcraft that had run in his family for generations, but resentment that his daughter, not himself, was the true heir to Phineas House? Might he also have erased his sister's name, as if to assert that he, not she, was the one fated to carry forward the line of inheritance?

Paula had said several generations had lacked whatever was the strange ability that defined the line. That seemed peculiar, too. Las Vegas, New Mexico, had been officially founded in 1835. The first family member listed on this chart had been born in 1813, making him a young man when the city was founded. Even if he'd hurried up, claimed the land on which Phineas House now stood, and started building, that left only two generations for his family to build what Paula had indicated was a formidable reputation. Four generations on, two off, then Colette, then me.

I suppose it would be enough, but I wasn't at all sure. I had this funny feeling that Paula had been talking about a lot longer span of time than from between the founding of Las Vegas to when Nikolai's grandmother had died. Then again, the Anglo history of the "American West" is so short that maybe it would have been enough.

I wasn't convinced.

I was about to go hunting in the vicinity of where I'd found the Bible when the phone rang. It was Chilton O'Reilly, reminding me about tomorrow's meeting. I thanked him and rang off, but that call made me think that there were other things I needed to do before tomorrow morning. The silent women kept the House far nicer than I could, but the front garden really needed some work if the place was going to be photographed.

I had to admit, if only to myself, that I needed a little time to think. Just over three months ago, I had been an orphan with little sense of where my ancestors had come from. Now I was discovering if not a family—for family is far more than shared bloodlines—at least my maternal heritage, a heritage that included, apparently, patricides and witches. It was a lot to take in, a lot more to accept.

And I still knew nothing at all about my father.

I was beginning to wonder if I really wanted to find out.

Despite my apprehensions, Chilton O'Reilly's visit went smoothly. The photographer was efficient, and admitted to being pleased to have a chance to take what he called "arty" shots. Domingo was surprisingly eloquent when Chilton interviewed him. The weather was what I was coming to expect as typically New Mexico—clear and sunny.

Chilton had kept his promise not to slight the neighbors, and soon everyone was trooping around in a small herd, watching the photographer do his work, and offering Chilton enough information on restoring old houses, local history, and the Painted Lady movement that he could have written a small book.

My mood was so good that after the photographer had packed his gear, I invited Chilton in for lunch. He accepted with pleasure.

"Maggie is at one of her clubs, needlepointing, I think," he said. "I was going to have a sandwich at home."

"I don't have anything fancier here," I warned, "unless Domingo and his crew are ordering takeout. I could check."

"Don't worry. A sandwich would be marvelous," Chilton assured me. "Company will be the sauce."

I waved him ahead of me down the front hall to the kitchen. I thought his gaze rested briefly on the door to my mother's office, but he didn't push. In the kitchen, I pulled out a variety of cold cuts and a loaf of dark rye bread. I had drinks, chips, and fresh fruit, even some of Chilton's candy left.

As we were making our sandwiches at the kitchen table, he gave an admiring look out the window toward the garden.

"You've gotten this place into wonderful shape," he said.

"The garden is Domingo's work," I replied. "His father was gardener here in my mother's time. Domingo kept up with it after."

"But Phineas House itself," Chilton said, "the painting outside, all the cleaning inside. It must be costing you a fortune."

"It's not as bad as you might think," I said. "Domingo has a way of finding good workers and materials. I've sold a few things here and there to raise the cash."

"Antiques?"

"Oh, no. Old appliances, mostly. It's amazing what you can sell online."

"There might be a story in that," Chilton said.

"If there is," I said, "you can consult me, but anonymously. I don't want people breaking in thinking there's a treasure trove here."

"Understandably. Let me run it by my editor. It might make a good followup to the piece on Victorians." He looked around the room with real appreciation. "Still, I reserve the right to compliment you, Mira. This old place looks great."

"I've had some help in," I said, not wanting to press his credulity, and wanting to give the silent women some credit. "And one person alone doesn't make as much of a mess, especially in a big place like this. In my experience, it's easier to clutter up a small apartment than a big house—and then the clutter makes cleaning harder, and . . ."

Chilton nodded. "That's how it is in my office at home. Maggie won't go in there anymore, and I don't do the best of jobs with dust. We have a maid twice a month, but she messes up my papers."

We laughed, and riding the general feeling of fellowship, I decided to tell him a few of the things I'd learned. Some of what I'd learned about Colette might be embarrassing, but it couldn't hurt anyone now—and I was curious what Chilton's response might be.

"I've learned a few things about my mother's past," I said. "I'll tell you about them, but only if you promise to keep them off the record."

Chilton paused, and I respected him for that. I was effectively asking him to sit on a story before he knew how juicy it would get. Then he nodded.

"I can do that. If it's really good, I reserve the right to try and talk you around."

"Done," I said with a laugh.

Chilton turned his shirt pocket out. "No hidden tape recorder, and my hands are busy with my sandwich. What have you learned?"

"I found out why some people said my mother had been born at Phineas House, while others claimed she'd only been there about ten years. In a way, both stories were right. Colette was born here, but she wasn't here for many years in between. Did you come across anything about her father's death?"

Chilton shook his head. "I was interested in her then, not her childhood. Wait. Didn't he die when she was young?"

"That's right. He fell down a flight of stairs when she was nine. Broke his neck." I took a swallow from my iced tea before going on, studying Chilton's face. There was nothing there to indicate he was hiding prior knowledge, so I went on. "The fall was ruled an accident, but apparently Colette claimed to have pushed him."

"What? Why would she have done that?"

"Apparently, Colette and Nikolai—that was my grandfather's name— didn't get along at all. I wonder if he might have beaten her. In any case, she was young enough to think she was showing her strength."

"Sort of a 'don't mess with me' statement?" Chilton asked. "It's a terrible thing to say, but that would be in keeping with the woman I remember. She had that attitude. Queenly. Arrogant."

I nodded. "Well, after Nikolai's death, my grandmother's brother came to help her run things. Then *he* had a fall . . ."

"He wasn't killed, was he? I would have heard about two deaths in such a similar fashion in the same house."

"No. He wasn't. The fall may not even have been mentioned outside the family, but Colette . . . Well, let's just say that Colette's behavior was such that her mother had no trouble getting her committed to the State Hospital. Colette spent something like ten years there. While she was committed, her mother died—natural causes, flu, I think, and so the estate came to Colette. Her case was reviewed, and she was let out."

"To become the town's eccentric, and vanish a decade or so years later," Chilton said. He sounded like he was trying out the words for print.

"This is confidential," I said. "I'm telling you because you cared enough to look for her all those years ago."

"I promise I'll keep it to myself," Chilton said. "Mental illness, especially of someone who could pay for private care, could be kept quiet, and if she'd been ruled sane after all—well, the hospital authorities wouldn't have been talking. Like most institutions of its type, it has been open to criticism in the past."

"Domingo told me a few stories," I said, "when we were out playing tourist."

"There are some good ones," Chilton agreed. "Speaking of good stories, how did you learn this one, Mira?"

I'd thought up a good answer to that one while I'd been talking. "I was looking through some family papers. I found some that told basically what I just told you. I think they may be copies of papers submitted to the State Hospital when . . ."

"When they were moving to have Colette committed," Chilton said, completing my sentence when he saw my discomfort. "That makes sense. I'd guess that Colette was interviewed, too. She must have said at least enough to confirm the claims she was unbalanced."

"I suppose so," I said. I ate a few potato chips to cover a moment of unexpected sorrow for that strange girl my mother had been. "And then she may have outgrown whatever it was, or at least learned more socially acceptable behavior."

"Or," Chilton said with brutal honesty, "she may have been treated in a fashion meant to make her behavior more socially acceptable."

Words like "lobotomy" and "electroshock" hung in the air between us, thought but not spoken. I left them there.

"In any case, I was wondering, there wasn't anything, uh, well, untoward connected with my mother's disappearance was there?"

"You mean bodies at the foot of staircases or anything like that? I can reassure you, Mira. There was nothing of the sort. The chief of police had someone check records for crimes in the area after it occurred to him that Colette might not have been disappeared, but rather have chosen to disappear voluntarily."

"That's a relief," I said. "I've been nervous about that possibility ever since I learned Colette had been accused of violence. She was never violent to me—cold, so cold that her disapproval could feel like a blow—but as far as I can remember, she never raised a hand to me or to any of the servants. It was hard to accept that she might have been, well, a murderess."

"And you don't have to accept that, Mira," Chilton said with a firm kindness I hadn't expected. "Colette may have been committed for other reasons entirely. You said there was an uncle involved. Might he have hoped to get his hands on the estate?"

"He might," I said. "I checked, and my grandmother was left Nikolai's personal property, but the House and its contents were left to Colette."

"Not uncommon," Chilton said, "when a property has been in a family a long time. Whatever games might have been being played at Colette's expense, they didn't succeed in the end."

"She lost ten years of her life!" I protested.

"I don't mean that," Chilton said. "I mean someone was acting for her interests, someone who couldn't do anything until she reached majority, but there was someone. You mentioned a trustee, didn't you?"

I nodded. "That's right."

I got up quickly to bring the tea pitcher from the refrigerator, letting motion cover my whirling thoughts.

*Trustees. That's something I have to look into. Trustees protected my interests. Now it looks like they protected Colette's as well. Mr. Hart came to warn Aunt May off her investigations—but he dropped hints, too, or at least she thought he did.*

I filled our glasses, then sat down again.

"Thanks for listening, Chilton. I've felt I owed you something, but I didn't expect you to accept what I told you."

"Reporters hear strange things," he said, "and many things that can't be allowed to get into print. I wonder sometimes whether we're like priests that way. We hear a whole lot more than we'll ever tell."

He laughed ruefully, "But unlike priests, our motives are far from divine. We know if we talk too much, we'll lose the trust of our sources and never get to do any more stories. And, speaking of stories, I have a big one to finish writing. It's going to be the Sunday spread after all, and there are hints that at least one of the wire services is interested in picking it up. They can sell it as a travel piece nationwide."

"That's great!" I said. "A real feather in your cap, though I expect at this stage in your career, you have enough to make a war bonnet."

"I've done all right," he said. "I'll tell you about it sometime when I'm not up against a deadline. Thanks again, Mira, and your mother's story is safe with me."

I watched him drive away, feeling real pleasure. The child me had liked Chilton O'Reilly, and the adult me did, too. I still thought he had an agenda of his own, but I thought my willingness to feed his curiosity had, ironically, served to defuse it.

When I went back into the kitchen, the silent women had already cleaned up the mess from lunch.

18

Color, sound, and taste were no longer separate and dis-
crete experiences, but parts of an integrated whole,
whose components could sometimes translate into one
another.

—Patricia Lynne Duffy,
*Blue Cats and Chartreuse Kittens*

## INSIDE THE LINES

Later that afternoon, I decided to continue trying to figure out why the connection to Phineas House, whatever it was, might have been interrupted in
my great-grandparent's generation—or if this was something that Paula
had not completely understood. After all, she herself had stressed she was
no omnipotent oracle. She only knew what she had observed. Maybe the
descendants of Aldo Pincas had decided it would be wise to hide their odd
talents.

But in looking at the chart, I found a possible reason for the interruption.
Isabela and Wallace Jefferson had had two daughters: Pinca, named for her
family, and Mercedes, possibly named for her grandmother. Somehow I had
the feeling that Wallace was either a nonentity or doted on his wife.

What I hadn't noticed before was that Pinca and Mercedes Jefferson were
twins. Could that have confused Phineas House? It might have, especially if
the girls were identical twins. I'd have to see if I could find any pictures or
paintings. I didn't know if it would matter, but since I had no idea what pre-

cisely this connection was that Paula claimed I had to the House, anything that indicated how the connection was made—or broken—could be useful.

That it was something that could be inherited, I had no doubt, but just what I was inheriting was anyone's guess.

Domingo came tapping at the kitchen door that evening as I was working on my laptop.

"Can I come in, Mira?"

"Please," I said. "Let me shut this down. I'm trying to keep in touch with folks I left behind in Ohio. Now that the school year has started, they're full of stories about mutual friends. Would you believe that the principal of one of the local high schools got married this summer—to a girl who graduated the spring before? True, he was young for his post, but really!"

"Seventeen-year-old girls get married all the time in northern New Mexico," Domingo said with deliberate obtuseness. "But maybe not to men old enough to be principals of their schools. Does hearing all the juicy gossip make you homesick?"

I sent off a sheaf of e-mails, then clicked off connections.

"Maybe a little, but I also feel a certain guilty pleasure that I'm not expected to be putting together lesson plans and grading assignments. It's much more interesting to be interviewed for newspaper articles and exploring Phineas House. Want to compare research?"

Domingo brightened. "I have a few things."

"So do I. I found the family Bible—and a family tree."

"Good! We can check our work against each other's."

"Coffee? I can make decaff . . ."

"Sounds good."

While I set up the coffeepot, I started telling Domingo what I'd learned, and what I'd deduced. I thought that maybe he'd be upset, that my finds would have made his own useless, but he only seemed interested, and if his fingers drummed against the file folder in front of him, it was with anticipation, nothing else.

When the coffee was done, we took cups into the library, and I pulled out the Bible so that Domingo could see the family tree. He ran his finger down the page, then opened his folder. The top item was a list of names with dates following them.

"Here," he said, "a bit more on your ancestors. I was lucky when I went down to the courthouse. One of the clerks is an older woman, a friend of my mother's. She won't retire, and, to be honest, she knows so much no one really wants her to do so. She helped me find what we needed."

"Didn't she think your interest was strange?"

"Not at all. She knows I live here at Phineas House, and she had seen the article about your coming home again. If she was at all surprised, it was that you had not come in sooner."

I'd been looking at the list as he spoke, and paused with my finger next to one name.

"Look, Domingo, here's my great-uncle Urbano. The family tree only gives his dates of birth and death, but you've found more. He was married, and had at least two children."

Domingo moved the top sheet to one side, and picked up another he'd headed "Urbano Bogatyr."

"I looked for further information on these children—after all, they would be your second cousins. I found nothing more, no marriage licenses or the like. My mother's friend, the clerk, cross-checked the real estate records and found that in 1936 Urbano sold a house on a street a few blocks away from Phineas House."

"It's a remarkable bit of luck that she found that," I said.

Domingo did not deny it. "She had been doing some research for someone else not long ago, and come across it. The reference stuck in her mind. She is amazing that way."

"I bet Urbano moved then," I said. "Las Vegas in the Depression would not have been a great place to try and raise a family. Obviously, he stayed in touch at least a little, or Colette would not have known when he died. He left two children . . ."

"At least," Domingo said. "Urbano was a relatively young man when he left Las Vegas. He might have had more later."

"I wonder if anyone of them ever came back?" I mused. "Probably not. What would there be to bring them back? Nikolai died a year later, and within another year Colette was committed. Phineas House was probably boarded up."

"Nothing in the courthouse will show us if Urbano ever came for a visit," Domingo said practically. "Bogatyr is not a common surname, though. It might be possible to trace him."

"I'm going to back-burner that," I said, "at least for now. Unless Great-uncle Urbano told his children stories about Phineas House, they couldn't help me much, and he has been dead since 1960—if the Bible is to be believed."

"I think it is," Domingo said. "The dates in it match what I found elsewhere. See, here are your maternal great-grandparents, Pinca and Ivan Bogatyr. I also found information on Pinca's twin sister, Mercedes."

"Ivan is listed as being born in Saint Petersburg, Russia," I said. "I wonder what brought him to Las Vegas, New Mexico?"

"Maybe Pinca did," Domingo said. "We have very little feeling for the lives your ancestors lived. They may have travelled a great deal."

I thought about this, then nodded. "I think they may have. Think about the furnishings in the House. There are Oriental carpets, fine musical instruments, paintings. True, some could have been shipped here on the railroad, but I'd say it's fairly certain that the family had access to something more than the Sears catalog for their shopping."

"True," Domingo said, turning a page. "Your grandmother, Chantal, was foreign, too. I found a copy of the marriage certificate between herself and your grandfather. Her place of birth is given as Paris."

"So we have some evidence that the descendants of Aldo Pincas, rooted as they were in Las Vegas, New Mexico, nonetheless got out and saw the world. That's something, but I'm not at all sure what."

Domingo reached across and squeezed my hand. "I have more. The courthouse was quiet today, and once my mother's friend got interested, she also got inquisitive. She remembered that at the time Colette disappeared there had been some gossip about a lawsuit related to Colette. It was old gossip, back from when Colette was a child. Given that it was bad form to discuss cases related to a minor, it never got beyond the clerks. She went and looked up files, and eventually found the jacket. It seems that Colette's maternal uncle brought suit on behalf of Colette's mother to have Ivan's will broken on the grounds that Colette was incompetent."

"He didn't succeed," I said, "but it's interesting to know he tried."

"More than merely interesting," Domingo said. "The information in the folder gave the names of the trustees for Colette's estate. There were three: Guillermo Jefferson, Amerigo Hart, and Ignatius Carney."

"Guillermo Jefferson!" I said, almost shouting. "That name's in my Bible. He was the younger brother of Isabela, my . . ." I counted back the generations, "Great-great grandmother, so he's my great, great uncle—or would that be great, great, great uncle?"

"It could well be the same man," Domingo agreed. "I thought this when you showed me the Bible. I didn't have time to trace back further than your great-grandfather, Ivan, but I did remember your grandmother Pinca's maiden name had been Jefferson."

"If it's the same Guillermo," I said, "he would have been in his seventies at the time of the lawsuit. That works, then."

I looked at the name of the second of the trustees. "Domingo, this second name rings bells, too, but you might not realize it."

"I did notice," Domingo said, "that 'Amerigo' is also the first name of your great-great-grandfather. It does not seem unreasonable that one of Amerigo's children—a daughter, perhaps, would have named her son for her father."

"That's just part of it," I said. "I've told you a little about my Aunt May's journals, haven't I?"

"A little."

"Well, although the conditions of my adoption were such that she and Uncle Stan weren't supposed to pry, Aunt May did anyhow."

"Like mother, like daughter," Domingo said, his eyes twinkling.

I grinned at him. "Right. Well, Aunt May wrote a bunch of letters to various people here in Las Vegas. She represented herself as interested in Colette's disappearance as part of research for a paper she was writing. She never got any answers. Then she had an excuse to go to Arizona by herself—a beloved cousin had cancer. She decided to use the trip to go to Las Vegas and ask her questions in person."

"Your uncle would not have agreed?"

"She was pretty sure he'd be furious. After all, she was gambling their custody of me against her curiosity."

"Does that make you feel uncomfortable?"

"Not a bit. Her journal makes pretty clear that she got interested at first because she was afraid Colette would show up and take me away someday. But I'm getting off topic."

"Go ahead."

"So Aunt May made reservations to go from Arizona to Las Vegas, but she did this through a travel agent in Ohio. The day she did this, a man shows up at her door—one of the three trustees for my estate. His name was Mr. Hart."

"¡Madre de Dios!"

"Or at least Mother of Hart," I said, trying to make a joke of it.

"Could they have been the same man?"

"I don't think so," I admitted. "Aunt May describes the man who visited her as the youngest of the three trustees. I think her Mr. Hart may have been a relative—maybe a son—of Amerigo Hart. This thing seems to run in families. I think you're absolutely right. Amerigo Hart is the son of either Belinda or Catarina Pincas. Although the House didn't go to one of them, still they were involved in its disposition . . . its fate."

"And the last man?"

"No way of knowing. He could be a son of the sister who didn't marry Whoever Hart. He could be a relative of Aldo Pincas from another branch. He could be some poor lawyer dragged in to do the paperwork, someone who has no idea how very odd a trust this is. Whatever the case, we're seeing that although Phineas House seems to bond with one family member per generation, whatever is going on is useful enough that other members make an effort to keep the House in the family."

Domingo lifted his coffee cup, found it empty, but continued to hold it, staring into it as if the brown smears at the bottom might hold the key to hidden secrets.

"Mira, what about your own trustees, the ones who arranged for your adoption? There was this Mr. Hart. What are the names of the others?"

"I don't think Aunt May mentioned them," I began, then tapped myself on the forehead in mute reprimand. "She may have, somewhere, but I'm sure the names have to be in that file folder Uncle Stan kept for me. Hang on."

As I headed from the room, Domingo called after me, "More coffee, Mira?"

"Please. There are cookies in the cabinet, too."

When I thudded down the front stairs a few minute later, Domingo had brought in two cups of hot coffee and the plastic bakery box of chocolate-chip cookies.

"Thanks," I said. "Read the Bible or something for a moment while I plow through this."

Domingo grinned. "I'll do that. I found a few more familiar names. I might as well confirm that they match up."

Uncle Stan had kept the file in order by punching each sheet of paper at the top and then clipping it into the file. Since this made getting at the earlier copies harder, I pulled the whole sheaf off.

"This is going to be a real nuisance to get back on," I muttered, but I wasn't really listening to myself. My eyes were skimming documents, looking for the names of my trustees. Funny. To this point that "my" had belonged to Colette—they were not "my" in the sense of men who worked for me or on my behalf. They were Colette's allies, assigned to me. Now I realized that Colette might well have had a fondness for the concept of trustees. Hers had certainly done more to protect her interests than her mother or father had done. In assigning my care to trustees, rather than to friends or to people I knew, had Colette been doing me a kindness, protecting me as she herself had been protected?

I found the names I wanted on a letter at the very beginning of the correspondence. It was the same one Aunt May had mentioned: the one that explained the terms under which the Fenns could have me to foster, and, if all went well, to later adopt. It was signed by three men, their names typed neatly beneath their signatures: Edgar Carney, Michael Hart, and Renaldo Pincas.

"Bingo!" I exclaimed softly.

"What have you found?" Domingo asked.

"My trustees," I said. "Jefferson has dropped out, but Carney and Hart remain—and Pincas is back. All men, but that's to be expected. I was born in 1952. There weren't many women in business then."

Domingo nodded. "Are we seeing a law firm of some sort here? One where family members are regularly given places, or some sort of club?"

"A club," I said firmly, "having something to do with whatever it is Phineas House does."

"But what is it that the House does?" Domingo said. "What is this 'witchcraft' of which Paula Angel spoke? Is it merely the ability to see ghosts and benefit from the talents of a strange building, or something more?"

"I think it's something more," I said, "but for the life of me, I have no idea what it is. However, sure as God made little green apples, I'm willing to bet that Colette's disappearance was connected to it."

Domingo looked at me, the excitement that had lit his eyes as we unravelled a bit of the tangle, darkening into worry. "So am I, Mira. Please, be careful."

"I think I've gone too far to be careful," I said. "I think now I have no choice but to be smart."

The next morning was Saturday.

A *week ago*, I thought as I walked down the hall to the shower, *I was out playing tourist with Domingo—wondering if he might like me just a little more than as a pleasant landlady. Now I've had beers with a ghost and am actually coming to accept that my family might have been some sort of sorcerers or whatever you'd call them. I don't know if I want to think about where I'll be a week from now. The thing is, I don't know where to go from here.*

When I went back to my bedroom, I found someone had offered me direction. A later volume in the series of Aunt May's journals lay open on my pillow. One of those old-fashioned weights used to hold books open had been laid across to hold it open. I couldn't miss the hint, nor did I need the sprig of Spanish lavender laid in the join of the page to tell me who had done this. The silent women—or Phineas House through the intermediary of the silent women—was offering me some advice.

"Aunt May figured something out, did she?" I asked the listening air. "Thanks for showing me. This is farther along than where I was reading. I might not have gotten here for weeks. I'll look at it after breakfast."

After I had dressed, I hurried downstairs to meet Domingo. I'd found a sort of braided bread with apricots and cheese in the folds, and was looking forward to sharing it. I wondered if I should tell him what the silent women had done, but decided against it. I hadn't quite gotten around to explaining about the silent women, and that would be a lot to go into before the workmen arrived.

Domingo and Blanco came out to the garden soon after I carried out the breakfast tray. The breakfast bread was just as good as I had thought it would be, and if Domingo had brought a few rosebuds in a little bud vase, well, that only made the repast sweeter.

"Will you paint today, Mira?" he asked. "We're about done with the exterior coverage, but there's lots of detail work to do. That's why some of the crew is here on a weekend. I'm going to act as if we'll get rain in a week or so, and lose time."

"Like washing your car or something," I agreed, looking up at the curves and curlicues that lined the gables. "Modern rain magic. I suspect that painting is going to be a seasonal job."

"Not to this extent," Domingo said, "but touch-up, yes, I think so. Still, it looks wonderful, does it not?"

"Anywhere else," I said, "it would look gaudy and overdone. Here, well, it looks just right."

I realized then, that I hadn't answered his question about my joining the paint crew.

"Let me do a bit of research this morning," I said. "You came up with some interesting angles. Also, now that I have names for the trustees, I may be able to track one of them down. We're no longer dealing with people from generations ago. Thirty years ago, they were at least passively administering my inheritance. Aunt May describes Michael Hart as the youngest of the trustees, although she doesn't specifically describe him as young. Still, from how she describes what he said to her, how they talked, there's a sense they were contemporaries. If Michael Hart was in his thirties, then, he'd only be sixty something now. The others could be alive, too."

"Are there addresses on the paperwork?"

"I didn't look last night. I was too overwhelmed, but I'm sure there must be. Who knows? They might be at the same address, even. Same phone number."

"Don't count on it, Mira," Domingo said. "A long time has gone by."

"I know," I said, "and I promise I won't get my hopes up too high."

"Promise, too, that you won't lock yourself away all day," Domingo suggested gently. "I can tell today will be lovely."

"I'll do my best," I said. "Promise."

Once inside, I dutifully put plates and such into the dishwasher. I knew if I didn't, the silent women would, and I felt guilty about that. My mother had frightened them. I remembered that clearly. I had no desire to be a more passive tyrant.

I took Aunt May's journal to the front window seat, the same one from which, as a child, I had watched people go by on the street. It was as comfortable as I remembered, and as most of the work was taking place at the back of Phineas House, it was peaceful, too.

I opened the journal. The entry was dated from the year I was a sophomore in high school—roughly five years after Aunt May had initially resolved to find out what she could about Colette. Aunt May had probably saved me a lot of dead ends. Offering a mental word of thanks, I settled in to see what Aunt May had to say.

## OUTSIDE THE LINES

Mr. Gilhoff was on the phone when I came into the bookstore, but he motioned for me to wait. That wasn't a problem. Stan's birthday was coming up, and I knew he'd enjoy a good book, preferably one filled with blue-prints and diagrams. I guess that's one of the big differences between men's work and women's work. If they're lucky, men get to do something they like, something that interests them. Women just get chores. For me, if I never have to deal with another dirty pot or pile of laundry, that would be just fine.

Maybe things will be different for Mira. I'd like to think so. She's doing very well in school. It would be a pity if the end result of all that work was, well, laundry.

Mr. Gilhoff ended his phone call before my train of thought could get too gloomy.

"Good morning, Mrs. Fenn," he said. "Looking for anything particular?"

I nodded, "Something for Stan's birthday. Architecture would be good—not a pretty coffee-table book, something with more meat on it."

"I can help you there," he said. "New or used?"

"Depends on condition," I said. "New, I suppose, but I'll take used if it lets my budget stretch."

"I have few ideas," he said, "while I look for the appropriate books, why don't you take a look at this one? It's not new. In fact, the theories have been around since the early nineteen hundreds. However, they've remained more of interest to scholars than to popularizers because they weren't translated into English until recently. I thought you'd be interested, though."

He handed me a book called *Rites of Passage* by someone named Van Gennep, and went off to find books for Stan. I took the customer's chair and started skimming. The writing style wasn't easy to get into. It wasn't that the author was being impenetrable, more that he assumed his reader would be familiar with his subject matter—a thing I wasn't.

Even so, within a few minutes, I thought I saw why Mr. Gilhoff had set the book by for me. Long ago, I'd asked him about the title "Mistress of Thresholds," and here was someone concentrating on the "between" states of things, the transitional moments. He used a word I'd never before encountered to define this transition: "liminal." Mr. Gilhoff hadn't come back yet, so I borrowed a dictionary and looked it up. It sent me off to the word "limen," and that definition set my heart thumping.

"Limen" was defined as "threshold." The dictionary went on about transitional elements and such, but the connection was confirmed. No matter how impenetrable this author was, I was going to read this book and learn anything I could about thresholds, about liminal things.

I skimmed chapter headings and much of what I read didn't really seem to apply. I wasn't interested in the "magico-religious" rites of various primitive peoples or territorial affirmation or ceremonies for burial. Still, the general theory, the idea that the times we pass between states are as much or more important than the states themselves seemed very pertinent. In fact, the more I thought about it, the more I realized how such rites still exist today.

I thought about the life-changing moments our own society celebrates: births, baptisms, marriages, even, in a sort of weird way, deaths. There are coming-of-age ceremonies, too, though I guess these are more common in religions than real life. Bar Mitzvahs. Confirmations. Then again, there are coming of age ceremonies in our society, too: getting the right to vote or getting a driver's license or reaching the legal drinking age.

It's funny, but I'd never thought about how each one of these involves not only the new state the person is coming into, and the older one that's being left, but a funny one that comes in between. Baptisms mark the entry of a child into a specific religion. Before that, the child is sort of like a stateless person. Some religions say that unbaptized babies don't get a shot at heaven, even though the little things can't have done anything wrong.

Basically, then, unbaptized babies can be looked at as being in a transitional state—but it happens to grownups too.

I mean, women are only brides for one day, but that transitional event when they pass over from being single to married is so important we give it its own name and surround it with superstitions and rituals. "Always a bridesmaid, never a bride." "Happy is the bride the sun shines on." "Something old, something new, something borrowed, something blue." "Carry the bride over the threshold. Be careful not to stumble."

That last one made my breath catch and my heart yammer under my breast. Thresholds again. Crossing over. Crossing into a new life, carried, presumably, by the one who will care for you the rest of your life. But the threshold itself is important. It's a place that's not one thing or the other. It's not in or out. What would a Mistress of Thresholds be then? Would she be some sort of doorman or something else entirely? Would she understand these liminal situations?

I was still thinking about this when Mr. Gilhoff came back with a pile of books.

"How much?" I asked, holding up the one I'd been reading.

"How about a quarter?" he said. "The spine's broken and it's had some hard use. Usually, I wouldn't even have bought it, but I thought you could use it."

"Sold," I said quickly, before he could reassess the volume's condition. It didn't look that bad to me. True, I might be able to find the book in my local library, but I liked having books of my own. "Now, what did you find for Stan?"

We sorted through the pile, and I ended up buying two very nice used books. Their condition was so good I suspected they had been bought as gifts for someone else, and never read—or kept as treasures. I knew Stan had neither of them, and imagined with pleasure him sitting up with one propped open on his knee, reading as Mira did her homework nearby. It was a pleasant image, one I treasured as I drove home to face the laundry.

## INSIDE THE LINES

*Liminal*, I thought, setting down Aunt May's journal. The term wasn't completely unfamiliar to me. I was pretty sure I'd heard it in relation to pop psychology used much as this Van Gennep apparently had, to talk about transitional moments in people's lives. "Liminal space" was the term I'd heard. The place you are when you're no place.

I had no doubt why the silent women had wanted me to read this passage. Aunt May's account didn't explain anything, yet, in a weird way, it did. It explained where I'd gone when I'd visited with Paula Angel.

Ghosts are pretty much a classic example of beings who exist in liminal space. Not only are they caught between life and death, they're caught between the present time and the time in which they originally lived. If you're religious, you could say they're caught between heaven and hell.

If I could see Paula Angel, that meant I could see into liminal space. If we could go to a bar and have a couple of beers, that would seem to indicate I could travel there, too. I'd needed a guide to do it—or had I? Had Paula Angel guided me to her? She'd never said so. If anything, she'd indicated the reverse. She'd said that Colette had been able to see her—not that she had been able to make Colette see her.

And that meant the same applied to me.

Liminal space. It was used in art to describe when colors blend so that you can't really decide whether you're seeing one hue or another. Blue-green, green-blue. Red-orange, orange-red. I remember crayons like that, and how I'd drawn lines with them, side by side, wondering just how much more yellow could be mixed in before you lost the primary color entirely.

Color. Aunt May hadn't mentioned it, but once you left those basic primaries behind, you were playing in liminal space. Color wheels try and draw neat little lines of division between colors, but those are fabrications. In nature colors shift and flow. They take color from each other, too. A blossom might seem white until you place it against snow. Then you can see the pale pink underlying the flower's white. There are no absolutes. Not even snow is really white.

Later, I stood on a ladder, painting a scalloped white border around a turquoise dormer window, relaxing into the simple, repetitive motion, doing what Domingo called "listening to what the House wants." All I felt was a general sensation of contentment that might well have been my own. I dipped brush into bucket again and again, stroking on the liquid color, losing myself in the motion, daydreaming a little.

When I heard the sound of horse hooves, I didn't even register them at first, or if I did, I thought they were some new twist to the paint crew's mariachi music.

*Clop-clop, clop-clop.* The hooves rose and fell in the rhythm of a well-disciplined trot, a gait that would cover ground without wearing out the horse too much. I listened, moving my paint brush to the rhythm, rising and falling along the curving edges as a bird's wings rise and fall in flight.

*Clop-clop, clop-clop.* I could almost see the horse now, a tidy little bay with a long white blaze that exploded into a star. She had good lines, but was more compact than lean. She looked mostly Morgan, but there was a touch of Arab in the daintiness of her face.

*Clop-clop, clop-clop.* I could hear a creak and hiss now, the wheels of the gig the horse pulled, moving over the road. Good wheels, rubber tires on them, for all the gig looked like something a dandy might have taken his sweetheart out in for a turn around the park in the days of Queen Victoria. The seat was high and I raised my eyes to get a look at the driver. I imagined him in a tailcoat of plum satin with darker facings on the lapels. He'd wear a stovepipe hat and a narrow mustache.

*Clop-clop, clop-clop.* The paintbrush faltered in my hand. I'd had the color right, plum satin, rich with reddish undertones that caught the sunlight. It was a good color for a woman with dark hair, raven-wing dark as this woman's was, worn piled high and held in place with glittering amethyst pins. She held the reins in one hand with perfectly competent confidence. She held something else in the other, and as I watched, she raised it to one eye.

*Clop-clop, clop . . .*

*Thump! Thud.*

I heard a shout, a loud, almost anguished cry.

"Mira! Hold on. Mira!"

19

From the second millennium B.C., the Chinese used color
to indicate the cardinal directions, seasons, the cyclical
passage of time, and the internal organs of the human
body.

—Sarah Rossbach and Lin Yun,
*Living Color*

## INSIDE THE LINES

"Mira! Hold on, Mira!"

The shout came a second time, and this time I recognized the source.
Domingo. His voice—and the panic in every note—pulled me back from
wherever it was that I had been.

I was suddenly aware that the ladder under me was swaying. The thump
and thud I'd heard had been my paint bucket falling off where I'd hung it
from the ladder and tumbling down to land on the ground two stories below. The white paint had left a trail like the droppings of an impossibly
large bird streaking the gaily painted side of Phineas House.

The ladder was tipping to one side, tilting back. I shoved my own weight
in the opposite direction, glad for once not to be slim and featherweight.
The ladder halted in its tottering. Then strong hands had it from beneath:
Domingo and Tomás, both men looking pale and frightened beneath their
outdoorsman's tans.

"Mira!" Domingo called. "Stay still while we make sure this is stable. Are you all right?"

"I'm fine," I called back. "Now. I don't know what happened. Maybe I drowsed off?"

Domingo forced a laugh. "Only you, Mira Fenn, could fall asleep on a ladder, paintbrush in hand. Just a moment more."

I felt vibrations as the two men made sure the base of the ladder was well-anchored. Then Domingo called, still shouting a little, as if I were farther away than at the top of an extension ladder.

"Can you come down now?"

For answer, I started picking my way down. I didn't want to admit it, but my legs were trembling. When I got down onto the lawn I gave both men impulsive hugs. Domingo held me a trace longer than was necessary, then moved me to arm's length.

"You, inside. I will come in and see that you are taken care of. Tomás, will you put this ladder away and see what can be done about the paint?"

"Sí," Tomás said. "Your nephew is here. I'll get him too clean up on the ground. I'll check the side of the house myself."

"Thank you, Tomás," I said, still shaky. "I'm sorry to create so much more work."

"No problema, Miss Fenn," he said with a grin. "Better you than one of us. You are paying us, after all."

His teasing did more than all of Domingo's anxious fussing to make me feel firmer on my feet. I insisted on walking under my own power to the kitchen—but I didn't send Domingo away either. I let him seat me at my own kitchen table and obediently drank the glass of water he put in front of me.

"Mira, do you think you got dehydrated?" he said, refilling the glass as soon as I had emptied it. "This is easy to do, this time of year. The weather is so pleasant compared to summer, you can forget how the dry air takes it out of you."

"No, Domingo, I don't think it's that. I've been careful. I don't like what the dryness does to my skin. If anything, I've been drinking too much. Domingo . . ."

I hesitated, then barged on. If anyone deserved to know the truth, it was Domingo. He had never laughed at me, not even when I told him about Paula Angel.

"Domingo, I . . . I guess you could say I had a vision. I saw my mother—

Colette—riding in the gig pulled by Shooting Star. I couldn't have imagined it. It was too perfect. I could see the details of her dress, the lace at the collar and wrists. I saw how her hair was dressed, even where it was a little mussed. I saw the trappings on the horse, what she held in her free hand. I think it was a vision of the day she vanished."

Domingo almost disappointed me. His brown eyes got very wide, and I saw the doubt in them. Then he shook his head, not in disbelief, but as if disbelief was a physical thing he could shake from him.

"¿Verdad? Well, if you say so, then so it must be. I wonder why you saw it now, there, up on a ladder. This is not a good place for visions."

Because, I thought, I was on a ladder, neither on the ground nor in the air—liminal space, of a sort. And because I was staring into the borders between the white trim and the turquoise paint, trying to get it right. And maybe most of all because Phineas House now knows I know more than I did, and maybe it tried to show me something.

I said none of this aloud. Aloud I said, "I'm not completely sure, Domingo. I have some theories, though. Can I invite you to dinner tonight, here, at the House? It's going to take some telling, and I'd rather not do so in a restaurant. I also have an experiment I'd like to try—one that definitely can't be tried in a restaurant."

"I will come," he said promptly, "on one condition."

"Name it."

"No more ladders for you," he said sternly. "Not today, maybe not for several days. I do not like how dying of broken necks seems to run in your family. I would prefer you not do so as well."

"Deal," I said. "Can I drive a car? I want to go to the grocery and pick up a few things for dinner."

"You can," Domingo agreed, "but better. Let me have one of the men drive you. I think we will need more paint thinner to deal with that paint splatter, and maybe even more rags."

"No need to worry about rags," I said. "I'm not sure that a square inch of fabric was ever thrown out in Phineas House. I have plenty, but I'll accept a driver—and gladly."

In fact, I admitted sheepishly to myself as I trotted upstairs to change out of my overalls, I think I was hinting that I needed one. I wonder if Domingo caught that, too. It would be like him.

After running errands, I went inside and busied myself with mindless domestic tasks. I'd decided on a nice baked chicken and herbs, with a side of brown rice and a big salad. Usually, I didn't like using the oven in the summer, but the new model I'd bought was so well-sealed that it released very little extra heat.

I juiced fresh lemons and made lemonade. I picked vegetables from the garden and worked on a salad. I forced myself to concentrate hard on every task at hand, a little afraid I might go slipping off again.

⊗

Domingo showed up when the chicken was about five minutes from being done, a pastry box in one hand, Blanco bounding at his heels. The chicken smelled wonderful, and you don't have to take my word for it. Blanco rose on his hind legs and danced in front of the oven door like somebody or other before the Tabernacle.

"I hope you don't mind that I brought him with me," Domingo said. "He can go out into the garden if you like."

"Blanco is fine with me, but chicken isn't fine with dogs, at least the bones aren't."

"Blanco lives to believe he will be fed table scraps," Domingo said. "I think it is very good for everyone to have a dream."

"And I," I said, reaching into a cabinet and pulling out a box of what I knew were Blanco's favorite treats, "thought I might have another guest for dinner."

We grinned at each other like a couple of kids, then I gave Blanco a few treats, and motioned Domingo to a seat at the kitchen table.

"I hope you don't mind eating in here. We could have done the whole grand dining room thing, but it seemed ridiculous for two."

"I like sitting here," he said. "You can look out at the garden. Did you eat here when you were a little girl?"

"No," I said, getting out a bottle of wine. I'd gotten a red, even though I knew it's supposed to be the wrong type for chicken. I'd always found the rich color sustaining. "I either ate in the dining room or—most of the time—in my nursery. That had a window that looked over the garden, too, but my table wasn't there. The garden window was in the bedroom part."

"The window that has the tigers and bramble roses around it," he said, accepting with a nod of thanks the glass of wine I handed him. "I remember."

"Funny," I said, putting my own glass down on the counter so I could pull the chicken from the oven. "I never knew what was there. The house was painted mostly white when I was a girl. It did nothing to show up the details."

"Perhaps that was the reason why," Domingo said reasonably. "Not everyone would like to live in a house that looks like it belongs on a fairground midway—or would if it was covered in flashing lights."

"Please, no," I said. "The bright colors are nice, but flashing lights . . . I don't think the neighborhood association would agree."

"Don't worry," Domingo said. "No one has suggested it."

I brought the chicken to the table in the bright amber Pyrex dish in which it had been cooked. A matching casserole dish held the fluffy brown rice, and a large salad was in the red bowl from the Fiesta ware set. I'd set my place with blue, Domingo's with green. It made for a colorful, but surprisingly harmonious, assemblage.

"It's sort of uncivilized," I said, "but the best topping for the rice is the drippings from the chicken. There are all sorts of herbs in there, plus onions, and garlic."

"It smells wonderful," Domingo said, "and not uncivilized at all."

We made it through dinner on small talk about cooking and our childhoods, but my near fall that afternoon and what I'd promised to tell him hung over the conversation. As I snapped on the coffeemaker and cleared away the worst of the mess from dinner, I launched in to my account.

"The reason I nearly fell today," I began, "I had a vision of my mother—my mother riding off on the day she disappeared."

Over coffee and blueberry pie, I told Domingo everything I had seen, stressing again how detailed the vision had been. Then I backtracked, explaining about liminal space, and how I'd been reading about it just before I came out to paint.

"I suppose that could have put me into a suggestible frame of mind," I said.

"Very likely," Domingo agreed. "If I understand what you are saying, that is. You are saying that you had a vision because the possibility of seeing between spaces had been put into your mind."

"Essentially, yes. You see, the one thing I hadn't told you was how I happened to be reading that section this morning. It's well ahead of where I was, in a different journal even. The night after I got so scared, when I came out of the shower, the journal was waiting for me on my pillow, open to that page."

Domingo cocked an eyebrow at me. "Do you think I had anything to do with that?"

"No, I don't. I locked the back door when I came in, so I know it wasn't one of the painters either. I think it was Phineas House herself who did it, the House or one of her agents. I'm not sure which, and I'm not sure just how much free will the silent women have."

"Silent women?"

I told him about them, about how they were the reason the House was so sparkling clean these days. How they had been there when I was a child, and how after I'd been back for a while they had reappeared.

"I don't see them very often," I concluded, "but there's no doubt they're here. This place is spotless. My bed is made for me. They don't do laundry or cook, but I wonder if they're just being polite. In my mother's day they were physically visible to everyone who came by. Your father and you probably saw them."

"There was a day," Domingo said, "not long ago, when I heard the vacuum cleaner running when you weren't home."

"That was probably one of them," I said. "They're not above using modern methods to do their work."

"So they're not ghosts, not insubstantial," he said.

"I don't know if they're ghosts or not," I said. "I don't know what they are. I just have a feeling they're connected somehow to the House and its care."

"That would explain," Domingo said, "why there were so few problems when the House was closed. I mean, dust accumulated, but there were no vermin, no major damage. I inspected the place, but I did very little to the interior."

"I thought of that," I said. "Accumulating dust might have seemed like a wise move to the House, though I have the distinct impression she is well . . . house proud?"

We shared an uncomfortable laugh at my pun, then I went on.

"I've been learning a lot, but obviously Phineas House felt I was missing something important. How she knew that what I needed was in Aunt May's journal . . ."

"Maybe one of the silent women read them," Domingo said practically. "If they can use cleaning appliances, well, certainly they can handle a book. Are you sure the silent women are extensions of the House?"

"No, I'm not," I admitted. "Maybe the relationship is symbiotic. The silent women keep Phineas House clean in exchange for something. I don't think they're enslaved to the House. The little touches, like the sprig of lavender on my pillow, go above and beyond servitude."

"And they were here in your mother's day," Domingo said, thought-fully.

"Yes." I hesitated. "But, Domingo, I don't think they liked her. In fact, I know they were frightened of her. That makes me wonder . . . Did Phineas House like my mother? I've thought she must have, based on what Paula Angel said, but now I'm wondering."

"We cannot know," Domingo said, "until we better understand the House and whatever heritage has come to you through it. Certainly, you inherited more than real estate."

"True," I said, "and I have a thought about that. Do you remember I told you that Colette was holding something in her hand in the vision?"

"Yes."

"Well, I think I know what it is. Are you done with your dessert? Would you come upstairs so I can show you something?"

Domingo nodded twice by way of answer, but as we cleared the last dishes away, he looked down at Blanco's hopeful face.

"But I think Blanco needs to go out into the garden. I will carry the chicken bones out into the trash, but that will not keep him from looking."

I brought out another dog biscuit. "Consolation prize, then."

Blanco went outside happily enough, and I couldn't blame him. The evening was lovely. The air in the garden scented with roses. I would have rather sat out there myself, but what I had in mind needed light.

When Domingo returned, we filled our coffee mugs and went upstairs.

"I want to show you something I found in my mother's suite," I said. "I could have brought it down, but I want you to see exactly what I found."

Mother's room was as immaculate as the silent women could make it, but nothing could make it inviting to me. I still felt like a trespasser. One of these days, I was going to have to make some redecorating decisions. Domingo followed me, his manners so perfect that I didn't even feel un-comfortable with the fact that I was taking him into a bedroom—well, maybe I felt a little overaware.

The better I knew Domingo, the more I was sure that if things had been different I would have already developed a massive crush on him. As it was, I couldn't decide whether or not I was glad that he was the one person in whom I could confide all this weirdness. On the one hand, it brought us closer, but on the other the peculiar intimacy made it impossible for me to tell whether any other kind of intimacy was possible.

Or something like that. All I knew was that I was very glad that my mother's room and the towering canopied bed where she had taken so many lovers did not seem at all tantalizing to either Domingo or myself.

"Over here," I said, taking him over to the vanity. "Drag a chair over. I want you to see things basically like I found them."

First I opened the drawer where the kaleidoscopes were hidden. Domingo was satisfyingly impressed both with the secret drawer and the treasure it concealed. He had too refined an eye for beauty to dismiss these as mere toys.

I handed him one to look through, deliberately not picking from the cabalistic seven. For all I knew, each of these was symbolically linked in some way, but of those I was certain. The one I had handed Domingo had an octagonal barrel adorned with stained glass patterned like a bouquet of purple iris. The object case at the end contained shifting pieces of jewel-toned glass in many of the same tones. I wondered if they were scraps left over from making the barrel. It seemed likely.

After making appreciative sounds at the patterns, and looking with a trace of innocent longing at the rest of the collection, Domingo tilted his head thoughtfully.

"Beautiful, yes, but I don't think that this is all you have to show. Nor do I think you are just showing them to me because you think they might be worth something to collectors."

"Right," I said. "I'm not going to put everything back in yet, but let me close that drawer for a moment, and open the one on the left."

I did so, and Domingo shifted his chair around to view the array of teleidoscopes.

"Similar, but not the same," he said. "What's this? One is missing."

I'd put back the teleidoscope with which I'd been playing earlier that day, and now the drawer looked pretty much as it had when I'd first opened it.

"That's right," I said. "One is missing, and what I saw in Colette's hand in my vision looked remarkably like the missing piece."

Domingo nodded, "So, you think that what Colette was holding in the vision was a kaleidoscope?"

"A teleidoscope, actually," I said. "Take a look through this one, and you'll immediately see what I mean."

Domingo did so, holding the end toward the light and exclaiming in delight.

"Wonderful!" he said. "That is amazing. The lamp shade, the wallpaper, even a bit of the rug."

He moved the teleidoscope, casting the end here and there, chuckling almost involuntarily at the array of images. When he lowered it, he was smiling.

"The kaleidoscope, that was lovely, but this is a marvel. The whole world becomes a picture—a bit art deco in style, perhaps, through this one, but marvelous."

"I like it, too," I said. "I've had that one in my room and have been viewing the room through it. Try the carpet. The pattern broken into patterns is really something else."

Domingo did so, then tried a few other things. When he caught Colette's portrait in the lens at the end, he lowered the teleidoscope and studied the portrait instead.

"But why would she take a teleidoscope with her on a carriage ride? Was she going to wait for someone and wanted something with which to amuse herself?"

"In my vision, I saw her driving the gig and looking through the teleidoscope," I said. "Now that I think about it, she reminded me of a sea captain looking through a telescope."

Domingo was neither slow nor stupid. "This is related to what you were telling me about liminal space, isn't it? The teleidoscopes take our normal world and shape it into patterns. You think she had some way of using those patterns to find something?"

"That's it," I said. "Mother had a thing about mirrors."

"Really?" Domingo said, looking around the room. "I would never have guessed this."

I stuck my tongue out at him and continued shaping my thought. "Mirrors are integral to how both kaleidoscopes and teleidoscopes work. I think it's all related somehow. I don't know exactly how, but I thought I might experiment."

"Experiment with the teleidoscopes, using them to locate liminal space, see what visions they bring?"

"Exactly. Would you be willing to stand by?" I said. "Last time I had a vision I nearly fell off a ladder. I don't think anything like that is going to happen here, but I want to be careful."

"I will stand by," Domingo said. "Only, if it is at all possible, can you speak aloud what you see? I understand this may be too distracting, but I would like to know."

I shrugged. "I can only try. If it's too distracting, I'll tell you."

"Fair," Domingo said, leaning back in his chair and extending the teleidoscope to me. "Whenever you're ready."

I took the teleidoscope and tried to get comfortable in the vanity's delicate little chair. It took a little shifting, but I managed. Then I held the teleidoscope to one eye and closed the other. Not wanting to complicate this with images of Colette, I focused instead on the carpet. The patterns were lovely, but I didn't see anything unusual. Belatedly, I realized I'd forgotten my promise to Domingo and started talking.

"You're right about the patterns being almost art deco. I wonder if any of those designers actually used teleidoscopes for inspiration. I think I've read about their doing that."

I found that speaking aloud actually helped me to concentrate. It kept me focused on what I was doing, rather than letting my mind wander through possibilities. I went on.

"The carpet doesn't seem to have anything hidden in it, so I'm shifting to the wall. Amazing the variations available in even an apparently monotone scheme. The least bit of color gets picked up and becomes the focal point for the design. Interesting.

"Trying the closet door. Amazing. The natural irregularities in the wood makes it look like a parquet pattern. That hint of gold from the bedspread becomes an intersticial note."

Domingo's voice spoke, so close that I jumped. "Do you see anything different. Anything you can't account for?"

I moved the teleidoscope around, occasionally checking to make sure my memory of what was there and what was not was correct. Things were distorted, sometimes almost beyond recognition, but I never found anything I couldn't find the original for somewhere in the room.

"Try another teleidoscope," Domingo suggested, "one you haven't looked through for a while."

I agreed readily, lifting one from the end of the row that I was pretty sure I hadn't looked through since my initial day of discovery. Except for the patterns being varied from the one I had been using—this one seemed to be a four mirror design—I found nothing new.

Even when I fell quiet and tried to let my mind slip into the cracks between the areas of the mandala figures, I didn't see anything unusual. Nor did I see anything other than the expected mandala patterns when I tried several others. Eventually, my head began to ache a little, and I set the teleidoscope aside.

"Maybe you didn't see anything unusual," Domingo suggested, "because there was nothing unusual to see. Remember, Colette took the teleidoscope away from Phineas House to use it—and you don't remember her roaming around the House peering through one, do you?"

I giggled at the idea, and some of my headache eased. *Tension*, I thought. *I'm trying too hard.*

"No. You're right. She didn't, at least that I remember. Of course, there was a lot of time she spent away from me."

"Still," Domingo persisted. "That the teleidoscopes would have been most useful away from the House makes sense in a way. You told me that you think both the teleidoscopes and the kaleidoscopes are in some way related to Colette's obsession with mirrors, right?"

"Right." I set the teleidoscope down and tried to join into Domingo's reasoning, finding enthusiasm as I did so. "And from what I can tell—at least in folklore—images in mirrors, other types of reflections, and shadows are all treated similarly—as versions of reality, tantalizing because they are alike yet not alike."

"Good," Domingo said. "Now, this liminal space, it exists between, right?"

"Right."

"Between anything?"

I nodded. "It's the 'between' in and of itself that's important. It can be a matter of spirit—like the state of an initiate between childhood and adulthood, but it can be physical, too. Thresholds are liminal. Windowsills are. Ladders, too. Certain types of terrain. I think mirrors create liminal space almost automatically. I keep think of *Alice Through the Looking Glass*, where the looking glass was a door to Wonderland."

"So," Domingo said eagerly. "Colette filled this house with mirrors—can we assume this was her doing?"

"Why not?" I agreed. "I should look to find some old photos for confirmation, but it makes sense."

"Colette filled the House with mirrors, creating perhaps, a great deal of liminal space, but when she went away from Phineas House she could not do this, so she used the teleidoscope."

"Possible," I said, "but I don't think that could be all of it. There's something else about mirrors, a trait they don't share with shadows."

"Oh?"

"Mirrors are associated with divination, with scrying ... With fortunetelling ..."

"Mirror, mirror on the wall," Domingo chanted.

"Exactly my first thought," I agreed. "But when you start looking in folklore compendiums, it's amazing how many types of fortunetelling or clairvoyance rely on reflections. Pools of water are really popular, but so are polished shields, bowls of blood, or oil."

I pointed to the righthand drawer again. "See that line of kaleidoscopes, where each one has a different planetary symbol on the case? I did some checking and, although I can't be sure without taking them apart, I think they're weird versions of the seven fortunetelling mirrors mentioned in cabalistic magic."

Domingo looking interested, but he shook himself away from temptation. "You must tell me more, maybe quite soon, but for now I will take your word on this. So you think that Colette was using the mirrors for divination rather than something to do with liminal space?"

"I think," I said, shaping my thought as I spoke, "that she was doing both. Have you ever really thought about Phineas House?"

"All the time," Domingo said simply. "Until recently, when I had a new distraction."

*Was he flirting with me*? As with cabalistic magic, I didn't think this was the time to explore that matter.

"Well, I think that Phineas House is somehow designed to exploit properties of liminal space. Think about it. It's got rooms going off at odd angles, thresholds all over the place, windows galore. Moreover, think about where it's built. Las Vegas, New Mexico, is set in liminal space itself. It's where the mountains meet the plains. It has had, for heaven's sake, two separate governments within a few miles of each other. It has two major languages: Spanish and English. Two populations that won't blend. It has a madhouse: sanity and insanity. There's got to be more, but I can't believe it's coincidence. From what Paula Angel said to me, my ancestors had a reputation as sorcerers. I think they chose this place because it was conducive to whatever form of magic it is that they do."

"Interesting," Domingo said. "There are other dualities you haven't mentioned. One is greatly related to another thing you have mentioned ... water. Las Vegas has a very confused relationship with water—even for the American Southwest, which is notoriously confused."

"Child of a rainless year," I said aloud.

"What?"

"Never mind. I'll tell you in a moment. Tell me about Las Vegas and water."

"Drought and flood," he said simply. "We have had both, and not after the fashion of dry spells and flash floods, but of crippling droughts and destructive floods. But it goes beyond this—just in case you think I exaggerate. Can you believe that Las Vegas once tried to establish a water carnival?"

"Here? Where rainfall is so unpredictable?"

"Here," Domingo affirmed. "I told you a little about the Hermit of Hermit Peak when we were driving. Did I mention that one of his miracles was that he was said to have created a spring?"

I shook my head. "Then there are the hot springs, too. So much in this area has been done because of those springs being here."

Domingo nodded. "They are a duality in themselves—natural water is usually cold. This is hot, bringing the core of the earth to the surface. Would you be surprised to learn that not far from the hot springs is a pond where ice was once harvested?"

"I see what you mean," I agreed, rubbing my temples. "Dualities with water."

"Now, what was that you said about 'child of a rainless year'?"

"It was something my mother used to say," I replied. "She claimed there was no rain the year she carried me, the year I was born. Sometimes she called me that—child of a rainless year. It was as if she was proud of it, but she never told me why."

"Very strange," Domingo agreed. He looked as if he was about to say something, then he looked more closely at me. "Mira, you look very, very tired. I think all of this—not to mention the adrenaline rush from nearly falling off a ladder—has worn you out. Are we done with your experiment?"

"For tonight, I think so," I said, realizing he was right. I felt nearly too tired to reassemble the secret compartments. I did anyhow. I felt safer when I did.

I walked Domingo downstairs, even though what I really wanted was to tell him to see himself out so I could collapse into bed. As we walked through the kitchen, the coffeepot had been washed, the crumbs from dessert wiped away. The kitchen was spotless.

Domingo looked right to left, taking it all in. His gaze when his eyes met mine held wonder and just the tiniest bit of healthy fear.

"Silent women," he said. "I see. Good night, Mira. Sleep well."

"Good night, Domingo. Thanks for everything."

He paused, and for a moment I thought he was going to kiss me, but he must have decided a gentleman did not take liberties on an overwrought and exhausted woman. Or maybe it was my imagination.

Instead, he gave me a little bow of his head, whistled for Blanco, and strolled off into the late-summer darkness.

## 20

Color is emptiness, emptiness is color. Color is not
emptiness, emptiness is not color.
—Sarah Rossbach and Lin Yun,
*Living Color*

### INSIDE THE LINES

The next morning over breakfast, I tried to apologize.

"I'm sorry I flaked out on you," I said. "It wasn't until I was turning out the light that I realized it was only nine-thirty."

"You needed to rest, Mira," Domingo said. "I think these things take more out of you than you realize—or maybe than you admit. Perhaps you should take a day or two to rest. Go to Albuquerque and visit your friend Hannah, maybe."

"Trying to get rid of me?" I teased. "Maybe so I won't be here to smear buckets of paint down the sides of the House? Seems to me that I managed to set us back from whatever progress having the crew work Saturday might have managed."

This morning, even with the quick clean-up the crew had done, it did look as if some gigantic bird had tried to shit down the side of Phineas House.

Domingo shook his head. "Never, Mira. If you wish to play pigeon on your own house, who am I to complain?"

"You're sweet," I said. "In all honesty, I want to kick myself around the block. Why shouldn't you? But, Domingo, I don't want to go anywhere. I have a sense of urgency. Maybe it's the fact that the monsoons never came and now it looks like that little bit of rain we had was just a taunt."

"Child of a rainless year? Mira, you aren't responsible. The southwest always has periods of drought. Ask any archeologist. And it rained when you were a child. I know I'd remember if nine years passed without rain."

"Still," I said stubbornly. "It's a feeling, and except for a few words from a ghost and Aunt May's journals, feelings are about all I have to go on. I don't want to leave."

"Then don't." Domingo sipped his coffee, staring out over the roses. "Do you plan to look at those kaleidoscopes again?"

"I've been thinking about it."

"May I be with you when you do? I think it would be a good idea if you had someone with you. I've been thinking about stories I've heard about crystal balls and magic mirrors. They aren't always safe. The more I think about them, the basic teleidoscope reminds me of some sort of weird crystal ball."

"You've watched too many horror movies," I said, trying to be brave. "But, well, why not? Last night's bull session really helped me put things together."

"Maybe not in the right order," Domingo agreed, "but certainly we made a pattern from what we had. It may not be all the right pattern. We may be missing a key piece, but still, there is something."

"Then this evening shall we look at the kaleidoscopes?"

"This evening or sooner," Domingo said. "You forget. Today is Sunday. No painting today."

"I had forgotten," I said. "That's what not having a job does to you. Makes you lose track of the days of the week. What are you doing here? We don't usually have coffee on weekends."

Domingo grinned. "I saw you when you went to bed, Mira. I thought you might forget, and decided to take my chance."

"For a free cup of coffee," I pretended to grouse. Hoping he'd say more. He only smiled.

"Have it your way then. I wanted to see what kind of coffee spirit women make. Did they make this?"

I stared at the cup in my hand. "You know, I think they did! I was too tired to set up the coffee last night, and this morning I turned on the machine without thinking. This is a first."

"They anticipate your needs," Domingo said. "Or maybe they didn't want you to break the carafe by turning the heat on under it while it was empty. You did say they were House proud."

"I did." I stared at my coffee cup, then decided to finish the contents. It was at least as good as what I made, probably better.

"I don't think I'm quite ready to deal with the kaleidoscopes right now," I admitted. "Why don't we do something dull? Walk around the yard. You can tell me what you're planning for the State Fair."

"That might be a good idea," Domingo said.

He cocked his head to one side, birdlike, listening. I listened too, and realized that I could hear cars on our quiet dead-end street.

"Your friend Chilton's article is bringing visitors," Domingo said. "It must be a slow day for news. Phineas House is featured in a little box on the front page, and then the full article is inside. We should put a sign on the gate, I think, or you will be running to the door all day."

I lettered two polite notes, one in English, one in Spanish, on a couple pieces of poster board. They stated that this was indeed Phineas House, that it was a private house, and there were no tours. People were invited to take pictures from outside of the fence, and have a nice day. Domingo hung them on the fence.

This stopped most of the potential visitors, but it was amazing how many still came in and knocked at the door. Finally, Domingo chained the gate shut, and, as the fence was waist-high, that stopped the visitors. The flow tapered off by late afternoon. Domingo's sister, Evelina called to say she'd seen the article, and wasn't that exciting, and did her brother and I want to come over for dinner?

We did, leaving Blanco to protect the yard from intruders. Later, when we were on our way home, I turned to Domingo.

"I think I'm ready now. I think I can handle looking at the kaleidoscopes."

"*Bueno*," he said, and his foot got heavy on the gas peddle. "I'm with you."

We went upstairs to Colette's room side by side on the front staircase where—just possibly—my grandfather had been pushed to his death by his own daughter, or worse, by a house his daughter controlled.

I tried hard not to think about this aspect of Phineas House. I was coming to love the place. In the months that had passed it was subtly becoming *mine*, not Colette's, and I didn't want to consider what the House might have done under my mother's rule.

*It's a little like having a boyfriend you knew had a steady or ex-wife he was crazy about and wondering what he did with her. The whole situation just feels twisted.*

I gave Domingo a sidelong look, remembering how I'd thought his relationship with the House was a little like a love affair.

*So, great,* I thought. *You have a thing for a guy—admit it, Mira, you do—you have a thing for a guy who you think might have a thing for your house. You can't help wondering, "Is he doing this because he's my friend or because I'm Phineas House's owner?" If he is flirting with me—and a couple of times I've been almost sure he was—then is he flirting with me because I'm me or because I'm a single, middle-aged woman who happens to own the House he's crazy about, and if he hooks me, he'll finally be a co-owner. Is New Mexico a community-property state? I bet it is. Well, before I sign any marriage certificate, I'll want a pre-nup making sure Domingo can't take Phineas House if we split.*

I was unlocking the door to Colette's room as these thoughts spilled through my head, and I wondered if she had ever had similar thoughts. In her time it was even harder for a woman to keep property—kids, she could have, but the valuable stuff, well, the courts seemed to figure a man was better at handling money and stocks and all that. Maybe that was why Colette had so many lovers. She wouldn't let anyone get their hooks into her—into the House.

*So who was my father, then? A one-night stand somewhere? Somehow, I just don't think so. Colette was too calculating for that. If I'm sure of anything, I'm sure she knew precisely who my father was.*

I walked across the room and started taking things out of the right-hand drawer where the kaleidoscopes were stored. Domingo reached to help me, and I snapped at him.

"I've got it."

"Sorry," he said, settling back in his chair.

"Sorry," I echoed. "This is making me nervous. I should feel, I don't know, foolish but excited, like a teenager trying out a Ouija board, but what I feel is tense."

"The difference is, Mira," Domingo said, "that the teenager doesn't really believe in the Ouija board. She hopes it will do something, but she doesn't really believe. If the arrows point to something that makes sense, then she gets more excited, because now she has a reason to continue with the game, not because she really believes."

"You sound like you know. Was Evelina interested in the occult?"

Domingo grinned and spread his hands in a self-deprecating gesture. "I could have said 'he' as easily as 'she.' Boys as well as girls play with such things."

"I never tried a Ouija board," I said. "No one I knew had one, but my mother—that is my Aunt May—and I bought some Tarot cards and tried them. Aunt May was interested in the occult, and I loved the brightly colored pictures on the cards. I considered collecting them for a while, but then I realized just how many different decks there were and, well, that they were all run off on printing presses somewhere. I think for something to be really magical, it would need to be handmade."

"Like these," Domingo said, gesturing toward the rows of kaleidoscopes I had just revealed. "Each of these is handmade, each a little love affair between the artist and beauty."

I looked at the kaleidoscopes, then at Domingo, wondering how I could ever have thought him a crude opportunist.

*This house is full of ghosts, Mira,* I said to myself. *Maybe the lines between your thoughts and Colette's long ago crossed as you stood on the threshold to her room.*

I suppressed a shiver at the thought, and reached into the drawer, picking up the first kaleidoscope my hand fell upon. The dominant colors on this one's casing were rose and crystal, accented by the silver solder used to hold the pieces of stained glass together. The object case was one of those external wheels you turn, this one a separate masterwork in stained glass. Cut crystals, teardrops of translucent glass in rose and pearl, and shards of glass had been delicately fitted together, the lines of solder spiderweb delicate, and spiderweb strong.

"I don't think I've looked through this one," I said. "I prefer the ones where the items in the object case are either loose or suspended in liquid. These color wheels are nice, but too predictable after a while."

"But the first time," Domingo said practically, "and the second and the third, even, they are not predictable at all. Moreover, these are perhaps the loveliest of all kaleidoscopes when not in use."

"Good point," I agreed, lifting the kaleidoscope to my eye and peering through the eyepiece. "And this one is truly lovely."

I spent a moment *ooh*ing and *ahh*ing at the varied images, handing the kaleidoscope to Domingo so he could share those I thought best. He in turn shifted the wheel and shared his favorites with me. I noticed he liked those where the darker pinks dominated, where I leaned toward lacework fantasies where the crystal fluted against the pinks and made the pinks—at least to my eye—more vivid by contrast.

"This is fun," I said after a bit, "but what should I try next, do you think? Another kaleidoscope?"

"Stay with this one," Domingo urged. "Relax and study. Talk to me as you did last night, if that will help. Otherwise, I will sit here and let you forget I am here."

As *if I could*, I thought, but aloud all I said was, "Sounds as good a plan as any I have, and better than most."

I raised the kaleidoscope again, then lowered it immediately.

"Maybe we should take one of the teleidoscopes down to the Plaza and see if we see Paula Angel. Maybe the teleidoscopes would help me show her to you. I've been worrying you think I'm crazy."

"It gets dark earlier now, Mira," Domingo said practically. "By the time we made it to the Plaza, it would not be good kaleidoscope light—and anyone walking by would think us both crazy, staring through kaleidoscopes in the twilight. I think you're nervous again. Would you rather wait until another day? Have me go home and let you rest."

"No and no," I said. "I don't want to wait—if I do it's going to hang over my head—and I don't want you to go. You're right. I'm nervous, but I'll give it a shot."

I raised the kaleidoscope again and focused very carefully. When I was comfortable, I started turning the color wheel at the end, small turns that changed the image by only the smallest amount. I didn't know what I was looking for, but I thought this was the best way to be sure I found it.

After one full rotation and then another I lowered the kaleidoscope and frowned at it, turning it front to back so I could study the stained-glass wheel at the end. Then, very carefully, I gave it a gentle shake, holding the barrel close to my ear.

"Something wrong, Mira?" Domingo asked.

"Maybe," I said. "Or something right. I've spotted something that doesn't fit."

"Doesn't fit?"

"A singularity in a world of multiplicity." Domingo made an encouraging noise, so I went on. "What I mean is every image in a kaleidoscope is multiplied by the mirrors. Even near the center where it can look like there is a single image, what you're seeing is several images overlapping so closely that they look like a single entity."

"Go on."

"But there's a single image—a white rectangle—that I have glimpsed a few times. I just looked at the object case here, and there's nothing on it that shape. I suppose there could be something loose in the barrel, but I didn't hear anything, and both ends of the barrel are sealed as they should be."

"Try again," Domingo urged. "Focus on that white rectangle. Is there anything else about it you can notice?"

I did as he requested, talking out loud as I looked through the eyepiece. "It's not there. No, wait. There it is. It's off to the right, middle of the panel—and there's nothing to match it anywhere else."

"A rectangle," I heard Domingo say. "Like a door?"

"No, not quite, proportions aren't right. More like a standard sheet of paper, eight and a half by eleven."

"Any writing on it?" I heard the laughter in Domingo's voice and knew he was making a joke.

"Actually," I said, "there's something."

I focused in, doing my best to eliminate the confusion of colors around the white rectangle. Either the white rectangle was getting larger, or my vision was getting better, because I was now certain that there was something written on the white. I felt myself focusing as I'd learned to do once I realized that nothing is just one color—that a lawn is made up of numerous shades of green and yellow and brown all intermingled to different degrees; that a newspaper cartoon varies in shade depending not only on the inks, but on the paper; that a computer image is made up of minute dots.

My mind fastened on the degrees of difference in a fashion that had nothing to do with the quality of my eyesight, and I realized that what I was seeing were handwritten words, blue ink against white paper. They said: "Mira, Since you can see this you need to call me. I strongly suggest you do so before you involve yourself further in matters whose consequences you do not fully comprehend." Then came a phone number with an area code I didn't recognize. "Please call me." The note was signed, "Michael Hart."

I stared at the note, mechanically reciting the phone number over and over again until I was sure I had it fixed in my memory, then I lowered the kaleidoscope. Domingo, pen in hand, was staring at me. The phone number—no hyphens, just a sequence of ten numbers, was written on a scrap of paper he had balanced on his knee.

"You want to tell me why you kept repeating this number?" Domingo said with that deceptive mildness some men use rather than shouting.

My head swam and I put the kaleidoscope down with very deliberate care. I felt wrung out, or tottery drunk, or like I was recovering from a high fever. Nothing seemed real but the colored patterns of rose and crystal still dancing against my memory.

"The white rectangle," I said, "was a note. A note from Michael Hart. He was one of my trustees when I first went to live with the Fenns. He said to call him."

"And this is his phone number?" Domingo asked, fluttering the piece of paper.

I nodded. Exhaustion was now blending with nausea. I didn't know whether I wanted to sleep or vomit. One thing I knew. I couldn't stay sitting upright one moment longer. I toppled to the side in the delicate vanity chair, wondering idly if I would hit the open drawer and break it.

Domingo reached to stay my fall—but it was the silent women who caught me. Two of them, dressed in housekeeping dresses from another era, their long hair pulled up and back, tucked under little caps. Their hands were firm and strong, and at their touch I remembered being dressed by them, being tucked into bed by them, even little pats on my head.

They bore me up and off. I don't think I broke anything.

I awoke the next morning to the sunlight streaming in my bedroom windows. Birds were singing. I closed my eyes and listened to the birds for a while, until the scent of coffee brought me fully awake.

I opened my eyes, half-expecting to see a cup of coffee waiting for me on a tray borne hence by invisible hands. What I saw was Domingo. He was sitting in a chair he'd pulled up alongside the bed, a mug of coffee steaming between his cupped hands, a worried expression on his face.

I smiled at him, and at his answering smile remembered what—or more appropriately, what not—I usually wore to bed. My hands flew to make sure the covers were pulled up for modesty's sake, and Domingo chuckled.

"You are decent, as the saying goes. Even more, sitting here on the bed-side table is a very nice piece of clothing, what I believe is called a bed-jacket. Would you like me to hand it to you? I don't see how you can have any coffee with the blanket pulled to your chin."

"Thank you," I replied with what dignity I could manage. "I'll take the bed-jacket, and ask you to turn your back."

"Even better," Domingo said. "I will turn my back, *and* close my eyes. Like elsewhere in this house, this room has many mirrors. Please applaud me for being a perfect gentleman."

"I will," I promised, accepting both the proffered item of clothing and his offer of courtesy. The latter thrilled me. You don't make a big deal about keeping your eyes to yourself if you haven't thought otherwise, do you?

The bed-jacket certainly wasn't anything I had brought with me, nor did it have the lavender and cedar scent of something stored away. The colors, a delicate violet floral print against the palest of blues, were flattering to my coloring. I had a mental image of the silent women who had sewn for my mother. Had they run this up last night while I slept? I was beyond refusing to consider the possibility.

Then again, they might have found it in a trunk in the attic and washed it. They might even have run the new machines. I could imagine their delight. I'd bought good ones.

"You may open your eyes and turn around," I said when I had myself suitably attired and propped up against a couple of pillows. "And you said something about coffee . . ."

Domingo bowed over his hand, then poured me a cup from the carafe waiting on one of the highboys.

"Good," I said. "Thank you. Thank you for the coffee and for your gentlemanly courtesy. May I ask what happened last night?"

"What do you remember?" he asked, his expression keen.

"I remember a letter from Mr. Hart telling me to call and giving a phone number. I remember being very tired and dizzy. Then I think I fainted. I felt hands catch me, but they weren't yours. They belonged to the silent women."

"So they did," Domingo agreed.

His voice, which could talk about the needs and desires of the House without sounding anything other than matter-of-fact, was alive with wonder now.

"They caught you, keeping you from crashing into the drawer full of kaleidoscopes—which would have been very bad for both you and for the kaleidoscopes. I might have caught you, but not without being much more clumsy. I offered to pick you up, and they accepted my offer with great politeness, directing me to carry you across the landing to your room. Once I had you on the bed, they ushered me out with tremendous officiousness, telling me that they could get you ready for bed, that they had done so often enough before. Then one showed me out, and told me I might call again in the morning. When I came by this morning, the kitchen door was open, but no one was around. I did, however, find the coffee things laid ready, and knew you well enough to take a hint."

I blinked at this speech, then shook my head in wonder.

" 'They,' you say. How many were there?"

"Two. Both ladies of uncertain age and race. They could have been taken for Hispanic or Anglo—although probably not for Indians, and certainly not for Negroes. They were dressed in long skirts, but moved in them as easily or practically as you do in jeans."

"And certainly more gracefully," I said ruefully. "Long skirts worn right do cover a multitude of sins. Modern girls make the mistake of walking in a skirt as if they are still wearing jeans and end up looking terrible."

"You," Domingo said, "never make that mistake."

"Well," I replied, pleased at the compliment, "I did grow up Colette's daughter. Poor Aunt May had to wean me of my taste for finery, and never did quite succeed."

"I'm glad," Domingo said. "I like seeing you dressed up."

He cleared his throat, suddenly, probably aware that he was flirting, if ever so delicately, with a woman wearing nothing but a bed-jacket.

"Tell me, Mira, are you going to do what that note said? Are you going to call Michael Hart?"

"I am," I replied with more firmness than I felt. "But first I want a shower and breakfast. Would you like to come back in about forty minutes and join me for something to eat?"

Domingo rose. "Unless you think you might need help in your ablutions. I would be happy to offer a steady arm to lean upon."

I smiled, but now that I felt certain of his interest, I had no desire to go at this ass-backward, and somehow I thought that, masculine male or not, neither, really, did Domingo.

"Come back for breakfast," I said. "I think we both have had ample proof that for some reason this House doesn't want me to fall."

Thirty-five minutes later I was in the kitchen. The silent women might have manifested last night more vigorously than ever before, but they hadn't yet stepped into the routine servant roles they had held during my mother's tenure. I found the kitchen clean, and the coffeepot washed and waiting in the dish rack, but no bacon sizzling or waffles emitting fragrant steam from the big, chrome-plated waffle iron I'd found in one of the cabinets.

I could make do, though, with what I had, and by the time Domingo arrived I was mixing up a batch of waffle batter, and bacon was defrosting in the microwave.

"Anything I can do?" he asked.

"I'd like more coffee," I said, "but it had better be decaf this time. That okay with you?"

"Just so. My nerves are dancing enough already, I think."

"Great. I'm making waffles. I found a waffle iron a couple weeks ago, and tested it. Seemed to still work, but if it doesn't I suppose we can have pancakes from the same batter."

"Wonderful," Domingo said, raising his voice to be heard over the coffee grinder. "And Blanco is certain that he smells bacon."

"He does indeed. We could cook it right in the microwave, but it never seems to taste quite right when you do it that way, not crisp enough. I thought I'd get a skillet going as soon as the waffles were started."

"Let me," Domingo said. "Tell me where to find a frying pan."

I did, and Domingo handled the bacon while I located syrup and butter, and set the table. The waffle iron worked as if it had been waiting for just this chance to show more modern appliances what they lacked, and I felt the last of my flagging energy restored as I devoured a couple of the rich, buttery squares. As I ate, I realized what had been missing in the morning sounds.

"Where's the painting crew?"

"I told them I had an emergency job for them else where. I thought you might need some privacy."

"Thanks. Did you have a job?"

"I found one."

I nodded. Unsure how to interpret this coddling, I changed the subject.

"I looked up Mr. Hart's area code in the directory," I said. "He lives in Minnesota—or at least he's taking phone calls there these days."

"When are you going to call him?"

"Right after breakfast, before I have a chance to think about all the reasons I shouldn't call."

"Good. Eat more. You're looking much better. When I came up to your room this morning, you looked so pale. I knew your skin was fair, but I never realized how translucent. It is amazing you haven't sunburned to a crisp."

"Aunt May taught me about good skin care right from the start," I said. "I think I've been first in line for each new generation of moisturizers and sun blocks."

"Wise," Domingo said. "I admired your skin from the first. I also like that you do not wear too many cosmetics, but are still interested in your appearance. Too many women, they go to one extreme or the other. Either they say 'no makeup,' and that means no anything else and dressing like slobs. The other way, I think they don't even know what their own faces look like."

"I know," I said. "It's such a part of female culture. 'Putting on my face,' like the one you were born with isn't good enough for public show. I want to scream and rant whenever I hear that song that starts with something about waking up and putting on makeup, like that's what she has to do to start her day. I don't mind when cosmetics are adornment. Then it's kind of wonderful, like the spread of a peacock's tail, but when it becomes disguise . . ."

I shivered, remembering, and my stomach twisted so that I pushed my plate away from me.

"Tell me about it," Domingo said. "This is more than feminist revolt against the patriarchal system."

I looked at him, arching my brows in surprise at his familiarity with the jargon.

"I have sisters," he said. "You've met Evelina. Then there's Sabrina, who you haven't met yet. She was quite a hell-raiser. Marched in protests, the whole thing. The bra-burning really upset my mother, especially since, well, Sabrina needs a bra."

I laughed. "It's funny how something that started out as a useful tool became a symbol of restriction, but let me tell you, some of those earlier garments were cages. My mother—Colette—had me wearing corsets before I had anything to corset. I'd forgotten that until just now. Girdles weren't much better. It's all part of the same thing. Somehow a man can be a man, grey hair, beer belly, lines all over his face, and that's just getting 'distinguished.' In a woman it's 'letting herself go.' Pisses me off."

"I can see why," Domingo said, "maybe more so now that the same impossibilities are being applied to men. Big muscles." He crooked an arm I knew was very strong, but no Popeye lump bulged forth. "Bad attitude, but, when needed, sensitivity and artistic sense."

Domingo gave an exasperated snort, then went on. "We have severe gang problems here in Las Vegas. Gangs create a whole other set of expectations, especially for the boys. One reason I like to keep my nephew Enrico around is I want him to see that there are choices. His father is a college man, a lawyer, member of the state legislature from time to time. If Enrico rebels against following his father's example, then he can see that there is no shame to working with your hands. But I still worry about the drugs— and the money that comes with drugs. My family is comfortable, but not rich. Evelina and her husband need to say 'no' very often."

It was my turn to slide a hand across the table, and I did this now. I won't deny it. My fingers tingled at the contact, the way they should when you've crossed a divide, but I felt more pleasure at how automatically Domingo's fingers wrapped around mine, accepting the comfort.

"I've taught for years," I said, "and there are versions of the same problems in Ohio. The town where I grew up is more prosperous than Las Vegas, though certainly not rich. Young people must contrast realistic expectations versus the dreams the media feeds a hundred different ways every day. Domingo, in some ways, we had it easier."

"I think so," he agreed, and as he said it, I remembered that he'd worked beside his father when he was a boy. "But I have distracted you with my stories of Sabrina. You were going to tell me why you are so . . . heightened . . . when you consider using cosmetics."

"It's just something I saw when I was small," I said, almost apologetically. "You know Colette was a great belle. One day I sneaked into her room when she was making up. I think it might have been the first time I'd ever seen her without any cosmetics on, and, well, it frightened me to see her 'real' face. She was much paler than you'd believe, and every feature was carefully constructed from the foundation up. Even her hair was colored that beautiful shining black. I suspect that without the dye it was as drab as mine."

Domingo didn't try to pretend that my not-blond, not-brown, not-really anything colored hair was anything else than what it was, and I liked him for it.

"And this frightened you?"

"It did. I remember thinking that she was using magic, that the colors were more than mere cosmetics, they were a transformation."

"Did it ever occur to you that maybe they were?" Domingo said. "I don't mean then, I mean now, now that you know so much more."

I blinked at him. "I don't understand."

"You know this house is not just a structure. You have spoken with ghosts. You are waited on by spirits. Your ancestors were thought to be witches. From there, the idea that maybe your mother worked some sort of transformation in front of her mirror does not seem impossible to me."

"It's just a kid's memory," I protested.

Domingo shrugged. "Maybe so, but one that has literally colored—or uncolored—your life, and Mira, you are very sensitive to color."

"I guess," I said, unconvinced, or, more honestly, unwilling to be convinced. There is only so much weirdness one can take all at once. Here Domingo was asking me to make yet another great mental leap.

Again I remembered the image of a couple of teenagers playing with a Ouija board. I wondered if, for all my certainly the night before that it wasn't so, maybe that's exactly what Domingo and I were, except instead of being teenagers we were two middle-aged, never married people, focusing on anything at all to avoid facing our attraction to each other—and the fact that for all that both of us had our past attractions, none of them had ever gone anywhere. Or at least not as far as love and marriage, a house and a couple of kids.

I took one more look at my now cold breakfast, decided I couldn't face it, and pushed back my chair.

"I'm going to call Mr. Hart," I said. "You can listen to my side if you want."

"How about I clean up the kitchen?" Domingo said. "I think you deserve some privacy."

So I went off into the library, picked up the extension, and hardly believing what I was doing, dialed—the phone was old enough to have an actual dial—a number I had copied from a vision in a kaleidoscope.

I more than half-expected to get one of those annoying noises phones make to punish you for dialing a number that isn't in use. The other half of me expected to be told I'd dialed a wrong number, so when I said, "May I speak to Michael Hart?" and the voice at the other end said, "This is Michael Hart," a long moment went by before I could say anything.

"This is Mira, Mira Fenn."

"Mira Fenn!" A small pause, then Mr. Hart said, "So, you got my number."

I realized he was hedging, waiting to see if I'd gotten his number in some other way. I could have, I realized. It might even be on some of Colette's paperwork, or maybe he was registered with some trustees' organization or the like. For a moment, I considered saying something like "That's right. I got your number from the Internet." Then I remembered drinking beer with a ghost in a tavern that quite probably didn't exist, of being caught by the hands of women who also might not really exist, and I knew once again that the time to run away back to the mirage that most people called reality was over.

"Yes. I was looking through one of Colette's kaleidoscopes."

I stopped there. Mr. Hart was going to have to give me more than he had given Maybelle Fenn when I was a girl.

"I see," he said after a long pause. "You were doing more than just looking—you were seeing. So, you're at Phineas House?"

"That's right. I've been here all summer. My parents—the Fenns—were killed in a car crash earlier this spring. I've taken a leave of absence from my job while I set several matters straight."

"I'm sorry about the Fenns," Mr. Hart said, and he sounded as if he genuinely did. "I always liked them."

"I am, too," I said. "You trustees did well by me when you set me up with them, but I think it's time I learned more about what happened when my mother disappeared. You know, don't you?"

"Not precisely. I have suspicions, yes. But I don't know."

"And how much of your suspicions are you willing to share with me?"

He answered with a question of his own. "Are you planning to keep Phineas House?"

"Possibly. Probably, even. I like it. I've had it painted. You won't recognize it when you see it."

"Oh." A long silence, long enough that I was fretting that I'd called him long distance, then Mr. Hart said, "I think we need to speak in person. I will need to see what arrangements I can make. Are you willing to wait on your, uh, explorations until we talk?"

"It depends on how long you want me to wait."

"No longer than the middle of next week. I will come to you there, in Las Vegas."

"I'd offer to put you up," I said, "but I think until I know you better . . ."

"Certainly."

Oddly, the fact that he didn't try and reassure me that he meant me no harm or tell me that he was an old man now actually did reassure me.

"I'll call you some time tomorrow," Mr. Hart said, "and tell you when to expect me. Please, until then, take care. If you could find my note, you are closer to things that—well, a car is not dangerous if you know how to drive it, but if you do not know, and climb behind the wheel when the engine is running . . . Do you understand me?"

I thought about my exhaustion last night, about nearly falling off the ladder, about other times since my return to Las Vegas when I had felt detached from the world around me, and, oddly, I did understand.

"I think I do," I said. "Not everything, but enough that I can wait until Wednesday."

"Wednesday or before," Mr. Hart assured me. "I will speak with you tomorrow. Thank you for calling me."

"You're welcome," I said, and hung up the phone.

I walked back into the kitchen to find Domingo polishing bacon grease off the stove top.

"Michael Hart is coming here. He'll be here by Wednesday, if not sooner. He asked me not to do any more experimenting until then."

"Did you agree?"

"I did."

"Do you trust him?"

"I don't know." I sat on the edge of my chair, twisting my fingers in and out of each other in a nervous basket weave. "Maybe he asked me to delay so he could set something nasty in motion, but I keep remembering that my mother's trustees were the ones who got her out of the madhouse, that my trustees found me Aunt May and Uncle Stan. I feel like I should at least try a meeting."

"Will you meet Mr. Hart here?"

"I think so," I said. "Whatever Mr. Hart has going for him—and he must have something, or he couldn't have left me that message where I found it—I think that Phineas House is on my side."

"So what now?" Domingo asked.

"I guess we wait," I said. "Mr. Hart said he'd call tomorrow."

"I have a better idea," Domingo said, taking my hand and drawing me up. "It's a beautiful day. Why don't we go for a drive, or maybe a hike. I can show you the trail up Hermit's Peak or something."

I let Domingo draw me up and stood almost within the circle of his arms.

"Let's go, then. Meet you in the garage in ten minutes."

"Why ten minutes?"

"I need to put my hiking boots on," I said.

21

The Hopis have six directional colors which are as follows:

Yellow refers to the North or Northwest.

Blue-green refers to the West or Southwest.

Red refers to the South or Southeast.

White refers to the East or Northeast.

All the above colors taken together refer to the Zenith or up.

Black refers to the Nadir or down.

—Harold S. Colton,
*Hopi Kachina Dolls*

## INSIDE THE LINES

Mr. Hart called late Monday after we were back from hiking and said he would be able to get to Las Vegas by Tuesday afternoon. I offered to drive to Albuquerque and pick him up at the airport—after all, it was a two-hour drive, and while he probably wasn't decrepit, he certainly wasn't young either.

"I have already made arrangements for transportation," he said. "But thank you. Would you like to come to my hotel?"

"If you don't mind, I'd like you to come to Phineas House and see what I've done with it. You say you'll be here in the afternoon. Why not come over when you're recovered from the trip, and we'll talk over dinner?"

"Very well. I'll call you when I get in."

So it was that late on Tuesday afternoon I was keeping myself very busy in the kitchen making preparations for dinner. I'd picked up some chicken and had it marinating, intending to cook it on the grill.

Domingo had oh-so-casually mentioned that he was going to Evelina's house that afternoon to help Enrico finish his project for the fair, and that he'd probably stay for dinner. I was grateful for his tact, since the garden was shared territory between us, but at the same time sorry that my one and only ally wouldn't be near.

To go with the chicken, I was making an elaborate pasta salad. I'd found tricolored twists at the grocery store, and was adding bright red peppers from the garden. They were sweet-hot, not too spicy, I hoped, for a Minneapolis palate. I figured if they worked for my Ohio one, they should for Mr. Hart.

By early evening, the green salad was made, and I'd stirred the pasta salad and put it aside to marinate. I was just coming in from checking the grill when the front doorbell rang. I rinsed my hands, put aside the dish towel I'd been using for an apron, and went to admit Michael Hart.

Michael Hart didn't look anything like I'd imagined. He was in his seventies, fairly short, his mouse-grey hair cut short to demonstrate textbook perfect male-pattern baldness. In comparison to Domingo and his painting crew, who'd made up most of my male companionship of late, Michael Hart was soft and pudgy. His handshake felt like unbaked bread sticks, but the gaze of his pale-blue eyes was direct and penetrating. His body might be soft, but he definitely was not.

"Come in," I said. "Thank you for coming all this way on such short notice."

"You're welcome," Michael Hart responded, stepping over the threshold and looking about the foyer with assessing interest. "I am glad to meet you at last."

"Then we never met?" I asked, taking his tailored windbreaker and hanging it on the mirrored coat-tree.

"We did not," Mr. Hart said. "I was the youngest of your trustees. The most senior member of that particular triumvirate, Renaldo Pincas, was the one who interviewed you. He died many years ago."

"Oh, I'm sorry," I said, rather automatically.

I was trying hard to remember which of the stream of adults who had questioned me after my mother's disappearance Renaldo Pincas might have been. I thought it might have been a very thin older man who had fascinated me not because of the questions he asked, but because of the elaborate network of brown liver spots on the backs of his hands. The fact that his questions had had more to do about me and my needs than with Colette made me think Mr. Spotty, as I had privately named him, had been my trustee, not a police officer. If he had told me so, the word had meant nothing at the time.

Mr. Hart was looking at me with a touch of bemusement, and I realized that my reverie had made me ignore my role as a hostess.

"I have dinner cooking," I said. "Would asking you to come sit with me in the kitchen be too informal?"

"Not at all," Mr. Hart replied with touching gallantry. "The food smells wonderful. Grilling? I thought so. You do your own cooking, then, no servants?"

"No cook," I hedged, not quite ready to bring up the silent women. I had a feeling that Mr. Hart didn't need to be told about them. He probably knew more about them than I did.

As I led the way to the kitchen, it occurred to me that my dinner guest, for all that he looked like an out-of-shape lawyer, was quite likely an accomplished sorcerer.

Once I'd settled Mr. Hart with a tall glass of iced tea garnished with mint from the garden, I went out and turned the chicken I'd already started grilling. Somehow, I'd known Mr. Hart would be on time, and when I came in, I reported that dinner would be ready to go on the table in about ten minutes. Unlike with Domingo, I hadn't felt comfortable with the idea of dining with my trustee informally at my kitchen table, and so had set two places at one end of the formal dining room table.

Needless to say, when I'd gone to wash it, I'd found the crystal and china was already spotless, and the silver polished to a soft, moonlit glow. If I ever gave up Phineas House, I was going to have lifelong nostalgia for the silent women.

Mr. Hart and I chatted about his trip in from Minnesota as I carried the side dishes out to the dining room. I brought the chicken in from the grill last, so we could enjoy it while it was still snapping hot. I was washing the inevitable smudge of grease from one wrist when Mr. Hart commented:

"You are very little like Colette, Ms. Fenn. I think she would be astonished to see what her daughter has come to be."

"No doubt," I said, a trace curtly, picking up the tray of chicken and leading the way into the dining room.

"I didn't mean that as an insult," Mr. Hart said, settling himself into the
indicated chair with the slight fussiness of a robin settling onto the nest.
"Nor did I mean to indicate that Colette would necessarily be disappointed. I think her lack of practical competence frustrated her. It may even
have been why she was so hard on the . . . servants. Employers most often
are when they realize how they need those who, ostensibly, are in their
debt."

"I wonder if the silent women knew that," I said, thinking aloud, as I'd
fallen into the habit since Phineas House seemed to listen.

"The 'silent women'?" Mr. Hart said, a slight chuckle underlying his
voice. It was not mocking in the least, but instead avuncularly amused. "Is
that what you call them?"

"Ever since I was a child, that's how I've thought of them," I said, and, as
if our discussing them granted permission, from the kitchen came the muffled sounds of the remaining mess from cooking being cleared away. "I
knew they talked among themselves, but they barely ever talked to me."

"They feared you, I suspect," Mr. Hart said, serving himself the largest
chicken breast with the air of a man who likes his food, and is certain he
will enjoy what is set before him. "They feared Colette, and since you were
so young, they would have seen you as her extension."

"Not hard to do," I said bitterly, "since that is how she seemed to see me."

If I had hoped Mr. Hart would say something to ameliorate this harsh
image of Colette, I was disappointed.

"Colette was a . . . difficult woman, but she had some reasons for being
so. Mira—may I call you Mira?"

"Please do," I replied.

"And if you would call me Mikey, I would be grateful. I know I am an old
man, now, but 'Mr. Hart' still evokes my father to me, and he was a formidable man."

"But, 'Mikey'?"

Mr. Hart grinned. "Ridiculous, perhaps, but a childhood nickname I
never shed. There were many Michaels in my family—heritage of a dominant patriarch in the person of my grandfather. Later, wherever I went, I
seemed to encounter other Michaels who had taken the more respectable

diminutives, or the dignified Michael. At least, I escaped Mickey, and attendant references to the mouse, a thing for which I am eternally grateful."

I found myself liking my dinner guest more and more. I'd prepared myself for someone rather like Chilton O'Reilly but stuffier, and with no childhood fondness to bridge the gap. I found this affable, doughy man quite amusing, and I was certain he was not putting on an act. The silent women would never have manifested if Phineas House didn't think well of Mikey Hart.

"Mikey it is," I agreed, and sliced into my own chicken with a great deal more appetite than I had anticipated.

"Well, Mira," Mikey said, "as I was about to say before I ran off on that last tangent, I'd prefer to discuss this entire matter in something vaguely like chronological order. I don't mean I won't tell you about your mother if you wish, but so many of the things that shaped her are related to earlier history. Marvelous chicken, by the way, and is the recipe for the pasta salad your own?"

"Thank you. Yes, it is. I can copy it for you if you'd like, though Domingo's garden contributed a great deal to the flavor."

I could see that any conversation with Mikey Hart was often going to run away into tangents. I no longer marvelled at his telling Aunt May about Queens of Mirrors and Mistresses of Thresholds. It now seemed a miracle that he hadn't still been there when Uncle Stan came home for dinner. I decided I'd need to bring us back onto topic, or doubtless Mikey would be asking me was Domingo suitable as a caretaker or where the garden was or even what we were growing in it.

"I've done some research," I said. "I know a lot more about my immediate family history at least. I've even come across the rumors that Colette was responsible for her father's death."

"Did Domingo Navidad tell you that?" Mikey asked.

"No, actually . . ." I trailed off, took a sip of wine to cover my nervousness, and went on, "it was the ghost of Paula Angel."

Mikey's response was nothing I could have anticipated.

"Pablita did always like Colette," he said. "I think she saw her as another rebel against the unfair, male-dominated system."

"And was she?"

"No, Pablita was . . ."

"I don't mean Paula Angel!" I said, not quite shouting, but coming close. "I mean Colette Bogatyr, my mother."

Mikey blinked owlishly with surprise, but as he helped himself to a third piece of chicken, I don't think I had offended him.

"Colette was . . . possibly a rebel, but she was also, quite honestly, less than completely sane and quite probably a parricide."

"But you," I fumbled for the right words, "or rather, her own trustees, they got her out of the insane asylum. Why would they do that if Colette was both insane and dangerous?"

"Because if they didn't, Colette would have left on her own accord. In fact, she had been doing so for years. The trustees merely put her in the position of being able to lay legal claim to Phineas House.

"I'm confused," I said, my elbows on the arms of my chair, my face in my hands.

"Well, it is easier to understand if I start at the beginning," Mikey said without reproof. "It's just that it's such a difficult beginning, and entails explaining things that have nothing to do with Colette—at least not with her personally."

He had finished the third piece of chicken, and though he looked longingly at the pasta salad, seemed prepared to make a valiant effort to resist fourths.

"I have dessert," I said, "and the silent women seem to have anticipated me and turned on the coffee. I made decaf, but I can put on caffeinated if you'd like."

"My doctor says I should cut back on caffeine and rich foods and get more exercise," Mikey replied. "Needless to say, I don't listen. However, your company is sufficiently stimulating that I can do without caffeine."

I smiled at the compliment. "The evening is lovely, and normally I'd suggest we take our dessert outside, but since I have a feeling that what you need to tell me shouldn't be overheard. . . ."

"Yes, that is probably best," Mikey said. "Tell me, is Domingo Navidad still living on the property?"

"In the apartment over the carriage house. He's been a gem. Lately, he's concentrated on getting the exterior paint job done."

"I noticed it," Mikey said, with almost incredible understatement; you'd have to be blind—and possibly deaf—not to notice that paint job.

"I won't ask if you like it," I said, grinning, "because I fear that what we're considering calling the 'Fairground Midway' style is probably an acquired taste."

Mikey rose, nicking one more pasta twist out of the salad. "It is an individual style, and says a great deal about you—more than that you are an art teacher. However, don't ask me what, because that would take us back to telling the story inside out."

"I have some suspicions," I said. "Like I said, I've been doing some research. Why don't we take the coffee and dessert tray into the living room? Then you can start telling me what you've come so far to tell."

*And the silent women can get on with tidying up. I suspect they might manifest for the purpose of frowning at me if I dared clear the table with our first formal dinner guest in the House.*

Once we had settled in, I tucked my feet up under me—something else Colette never would have done. She might have done a Cleopatra lounging upon her gilded divan routine for one of her lovers, but never just tucked bare feet up under the hem of a loose silk skirt.

Mikey indulged in both a brownie and a cookie, but he was more focused now than he had been before.

"You found the kaleidoscopes," he said, "and, more importantly, you somehow figured out how to use them. I know this, because you found my note. That phone number was given out in one place, in one way, precisely for that reason."

I nodded. "You said something to my Aunt May about Colette being a Queen of Mirrors, a Mistress of Thresholds. Did you do it knowing she would start researching?"

Mikey sipped his coffee, to which he'd added enough cream and sugar that it could qualify as another dessert.

"I . . . suspected she would, yes. Maybelle Fenn was a remarkable woman. She was well on the way—not to finding out where Colette had vanished; that would have been unlikely even for her—but to making some inquires that could have caused difficulties."

"For you?" I asked mildly, when what I really wanted to scream was *Where did Colette go! What happened to her? Is she alive?*

"No, Mira, actually, the difficulties would be for you. I'm going to need to go back before Colette was born for you to understand just how difficult matters could have become. Shall we suffice to say it has to do with inheritance?"

"I can deal with that," I said. "My own research has shown me that Phineas House seems to be an important piece of property. Did you tell Uncle Stan not to sell it?"

"We did not, not precisely. We did indicate that we would assist with the long-distance administration of the property if he would agree not to sell it. He was eager to cooperate, to prove he was not interested in adopting you for your inheritance."

But *someone else might have been*, I thought, feeling suddenly cold. *That's what Mikey's hinting at. Someone or someones wanted Phineas House.*

"Am I to understand then," Mikey went on, "that you learned what you did that enabled you to use the kaleidoscopes from Maybelle Fenn?"

"Not quite," I said. "Aunt May never told me about her research, but she left journals. Research journals, I guess you could call them, though they cover a lot more. She made sure that I would get them after she died. Her journal is where I first encountered the term 'liminal space,' and some of the theory. I put that together with some of what I'd found here at Phineas House, and decided that maybe the kaleidoscopes weren't just ornamental."

Mikey nodded approval. "You did very well. Now, though I'm risking putting you to sleep after that excellent meal, I'm going to lecture you. You see, liminal space is where all of this begins, and until you understand that, you are going to have difficulty understanding how this all applies to you."

"Is liminal space a place then?" I know I sounded puzzled. "That doesn't seem quite to fit."

"No, liminal space isn't a place. By definition, liminal space can't be a place because the tenuous virtue of betweenness is what creates liminal space. When liminal space becomes a place, it ceases to be liminal."

"I'm with you," I encouraged him when he looked at me, obviously wondering if I'd accepted this convoluted logic.

"Liminal space—for all that it is, by definition, most itself when it almost isn't," Mikey went on, "is a very potent thing. It can be channeled in a wide variety of ways, but the most obvious way to use it is for scrying, for looking into probability."

"That would be because anything that is liminal, that is on the border between two edges," I said, shaping into words ideas I'd been puzzling over, "is sort of a crossroads where various outcomes can all be seen as probable—if not equally probable."

"That's right," Mr. Hart said. "Scrying through liminal space is not easy. For one thing, it takes a while to learn how to deduce which of the various futures is most probable, but the technique does work. Trust me on this."

"Okay."

"Another possible use for liminal space is for travel."

"Travel?"

"That's right. To one who has the talent and the training, liminal space can be used to violate the charming principle that the shortest distance between two points is a straight line."

"It isn't?"

"Not when liminal space is involved. Probably everyone has used liminal space at least once. It's easiest to use it accidentally, in a familiar environment where you are, to use the modern term, 'on autopilot,' not really paying attention to what you are doing. Don't tell me that you've never been walking or driving somewhere and found yourself at your destination with no real sense of how you got there—and often with time to spare."

"More times than I can count," I laughed. "I always found it most awkward when I was going to visit someone and got there early. There were a few times when I was teaching and I'd find myself opening a multipurpose classroom and walking in before the previous class was over."

"What you did then," Mikey said seriously, "was use liminal space. You unconsciously crossed into a liminal area where various borders met and chose the route you needed. An adept in the skill can do this consciously."

"And Colette knew how to do this," I said, thinking of something Mikey had said earlier, "and that's how she'd leave the insane asylum."

"Bingo," Mikey said, but despite the flippant term, he looked a little sad. "Because she had been severed from Phineas House—I'll get back to that, I promise—she chose some very dangerous routes for her escapes. That's one of the reasons her trustees wanted her released."

"Because they thought she'd hurt herself?"

"And because of the things that might have been created by her on her journeys," Mikey said. "When you are dealing with probability, for everything you could have done right there are dozens of ways you could have done the same thing wrong. Colette would use one of these wrong ways, correct to make it right, but still, sometimes fragments of the wrongness would get out there."

"I don't understand."

"Good girl, and honest," Mikey said. "Let me tell you a bit about Phineas House. It may help."

"Go on," I said, suddenly eager, sitting very still, as if my slightest move might distract him. "I can't wait to hear."

## 22

This was a land of vast spaces and long silences, a desert land of red bluffs and brilliant flowering cactus. The hot sun poured down. This land belonged to the very old Gods. They came on summer evenings, unseen, to rest their eyes and their hearts on the milky opal and smoky blue of the desert. For this was a land of enchantment, where Gods walked in the cool of the evening.

—Marian Russell,
*Land of Enchantment: Memoirs of Marian Russell*
*Along the Santa Fe Trail*

## INSIDE THE LINES

Mikey Hart stirred his coffee a couple of times, the spoon ringing against the side of the china cup like a chime. I sat in silence, willing him to start talking again. At last he did.

"Since you are willing to accept the possibility that liminal space may be more than a psychological construct, then it is not a great leap to ask you to accept the idea that those who are aware of liminal space as something that can be used, rather than merely experienced, would construct tools to enable them to better use it. Phineas House is one such tool. The kaleidoscopes and teleidoscopes you found are others. Phineas House was the brainchild of one Aldo Pincas."

I nodded to indicate that the name was familiar to me, and Mikey went on without asking any questions. I liked that he accepted I would have come across the name in my own research.

"Now, again, I need to stop and lecture," Mikey said with a rueful smile. "There are places where the use of liminal space is easier. This area—Las Vegas, New Mexico—is one. Physically it has useful qualities."

I bit down on my lower lip to keep from spouting out what Domingo and I had deduced, wanting to hear whether Mikey would confirm our guesses.

"It is an area where mountains meet the plains," Mikey said, "not gradually, with a fading into foothills, but comparatively abruptly. Another useful quality is the degree of geothermal activity simmering beneath the surface. If the pressure broke out into active eruption, it would not be as useful, but the hot springs offer a nice blend and emerge within a few yards of an icy mountain stream. The weather is also classically liminal—a temperate zone that experiences the seasonal borders, but is not defined by them. It is an area that knows both drought and flood; that is divided by a river, but not defined by that river.

"Moreover," Mikey continued, "the dry places of the earth have always been especially transitional. Living things cannot exist without water, and so deserts regularly move between the appearance of death into the vitality of life. Desert plants bloom apparently from nothing after a rain. Brown shifts into green; then, as the water is withdrawn, it shifts back into brown once more. Human occupation only intensifies the situation, for frequent rituals meant to bring rain, meant to alter one state into its opposite, create liminal states.

"In Las Vegas specifically, the coming of humans only intensified the multiplicity inherent in the natural landscape. Because of the hot springs, a wide variety of native peoples shared the area in relative peace, each bringing their own customs and traditions. When the Spanish arrived, the complexity increased. Later, Las Vegas was part of Mexico, later still part of the United States. Each change was made in a fashion that increased the complexity of the situation without wiping out previous influences."

I nodded and Mikey looked at me narrowly. "I can see from your expression that you've thought of some of these things yourself. I am impressed."

"I hoped I wasn't showing it quite so plainly," I said, "but you're right. I had wondered why Phineas House should be in Las Vegas, New Mexico, of all places. As history maps the world, Las Vegas has been passed by more than otherwise. In fact, it's almost defined by the number of times it has been passed by."

Mikey nodded. "That passing by is not accidental. Even before Aldo Pincas built the house that would evolve into this Phineas House in which we sit, the Las Vegas area was on what . . . Let me start over. Are you familiar with the concept of trade winds and currents—natural phenomenon that helped define how the ocean travel evolved?"

"A little. Enough to see what you're getting at. You're saying that Las Vegas is on the liminal current."

"That's about as close an analogy as I can give you," Mikey said. "It's nothing like, of course, but helpful in what I'm trying to explain. Aldo Pincas decided that he would like to be able to use the Las Vegas current more effectively. The city of Las Vegas was young then, hardly more than a tidy collection of adobes. Aldo found it easy to acquire the precise piece of land he wanted, and he built Phineas House. The House is placed to take advantage of all sorts of things. You've heard of feng shui?"

"Chinese geomancy," I said. "It's dreadfully trendy these days."

"And most feng shui is nonsense, but like most occult sciences, it has a germ of truth to it. Aldo Pincas used feng shui–like techniques to harness the current. This didn't prevent others from using it, but did weaken it—like running a stream through a mill wheel slows It down without stopping it."

"I bet other liminal sorcerers, or whatever you want to call them, weren't crazy about that."

"They weren't, but that only touches on what I'm telling you—though we may come back to it. Let me stay with Aldo for now."

"Okay."

"What Aldo had not anticipated was that in channelling the liminal current through Phineas House, he would slow the very force from which he wanted to benefit. Once he realized this, Aldo set out to make sure the part of the environment he could influence would create more dualities—thus the checkered history of Las Vegas. I won't go into all the examples, but if you were to go and read the minutes of the meetings discussing the placement of the first rail line, you would discover Aldo's influence. Later, he would encourage the split that lead to the creation of the two towns."

I frowned thoughtfully, remembering that the Bible had listed Aldo's date of birth as 1831. He would have been a man in his prime during the events Mikey was relating. It fit.

"What about the State Hospital—the one that treats mental patients. Did Aldo have something to do with that?"

"He and his son Amerigo were influential, yes. Pincas family members helped encourage the founding of the Normal University as well. There's nothing like an institution of learning to intensify liminal space. That's one reason that, for a town so small, Las Vegas has had so many. The nice thing, from the point of view of the Pincas clan, is that unlike geographical features, educational ventures tend to encourage the creation of other, competing ventures."

For a moment I almost felt the fragmentation going on around me, as if I was a spider in the middle of a web of thin, flexible, but very strong strands. I understood why Mikey had been reluctant to use the trade winds analogy. Liminal space was more like a web spun by a host of spiders on LSD.

Mikey was studying me thoughtfully, and I suspected he had been aware of my insight, making me think what I had understood had not been intellectual, but actual perception. He did not comment, and I, eager that the tale of Aldo Pincas and Phineas House not be truncated, held my peace.

"Now, you must understand that Phineas House is not the only structure of its kind or the oldest or anything like that, but it is an important one. Aldo was a proud and arrogant man, and he was determined that his masterwork would not leave the control of his family. Therefore, he—to use another not completely accurate analogy—mixed into the very mortar of Phineas House bindings that would tie the House to one member of his family. Those bindings did not prevent others from benefiting from Phineas House, but only one person in each generation would possess the full power.

"Because this was a chancy thing to do, Aldo also made the House determined to care for and protect the person to whom it was bound. To ameliorate hurt feelings, Aldo set in place the tradition of trustees for Phineas House—and therefore of its partner. The trustees received certain benefits, and as these came to them through their fidelity to their trust, they had every reason to perpetuate the scheme."

I nodded. "I'd forgotten. I realized when I saw the names of Colette's trustees and then mine that you and I are probably related somehow."

"That's right," Mikey said. "My father was your mother's trustee, Amerigo Hart. His mother was Catarina, the youngest daughter of Amerigo Pincas, who, in turn, was the son of Aldo. Your great-great grandmother, and my grandmother were sisters. I suppose that makes us cousins by several removes."

I grinned. "I must have lots of cousins. Amerigo Pincas and his wife had a mess of kids. The tendency seems to have decreased, though."

"Actually, only in your line," Mikey said. "It may be the House's influence, indirectly. You see, the system worked well for several generations. Amerigo Pincas was a bit surprised when the House showed preference for Isabela over his first-born, a son named Urbano, but there was no fighting it. Urbano was as sensitive to liminal space as a man born blind is to color.

"However, when Isabela gave birth to identical twins, Pinca and Mercedes, Phineas House didn't know what to do. That was a bad time, let me tell you. Eventually, the House was convinced to fix on Pinca, the elder of the twins by a minute or so. It's said that her name was given to her specifically to assist. Initially, she was to have been named for Belinda, Isabela's younger sister."

I thought about the Bible chart. "It didn't get better, though, did it? There were problems in the next generation, too."

"Perceptive," Mikey said.

"Well, I was helped by something Paula Angel said," I admitted. "She told me that one of the reasons Colette had problems with her father was that while Phineas House had wanted nothing to do with him, it bonded with Colette. He resented this, and took it out on Colette."

"It's a little more complicated than that," Mikey said, "but there's truth in what Pablita told you. Pinca married a Russian named Ivan Bogatyr. Their first born was a girl that, maybe for insurance reasons, they named Pinca as well. Phineas House liked young Pinca, but even the best efforts of a guardian cannot prevent death. When she was in her late twenties, Pinca Minor died in a road accident.

"Apparently, Pinca's younger brother, Nikolai, expected Phineas House to take him on—this in spite of the fact that he had only the most minimal sensitivity for liminal space, hardly more than what is usual in the average person."

"Then it is an inherited trait?" I asked.

"Yes. There is some evidence that the tendency to develop the sensitivity can be encouraged by environment—or, equally, discouraged by the same, but then biologists are discovering the same is true of many genetic traits. What a mother eats while the child is being carried can influence what genes turn on or off. A child who is never exposed to art, or is discouraged from making art, may never learn she has the potential to be a great artist."

Mikey's last sentence came so close to my own situation, I wondered if, as when he mentioned the terms "Queen of Mirrors" and "Mistress of Thresholds" to Maybelle Fenn, Mikey Hart wasn't dropping a hint of sorts. I filed it away for future meditation.

Mikey went on without pause. "Growing up as he did in Phineas House, Nikolai had what little gift he possessed encouraged, but it didn't amount to much. Therefore, the only one who was surprised when Phineas House passed him by and chose instead his infant daughter, Colette, was Nikolai himself."

"There was another sibling, wasn't there?"

"That's right, a brother named Urbano. He had even less talent than his brother, and, perhaps as a reaction, developed an aversion to anything that smacked of the occult. At a young age, he married, left Las Vegas, and, except for an annual Christmas card, pretty much didn't keep in touch with his family. Urbano Bogatyr died of liver cancer when he was fifty-one. He left a wife and a couple of children. I think they're all still alive, though his wife would be quite elderly by now."

It still felt odd to hear about people dying younger than me. I made yet another mental note, to get Mikey to give me as list of what had killed my various relatives. Up to this point, I'd lacked that vital information, and had never known whether I was at risk for, say, breast cancer or heart disease.

*Of course*, I thought cynically, *knowing your grandfather died from being pushed down a flight of stairs isn't helpful in quite the same way—though it does give insight.*

"Again," Mikey went on, "Phineas House may have played a role in Urbano's desire to leave, in Nikolai having only one child. The House isn't like a human or even a cat or dog, but it is certainly sentient in its own way. It was created to give order to something that, by its very nature, is outside of the usual order. It has been speculated that Phineas House was shaken by the birth of the twins, and from that point forward did what it could to assure that it would not be faced with a similar confusion."

"I guess," I said, hesitantly, "it could meddle easily enough, especially since the owners tended to live within its walls."

"That's right," Mikey said. "In fact, I think that the selling of some of Phineas House's property was done less because of financial need than in an effort to curtail the House's growing power, its sense that it was entitled to shape the lives of those who lived within it and benefited from its power."

I drummed my fingers on the sofa, trying to arrange a thought. "Does this happen frequently, I mean, with the other structures of this type?"

"Sometimes, but not in the same way. You see, Aldo Pincas created the situation by his strong desire to keep Phineas House in his personal line. The House was built with that desire in mind, and has ever since attempted to be faithful to that need."

"Like a computer program or something?"

"More like a herd dog," Mikey said. "A computer program is limited in what it can do. A herd dog is inventive and has the inbred imperative to herd."

"I know what you mean," I said. "I had a friend who had a lovely border collie, but there aren't a lot of sheep in my part of Ohio, so the poor dog took to herding anything it could—pigeons, small children, other dogs. When my friend had triplets, the dog was perfectly content keeping them in line."

"Now imagine," Mikey said seriously, "if the dog had been able to *make* your friend have triplets. That's what we think Phineas House did to the later descendants of Aldo Pincas—restricted their ability to confuse her."

I looked up at the ceiling. "She's going to have trouble with me. I'm too old to start having kids. It wouldn't be fair to them—even if I managed."

"Right now," Mikey replied, still very serious, "I don't think it has occurred to her. She's too happy to have someone living here. Tell me. Have you considered returning to Ohio permanently?"

"Several times. After all, I have friends there. It's more my home than here."

"But you haven't gone. You even took a leave of absence from your job."

I saw where he was headed, and didn't like it much, even though the idea wasn't completely unreasonable.

"And you think the House encouraged me to stay."

"That's right."

I drew in a deep breath. "I'm not going to say that's impossible. I can't. It's unsettling, though. What do you think will happen when the House realizes she has a middle-aged lady here, not a fecund maiden?"

"I don't know," Mikey said. "There's a lot I don't know. Let me continue telling you what I do."

I nodded.

"There's not too much else, and I wouldn't even mention it except that it may relate to Colette's eventual disappearance. I'm sure you realize that not everyone in Aldo Pincas's family was happy with how the patriarch had set up matters of inheritance."

"That's natural. He took the family's biggest asset and gave it to one person—even if he did make provisions for the others."

"Right. In the first generation, there wasn't too much of a problem. It was still a time when first-born regularly inherited most of the estate—though in the Spanish tradition, this was less common than in other parts of Europe. The next generation was a bit more of a problem."

I mentally traced the family tree. "That's the big group, the one where Isabela was the heir."

"Right. Urbano was blind to liminal space, and there were other properties for him. Belinda married the older brother of Isabela's husband. Her talents, combined with the fact that this was the boom time for Las Vegas, meant they were fairly well-to-do. The younger two, Guillermo and my own grandmother, Catarina, were less content. At the time, matters were eventually ameliorated by drawing two of the trustees from their offspring."

"Two of my mother's," I said. "I'd thought Guillermo Jefferson was somehow related to Isabela, but I admit I was confused."

"Natural, but it is not unheard-of for sisters to marry brothers, and that's what happened there."

"And everything worked out with your family, too," I asked, a bit anxiously, I admit. I'd gotten to like Mikey, and didn't really want to be at odds over something a common great-great-whatever grandfather had done."

"All fine," Mikey assured me. "I rather prefer not having to live in Las Vegas, to be honest. But back when the resentment was more current, efforts were made to dilute the effects of Phineas House. We skipped over discussing the Montezuma Hotel earlier, but it, too, fits into the story. All the histories say that it was built by the Santa Fe Railroad, and that is correct, but only as far as it goes. Part of the reason the hotel was built where it was, and as elaborately as it was, was in an effort to counter the effects of Phineas House."

"Are you serious?"

"Completely. What do you know of the Montezuma's history?"

"A fair amount, actually. Domingo and I went and played tourist a couple weeks ago. He knew the background of the place pretty well."

I thought about mentioning how Domingo had worked on the renovation, then remembered Domingo's own odd superstition that Phineas House might not like that he'd done that. Given what I'd just heard about the House's rather proactive role in the lives of my family, I no longer thought the superstition odd.

"So you know that the hotel suffered a rather astonishing series of disasters."

"At least two wholly destructive fires," I said, "despite the fact that the architect's designs were specifically designed to be fireproof. It seems to me that Domingo also said—or maybe it was in one of the books I read—that the hotels showed an incredible inability to turn a profit."

"Right. And, yet, despite this, the Montezuma Hotel was not only repeatedly rebuilt, but repeatedly invested in, and monumental efforts have been made to keep it open."

"You're saying that this persistent desire to keep a structure on that site had something to do with Phineas House—or rather, an attempt to counterbalance Phineas House."

Mikey nodded, and I noticed he was beginning to look tired. I glanced at the clock and saw that it was getting late.

"Did the attempt work?" I asked.

"It may have," Mikey said. "It's one of those largely theoretical matters, since it's hard to find a control for the experiment."

I noted he said "hard" without irony or humor, and wondered if perhaps somewhere in liminal space it might be possible to find a control for that experiment. Why not? It seemed as reasonable as a house doing genetic engineering on its occupants.

"However," Mikey went on, "it did seem that the Montezuma resented being used as a 'for-profit' venture. This may have to do with the nature of its mission. It has done much better since it's been turned to not-for-profit or educational uses."

"You're kidding . . ." I began, then stopped myself. He wasn't, and I was being an idiot if I didn't admit the possibility. "No, you're not, but I'm afraid I don't understand."

"Phineas House was built to enable Aldo Pincas and his descendants to profit from the charged qualities of the surrounding area," Mikey explained. "The Montezuma was built to counter Phineas House. My best guess is that in their desire to counter Phineas House, the builders of the Montezuma inadvertently gave the 'spirit' of the Montezuma a sense that profiting from the area's qualities was somehow wrong."

"So it kept burning itself down?"

"Not quite," Mikey chuckled. "My guess is that the fires were . . . well, not started, but rather instigated by the friction between Phineas House and her rival."

I blinked. That was a lot to take. Mikey saw my expression and began to clarify.

"Phineas House is specifically positioned to exploit the area. Even when the House's geomantic qualities were reduced by selling off portions of her lot, she was still a potent force. The Montezuma was a newcomer—and her site was initially not well-chosen."

"That's right," I said. "After the first fire, the hotel was moved further up the hill, but that one burnt, too."

"Because of badly positioned fire hoses," Mikey said, almost dreamily. "I'd love to see a roster of the builder's crews. Did someone deliberately do that, maybe by choice, maybe coaxed in a dream?"

"That's creepy," I said.

"It is," Mikey agreed, "but Phineas House is a tool, capable of being used for either creation or destruction."

I nodded, feeling a trace of the uneasiness I had felt when I had first learned how my grandfather had died. I decided to change the subject, just a little.

"You said the Montezuma Hotel might have had something to do with Colette's disappearance."

"I did. As you certainly have noticed, when she vanished, she was reported as driving her gig in the direction of the Montezuma Hotel. That may not have been her final destination, but she was heading in that direction. At that date, the Castle was in use as a Catholic seminary. That would not have kept it from serving as a damper on Phineas House's power. I have often wondered, was Colette going to the Montezuma Hotel?"

"Could she have been meeting someone there?"

"Possibly," Mikey said, "though as the Hotel was not constructed as a channel—as Phineas House is—there is no benefit to be gained by living there. If anything, someone with the ability to use liminal space might find it obscurely dampened."

I was just tired enough myself to be blunt. "So if you don't think she was meeting someone, what is it you're hinting about?"

Mikey sighed, and I saw his gaze flicker up to the ceiling, as if he was trying to see if Phineas House was paying attention to his words.

"I have wondered," he said slowly, "if she might have been intending to use the Montezuma's qualities to her own advantage. If so, what did Colette intend to do that she did not want Phineas House—or possibly those tuned to Phineas's House—to know about?"

It was a startling conjecture.

"Did you investigate this theory?"

"As best as I could, but, Mira, there was a tremendous amount of turmoil then—and we had no more luck tracing Colette than did the police. Moreover, we had immediate problems to solve. If Colette was dead, then you would be heir to Phineas House, but control of the House did not transfer to you. Did that mean Colette was alive, or that she was dead, but that the House was unaware of her fate? Had someone harmed Colette, or had she voluntarily vanished? Some even theorized that she had finally fallen afoul of her tendency to go by routes more careful souls would avoid."

"I see," I said, then voiced only one of the many questions clamoring in my head. "Does the fact that Phineas House seems to be responding to me indicate that Colette is indeed dead?"

Mikey was blunt. "Quite possibly, but it also could mean that the House is lonely, that it feels abandoned—or that it hopes that with your return you will find Colette. You admit to feeling an imperative to do so, don't you?"

"Imperative? I don't know. Curiosity maybe."

But I was remembering the vision I'd had while up on the ladder, the one of Colette in her plum satin gown, driving her gig steadily along a road. Had the House been trying to show me something? To give me a message? To get me to do something about that old mystery, now that I'd finally learned about liminal space?

The possibility made me uncomfortable. I honestly wanted to know what had happened to Colette, but I didn't like the idea of being pushed into making those discoveries—not even by Phineas House.

It was late by now, and I could see that the hour was preying on my guest.

"Mikey, maybe we should resume this in the morning."

He politely patted back a yawn. "I wouldn't mind some sleep. It was a long trip, and excitement carried me along to this point, but even a good meal can't replace honest sleep. When may I call tomorrow?"

"I'm usually up early. Domingo and I have breakfast and review the day's work on the House. You're welcome to join us."

"Perhaps I will. However, I'd like the opportunity to sleep late. May I call after I'm awake and come over then, or would that be asking you to wait around for me?"

"Not at all," I assured him. "I'm usually home. There's quite a lot to do."

"Then I will call," he said. "Until tomorrow, then, Mira."

"Until tomorrow," I replied.

I went to bed that night, aware that I was digging in my mental heels. I'd wanted to learn what had happened to Colette. I still did—in a way—but I didn't like the idea of doing so for any reasons other than my own. If Mikey Hart was to be believed, Aldo Pincas had attempted not only to shape, but to secure forces that by their very nature should neither be shaped, nor secured. That Grandfather Aldo had not anticipated the House evolving its own agenda seemed clear. Equally clear was that the House did have an agenda—an agenda that frightened me because I didn't know where I fit in.

The kitchen was clean when I went in to check the lock on the back door. The coffee for tomorrow morning was already set up. I made a point of putting the coffee mugs Mikey and I had used in the dishwasher, along with the cookie plate. Before tonight, this would have been a quiet act of thanksgiving. Tonight a hint of rebellion underlay my actions. I appreciated Phineas House's help, but I wasn't dependent on it, not for cleaning, not for anything.

Wondering about Grandfather Nikolai's death had become almost reflex whenever I went up or down the main staircase. Tonight, however, rather than asking myself did Colette push him or did the House itself do something on her behalf, I found myself wondering "And if Phineas House did help Colette, what then was the price?"

It was an unsettling thought. The Fenns had reared me with good, old-fashioned values, one of which was that nothing was free—there was always a price. Uncle Stan had even made clear that things that apparently had no cost—whether in accepting charity or letting someone else do what you knew you should be doing—was its own form of cost. In these cases many times the coin in which you paid was pride.

I thought about that as I washed my face and brushed my teeth, as I used a toilet I hadn't had to scrub for weeks because invisible hands kept it sparklingly clean. I hadn't thought about the price for these services. Was I losing my own will to act? Was I becoming a bird in a gilded cage?

When I went into my room, I nearly threw the sprig of Spanish lavender onto the floor in a sudden surge of revulsion. Instead, I did with this piece what I had done with all the others, added it to the sweet-scented bundle that had gradually accumulated in my bedside table. There was no need to reject grace and kindness, just because I wondered at what motivated it. That would be as foolish as accepting without question. Walking a middle line was the only reasonable solution.

And, Mira, I thought to myself as I drifted off to sleep, *if what Mikey says is true, well, then, walking lines, through them, along them, in between them, that's something you should be very good at indeed.*

23

Winter in Ohio was especially rough if you had an appetite for color.
—Toni Morrison,
*Beloved*

## INSIDE THE LINES

My dreams that night were a continuation of the vision that had nearly toppled me from my ladder, only more vivid. Gowned in plum satin, Colette continued to drive her stylish gig along a winding road. Shooting Star continued to trot along, steady but obviously aware of being part of a stylish turn-out. Neither of them seemed aware that they were travelling through a landscape right out of one of M. C. Escher's nightmares.

The road along which they traveled split: one becoming two, two four, four eight, eight sixteen, sixteen thirty-two, thirty-two doubtless sixty-four, and sixty-four one hundred and twenty-eight, though by then I had long since lost count. Each road was identical, each route carried its own Colette, its own gig, its own tightly trotting bay mare.

The skies above were no longer pure New Mexico blue, but were the hue of a two-day-old bruise. They were livid, shot through with lightning bolts in neon orange and lime green. The thunder from the lightning's passage cracked and screamed like breaking glass.

None of the infinitude of Colettes noticed. They drove on, each along their own road, each fanning out farther from the others, their roads slim spokes in an increasingly attenuated wheel. I thought of my earlier image of liminal space as like a spiderweb, and looked to see what spider sat at the center of this web, what stable basis provided the hub.

I expected to see Phineas House, but what I saw instead was emptiness, a dark red void, colored like the afterimages left when you rub your eyes too hard. I stared into that void, certain that something must be concealed beneath the viscous red, but there was nothing but the dull, bloody glow.

When I looked down the spokes again, the Colettes had traveled far enough down their roads that their images were the size of pinpricks, yet these pinpricks were still perfect in every detail, as if the Colettes had lost size and volume rather than moving along, but the images defied this interpretation, for Shooting Star's legs moved in their steady, rhythmic trot, the rubber-tired wheels spun, and Colette after Colette shook the reins impatiently, and focused on the landscape through a teleidoscope held in an elegantly gloved hand.

I looked in the direction in which she pointed the device, trying to see what she did, but all I saw was a chaotic scream of neon brilliance against that bruised sky. I fell into deeper sleep wondering if Colette had seen anything different.

Mikey did not arrive in time to join me and Domingo for our breakfast in the garden. Although I had genuinely liked the man, I found myself relieved. Mikey himself might be good company, but the stories he had told me had been—to say the least—disquieting.

I filled Domingo in on some of it, and if I emphasized the points where our guesses had been correct or mostly correct, rather than the unsettling evidence that my mother had been the insane conclusion of a family who sought to control time and space for its own benefit, well, can you blame me?

"Do we continue the painting today?" Domingo said. "I did not tell the crew not to come."

"Continue," I said, a note of defiance in my voice. "Phineas House may want this paint job, but, you know, so do I. Somehow it's impossible to be afraid of the House in daylight—especially as it becomes more impossibly gaudy."

Domingo dropped his hand to accept the stick Blanco had brought him, and tossed it across the yard. It fell at the edge of a patch of squash, and Blanco paused to bark aggressively at something hiding beneath one of the large leaves—probably a toad. The garden's dampness drew them. Any wise gardener welcomes toads, but Blanco did not share our appreciation.

"Tell me, Mira," Domingo said in that voice that always seemed soft, even when he was shouting orders up to the painters, "do you fear the House?"

"Sometimes," I said. "You know that. You gave me a bed one night when I was too scared to go back inside."

"Sometimes," he said, and this time his voice was truly soft, "I also fear Phineas House, but long ago I reasoned that there is nothing at all wrong with fear when it is merited."

I blinked at this, but there was really no need for me to answer. Domingo and I understood each other too well where the House was concerned. In other ways, we might still almost be strangers, but not in this. The phone ringing in the kitchen saved me from the need to shape an unnecessary reply.

"That's probably Mikey," I said, running inside. Blanco, who like every dog saw a running human as an invitation to chase, came after me, and I let him inside. Domingo remained outside, sipping coffee and looking thoughtfully at the rosebushes.

"Hello?"

"Mira? This is Mikey Hart. I'm finally awake, but not yet dressed or show-ered. How about I drop over in say an hour and a half? I'll eat here at the hotel, and give you a chance to get your morning in order."

"Fine," I said. "When you get here, just come in the gate and walk around the side of Phineas House. Someone will tell you where I am, and I might as well do some painting."

"I'll do that," he said. "See you in a bit, then."

I came out and told Domingo the gist of the conversation.

"So," I concluded, "I'll have a chance to help paint out the bird poop someone spilled down the side the other day."

Domingo grinned at me, but shook his finger in an admonition that was only in semi-jest.

"I'll let you do it," he said, "but no daydreaming. I will not have my meal-ticket fall off a ladder and break her neck."

"I promise," I said, growing suddenly serious. "I think I dreamed enough last night."

———————

Mikey arrived as I was wiping paint off my fingers with a rag. With the help of Tomás, I had repaired most of the damage caused by my spill, and I thought the House looked quite good.

"Good morning, Mikey," I said cheerfully. "You look rested and well."

"I am indeed," he replied, "and if I thought Phineas House looked impressive in evening light, in full daylight . . ."

He trailed off in what I chose to take as admiring astonishment. I dropped the paint rag with its fellows, and motioned for Mikey to follow me.

"Let me introduce you to Domingo Navidad. You know of him, of course, but I have the impression you have never met."

"We have not," Mikey said, "but I'd be glad to remedy the situation."

"Good. Then I'll let him give you the grand exterior tour while I get out of my coveralls. You've had breakfast, I know, but can I offer you anything?"

"A glass of iced tea, perhaps," Mikey said, his gaze still moving over Phineas House's exterior, resting for a moment on an ornate frieze or window frame, then moving on.

Introductions went smoothly. When I emerged from the House, wearing an olive-green broomstick skirt and an off-white peasant blouse embroidered with wildflowers, most of the paint off my hands, I found the two men discussing the work. I waited until they had finished comparing the very different needs of Minnesota and New Mexico, then motioned for Mikey to come inside.

"The painters like their music while they work," I explained, "and I don't feel like competing with guitars and trumpets."

Domingo gave us both a casual wave as he returned to his ladder. "Perhaps we will talk more later," he said to Mikey. "I am glad you like the paint job."

Domingo's tone told me, as I knew he had intended it to, that he also liked Mikey Hart. I felt unaccountably relieved. It wasn't like Domingo was the most normal fellow I had ever met, but he seemed a good judge of character.

Mikey huffed slightly as he followed me up the stairs into the kitchen.

"Domingo is a fascinating fellow," he said. "I'd wondered about him for a long time."

"He's done well by Phineas House," I said.

"Better, maybe, than either you or he know," Mikey said cryptically, and something in his tone told me I'd be wasting my breath asking for clarification.

Today I invited Mikey to sit with me in the library. For one thing, the family Bible with its odd version of a family tree was there. For another, the chairs were really very comfortable. I had gotten over my childish feeling that the room was "Mother's office." Now it was simply another room, one more useful than most.

I offered Mikey a deep leather armchair, and seated myself in its mate. The desk remained untenanted, except by my memories of Colette. Mikey had carried in his own glass of tea, and now he set it on a sandstone coaster on the table beside him.

"Last night," he said, "I recounted a lot of history. Today, if you don't mind, I'd like to start by explaining why you were placed with the Fenns, rather than left here."

"Sounds good," I said. "I hope you'll also explain something about the extraordinary conditions you placed on the Fenns. I know that Aunt May lived in fear you'd come and take me away."

"Not too much fear," Mikey reminded me. "It wasn't enough to stop her from being nosy."

"True," I admitted, "but you have to admit, those were extraordinary conditions."

"Perhaps, perhaps not. We had two reasons for setting those conditions, Mira. Both were intended to protect you."

"Oh?"

"You heard what I told you last night," he said, and for the first time since I had met him he seemed impatient. "If the Fenns had investigated your past too closely they would have learned that your mother had done time in a mental hospital. That would certainly have prejudiced them against you. They might even have learned that your grandfather died under rather odd circumstances. Gossip about the less attractive aspects of the Bogatyr family history was at its height for a year or so after Colette's disappearance, while the investigation was most active."

I made an apologetic gesture. "I understand. I really do. Before you explain your second reason, I wonder why it was so important for me to be adopted outside of the family. Until I got here, I thought that maybe I didn't have any family left, but now it seems that I must have had family. If I may be blunt about it, you and the other two trustees were family, if somewhat distantly connected."

"I think you already know the answer," Mikey said, "but if it helps, I'll spell it out. If anyone did make Colette disappear—murdered her, kidnapped her, led her astray in some fashion—then the likelihood was fairly high that whoever did it was family.

"Even your maternal line—your grandmother Chantal's family—was suspect. Chantal resented not inheriting more of her husband's estate. That resentment could have been passed down. Once Colette was out of the way, well, you were the only one left. Chantal's family would have known that your father's siblings were both dead. Nikolai had alienated himself from his cousins by his resentment of his own daughter, so it wasn't like there were tremendous Pincas family reunions.

"We had to be uniformly suspicious, even of each other. There's a reason there have always been three trustees, you know. As Caesar and his buddies knew too well, in a triumvirate it's harder to violate the basic contract. Anyhow, in the end, we decided that placing you with an unimpeachably neutral family was the best course of action."

"Thank you," I said with what simple dignity I could manage. "Both for the explanation, and for doing so well by me. I'm beginning to understand better what you said last night about the time of Colette's disappearance being one of turmoil. You didn't just mean on whatever level of all that liminal stuff, you meant within the extended family as well."

Mikey nodded. "It was a bad time, everyone looking at everyone else sideways, people making snide hints, and trying to shift blame. The thing was, Colette vanished so completely. I know you did some looking into the police side of it. Matters weren't much better from our end."

"I can see that," I said. "Can you bear one more question interrupting your organized presentation?"

Mikey grinned. "That's the first time anyone has called me organized in a long while. Someday I'll have to introduce you to my wife, just so you can tell her that. Go on."

"How did you know Aunt May was nosing around?"

Mikey looked thoughtful. "Frankly, we paid a handful of people here in Las Vegas and in a few other places to let us know if certain circumstances occurred. One of these was a fellow in the post office who sorted the mail. He was asked to look out for letters going to the police, local paper, and a few other places postmarked from Ohio. He was our most useful source—and interested enough in a supplemental income to divert those letters to us."

"He missed a couple," I said smugly. "Aunt May got clippings from the *Optic*. What if she had phoned?"

"We'd paid a few people at the police and paper as well," Mikey said.

"Our interest was pure and above suspicion. We were your trustees after all, and had let a few people know in confidence that we feared that whatever had happened to Colette might happen to you as well."

"Simple," I said. "So simple."

"Simpler then than it would be today," he said, "what with machines sorting the mail, and Internet connections for research. We might never have gotten wind of Maybelle's interest if she'd been able to read articles on line. If she'd contacted someone, though, we still might have managed to learn what she was doing. Humans remain the eternal weak point in any secure system."

"Good," I said. "I'm actually glad in a way. I hated the idea of Aunt May's letters merely being tossed in the circular file. Now, to backtrack, you said there were two reasons for setting those conditions on the Fenns—conditions that included asking them to change their name. One was that you were protecting my reputation."

"The other was we were protecting you personally—your continued physical existence," Mikey said without the least trace of melodrama. His matter-of-factness on such an issue made my skin crawl. "As I mentioned before, we didn't know who to trust. We decided to trust no one. We even did our best to remove from Phineas House anything of yours you did not take with you."

"That's why the nursery was stripped!" I said.

"That's why," he agreed. "I've told you that one of the uses liminal space can be put to is scrying. Scrying works better for some people if they hold something that belonged to the person they're investigating. We did our best to move you into protective custody—on all levels. Again, if the Fenns had decided to ask questions or take you to Las Vegas to find your roots or something . . ."

"That would have ended any protection you could have given me," I said, finishing the thought for him. "But why did you trustees drop out of my life so completely? I mean, as time passed, so did the risk. Uncle Stan gave me information on my inheritance when I turned twenty-one. Why didn't you?"

Mikey raised his hands as if to physically stop the flow of words. "Those questions have very different answers. To answer the first, we didn't drop out of your life. We regularly reviewed how you were doing, both with the Fenns, and by more objective means. We saw copies of all your report cards, your health records, even talked to your teachers or neighbors, when we could do so without arousing suspicion. Your Uncle Stan practically demanded we inspect your financial standing.

"We didn't stop with those annual reviews," Mikey went on a trace smugly. "Edgar Carney made a point of making visits to see things you had done. Remember when you won first prize in that art show when you were in high school? Ed went to that. He went to school plays, to public recitations. We picked him because you were showing an interest in art, and he had one, too, enough that he could tell us you had real talent. He also told us that you were stepping on that talent, that you could have been a professional, but for some reason chose to teach instead. Do you mind telling me why?"

I looked at Mikey, rubbing my hands against my brow as I remembered. "Edgar Carney himself was partly to blame. I saw him twice, both times looking rather intently at my art. One time was at that show you mentioned, now that I think about it. Nine isn't so young that I hadn't wondered about why I'd been taken from my home and placed with strangers. I'd even come up with something like the protective custody theory on my own—though I thought Colette was involved with criminals rather than . . ."

"Sorcerers? Wizards? Practitioners of occult arts?"

I nodded. "But seeing Mr. Carney wasn't the main reason I 'stepped on' following a career in art. From the time I was small, I've always felt funny about my interest in art and color. I thought—knew—Colette wouldn't like it. I guess Mr. Carney's interest just gave me an excuse to follow my own inclinations to hide my art. I couldn't leave it entirely, so I turned to teaching."

"Fascinating," Mikey said. "Colette didn't like you doing art?"

"She didn't know I did art of any kind," I corrected. "I hid my interest from her. I sensed she'd disapprove."

"Let me think on that," Mikey said. "That's very interesting, very interesting indeed."

Mikey rubbed his hands across his pudgy face, the flesh moving under his hands like modeling clay, but falling back into its usual lines when he dropped his hands back into his lap.

"Sorry," he said. "Travelling takes a bit out of me these days. I'm not as young as I was."

"Who is?" I said. "Let me make coffee, and, as I promised, you can tell me what you intended, rather than answering my questions."

"Those questions haven't been completely useless," Mikey insisted, following me into the kitchen. "Some of your questions anticipated matters I had planned to bring up."

When I had ground the coffee beans, I shook them into the basket of the coffeemaker.

"So, go on. Or are you done?"

Mikey shook his head. "I'm not done. It's just, the next item on my agenda isn't merely a background report."

"Go on."

"We have discussed your desire to find Colette. I think that's a valid and important issue—and one in which you may have more luck than anyone else."

"Oh?"

"Yes. You are her daughter. No matter how you feel about her, that creates a tie. Also, while Phineas House may have resisted or blocked other attempts to trace Colette, it does not seem inclined to block you."

No. I thought. *You actually think it's encouraging me.*

"Colette was a very dominant personality, so much so that you may have forgotten you have another parent."

"I haven't," I said dryly, "though I think Colette did."

"I simply feel it is important to remind you that your father—whoever he is—should not be forgotten. I'm not saying you should try and trace him . . ."

"Let me guess. It's already been done. No luck."

Mikey grinned. "That's right. However, we've no idea why Colette vanished when she did, but it is not impossible that your father had something to do with her disappearance."

"He kidnapped her, you mean?"

"Or she fled him. Or, even she chose to go somewhere with him, rather than remaining here. The last seems unlikely. If Colette had known she was going away for an extended period of time, she would have taken things she valued."

"Like her jewelry or the kaleidoscope collection," I said.

"Actually, I was thinking of you," Mikey replied gently. "Whatever her failings as a mother, Colette did value you."

I didn't answer. Childishly, I wanted to deny the truth of this statement, but I couldn't. The problem was, I couldn't deny that I felt my value had been more in the line of an ornament or accessory, rather than as a person.

Mikey went on. "So, what are you going to do?"

I turned sharply from where I had been getting coffee cups out of the cabinet.

"Do?"

"Are you going to look for Colette? Go back to Ohio? Stay here in Las Vegas, and paint Phineas House into the paean to color you have denied yourself all your life?"

That last hit me like a physical blow. I'd thought I was responding to the House. Had she been responding to me? I tried to remember when Domingo said he had undertaken his ambitious project. Was it before, or after, I had learned I owned Phineas House. Before, surely.

But what if the House had sensed my impending return? It had been constructed to be a hub for liminal space. What was more liminal than time? Past, present, and future shift with every breath, every second, every heartbeat. Might Phineas House have sensed my coming as wild animals sense the shifting of the seasons?

Might it . . . my heart froze in my chest at the thought . . . Might it have done something to make me come? Uncle Stan was not young, so easy to create a ripple in probability and make an older man have an accident. The police had been so vague about the cause of the accident.

"Mira?" Mikey said. "What's wrong? You've gone all pale."

"I just had an unpleasant thought," I said, setting the mug on the counter with incredible care. I feared to speak my thought aloud, but a perverse sense of defiance made me do it. "What would Phineas House do to get itself a human focus again? You've already said you thought it might push me to go after Colette. Would it do something to make me come here? Uncle Stan tried to get me to take over managing my estate when I turned twenty-one. I refused. It was, well, it was too much like putting Colette in her grave. I couldn't do it."

"And Stan Fenn continued to administer the estate for you—including Phineas House."

"Which I didn't even know I owned."

As he had once before, Mikey looked up at the ceiling, as if there he might see the House's face.

"Mira, I don't know, but I don't think the House is capable of doing such a thing. For one, you are among those it is meant to protect. Harming your parents would not be protecting you."

I poured the coffee with a hand I forced not to shake. "Unless the House is still protecting Colette, rather than me, and got tired of waiting. After all, I'm not young. I have no children. What would happen when I was gone?"

"I'd wondered about why you're not married," Mikey said, almost diffidently. "You're a very nice woman, very sweet, and not at all unattractive. Is there a reason you haven't married?"

I started to give him all the usual reasons—never the right man, bad luck, too busy—but what I said cut through all the deceptions, even those I'd made for myself.

"I couldn't, not without knowing more about myself. You protected me, Mikey, but you also robbed me of a past. There were things I just couldn't bring myself to talk about, not to anyone . . . That made a barrier I've never gotten beyond."

"I'm sorry," Mikey said. "It must have been very lonely."

Again, I couldn't say the polite things. I remembered he had mentioned having a wife. Did he have children, too?

"Yes," I said, bluntly, coldly. "It has been very lonely."

Mikey looked uncomfortable, but had the wisdom to change the subject.

"Mira, on this issue of what Phineas House did or didn't do, may or may not be capable of, don't make it worse for yourself. There is one way to resolve some of this uncertainty. Find Colette—or at least find what happened to her. Then you'll know who the House serves. You'll know if you have enemies. You'll know things you can't learn from me for the simple reason that I don't know them."

I set the coffee mugs on the table, and looked down at him.

"Finding Colette has always been one of my goals. However, I don't have the least idea how to go about it."

Mikey lightened and sweetened his coffee, the spoon clinking with metronomelike regularity against the sides of the cup.

"There are," he said, almost hesitantly, "the kaleidoscopes."

"The kaleidoscopes," I repeated. "I figured out that they must have something to with scrying. That's what I was trying to do when I found your note. Are you suggesting I scry for Colette?"

"Something like that," he said. "However, to be completely honest. I don't know what you have access to."

"You mean, you don't know about her collection?"

"I do and I don't," Mikey said. "No. I'm not trying to be difficult. I'm being precisely honest. Let me start over."

He sipped his coffee, as if the act would permit him to physically readjust his thoughts.

"We haven't really talked much about Colette's fascination with mirrors, have we?"

I shook my head. "I've thought about it. Reflection and reality are very liminal concepts, like shadow and substance. Which is really real? Peter Pan's shadow had a life apart from him—Alice went through the looking glass."

Mikey smiled broadly. "I can see I don't need to give you the basic primer. Good. Let me jump ahead then. To start, before Colette's return from the mental hospital, Phineas House was not decorated all over with mirrors."

"No?"

I glanced around the kitchen. The omnipresent mirrors seemed so normal now that when I visited somewhere like Evelina's house, the walls seemed somehow dead. I no longer felt any desire to cover them. In fact, I'd found myself toying with the idea of getting some fabric like my mother had owned, the type trimmed with tiny mirrors.

"No. The mirrors were Colette's idea, and she cultivated it with enthusiasm. Her trustees were mildly appalled, but as no harm seemed to come from it, and Phineas House did not seem in danger of being damaged, they did nothing to try and stop her—and, to be honest, they would have been on thin ground if they did."

"Damaged?" I said. "How could mirrors damage a house? I don't think you're talking about walls falling down from the weight."

"I am not," Mikey agreed. "Phineas House was built to focus liminal space. Mirrors create liminal space. In setting up so many here, placing them where they reflect not only their surroundings but each other, Colette created something of a resonance chamber in which waves flowed in, bouncing off of each other, shattering, and taking new forms."

He spoke of "waves," and I think he meant to evoke sound waves, but the image that sprang to my mind was of a storm-tossed ocean, an ocean in a house-shaped bottle, the trapped force splitting and reshaping, splitting and reshaping, sometimes coming into the same forms, but more often creating an infinitude of foam and chaos.

"And Phineas House was able to handle this?" I asked.

"It has," Mikey said. "Maybe for Phineas House, the multiplicity of mirrors was no more a strain than the numerous thresholds, rooms, and corridors, no more than the multiplicity of carvings on the exterior . . ."

"Or the broken rainbow of color?" I added. "I think I see, but we were talking of kaleidoscopes."

"Yes," Mikey agreed. "We were. You know how kaleidoscopes work—that they have an interior mirrored chamber."

I nodded.

"Well, Colette's obsession with mirrors extended to kaleidoscopes and teleidoscopes as well. That was common knowledge. Many of us knew that she was amassing a collection of them, and that among that collection were pieces that were . . ."

"Enchanted?"

"Why not? It's as good a word as any. In any case, created for a specific purpose. That's why I placed my message to you as I did. It was set to intercept you if you did any mirror scrying, through the kaleidoscope or not."

"How?"

He waved his pudgy hands. "It's very technical, and, frankly, you don't have the vocabulary to understand what I did. Will you accept that I know how to place things at liminal crossroads? I located the road you would need to travel to begin scrying, and set my marker there."

"I'll take your word for it," I said. "So if I had tried gazing in a pool of water or an oiled shield or whatever, your note would have reached me?"

"Only if you did it with a conscious knowledge of what you were attempting," Mikey said. "Idle studying of your face in the mirror would not have done it. Scrying with some sincere belief that such could be done would—and did."

"Tell me," I said, "what would you have done if I had tracked you down in some more usual fashion? I had already decided to do so when I, uh, intercepted your message. I had your name, and even a few addresses and phone numbers. It might have taken me a while, but I figure I could have tracked down you or one of the others."

"Only me," he said sadly. "I am the sole survivor of your three trustees. We are not an extraordinarily long-lived family, though seventies, and even eighties are not unusual."

"But what would you have done if I'd phoned you not on the special scrying line?"

"I would have been happy to hear from you, made arrangements to come see you, much as I did, and then tried to get a sense for how much you knew, and how much you could handle knowing. I might even have found a way to see that you came across certain books or articles. Or, if you were obviously uninterested or unable to comprehend such odd concepts, I would have done my best to make sure you were comfortable, and then reported to what, for lack of a better term, I'll call the 'Family Council' that Phineas House might be on the market."

I had a sneaking suspicion how Mr. Gilhoff, the bookseller, might have acquired some of those books that were so fortuitously useful in guiding Aunt May in her studies, but I didn't ask. Colette wasn't the only rebel in Aldo Pinca's line. I thought that, for all his pudgy body and cheerful demeanor, Mikey Hart might be one, too. There was no need to put him on the spot about what was done and gone. He'd probably simply reply that it had been another of his ways of looking out for my interests.

"We've gone off on another tangent," I observed. "I suppose that's another form of liminal space, isn't it?"

"You could see it that way. I prefer to think of it as a sign of active curiosity and a healthy mind. Now, kaleidoscopes. Phineas House did not exactly encourage prying after Colette's disappearance. It didn't do anything like drop pictures on us or make the carpets rumple and trip us, but it had a distinct way of making us uncomfortable.

"Moreover, making an inventory of the property wasn't our job. Therefore, although we did look for the kaleidoscope collection, when we didn't find it, we didn't look too hard. I take it you did find it?"

"Hidden in the drawers of my mother's vanity," I said.

"Appropriate," Mikey said. "Kaleidoscopes and teleidoscopes, both."

"That's right."

"And were there any particularly unusual ones?"

I rose and pushed back the kitchen chair, outside the sound of a Spanish-language talk show drifted in from where the painters worked.

"Why don't you come with me?" I said. "It will be easier if I show you."

## 24

They stript Joseph out of his coat, his coat of many colours.

—Genesis 37:23

---

## INSIDE THE LINES

"This is an amazing collection," Mikey said, looking up from his inspection of the kaleidoscopes.

We had lifted the trays from their drawers in the vanity and carried them into my mother's front parlor. While Mikey systematically inspected each kaleidoscope and teleidoscope, I idly lifted one or another out at random, enjoying the shifting patterns, determinedly *not* trying to see anything but the pretty colors.

"As I'm sure you realize," Mikey said, "these seven are the most remarkable of the lot."

I liked that he didn't try to lecture me, and answered easily. "I did notice the symbols on the casing, and lucked into some information in one of Aunt May's books that helped me realize what they are. They're an adaptation of the cabalistic seven mirrors of divination, aren't they?"

"That's my guess, too," Mikey said. "I haven't studied the cabala in any detail, but I have an interest in scrying. In my opinion, this is a particularly lovely system: a different mirror for each day of the week, each made of specific materials, and meant to provide information on a specific type of question."

"But are they really ensorcelled?"

Mikey shrugged. "Mira, that's an almost impossible question to answer. Magic—to use a word I'd rather not—is not as simple as technology. Anyone can turn on a radio or flip a light switch. Magic takes training. A violin, for example, is an elaborate construct, but where one person can use it to create lovely music, another will make only scrapes and screeches."

I lifted one of the kaleidoscopes and rolled the barrel between my hands, listening to the rainfall hiss as the items in the object case shifted against each other.

"So you're saying that items created for magic are more like violins than radios. The virtue in them is as much in the user as in the item."

"Precisely," Mikey said. "As with violins, there are varying degrees of quality. The majority of these kaleidoscopes are the Stradivariuses of their kind, but just as an amateur handed a perfect violin would not become a perfect violinist, so these cannot create visions for someone who lacks both talent and training."

"I see." I picked up the rose-colored kaleidoscope. "When I used this and found your message, I certainly wasn't trained, so I was going on raw talent?"

"That's right. You mentioned how doing so wore you out so much that you fainted. That's because you didn't know what you were doing and, for lack of a better analogy, pulled a muscle."

"Pulled a muscle? Playing a violin?"

"That was only a comparison," Mikey said, "and the dangerous thing about comparisons is that they can be taken literally. Let me use a more physical one. Think of the kaleidoscopes as skis."

"Like for sliding down hill on snow."

"Right. Again, anybody can strap skis on their feet and slide over the snow, but an amateur is going to fall, pull muscles, and wear himself out, even on the bunny slopes. In contrast, a professional will perform far more ambitious acts and hardly break a sweat. Even a potentially talented skier needs to learn how to balance, how to shift his weight, how to push off right . . ."

"Do you ski?" I asked, eyeing his soft, flabby body with distrust.

"I do not. I have weak ankles. However, I have spent many hours drinking hot cocoa and watching various family members exert themselves." Mikey grinned. "Now, do you understand a bit more about the nature of magical items?"

"It sounds to me like they're not magical at all."

"Remember Phineas House," Mikey said. "Tools created to conduct forces sometimes acquire virtues in themselves."

I thought about it, "Like a favorite paintbrush or whatever will seem to work better for you, even though there's no particular reason."

"We'll leave it there," Mikey said. "I'm fresh out of clever analogies. As long as you understand that using these marvelous kaleidoscopes and teleidoscopes will not be like turning on a radio, I am content."

"Okay, I accept that."

Mikey gestured toward the Cabalistic Seven. "These seven kaleido-scopes were created for specific purposes, and that may make them easier for you to use. Think of skis again."

"I'd rather not," I laughed. "I've never skied in my life. I think I see where you're going, though. It's like paintbrushes. There are different brushes for different purposes, and the differences don't just have to do with width and length of the bristles. Bristle materials make a huge difference, so does quality, so does the angle at which the brush is trimmed. A long time ago, I was advised to buy the best brushes I could for a specific task because what I'd spend in money, I'd save in effort, clean-up, and even paint."

"Wonderful!" Mikey said. "I've never painted, either, but I'll have to add that one to my list of examples. Very well. Since these seven kaleidoscopes have been crafted to make certain types of inquires easier to do, in using them, you will save effort. However, you will lose generalities."

"Generalities?"

"Do you remember card catalogs?" Mikey asked.

"Sure."

"Well, computer databases are wonderful, but the one thing you lose when doing a computer search are the generalities. The computer takes you to a specific point, whereas in leafing through the card catalog you would see the surrounding entries. Sometimes, at least in my experience, these would be as useful as the one you had intended to find."

I grinned. "I know exactly what you mean. Especially when I'm research-ing something nonfiction, I write down the numbers for the topic and then scan the entire shelf, looking for what else I might find. That's why I don't like researching something new over the Internet. Even the best search en-gines can't match what my own curiosity might find."

"And that will be the limitations of these kaleidoscopes," Mikey said. "Let's see, today is Wednesday, right?"

"Right." I'd grabbed the appropriate volume of Aunt May's mythology dictionary on our way up, and looked up the entry for mirrors. "Wednesday is Mercury, crystal, and money. So if we looked into it and inquired after Colette, we'd get nothing."

"Right," Mikey said. "Is there one that is meant to help with finding lost objects?"

I scanned the entry. "Saturday. Lost articles and secrets. Let me guess. If we tried it today, we'd get nothing."

"I'm afraid so. That limitation is one of the prices of precision. What are tomorrow's and Friday's?"

"Thursday might be interesting," I said. "Jupiter, tin, and probable success. Friday probably won't be much help. It has to do with Venus and love."

I thought about Domingo, and wondered if I might take a peek on Friday, run a search, so to speak, for my true love. Would that be fair?

"Friday might be more useful than you imagine," Mikey said. "You might be able to inquire after your father by inquiring after Colette's love."

"She had lots of lovers," I said dismissively, "and there's no proof she loved my father, just got a child with him. Mikey," I said, deliberately changing the subject, "you keep saying 'you.' Aren't you going to use the kaleidoscopes? After all, I may have some talent, but I have no training."

Mikey shook his head. "I could, I suppose, but you are the one who needs to find Colette. I had planned to coach, but I think you would have a better chance of getting good information."

"That mother–daughter bind you mentioned yesterday?"

"That, and that these are her tools, and this is her house, and many other things that I can't go into without being confusing. Suffice to say that the probabilities are better if you do the scrying."

I started to protest, but stopped. Liminal space was supposed to be useful for probability analysis. Had Mikey already made some inquiries? I thought, too, about how Mikey had been able to place his message where it would intercept me. Had Colette—or her abductor—placed barriers against pursuit? Might my relationship to Colette be sufficient to enable me to move those barriers?

Instead of protesting, I nodded. "I accept that, Mikey. However, I'd appreciate some training, if you can give it. Last time I fainted and slept like I was dead for over ten hours. If I'm going to be useful at all, I'd better not pull any more muscles."

Mikey gave a crisp bob of his head. "That's wise. Unless you're interested in inquiring after money . . ."

"I'm not."

"Then why don't we put these away. Keep one kaleidoscope out, one you haven't looked at much, and that will be it for now."

I chose a kaleidoscope whose stained-glass barrel held hues ranging from deep teal to a sea foam so pale that the greenish hues were almost lost in the white. Its object case was, appropriately, one of those in which the items within were suspended in a thick liquid. The images here would shift even without my turning the case, but slowly, like dancers in a dream.

The rest of the day drifted by in a fashion that itself seemed rather like a dream. Mikey was right. There simply aren't words to explain the sensation of drifting between things, riding with that betweeness without forcing it to become something by your use. It's hard. More than once I concentrated so intently that I solidified a line, a sensation rather like being inside water as it freezes, though not in the least cold.

I grew tired, and ate a late lunch that would have satiated a football player. I napped, and woke up ravenous. Mikey and I continued my training until late afternoon, then he invited me to an early dinner.

"You shouldn't have to cook, after all of that. Tell me, would Domingo Navidad be interested in joining us? I'd like to get to know him better."

"We can ask," I said. "He's usually out back around this time, watering the garden. The painters usually knock off in late afternoon to give them time to clean up."

"Let me go ask him," Mikey said. "You rest."

I was tired enough to agree, leaning back in the leather chair in the office where we'd been working. When I heard the soft clink of a glass onto the coaster on the desk, I said, "Thank you," without opening my eyes.

"You're welcome, Mira," said a soft, female voice.

I opened my eyes quickly enough to see one of the silent women leaving the room. She used the door, just like any person would. Was that habit or necessity? I didn't seem to have the energy to worry about an answer.

Dinner, which we had at the Landmark Grill in the Plaza Hotel, did a great job of restoring my energy. Over dinner, Mikey and Domingo carried most of the conversation, discussing home repairs and restoration, mostly.

Mikey's hobby was carpentry, and I enjoyed listening to the two men talk. They did so without the one-upmanship that is so common in man-to-man conversations among near strangers, each feeding the other's tale with one of his own.

After a while, I started participating, for although I hadn't done much renovation work until I came to Phineas House, I was a builder in my own way. We chatted through dessert and coffee. Then Domingo, after glancing at me and assuring himself that I was no longer on the verge of collapse, suggested we go for a stroll around the Plaza.

"There are some very interesting buildings there," Domingo said. "I worked on a few."

Mikey agreed, though I suspected that a stroll around the Plaza area would be just about his limit. He really was in astonishingly bad shape, but I put that down to living where the weather was cold enough to make Ohio seem tropical. If you didn't like winter sports, just how much exercise could you get?

Domingo gave his tour-guide spiel much as he had done for me, though with more attention to specific details of structures rather than to local history. I trailed behind, enjoying seeing the buildings again, my gaze scanning the Plaza for a structure that shouldn't be there.

I found it. The windmill overlaid the gazebo and other structures, complete in every detail, but translucent. Paula Angel sat on the base, swinging her long legs beneath her ruffled skirt. Without saying anything to the two men, I walked over to her, marvelling that as I did so everything became more solid, so that by the time I reached the ghost's side, the modern Plaza was less substantial than the windmill's rough wood.

"Hey," Paula said. "Walking out with a couple guys. Not too bad."

"Not too bad," I agreed. "How are you?"

"Making do, making do. Not a hell of a lot changes here, y'know. I drift."

"Drift on over to my place some time," I said. "You've got to get bored here. I could use some girl talk."

"Girl talk is about guy talk," Paula said with a laugh. "You gotta guy you can't figure out?"

"Something like that," I admitted, "but mostly I remembered what you said about being bored. You helped me out with what you told me about my mother. I guess I wanted to help you in return."

"I'll remember that," Paula said. "Hey, the fat guy. He looks familiar, but I don't know why. He been around here before?"

"He has," I said. "Seems to know you. Calls you Pablita, not Paula, though."

She narrowed her eyes, her lips curving in a sensuous smile. Then she laughed.

"I remember that one. Mikey, he called himself. Fat kid. Shy with the girls. I told him a few things. Tell him to come visit some time."

"I will," I said. "I'd better get back before they miss me."

"Oh, they miss you," Paula said. "One more than the other, I think."

She laughed again, mocking, wicked, innocent, and faded away wherever ghosts go when they're not where you can see them.

Thursday, Mikey suggested that I practice with the Jupiter kaleidoscope. I was hesitant.

"Success seems like a strange thing to augur for," I protested. "Abstract. At best I keep imagining one of those Magic Eight Ball toys: 'Answer cloudy, try back later.'"

"Well," Mikey said. "That would be useful, wouldn't it? I doubt you'll get anything so clear."

"I know," I said. "That's why I'm not sure that I'm up to it. Something more concrete would be easier."

"Like your true love's face?" Mikey asked mischievously, fingering the copper case of the Venus kaleidoscope. I'd polished it since my initial discovery, and now it glowed as warm and welcoming as a lover's kiss.

I made inarticulate sounds of protest and Mikey laughed.

"Relax, Mira. I was only teasing. Honestly, love is probably the first thing anyone ever augurs for. Did you ever think about how many little rituals there are for it—from pulling petals from a daisy to those intricate games that involve counting the letters in your name and rearranging them to find the initials of your future sweetheart's name? I bet the first question you ever asked one of those Magic Eight Balls was whether some fellow liked you."

"I think it was about whether I'd passed an exam," I fibbed. "Still, we weren't talking about auguring for love, but for success. How would I scry for something so tenuous?"

"If it were me," Mikey said, "I'd find some very precise way of phrasing the question in my mind, then I'd look into the kaleidoscope with the intention of seeing the answer as a visual image."

"You do it then," I said, childishly stubborn.

Mikey laughed and shook his head reprovingly. "I told you, Mira, you are more likely to learn something than I am."

I drummed my knuckles lightly on my forehead as I considered this. What, after all, did I have to lose?

*Certainty that you will find out what happened to Colette*, came the answer, drifting from the depths of my subconscious. *If you don't get an answer, you will fear that success is beyond you. If you do . . . well, then you're committed.*

I turned the kaleidoscope in question over and over in my hands. The outer case was pierced tin through which gold shone softly. I recalled that the colors within were dominated by azure and blue, that little figures of lightning bolts were mixed in with the more usual gems and irregularly shaped pieces of glass. It hadn't hurt me to look through it then. Certainly, it couldn't now.

"Okay," I said. "I apologize for being difficult. I'll give it a try."

"Thank you, Mira," Mikey said seriously. "Actually, I prefer your reluctance. Usually, when I tutor someone in these arts my problem is the reverse—too much eagerness, too little thought."

*Tutored others?* I thought. *Of course he has. Didn't he say that these talents are inherent in almost everyone, but that they can run stronger in families? He's a descendent of Aldo Pincas, too, so obviously he has gifts that he could pass on to his own children and grandchildren.*

I raised the kaleidoscope almost to my eye, then lowered it again as I thought of a question.

"Mikey, would I have managed to learn these things if I'd never come to Las Vegas?"

"Maybe," he said. "Maybe not. Much would have had to do with your frame of mind. Frankly, as long as you were blocking yourself artistically, I think you would have blocked yourself in other ways, too. If you had ever let go and expanded your potential, I suspect you would have found yourself taking a lot more unexpected shortcuts or having insights into things. Whether you would have realized you were employing liminal space to do this or not . . ."

He shrugged.

"I might have just ended up one of those 'wise' people," I said, "or maybe lucky in my finances and relationships, except it wouldn't have been luck at all."

"And you might not have always had true visions," Mikey said. "There are all sorts of edges out there, and not all of them are the edges between what might happen and what will, some are simply between mights."

"You're making my head ache," I said with a laugh.

"So look through the kaleidoscope and see what you see," Mikey said. "Give yourself a rest from questions."

I lifted the kaleidoscope, and this time I did as Mikey had commanded. I relaxed, studying the shifting images, looking as I had learned to do for the unique element amid the shifting multiplicities. As I did so I repeated over and over in my mind: "I want to find out what happened to Colette. Will I succeed?"

Amid the drifting lightning bolts I found one that wasn't like the others. I focused in on it, watching as it grew within my line of sight. The others had been represented like jagged lines, longer top to bottom as lightning bolts rain from the skies. As I focused on this one, it drifted onto its horizontal axis, the jagged length transforming into a road that jolted violently across a dark landscape.

Then, even as in my dream of a few nights before, the roads multiplied: two becoming four, four eight, eight sixteen, sixteen thirty-two, thirty-two sixty-four. Each road was the violent blue-white of a lightning strike in a summer storm, each seared my retina with a vivid black afterimage, so that the jagged roads multiplied even more.

I struggled to focus in on one road, the road I thought was the original, watched as it stretched on to the horizon. I realized that this road and its multiplicity of fellows were curving slightly downward, each jagging back and forth, back and forth, but bending slowly and almost imperceptibly down. Before it happened, I knew what they would do.

The roads joined again at a hub an infinity of distance below their point of origin, the whole pattern forming an enormous globe, fit together puzzle-piece tight, puzzle-piece perfect, fusing into one eye-achingly blue-white ball and its dark afterimage. The roads went nowhere but to themselves, to their source.

The image held for a long moment, then either I lost my concentration or the show was done, for the twin globes vanished and I was again watching the shifting patterns of gentler blue and white mingled into pretty mandalas ornamented with stylized lightning bolts.

"So what did it mean?" I asked Mikey after I'd taken two aspirin, and told him as precisely as I could what I'd seen. "Yes or No?"

"I'm not certain," he said somberly. "Iconography is very personal, but usually there are enough common symbols that I can interpret visions. This one started out clearly enough. You saw a road, but that multiplying . . . You say you saw something similar in a dream?"

"I did. Colette and her gig going down a bunch of identical roads."

"Did they end up in a globe in that dream?"

"I don't know. I can't remember clearly. Something about a hub and a void. That's it."

"And we probably shouldn't make too much of it, either," Mikey said. "After all, the last time anyone saw your mother she was driving her gig down a road. It makes sense you'd dream of her."

"And this vision, the one in the kaleidoscope," I asked.

"I'd guess that it means that there are still too many options left undecided for a clear vision of success or failure. You could try scrying to refine the options . . ."

"Not now," I said. "Maybe later. My head hurts and my eyes feel like I really did stare into a lightning storm. Mikey, can you bear with me if I just go take a nap?"

"Certainly," he said.

"Mikey?" I asked, my voice sounding like that of a very little girl.

"Yes."

"When do you have to go back to Minnesota?"

"Not until after Saturday at least," he assured me. "After that, we'll talk."

Friday morning I woke early, probably because Thursday's afternoon nap had extended into the evening. I'd crawled out of some very vivid dreams into that cloudy, foggy state that's so annoying because you're neither awake nor really asleep. I'd managed to awaken enough to thud down the hall to the bathroom.

When I staggered back into my room, I had found a tray at my bedside containing an array of perfect invalid food, including English muffins and thick strawberry jam. I smeared half of one muffin with butter and jam, and as I was chewing my first mouthful I had noticed two neatly folded notes on the tray next to the teapot.

One was from Mikey, telling me he'd gone back to his hotel, and that I could phone him if I woke up and wanted company, but that I should sleep as much as I wished, that he could easily entertain himself. The second note was from Domingo, offering to run any errands I might need taken care of, and urging me to take it easy.

Half an English muffin had been almost more than I could handle, and after rinsing away the worst of the stickiness with a conveniently placed glass of water, I apologized to my teeth—I simply couldn't make the trek back to the bathroom again—and crashed back to sleep.

So it was that Friday morning I awoke after something more than twelve hours of sleep feeling bright-eyed and energetic, though with a mouth that tasted awful. The tray had been removed, but the tumbler of water had been refilled. This I drained in a couple of large gulps. The inside of my mouth still tasted like the death of all strawberry factories.

I rose and headed for the bathroom, marvelling that the same trek had been nearly impossible to manage the night before. I sang as I showered, dressed in a bright patchwork skirt and green blouse, and headed down-stairs to make coffee. Domingo wouldn't be by for breakfast for hours yet—if at all.

Over bacon and eggs—cooked by me, though I thanked the silent women for their service the night before—I caught up on my e-mail, rapid-firing messages off to various friend, including Hannah in Albuquerque. I'd mentioned earlier that I was planning to go to the State Fair with Domingo, and she'd suggested we pick a day and meet up. It sounded good to me, al-most as good as her casual assumption that Domingo might be more than a handyman playing local guide.

After I'd sent off the messages, I found myself thinking about Domingo. My thoughts had a copper tinge, and I knew why. Today was Friday, and the reigning kaleidoscope was the copper-mirrored one dedicated to Venus and matters of love.

I walked upstairs with steady purposefulness. I knew how to use the kaleidoscopes now, and I even had a suspicion that asking a question about my love life wouldn't drain me as had inquiring after Colette. This was simple and straightforward, surely. There would be one of two answers: Yes or No. I supposed that if Domingo himself wasn't sure about his feel-ings there could be a "Maybe," but even that wouldn't be too bad.

The kaleidoscopes weren't in the upper parlor where Mikey and I had been looking at them the day before. I found them back in their secret com-partments, neatly locked away. I wondered if Mikey had done it, or the silent women. Somehow I thought Mikey had. For all that he knew so much more than I did, he was very polite, even respectful, as if the mere fact that I had inherited Phineas House was a matter to respect.

I slid open the right hand drawer and looked down at the kaleidoscopes. All were there, each in its correct place. My hand drifted toward the copper casing, moving slowly, so I could see my fingers reflected in the shining metal.

I stopped a few inches short of picking it up and stood there in that attitude long enough that I became aware of the wood creaking as the House warmed with the rising sun. Then I straightened, leaving the kaleidoscope in its place.

Using it to inquire after Domingo's feelings wouldn't be right. It would be too much like spying on him, worse really. If I peeked in his window, all I could see were details of his exterior life. Using the kaleidoscope would be like peering into his heart.

I went down the kitchen and set up a fresh pot of coffee. Then I wandered out into the garden. The early morning chill was giving way as the sun rose higher, but all the plants continued in their early morning freshness. Without volition, my fingers found something daisylike growing among one of the borders. I plucked away the petals one by one: He loves me. He loves me not. He loves me. He loves me not.

The last petal was torn in two or perhaps it had partially been eaten by some bug. I stared down at it feeling dismay all out of proportion to what I was seeing. I was still looking at the partial flower petal when I heard the gate open and Blanco's yap of greeting.

I crushed the flower into my palm and moved quickly—though whether to greet Domingo or to hide what I had been doing, I don't know.

"Good morning," I said brightly. "Let me run inside and turn on the coffee."

## 25

However, researchers discovered that not only did synesthesia take different forms within the same family, but that even when it took the same form—colored letters, for example—the colors perceived varied greatly from one family member to another.

—Patricia Lynne Duffy,
*Blue Cats and Chartreuse Kittens*

## INSIDE THE LINES

Mikey called while Domingo and I were on our second cup.

"How are you feeling, Mira?" he asked.

"Much better. Sorry about pooping out on you yesterday."

"Don't worry about it. I had a pleasant afternoon. In fact, I learned a few things. Would you mind if I came over and shared them with you?"

"Not at all. If you'd like, we can have lunch."

"That would be wonderful. Tell me. Is Domingo available to join us?"

"He'll be out with the painters," I said. "It is a work day."

"If Domingo can take a break," Mikey said, "I really would like to speak with him."

"I'm sure he'll leave off if you want to ask him something."

"Good. I'll be there in about fifteen minutes."

We rung off and I went back out into the garden. Domingo was busy pulling grass from between the border stones of the garden. His fingers remained busy as he listened to my question.

"I'll be here all day," he said. "I will tell the crew that the trustee for your estate wants to review my custodian work. They will pity me, and maybe even work harder so that I'll look good."

I chuckled. "You're probably right. Come on in as soon as you can take a break after Mikey gets here."

Mikey arrived slightly more than fifteen minutes later, but the reason for his delay was explained along with the heavy grocery sack he carried into the house.

"I thought I really have been imposing on you," he said, "so I went and picked up a few things to add to lunch."

I peeked in and saw neatly wrapped packages of deli cold cuts, some chips, and a small bag of apples.

"You're not imposing," I said truthfully. "I feel that I'm imposing on you—especially making you stay in a hotel."

"I've been drawing my fee as your trustee for a good number of years now," Mikey said, "and this is the first time since you were settled with the Fenns that I have had to do more than review a little paperwork. And I assure you, staying in the hotel is no burden. Large as this house is, I think that right now you need your space."

"There has been a lot for me to adjust to," I admitted, leading the way into the kitchen. "Tell me, Mikey, will using the kaleidoscopes always hit me so hard? I mean, I feel like a kid riding a bike that's too big for her. It takes more effort than I have to give."

Mikey looked grave. "In order to use power, you must give something back. That's one of the oldest principles of magic, found in every tradition there is. It's the true meaning behind the tale of Adam naming the animals. In doing this, he asserted his sovereignty over them, but he also gave them names—individual identities. In many magical traditions, knowing the true name of something is knowing how to control it. That's why true names are kept secret."

I wrinkled my nose, feeling doubt. "But Adam named the animals. Doesn't that mean he knew their names and so still kept power over them?"

Mikey chuckled. "Adam also named Eve, and how much control did he have over her?"

I shared his laugh, but didn't let myself be distracted from how this applied to me specifically. "Leaving out Adam, Mikey, should using this ability stay so hard for me?"

"I don't think so, but I honestly don't know. Mira, I sense a great deal of ability, power, whatever you want to call it, inherent in you, but I will admit, I have been puzzled by the effort it takes you to use it. It's almost as if something is blocking you."

"Phineas House, you think?" I asked, finding myself glancing up at the ceiling as I had noticed Mikey doing a couple of time.

"No. I don't think so," Mikey replied. "I'm something of an expert on Phineas House—at least as much as anyone who is not keyed to it can be—and my feeling is that it is pleased with you. Certainly the behavior of the silent women would seem to bear witness to this."

"They took care of me last night again," I said. "Brought me a tray and your note. But if it isn't the House, what then?"

"I've been wondering if it's something that Colette put in place," Mikey said. "Her behavior toward you was always strange—protective and antagonistic at the same time. Her father viewed her as a rival. I wonder if she feared that Phineas House would pass her over in favor of you once you had developed some skills. Maybe she did something to prevent you from coming into your potential."

I thought about this as I put the extra groceries away.

"Maybe," I said. "Maybe. In any case, we don't need to worry about it until we can use Saturday's kaleidoscope."

Mikey didn't press me to try using Friday's to garner hints about my anonymous father. I think how hard I'd been hit by our sessions had made him cautious.

Domingo knocked on the kitchen door about fifteen minutes after Mikey's arrival. He'd clearly taken time to go back to the carriage house and clean up from painting. He was wearing slightly faded blue jeans and a collarless button-down shirt. His hair was slightly damp, as if he'd just gotten out of the shower, and I found myself thinking of that indecisive daisy petal.

The men exchanged their greetings and some small talk about the work on the exterior of Phineas House. We made elaborate sandwiches, and continued our small talk through an early lunch. Afterward, Mikey turned to me.

"Mira, would it be possible for us to adjourn to your library? I have some papers to show you, and the desk would be convenient."

I nodded. "Refill your drink and come along. There are three chairs there. I'll let you have the one at the desk."

When we were settled in, Mikey began without preamble. "I knew that we had found a reliable caretaker for Phineas House, but it wasn't until I met Domingo that I realized what an extraordinary person he was."

Domingo shuffled his feet in the carpet, obviously uncomfortable with this effusive praise—and perhaps suspicious of it as well.

Mikey went on. "Domingo, Mira has told me that she has confided to you a great deal about the—oddness—both of her own history and that of Phineas House."

"That's right," Domingo replied a trace defensively.

I didn't blame him. I was feeling defensive, too. Mikey was leading up to something, and I wasn't sure I was going to like whatever it was, but Mikey was still smiling and still being his affable self. I made myself listen without saying anything.

"As we've discussed your work on Phineas House," Mikey said, "one thing has become clear to me. This extraordinary paint job was not Mira's idea, was it?"

Domingo shook his head. "I have never said so, nor has she. It was the House's idea. Mira was kind enough to think it was a good idea, and encouraged me to complete it."

"Tell me," Mikey said, addressing us both. "Neither of you thought it the least odd that Domingo should be so in tune ·with Phineas House's wishes?"

Domingo let me answer first.

"Not at all," I said. "At first, I didn't know Phineas House could have wishes. I took Domingo's statements as figurative. If you'd been around as many artists as I have, hearing that an ornate house—one whose current paint scheme was clearly at odds with the demands of the structure, let me remind you—anyhow, hearing that that ornate house 'wanted' a more suitable paint job seemed pretty normal, like hearing a sculptor talking about there being a fox or a child or a naked woman in a chunk of marble."

"And, later," Mikey asked, "when you realized that Domingo wasn't speaking figuratively? It didn't strike you as odd then?"

I shrugged. "How I realized Domingo wasn't speaking figuratively was when I started experiencing the same prompting. You've got to understand, Mikey, it's not like Phineas House says 'Paint those dragons crimson, would

you?' It's just that if you look at the house long enough and let your imagination drift, pretty soon you get a strong feeling for what combination of
colors is, well, right. After that, anything else seems wrong."

"And you, Domingo?" Mikey asked. "Was it like that for you?"

Domingo shook his head. "No, not quite like that. Choosing the right
colors is not so easy for me. I have to concentrate a lot, even try samples. I
have a computer program for this, but sometimes I have come out and
tried a splash against the wood and looked at it. I have a cousin who works
at a paint store, and he's okay about giving me samples because he knows
that when the time comes I'll be buying a lot of paint."

"I don't just mean," Mikey said, "how you select the paint colors, I mean
how you communicate with the House."

"Like Mira says," Domingo replied, "it's not like talking. It's just a feeling.
I've always had it, from when I was small and coming here with my father to
tend the gardens. I could feel how the gardens should be, and that those
fences in between shouldn't be there. Later, I could tell that the House felt
sad because she was colored so dully. Even later, when Colette vanished and
Phineas House was shut up, I felt the House becoming more and more quiet.
I would come here sometimes to trim the lawns and make sure nothing had
broken in, and it felt like the gardens surrounded a great sleeping creature."

Domingo looked at Mikey, then at me. "I'm not crazy. I know some people think I am, or even that maybe I am a little slow, a little thick, but I am
not. When the real estate company offered me the job of caretaker rather
than just groundkeeper, I was very pleased. I took jobs in renovation so I
would know what an old structure needed. When in the early 1980s the
Montezuma Castle grounds were taken over by the United World College, I
was offered work there, and I took it because then I could better serve
Phineas House's needs."

"When was this?" Mikey asked.

"Early 1980s," Domingo repeated. "That's when the college bought the
land, but they didn't use the Castle right away. It was in too bad shape.
They used other buildings. The big renovation was more recent—I think it
started in 1997 or maybe 1998. The rededication of the Castle was just a few
years ago. It was a huge event with celebrities from all over the world coming. I met a queen, even, Queen Nur of Jordan."

"Bingo . . ." Mikey said very softly, but he didn't elaborate. Instead, he returned his genial attention to both of us. "Well, despite the capacity of the
two of you to take the extraordinary as if it were quite usual, it is not usual

for people—even the 'liminally talented'—to get messages from Phineas House. Yet I do not doubt for one moment that this is what Domingo has done."

"And me?" I asked.

"Of course you," Mikey said. "You're the heir to the House. In a very real sense, you're the one person I'd expect Phineas House to talk to. That's why Domingo's ability, which I could sense for myself, struck me as unusual. So, when Mira didn't need me, I took advantage of my free time to do some research. Would either of you be very surprised to learn that Domingo is also a descendent of Aldo Pincas?"

We were, but neither of us said anything. We just stared at Mikey, waiting for him to clarify.

"Aldo Pincas, the builder of Phineas House, and his wife, Rosamaria, had three children. The first was Amerigo, who inherited the House. The other two were Carlta and Fernando. I've done some checking through old records here and elsewhere—the Net is really wonderful—and confirmed to my satisfaction that Domingo is a descendant of Fernando Pincas."

"Really?" I asked. Domingo was too astonished to say anything.

"Really," Mikey confirmed with a crisp nod. He started unfolding papers, spreading them on the cleared portions of the desk. "When he was a young man, Fernando went to seek his fortune away from Las Vegas. He never returned, but years later his daughter, Florencita, returned with her new husband. As far as I can tell, Florencita did not associate very much with the residents of Phineas House. They were cousins, true, but they had been raised apart and had little in common. I do not even know if Florencita had any talent beyond the normal for sensing liminal space. In any case, some of Florencita's descendants have remained in Las Vegas, but where Amerigo's children married Anglos, Florencita's alliance was to the Spanish town. I wouldn't be surprised if by the next generation, the two families had so little in common they did not even associate."

"Another duality," I said, my voice hardly louder than a whisper. "Two branches of the same family living side by side in the same small town, gradually forgetting they were related. It's weird . . ."

"Weird," Mikey agreed, "but interesting. What do you think, Domingo?"

"I'd like to see your records," Domingo said, rising to bend over the spread papers, "but I am inclined to believe you. The name Florencita remains a family name for us. My mother's sister is Florencita, though mostly she goes by Florie."

"Look as much as you want," Mikey said. "Copiers are wonderful, too, especially when," he twinkled mischievously, "you can slip in after hours and copy things not usually available to the public."

I didn't bother to ask about how Mikey had managed that. For all his friendly affability, Michael Hart was a sorcerer or something very like, and a locked door or two probably wouldn't stop him from going where he would.

We all poured over the papers for a long while, tracing lines and deciding that Mikey's leaps of faith—which he had been forced to make from time to time as the old record keepers seemed to have been rather cavalier on matters of spelling—weren't large enough to make it seem that the connections had been forced.

"Happily," Mikey said, folding up the records, "genealogy is a hobby of mine. Some of us who use liminal space are still trying to figure out exactly what makes it likely for the trait that allows conscious use of liminal space to be passed on between generations. Not all my children have it, but I'd like to know if one of their children might. In any case, it seems that Domingo still carries traits inherited from his great, great, great whatever grandfather Aldo Pincas, and that Phineas House, desperate in her abandonment as she had never been before, reached out and connected with him."

I sat staring at Domingo. The blood connection was tenuous enough that it wasn't even like we were real relations, but still it was a great deal to take in. Domingo wasn't looking at me. He really wasn't looking at anything in the room but back across time and the ebb and flow of generations. When Domingo's gaze focused again, he was looking at Mikey.

"Could I have a copy of those papers?" Domingo asked. "My family has never been too into written genealogies, but there are old Bibles and the like. I could probably confirm at least some of this."

Mikey bent and pulled a fat manila envelope from his briefcase. "I thought you might like a copy, so I made you one."

I understood why Mikey hadn't handed the copy over immediately. Domingo might have resisted knowing that he was related to the family that, in the present day, he was employed by, the same family that had not let his father over the threshold, even into the kitchen.

I wondered about that now. Initially, the restriction had seemed just another example of Colette's snobbishness. Had she, in fact, sensed a connection, and decided not to risk attenuating her connection to Phineas House? It seemed possible, but then again, the way things were going it also seemed possible that the full-length portrait of Colette that still hung in her bedroom would come to life and begin ordering around the servants.

Right now, just about anything seemed possible, and I felt the dull throb of a developing headache. I shook it away, exasperated. So what if the universe was more complex than I had ever imagined? It was also a whole lot more interesting.

Eventually, Domingo excused himself to return to supervising the painters.

"I would rather remain," he said in gentle apology, "but this is Friday, and I think I should make certain that they do not grow sloppy as the weekend beckons."

We assured him that we understood, and with a slight bow Domingo rose and departed. When he was gone, Mikey looked seriously at me.

"Mira, is that door tightly closed?"

I checked, and it was. "There's a window open behind you, though. The House isn't air-conditioned, you know."

Mikey nodded. "Yes. I recall. Perhaps it would be wisest if we adjourned to that upstairs parlor again. No one is working on that side of the House, are they?"

I shook my head. "No. The front of Phineas House was the first part Domingo painted—a brave face to the world or something like that."

"Good."

We stopped by the kitchen long enough to refill our glasses, and I excused myself to use the bathroom. As I washed my hands, I frowned at my reflection in the mirror over the sink. What did Mikey have to tell me he didn't want overheard? For the last half hour or so our conversation had been general, so that implied it was something he didn't want Domingo to overhear either. That didn't please me, but I kept my suspicions to myself as I joined Mikey in the front parlor.

He was seated on one of the love seats, looking around at the elegant room where Colette had most often held court with her favorite of the moment.

"Your mother didn't share your love of color, did she?" he commented. "She didn't redecorate the House in full, but in her private rooms, she preferred muted colors or white."

"It's elegant," I said. "So was she, and she certainly didn't avoid rich col-

341

ors in her personal attire. She revelled in them. I remember how her clothing almost seemed to sing it was so vivid."

Mikey smiled. "It might well have, you know. Has it ever occurred to you that you are likely a synesthete?"

I knew the term. It was common enough in artistic circles where the idea that color might be heard or that sounds might have colors and shapes was a provocative one.

"I hadn't really," I said. "Certainly, I don't show any of the usual signs— no colored or textured alphabets or numbers."

"Even so," Mikey said. "You frequently refer to colors as making sounds. I suspect that as a child you were more acutely aware of it. Apparently, synesthesia is more common in children than in adults."

"It's that liminal space thing again," I said with sudden insight. "A child doesn't draw the same distinctions as an adult does. I remember thinking quite firmly that numbers had gender—that one and five were boys, while two and four were girls."

"What about three?" Mikey asked.

I laughed. "I don't remember, a boy, I think."

"So boys are odd," Mikey chuckled. "That sounds like a healthy female attitude."

I stuck my tongue out at him as if I were a girl, not a mature woman past her fiftieth birthday.

Mikey forbore to return the gesture. "Seriously, Mira, synesthesia is a documented phenomenon. No one doubts the reality of it—though not all who claim to possess it do. I think you are a synesthete, but rather than your brain assigning colors to abstract concepts, your colors have sounds."

"Or did," I said a little sadly. "I seem to have outgrown it. This room is quiet enough."

"Don't be so hard on yourself, Mira," Mikey said, almost scolding. "As I said, your own words gave me indication of your probable tendency."

"But, that's not why you had me come up here, is it?" I asked. "We could have discussed synesthesia downstairs as well or better than here. I think there's a book or two on the subject on the shelves."

"Interesting," Mikey said, "but, you're right, that isn't what I wanted to discuss with you. It's a sensitive matter. I even thought about asking you to take me for a drive, but I think that in the long run it's better we air it here."

"What is it?" I said. "Have you found something out about Colette?"

"No. Not Colette. And it's not something I'm even sure about." Mikey looked very uncomfortable. "It's about Domingo."

"More about Domingo? And this is something you couldn't say in front of him?"

I know I sounded angry, but I didn't apologize, nor did Mikey seem to expect an apology. If anything, he seemed relieved that I would stand up for Domingo.

"Yes. About Domingo—and as for saying it in front of him—I wanted to see how you wanted to approach the matter. He's your handyman, your caretaker—and, more importantly, your friend."

This didn't sound good.

"What is it? Something else you uncovered in your research?"

"Yes and no. Remember our discussion about how Phineas House was placed where it could ideally take advantage of the area's feng shui?"

I nodded.

"And how," Mikey went on, "the shape of the lot played a part in Phineas House's effectiveness?"

I nodded again. Mikey waited a moment to see if I would say anything, then continued.

"We probably will never know for certain if the truncating of the lot was done deliberately, or merely to raise money. There might even have been a combination of motives—money was needed, and someone who hoped that changing the shape of the lot would effect Phineas House's effectiveness prompted the sale."

"Whatever," I said. "That's how it was when I was a child. The lots had been sold off. There were houses close on either side, and one along the back. We didn't have much more of a backyard than what is the courtyard today."

"But today you have back the entire property," Mikey said, "because of three providential fires, and trustees who thought to take advantage of them."

I managed a thin smile. "And I thank you for it. I can't imagine Phineas House in its current loud paint job squashed between two other houses."

"Nor can I," Mikey agreed. "Mira, I was one of your trustees when the properties came up for sale. The first fire was to the property in the rear and occurred in the early eighties. That had always been a peculiarly shaped lot, and no one was really interested in it. The owners let it go rather than pay taxes on it, and we bought it from the city.

"The second fire occurred a year or so later to the house on the left of

Phineas House. This house had been on the market for quite a while, and hadn't been occupied for several years. We had considered buying it as an asset for the estate, but the asking price was quite high, especially after the owners learned that the offer came from the owner of the neighboring property."

"So?"

"We had already dropped negotiations when the structure caught fire. It was wooden, and went up so fast that the trees closest to it were singed. Police had some suspicion that arson was involved."

"Oh?"

"The electricity and gas had long been disconnected. There were no lightning storms that might have caused the fire. The house itself was empty—no fuel in the heaters. No piles of rags lying around. It seemed that someone might have set the fire."

"Did the city investigate?"

"Not in any detail. The prevailing theory was that sometimes wooden houses burn for no apparent reason, especially in such a dry climate. The second theory was that some bums might have been squatting in the house, and caused the fire by accident. It wasn't until the third fire that the city began to seriously consider there might be an arsonist operating."

I didn't like where this was heading, but I continued to listen politely.

"After the fire, we bought the vacant lot for the estate. It was going cheap, and the property did belong to Phineas House's configuration. We thought about inquiring about purchasing the remaining house and lot, but we'd had to answer more than a few questions from the police after the house on the other side had burned—some bright mind thought we might have done it when we couldn't get the property any other way. When we proved that we had been out of negotiations for over a year at that point, and noted that we had no plans to build anything on the vacant lot nor to sell it, the investigation into our possible involvement ceased."

"After all," I said, "what motive would you have to buy a lot adjoining a house that was vacant? If you'd wanted to build a new house there, or sell the lot at a profit, well, maybe there would be some reason, but buying a lot and paying taxes on it just to improve the feng shui of Phineas House?"

"You're being flippant," Mikey said, "but I think that was pretty much what the police thought. Had Phineas House been occupied immediately thereafter, they might have had reason to question again, but this was almost twenty years ago, and the House would remain empty for a long time to come."

"There was a third fire," I reminded him, "and you said this has to do with Domingo."

"The third fire," Mikey continued imperturbably, "did not occur until three years later. By this time, the structure to the right of Phineas House was no longer inhabited and was on the market. Like the second fire—like the first, if we're being completest—it was quick burning. No one was hurt, no other property was damaged. This time, however, the police were certain arson was involved. They found tell-tale marks that showed where gasoline or some similar liquid had been poured. However, they could not find a motive for the fire, and eventually the fire was dismissed as hooliganism."

"Were you questioned this time?" I asked.

"No. We were not," Mikey said with a smile. "We had not offered on the property when it went on the market, nor did we offer after the fire. We finally bought it when a real estate agent, acting on behalf of the seller, came to us."

"So," I said, "three convenient fires . . . but you think there is something more. You think Domingo set those fires, don't you?"

Mikey didn't try to deny it. "I have no proof, Mira, but circumstances are very interesting. The early 1980s are when the Montezuma Hotel was bought by the United World College. As you must remember, the Montezuma Hotel—most specifically, the Castle—was built in an attempt to curtail the ability of Phineas House to channel local currents. I've done some investigating, and although the Castle was not immediately put into use, from the time the property was purchased, even after the formal dedication of the college in 1983, there was considerable construction on the property."

"Construction," I said, "that you think did something to negate whatever influence the Montezuma had on Phineas House."

"If not negate," Mikey replied, "at least ameliorate, moderate, reduce. Remember what Domingo said earlier? The early eighties is when his attachment to Phineas House increased, when he began to think of learning skills that would serve the House, when he began to define himself not as a man who viewed his caretaker position as a job that brought him a place to live and a small salary, but as his vocation."

"That's a little strong," I said, "but I admit you have a point. Do you think Domingo learned that Phineas House had once had more property, and deliberately set out to rebalance the lot? I can't believe that. Even if he did burn down all the surrounding structures, he had no guarantee that you trustees would conveniently buy up the land."

"No, I don't believe that," Mikey said. "What I think is more likely is that Phineas House, well, put the idea in his head. It must have been aware of fire, given the number of times its rival the Montezuma burned."

"You mean Domingo was the House's puppet? If it wanted puppets, why wouldn't it use the silent women?"

"Domingo may have been a puppet, though it is hard for me to imagine the House having the volition to actually control a living person. As for the silent women, they are extensions of the House's desire to serve its inhabitants. Without inhabitants, I suspect they do not fully manifest."

"So what do you think happened?"

"I think what happened was in between Domingo being a deliberate arsonist and being the House's puppet. I think the House dreamed and Domingo shared those dreams. Eventually, Domingo acted on those dreams. When you think about it, the fires were all quite like fires Domingo would set. They were well-planned, no one was hurt, no surrounding property was hurt. The only thing that happened was an obstruction to the House's perfection was removed."

"I don't like it," I protested. "Domingo is a builder, not a destroyer."

"But he'll rip out old wood that's grown weak or rotten to put in new. He'll tear out weeds that are choking his plants. Really, there's not a lot of difference between the destroying and building—at least from the point of view of the weeds."

I glowered at Mikey. "You aren't going to talk to Domingo about this—not without a lot more proof than you've given me."

"That is why I wanted to speak with you about the matter," Mikey said with deceptive mildness. "I wanted your opinion on how to handle the matter."

"You won't bring it up," I repeated stubbornly. "I don't care if your theory is correct—and I don't know if it is—or not. This is slander of the worst possible type."

Mikey held up his hands in a gesture of surrender.

"As you wish, Mira, as you wish. I will not speak a single word on the matter, but I felt I had to tell you. Aldo Pincas created more than he imagined when he had Phineas House built. None of us really understand it or what it is capable of."

I heard the warning in Mikey's words, and nodded stiffly to acknowledge it.

"Fine. But we say nothing of this to Domingo. Nothing."

## 26

Hellerer describes a sensation of literally feeling herself "in" time, moving *inside* an hour or a day, walking within a week, looking behind her at the "smaller" previous days or weeks as they recede in the distance.
—Patricia Lynne Duffy,
*Blue Cats and Chartreuse Kittens*

## INSIDE THE LINES

Saturday's kaleidoscope, the one holding the leaden mirrors of Saturn, wasn't cased in lead—as Venus had been in copper or Jupiter in tin—a fact for which I was grateful since I was going to be handling it. Nor was the tube dull grey. I guess after iron, tin, and silver, Colette had wearied of that hue. Instead, the casing was thick enamel that flowed like watered silk through all the shades of yellow, from sunny brilliance to the pale tint found in the inner petals of grass flowers.

But what first caught the eye was not the yellow casing, but the elaborate object chamber. A handblown sphere had been filled with golden-orange liquid in which glitter in the same shades had been suspended. The sphere was ringed around with flat pieces of enameled metal, richly colored after the fashion of Saturn's shifting rings. I'd been too overwhelmed the first time I'd inspected the cabalistic kaleidoscopes to think about the artistry of this piece, but now I took time to give it the appreciation it deserved.

Saturday midmorning once again found Mikey Hart and I in the downstairs front parlor. I sat in the window seat that had been my favorite when I was a child, feeling still some of the same sheltered protectedness of the spot. I needed that feeling, for I realized I was scared stiff to look through the eyepiece and see what the kaleidoscope might reveal.

Mikey patiently waited out my fidgeting, then said, "Well, Mira, how well does lead reflect?"

It was exactly the right question to ask me, for it engaged my curiosity. I knew I'd glanced through the lens at least once, but the impressions were intermingled with impressions from the others I'd inspected that day. Hard as I tried to remember, I couldn't recall how the lead mirrors had managed to act as reflectors.

I lifted the kaleidoscope to my eye and turned toward the window, discovering as I did so that within Saturn's sphere, when light reflects off of lead, it becomes gold, golden light breaking into nearly monochrome mandalas.

*Sunflakes*, I thought, *like snowflakes, sparkling with color, singing with light. It wasn't like this before, I'm sure I'd remember if it had been. I guess this means it's ready to be used for scrying.*

I gasped as a particularly beautiful sunflake took form, and reflexively started to lower the kaleidoscope so Mikey could have a look. In my peripheral vision I saw him making shooing motions.

"You keep it, Mira. Take a good look. This is the one that is supposed to reveal lost articles and secrets. Lost a sock lately or maybe your glasses? This is the time to find them."

I didn't wear glasses, and a sock had hardly touched my foot through New Mexico's warm summer. I knew Mikey was teasing me. I was surrounded with puzzles and secrets enough, including and especially the mystery of wherever it was that Colette had gone when she vanished.

But was a person a lost object? I didn't know, and maybe I was just a little fearful of what I might find out. After all, what if she was dead? Would I see her corpse in a grave? Her ashes scattered on the winds? Her bones gnawed by scavengers spread about some isolated arroyo?

Instead I concentrated instead on learning one of Colette's secrets, focusing with all my might on finding the solution to the question I had never asked her.

"Who is my father?" I thought—or maybe I said it aloud. I don't really know. "Who is he or was he?"

I turned the kaleidoscope in my hand, peering through the golden mandalas, watching them shift and change until I felt drawn into a blizzard of golden light. The golden light was easy on my eyes, not in the least harsh or glaring. My earlier fear slowly ebbed, exhilaration taking its place as I walked, penetrating deeper and deeper into the glittering field, catching sunflakes on my tongue and listening to their bell-like chime as they fell in drifts about my feet.

Gradually, I became aware of an intrusion into the omnipresent golden light, something in shades of grey and black, a rhomboid shape, nearly square, flat and two-dimensional. I moved toward it as the one anomaly in the golden haze. I'd forgotten to concentrate on a question, forgotten everything but my pleasure in my surroundings. So it was that I was rather surprised to be confronted with a photograph framed in a stolid walnut frame: a head and shoulders shot of a man who was staring into the camera with a stern and solemn expression.

The man depicted within was young—in his mid-twenties, perhaps— but had about him a sense of stolidity. You didn't need to look at him for long to know that for all his youthful leanness, he would be stout and stodgy come middle age. He wore his hair in a stiff brush-back. His face was adorned with a thin, somehow military seeming mustache, though he didn't wear a uniform, but instead what seemed to be a suit with an old-fashioned stiff collar.

Now I remembered the question that I had carried with me into the golden mandalas and I asked aloud in pure amazement, "That's my father? I don't believe it!"

The golden light went ruddy, as if flushing with anger, but then paled again into more comfortable hues. The photo in the frame changed, showing the same man in successive images, each slightly older than the last. The man's hair receded, his figure broadened, his expression grew sterner and more self-confident. He wore glasses or the vague expression of someone who is accustomed to glasses but has put them by for vanity's sake.

The photos were never candid, and always focused on the head, so that I could see little of the man's costume, but from what I could see, it always remained formal, the style old-fashioned. The photos themselves seemed old-fashioned, though I was pressed to say why. Good photography is something I admire, but have never pursued, perhaps because I so much enjoy creating with my hands.

Then abruptly, the sequence ended with a picture that showed this man—my father—no older than maybe forty, and I was willing to bet younger than that. I continued to stare at the frame, and the golden light obliged by beginning the sequence once more. This time I garnered a few more details, including a strong sense that the man's hair was probably dark blond or light brown, that his eyes were also light, grey maybe or pale blue.

After this second showing, the frame lost cohesion, its browns, blacks, and greys breaking into minute particles that dispersed into the surrounding golden light until they were lost. Then the blizzard in which I had so joyfully ventured began to cohere and solidify, becoming again the sunflake mandalas, and I was aware again of my body sitting on the window seat, my feet curled beneath me, my back leaning against the wooden window alcove.

I lowered the kaleidoscope, too confused to even feel tired. Mikey set down the book he had been reading, an action that made me feel certain I had been walking amid the sunflakes for a long while.

"Well?" Mikey asked. "You were entranced for quite a while—well over an hour. Except for two things, you said very little."

"What did I say?" I asked, carefully setting the kaleidoscope on a nearby table and rising. I was certainly stiff enough to have been sitting motionless for an hour or more.

"The first thing was mumbled," Mikey said, "but I caught the word 'father.' The second was rather more clear. You said in complete astonishment 'That's my father? I don't believe it!' Then you fell silent again, right up until now."

I walked over to where a pitcher of iced water, the ice nearly melted now, had been set on a tray. I poured myself a tumbler full, taking delight in the deep reds of the glass, using them to draw myself back into a world other than one filled with golden light.

Mikey waited with astonishing patience, but then he probably had experience with this disconnected feeling, the feeling that nothing around you is as vivid as the images moving in your mind's eye.

"I saw," I said at last, "a picture frame, and in it the image of a man in his mid-twenties."

I described the man as best as I could, including in my description how, after I had expressed doubt the image had shifted, showing the same man at various ages.

"You say the images stopped when he was maybe forty?"

"Forty or a bit younger," I concurred. "I thought forty at first because he seemed so, well, stolid. The second time through, I looked more carefully.

He had lines on his face, at the corners of his mouth and near his eyes, one between his brow, but none of them were at all deeply graven. They were almost proto-lines, showing where he would have deep lines in another ten years. Know what I mean?"

Mikey nodded, touching his own face where habitual expressions were deeply etched. "I do indeed. Now, remember, sunscreen and moisturizers are modern obsessions. A man of your mother's generation not only wouldn't have had access to them, he probably would have shunned them as unmanly if he did. Then there's the question of lighting. Photographers didn't always have access to bright lighting. The man in the pictures might have been older than you think, the lines on his face recorded more softly than today's unforgiving cameras are likely to do."

I shook my head. "You're right, Mikey, but I think I've got the age right. It's just a feeling, which isn't much to go on, but still . . ."

Mikey's nod acknowledged the potential validity of my feelings. "I wonder why you were shown static images rather than the man himself."

"You know perfectly well why," I said, "but are too kind to say so. Obviously, the man is dead. My guess is that the first image was from the year I was born—remember I asked to see 'my father' not Colette's husband or lover—and that would be the year he became my father. Only after I protested did the other images appear, almost like annual shots right up until the year of his death."

"I don't suppose," Mikey said, "you recognized him."

"No," I started pacing, aware even as I did so that my body ached with a preternatural fatigue. "I didn't. I'll tell you something else that puzzles me even more than that. He didn't seem at all Colette's type."

"Type?"

"You'd know if you'd seen the pictures," I said, "especially since you knew Colette. This man was stiff, stuck-up, self-absorbed. You could tell from how he looked at the camera, from how, except for a couple of pictures, he didn't wear his glasses. Colette's lovers—and I remember a good number of them—were all, not playboys exactly . . . Dandies, young gentlemen about town, men who knew how to have a good time and liked doing so in the company of a pretty woman. The man in this picture looked like he'd try to be dignified while eating birthday cake."

"Maybe Colette's experience with him," Mikey hazarded, "turned her away from the serious types, especially if he rejected her when he learned she was pregnant."

"Maybe," I said. "It makes as much sense as anything. Mikey, why is it whenever we find an answer, it just raises more questions?"

"Because you haven't answered the question that's at the heart of this," Mikey said, his expression kind but stern. "You came here to find out what happened to Colette, and that question remains unanswered. I admit, I thought that your father had something to do with it, but if he died young . . ."

"Those photos seemed to span about ten years," I reminded Mikey. "That's long enough for him to have had something to do with Colette's disappearance."

Mikey nodded. "You're right. You were nine when she vanished, weren't you?"

"That's right." A strange thought came to me then. "Do you think he—my father—was killed by Colette and she fled to escape the consequences?"

"It's possible," Mikey said. "It's also possible that he died trying to do something to Colette, or even that he kidnapped her and then died and for some reason—amnesia maybe—she never returned. Let's not place the blame for his death on her. It might be a coincidence."

"I'm fine with that," I said. I'd paced back in the direction of the window seat, and now I sunk down onto the cushioned surface once more. "Mikey, I'm beat, but I'm also not going to wait another week to ask after Colette. Maybe a person isn't included in 'lost articles,' but I have to try."

"What do you want to do?" Mikey asked.

"It's past lunchtime," I said. "Let's get something to eat. That sandwich I had earlier is less than a memory. Then I'll take a nap. If I haven't gotten up by, say, four, you promise you'll wake me?"

Mikey nodded. "I promise. That will leave eight entire hours for you to experiment with before Saturday's mirror falls inert—and even time for a dinner break."

"Good," I said. "I'm so tired I could fall asleep right now, but I'm going to make sure I eat something."

"Want a tray in bed?" Mikey asked.

"No. I'd fall asleep in my sandwich." I patted back a yawn. "Come on."

As we made our sandwiches, I had a thought.

"Mikey, you knew Colette far better than I did. Maybe you'd recognize the man I saw."

"I might," Mikey said, smearing enough mayonnaise to explain his girth on a slice of dark rye. "But I'm reluctant to use the kaleidoscopes. They have been working for you—I'd hate to . . ." He piled sliced turkey on his bread, searching for the right term. "Uncalibrate it. That's the best word I can come up with. If we don't get anywhere this evening, I promise to try. Sunday's kaleidoscope might work. Certainly this man is a 'great person' in our current difficulty. Tuesday's might work, too, if he was an enemy of your mother, and perhaps of you."

The sandwich tasted wonderful, as if my body was soaking up the nutrients and singing hosannahs as it did so, but even so I was almost too tired to think.

"Okay. I see your point. Can you keep yourself busy for the next couple of hours?"

"Certainly," Mikey said. "There are any number of novels here, and I'll probably call my wife and bring her up to date."

"Good," I said, forcing myself to my feet. The idea of putting my head down on the table was beginning to seem too attractive. "Remember, if I'm not up by four, you'll wake me. Promise?"

"Promise," Mikey replied solemnly. "I promise."

Mikey not only kept his promise, he had put together another meal, one more substantial than sandwiches and chips.

"This violates," I said, laughing as I lifted a forkful of breaded chicken in a rich butter and cream sauce to my lips, "every diet out there. And did you have to make a cheese sauce for the broccoli?"

"There is devil's food cake for dessert," was Mikey's response, "with or without ice cream if you prefer. I spoke with my wife about your problems with exhaustion, and she suggested the menu. I," he added with complacency, "cooked it though."

"It's good," I said, "very good, and it hits the spot. Tell me, is your wife . . . I mean does she . . ."

"Have an awareness of liminal space?" Mikey completed for me. "A little. We met when I was in law school and she was taking teaching courses at the same university. The lecture halls were in the same building and we both had a tendency to arrive early."

"A teacher?" I asked. "What was her subject?"

"English: grammar and reading. Like you, she taught at the grade school level, so she learned to be a bit of a jack-of-all-trades. She's retired now, of course, like I am."

We talked a bit about Mikey's family, and then Mikey said almost awkwardly. "I called Domingo for help because I wasn't sure I could find the grocery store. He asked after you, and I filled him in. He wanted you to know he's thinking about you, and wishes you well."

"Thank you," I said, then grew guarded. "You didn't tell him anything else, did you? Like about fires?"

"Nothing," Mikey said, making a "cross my heart" gesture over his chest. "He did ask more about the Pincas family, though, and I filled him in where I could. I don't know a great deal about Fernando's branch. My interest has always been with Amerigo's."

"Makes sense. How's he taking it? I mean, finding out he's sort of related to Phineas House."

"Fairly well," Mikey said. "Actually, I think the information was something of a relief. He's felt a connection to the House for so long, finding there was a reason was a good thing."

"He's not . . . well, envious that I own it, not him?" I hated to ask the question, but there was no avoiding it.

"I don't think so," Mikey said, "but then I wouldn't be the one he'd tell, would I?"

"You being my trustee and all," I said. "No. I guess not."

When our early dinner was completed and the kitchen tidied, if not cleaned, we adjourned to the front parlor again. I felt good. If the morning's experiment had been a disappointment in many ways, it had at least banished my fear of using the kaleidoscope.

"Ready?" Mikey asked.

"I'm going to ask," I said by way of reply, "to have the answer to what happened to Colette. I think that's better than searching for her as if she's a lost shoe."

"Good idea," Mikey said. "Since no one but Colette knows why she rode out that day, that certainly qualifies as a secret."

"No one but Colette," I said, raising the kaleidoscope to my eye, "and whoever she was going to find—if it was someone, not someplace she was seeking."

"True," Mikey said, and the single word echoed and re-echoed in my ears as I let myself sink into contemplation of the slowly moving golden mandalas.

I lost myself in their shifting beauty, moving deeper among them until they turned like pinwheels on all sides.

"What happened to Colette?" I asked. "What is the secret of her disappearance?"

The pinwheels spun around me, faster and faster, until I could hear the buzz of their edges against the wind. Their patterns vanished, replaced by isolated blurs of golden light that surrounded me like a host of miniature suns. Then the individual suns exploded, their lights overlapping, washing me in a golden tide, overwhelming me.

I closed my eyes, but the light penetrated my eyelids, permeating every cell of my body, searing my optic nerves with a shrill ecstatic cry before ebbing. When I dared open my eyes again, I thought I would be blind, but my sight was perfectly clear. I was standing at the edge of a dirt road, and a stylish gig I knew very well, drawn by a familiar bay horse was coming down the road in my direction.

Colette, teleidoscope in hand as if she had just been peering through it, held the reins.

I stood there on the side of the dirt road, shifting my foot when a bit of gravel dug into my instep. My gaze greedily devoured every detail of the woman driving the gig, finding her both like and not like I remembered her.

One difference was so obvious I almost laughed aloud for not expecting it. Colette was shorter than I remembered. It was hard to judge for certain with her seated, but I guessed she was no taller than my adult self. She also looked younger than I recalled, but, again, that made sense. She had been in her midthirties when she had disappeared, almost twenty years younger than I was now.

Other things were precisely as I recalled them: her elegance, her grace, her haughty arrogance, the angle at which she carried her head, the piercing sharpness of her gaze. There was something else that niggled at my memory, something I could not lay hold of, and I let it go, captivated by the moment.

Colette was drawing closer now. I could hear the squeak and jingle of harness leather. I thought I could catch the scent of Colette's perfume even over the odor of horse sweat, but that was almost certainly my imagination.

I glanced down at myself. I was dressed in the clothes I had put on after my nap: a loose ankle-length skirt in a silver-shot green, a scoop-necked cotton tee in pale grey. I'd put on earrings, long dangling ones strung from freshwater pearls and jade beads, but no other jewelry. My feet were bare.

I knew Colette. Those bare feet alone would be reason not to acknowledge me, but a style of dress that in the late fifties would have been defined as bohemian at best would also mean her gaze would pass over me as if I were nothing more than a lizard sunning myself on a rock. Colette was not one to nod to passersby.

I must speak first, that was clear, but what could I say? What should I call her? Certainly not "Mother." If I was indeed intercepting her on the day of her disappearance, her only child was nine year's old. At best she'd think me flippant, at worst some inmate gotten loose from the mental hospital.

"Mrs. Bogatyr!" I said as the gig drew closer. "Mrs. Bogatyr! I have a message for you."

Colette raised the teleidoscope to one eye, I thought to look at me, but the slow scan of the crystal sphere passed over me as if I wasn't there.

Angered at this rudeness, I called again, raising my voice to be heard over the steady fall of Shooting Star's hooves.

"Mrs. Bogatyr! I need to speak with you. It's very important."

The gig drew abreast, but Colette did not pull up the horse, did not slow in the least.

"Mrs. Bogatyr! Colette! Mother! For heaven's sake, listen to me!"

No pause, but in the gig's shining metal trappings, I saw the truth. I cast no reflection. I wasn't there except as an observer.

I should have known. Mikey had confirmed my deduction that the kaleidoscopes were meant for scrying, and scrying was watching, looking. It was nothing more. The gypsy did not slide into the world in her crystal ball. I was not Alice, gone through the looking glass.

Even as I accepted this, I came to the realization that though I had made no effort to do so, I was keeping up with the gig. I had resumed my point of view slightly ahead of the gig, watching it come on toward me, never reaching.

Periodically, Colette would scan the landscape through her teleidoscope, but she did not seem to find whatever it was she was seeking. At least she never paused nor changed her course, but continued riding on.

I don't really know how long I stood there alongside the road and watched. All I know is that I had been watching for a long time when I noticed something strange. Hadn't the gig passed that field before? I was certain I remembered the colorful if rather tattered shirt that adorned the scarecrow. It had caught my attention, not only for its color but because I wondered why a scarecrow was set up so early in the season, and had decided it must have remained from the summer before.

Alert now, I glanced about me, certain that a house, a heap of stones at the roadside, a patch of straggly wild flowers were all familiar. At last I thought to glance up at the sun. It had changed position, and stood exactly opposite where it should be in the sky. That last confirmed it. Somehow Colette had reversed her course without my ever seeing her turn the gig. She was no longer heading away from Las Vegas, but back toward it.

I had no choice but to accept this, spending my energy instead on looking for other alterations in my surroundings. I found them almost immediately. When I had first encountered her, Colette had driven through a living landscape. What she travelled through now was more a semblance of one, an extraordinarily vivid painting, a film that continued to unwind but without sound other than what Colette and her assemblage made. The steady sound of the horse's hooves had fooled me, but there was no birdsong, no insect chatter.

When we passed a field where a farmer was mending the fence that protected his field of greening crops, there was no sound though he was busy with hammer and nails. There was no scent either, though there should have been that of crushed herbage and maybe even the rank odor of male sweat.

*So Colette has passed into some liminal space where she's paralleling the real world, moving alongside its borders. I wonder if I am in some similar state in relation to her? I wonder if I could bridge the gap.*

I tried, but I was like a child trying to drive a car. Just as the child knows the car should move, even knows what the gas pedal and brake do, how the steering wheel is used, even that the key turns in the ignition, still this is not enough.

*And I don't even have the car keys. I guess I'll just have to watch to see where she goes, then see what happens to her there.*

That's what I did, letting my point of view draw me along through this land on the edge of a land I almost knew. That almost became increasingly important as I watched, especially when we reached town. That what I was seeing was Las Vegas, New Mexico, I was certain—although I'll admit it took passing several landmarks and reading a dozen or more street signs for me to be certain. Las Vegas this certainly was, but it wasn't the Las Vegas I knew.

Which Las Vegas it was was not easy for me to decide. There were cars, but these were older models, older even than the cars I remembered from my childhood. I noted details, figuring I could sketch them later. Mikey would probably know their types, and if he didn't I could check at the library.

The attire of the people walking on the street was also old-fashioned, but I wasn't enough of a clothing historian to be certain just how old-fashioned it was. Again I made mental notes. Seeing a man walk by with his nose buried in a newspaper gave me the bright idea of going to check the date printed on the paper, but I found I was limited to the vicinity of Colette's gig. I could stay slightly in front of it, draw alongside, or trail a few paces behind, but that was my range.

After a bit, I recognized the neighborhood into which Colette was turning her carriage as the very one in which I was currently residing. Many of the houses were recognizable as ones I knew, but very few resembled their modern counterparts. They were painted different colors, window treatments weren't the same, plantings were arranged in different patterns. In a few cases I saw young trees where in my day towering giants stood. In other cases, the trees that shaded street or yard were long gone in my day.

I was not at all surprised when Colette drew her gig to a stop in front of Phineas House. This was neither the wildly colored House of my present, nor the paler one I remembered from my childhood, but instead it wore a color scheme that was somewhere between the two. The background color was a pleasant sunny yellow, the shutters and window casements were a darker harvest gold. The numerous carved details were neither ignored as they had been during Colette's tenure, nor accented as they were in mine. Instead they were brought out just a bit, often in shades of ivory or lighter yellow. The effect wasn't as dramatic as my "Fairground Midway style," but it worked.

As Colette drew her gig to a stop and gracefully dismounted from the driver's box, all sound but Shooting Star blowing and shaking her trappings ceased. Then Colette dismounted the box, and went to the gate. She didn't walk through it as I thought she might, but when she opened and closed it, there was no sound.

The same routine was followed at the front door, which, evidently was unlocked. I expected my point of view to follow Colette inside, but I was stopped at the front door, unable to penetrate further. It wasn't as if I was anchored to the gig, but rather as if a strong wind—one that politely didn't muss my hair or stir my garments—pressed me back.

I remembered that Mikey had said Phineas House had been created to channel the currents of liminal space, and that while the channelling had greatly benefitted Aldo Pincas and his family, it had not benefitted other liminal travellers in the least.

"But why can't I get through?" I said to myself. "I'm a member of the family. Could it be because I haven't been born yet? Colette could get through, though. Does this mean that she has returned to the past—for certainly this is the past—but within the span of her own life?"

That made sense. Paula Angel had told me that Nikolai Bogatyr had held but the lightest of holds on Phineas House, and that upon Colette's birth, the House had bonded with her. Therefore, unlike earlier heirs who had taken over upon their parent's death, Colette had the bond from her birth.

I kept trying to get in without success. Had Colette gone into the past and been killed there? That would explain why she hadn't returned, and why there was no record. Nikolai and Chantal Bogatyr would not have recognized their daughter in this elegant woman dressed, even for their time, in out-of-date styles.

I began to think that I would keep a fruitless vigil right up until midnight when, presumably, Saturday's kaleidoscope would cease to show its vision and I would be thrust back into the front parlor in the Phineas House of the present day. With a long wait in mind, I'd taken a seat on the high curb, leaning back against a tree that wasn't there in my time, but here and now provided fine shade from the late-spring sun.

I'd gotten comfortable, and my feet—which felt like I'd been on them all this time, for all that I must have been here only in spirit—had lost their ache, when Colette came back out the front door and made a beeline for her gig.

Although Colette moved with her usual grace, there was no doubt that my mother was furious. Her hands in their kid gloves were clenched into tight fists, and her mouth pressed in a line so thin that her full lips became a slit. She mounted the driver's seat with abrupt jerking motions, and when seated slapped the reins across patient Shooting Star's back so that the mare looked back at Colette in equine rebuke before breaking into a trot.

Leaving Phineas House behind, Colette began to retrace her way through the streets of Las Vegas. When I saw her lips moving, I brought myself alongside the gig in case I might overhear something interesting or useful. Most of what she said was inarticulate, little hisses and snorts, punctuation in an internal dialogue to which I was not privy. Only once did she say something aloud.

"I suppose I'll need to return the one before I can have another. What a bother! I've made the trip twice now, and hoped never to risk a third."

Colette said nothing further to clarify this. Over time her supreme self-control reasserted, so even the indignant hissing ceased and her mouth resumed a semblance of its usual lines. Only her eyes narrowed with calculation showed she was anything but a well-born lady out for a drive.

I think I noticed before she did that something wasn't right, but I could be wrong. Self-control was always one of Colette's strong points. In any case, before long we both had registered that the gig was no longer travelling either through the streets of Las Vegas or through the surrounding countryside.

The landscape was familiar, yet it was not. There were mountains in the right place, but they weren't quite the right mountains. Key features looked just the littlest bit off. The dirt road was the same, but the flowers that grew along the edge were too far advanced for late April. These were the sunflowers and asters of late summer. The fields showed signs of harvest, cut to the ground in some places, bailed hay waiting to be hauled to shelter.

There were other indications, but they all came down to the same thing. Colette Bogatyr was lost somewhere between the past and her present. Belatedly she pulled out the forgotten teleidoscope and sought to chart her course back to familiar ground. Although I understood nothing of what she was doing, I could tell she was unsuccessful.

My mind filled with the image I had encountered in various forms in dreams and visions, Colette travelling further and further down a road that fragmented with possibilities, growing more and more lost with every choice she made.

When a swirling of sunflakes heralded my return from vision to my own time and place, Colette still had not found her way back. Her expression was becoming increasingly frantic, the hand holding the teleidoscope was beginning to shake.

For the first time in this mad venture I was glad I couldn't speak to her. I felt shamed and yet relieved that I did not have to be the one to tell her that she would never make her way home.

27

Surrealist artists were fascinated by psychological mean-
ings of colors. Oddly, each hue has both a positive and neg-
ative connotation in most cultures. For example, consider
the following: White: innocence *and* ghostliness; Black: restful strength *and* depression; Yellow: nobility *and* treason;
Red: ardent love *and* sin; Blue: truth *and* despondency; Purple: dignity *and* grief; Green: growth *and* jealousy.
—Betty Edwards,
*Drawing on the Right Side of the Brain*

## INSIDE THE LINES

I came out of my trance to hear the grandfather clock on the upstairs landing chiming the strokes of midnight. Mikey Hart sat, or rather slouched,
half-asleep in one of the comfortable padded chairs. To my surprise, a
much more wide awake Domingo Navidad sat in another, and when I lowered the kaleidoscope from my eye, he was across the room and taking it
from my hand, setting it on the table, pressing my hands between his own.

"Mira? Mira? Are you all right?"

Sunflakes still spotted my vision, like the afterimage of a camera flash or
a bolt of lightning. The room reeked of strong coffee, undertoned with male
sweat.

"Coffee," I said weakly. "Water. Aspirin. Bathroom first."

I tried to get to my feet, but I felt wrung out. Unfairly, for someone who had been sitting for the last several hours, my feet hurt, just as they had in my vision. When I tried to stand, my left ankle buckled.

Domingo caught me, his arms around me feeling very good. I restrained myself from an impulse to giggle, knowing full-well I was overtired and punchy, not wanting to say or do anything that I would regret later.

By the time he had escorted me to the bathroom, I was steady enough that I gently pushed him back.

"Thank you," I said, "but I think I can handle this."

He nodded, but as I closed the bathroom door, I noticed he watched very carefully to make sure that I didn't fall. I managed to pee, then drank several glasses of water and swallowed two aspirin. When I opened the bathroom door again, Domingo was waiting at a polite distance. Mikey stood beside him, a mug of coffee in his hand.

At the smell of the coffee my head pounded harder and my stomach roiled. I waved it away when Mikey would have brought it over.

"No. Sleep. I'm sorry. So much to tell . . . Too tired. Too damn tired."

I was nearly asleep on my feet, and I didn't even want to protest when Domingo came and helped me into my bedroom. I know that he and Mikey were there when my head hit the pillow. After that, I don't remember anything except for a host of odd, golden-hued dreams.

I slept ten hours, and I'm not sure I even rolled over once. When I opened my eyes, Domingo was waiting in a chair by my bed. I grinned weakly at him.

"Making a habit of this?"

"I hope not," he said seriously, "at least not quite this. How do you feel?"

I yawned, remembering belatedly to cover my mouth, and as I did so ran a mental check through my body.

"Pretty good," I said. "No headache. Starved though."

Domingo smiled. "Mikey Hart slept at my place last night—so did I, in case you wonder. The silent women escorted us out, but they let me come back in this morning. Mikey hasn't gotten moving yet. He's not young, and though he hasn't said anything, I'm sure this hasn't been easy on him."

"Go check on him," I said, "while I shower and get respectable. Then come back over for breakfast. Oh, and tell Mikey he should check out of his hotel and come stay here. The silent women won't throw him out if he's a guest, and I'd feel safer with someone in the House."

Domingo quirked the corner of his mouth. "I hope you're not afraid of me. Even the silent women know I'm harmless."

"Harmless?" I teased. "I hope not. That would be too boring. You can stay here, too, if you want, but you have a perfectly good house within shouting distance. Look. This will all make sense when I've had a chance to explain what I saw last night."

"Do you know, then, what happened to Colette?"

"Sort of," I said. "Not quite. It's very strange."

"What about this hasn't been?" Domingo said. "I will do as you say, but first . . ."

He leaned down and kissed me squarely on the lips, and though he made no effort to prolong the contact, there was nothing brotherly about it. Lightning shot right through me at the contact, and I know I blushed right up to the roots of my hair.

"I'm very glad you're feeling better, Mira," Domingo said, and then he made his way briskly, but not hurrying, out of the room. I lay there listening to his feet on the stairs, thinking of falling daisy petals.

Then, practical soul that I am, I got up and headed for the shower.

I told Mikey and Domingo about my vision of the night before over a very substantial breakfast.

"These car models," Mikey said, looking at the sketch I'd drawn. "Late twenties, early thirties."

"Colette was born in 1928," I said. "That would be about right then, at least if my guess that she could enter Phineas House without resistance because it was, effectively, her house. The House has intelligence, in its own way, but I'm not sure it has enough to sort Colette from Colette."

"Wouldn't it sense two Colettes?" Domingo asked. He'd made no comment about that kiss—and well, neither had I—but insisted on doing most of the cooking, and had hovered over me until it was quite clear that I was feeling fine.

"Maybe," I said, "but I've been thinking about that. Maybe the signatures, well, sort of blend, like if you add ocean water to ocean water. It's not possible to sort it."

Both Domingo and I looked at Mikey, but our expert only shrugged.

"Time travel through liminal space has always been theoretically possible, but I've never tried it, and I've never known anyone who has success-fully done much more than retrace a couple of seconds. The farther back you go, the more possibilities there are, complications that make it . . . The best word I can find for the sensation is dizzying. The times I tried I felt sick, disoriented, with a touch of vertigo thrown in."

I nodded. "But you did say that Colette had learned to use routes most people never dared. I think that's what she was trying to do here—and that she'd done it before, made it there and back successfully. What messed her up this time is that she was so angry she forgot to plot her course, and when she realized what had happened, it was too late."

"But what happened in the House," Domingo asked. "What did she see that upset her so much?"

"I wonder if she witnessed her father's death?" I suggested, then I shook my head. "That can't be right. This was the middle of the day. Didn't that happen at night?"

"So the reports say," Mikey agreed, "but those need to be taken with a grain of salt, since we know a cover-up was involved. I'm interested in what you overheard. What did she say again?"

" 'I suppose I'll need to return the one before I can have another.' " I quoted from memory, though I'd written the words down, for future refer-ence. " 'What a bother! I've made the trip twice now, and hoped never to risk a third.' "

Mikey frowned. "It sounds to me like she'd actually succeeded in bring-ing something forward from the past into her time. I wonder what would be worth the risk? She would have inherited everything the House con-tained."

"We can theorize forever," I said with more confidence than I felt. "There's only one way to be sure—I need to use today's kaleidoscope and see if I can learn more. You yourself mentioned that Colette is a 'great person' in my life, especially right now. I'm hoping that kaleidoscope is set to show not only great people, but great events—like the murder of Julius Caesar or something. I'll ask to see not only Colette, but what happened to her that day in Phineas House."

"Do you think it will work?" Domingo asked, as much of Mikey as of me.

Mikey only shrugged as if saying the kaleidoscopes were not his to as-sess, so I answered.

"I think my mistake—and it wasn't really a mistake—last time was in asking to see what happened to Colette. The kaleidoscope did as requested. It showed me going into the past, then that she got angry, and whatever made her angry led to her making a mistake that put her off course so she got lost."

"And since the fact that she got angry—not what she got angry about," Domingo said, following my logic with flattering speed, "was what was the key to her getting lost, the kaleidoscope did not bother to work through Phineas House's currents to show you the specific incident."

"That's what I guess," I said, "but I won't know until I try."

Mikey spread jam on a slice of cold toast. I'd thought I had a sweet tooth, but Mikey was making me feel positively virtuous.

"How soon are you going to try scrying again, Mira?" he asked, looking down at the shining surface of the strawberry jam as if he could see omens in it. For all I knew, he could.

"Pretty much immediately," I said. "I'm rested, fed, and if I do this now and learn something that makes me want to refine my scrying I'll still have time to try."

"Good planning, except for one thing," Mikey said. "Last time what you asked the kaleidoscope to show you essentially had no end, so you remained enthralled until the kaleidoscope reached its limits—and we were lucky that wasn't beyond your physical limits."

Domingo leaned forward, his gaze intent. "Watching you was a little frightening, Mira. You hardly moved. You sat there like you'd been carved from wax, hour after hour. The only thing that changed was that you grew more and more pale, and circles formed under your eyes. There was no doubt the process was draining you."

I acknowledged their concern with a brief nod.

"I can see your point, but what I want to scry for this time is definitely a matter of limited duration. Colette was not in that past Phineas House for more than an hour."

"How can you be sure?" Mikey countered. "I suspect your sense of time was distorted."

"It may have been," I replied, "but the odd thing was that I felt as if I had my body with me. I mean, my feet hurt after I'd been standing for too long—even though here I'd been sitting. How about my using those signals my body gives to let me know if I'm pushing too hard?"

Domingo shrugged. "I don't see how we have much choice, but, please, take care, Mira. These kaleidoscopes are wonderful tools, but you cannot forget that they take a toll on you."

"I'll be careful," I promised, "but what happened in there is important. I feel it in my bones."

The two men looked at each other, exchanging glances that said, "Well, we warned her." About a half hour later, we once again adjourned to the front parlor.

I hadn't bothered to tell Mikey and Domingo that I sincerely doubted the experiment would work at all, that we might be left waiting until later in the week, maybe all the way to next Saturday to do our follow-up research. My dictionary defined Sunday's mirror as used to scry "great persons on earth." I wished I knew more. Did that category include great persons living and dead? Did it include past events as well as present?

I'd decided to press ahead as if it did, remembering stories of legendary seers who impressed their clients by showing them views of famous historical personages, but I wasn't confident that my kaleidoscope embraced the ability to do the same. Maybe that was why the two men's cautions didn't seem important. I didn't believe today's attempt would achieve anything.

Making myself comfortable in my chosen window alcove, I picked up Sunday's kaleidoscope. The hand-beaten gold case was comfortable in my hand, the little dimples in the metal kissing my fingertips.

As I raised the kaleidoscope to my eye, I spoke my purpose aloud. "I want to see my mother. I want to see what happened when Colette went into Phineas House that day."

Somehow I felt certain the kaleidoscope would know what I meant by "that day," but I clarified, "The day I viewed yesterday through the kaleidoscope with mirrors of lead, the day Colette left here and never returned."

The object chamber for Sunday's kaleidoscope held a rattling assortment of multifaceted topazes in shades ranging from a yellow-gold so pale that the stones were almost clear all the way to dark amber. Interspersed among the topazes were infinitesimally small rubies. Scattered among the stones was a haze of gold dust.

The combination made for beautiful mandalas, flower-shapes whose golden petals were streaked with red. Occasionally, when I turned the kaleidoscope, red would dominate, creating tiny red wildflowers against fields of gold. I walked into this garden, moving here and there to enjoy each new delight as it materialized, gradually losing awareness of the me who sat in the window seat, a dimpled metal casing rolling slowly between my fingers.

I was in the garden behind Phineas House. A woman wearing old-fashioned clothing, her shining brown hair parted in the middle was there with me. She had the gravitas of a matron but the fresh, unlined skin of a girl. In her arms she cradled a very young infant wrapped in the lace-trimmed flounces of another day.

"Chantal," a man's voice called down from us, "I know you are weary of being shut indoors, but I think it is too cool yet for the baby. Come inside now."

"Oui, Nikolai," Chantal replied with tranquil patience. "See? I have wrapped her up very well, but I will come in as you say."

"Very good," the man's voice said.

I heard what sounded like a window closing, and guessed that the speaker—my grandfather Nikolai—must have been upstairs, looking out into the garden. This then would be my grandmother Chantal, and the baby in her arms could be none other than Colette.

While listening to this brief exchange, I had confirmed that, as with my previous day's vision, I was limited to the vicinity of the mother and child, so I followed as Chantal walked around the house rather than going in the convenient kitchen door. I wondered if she would not use a servant's entry or if this was her way of prolonging her time outside without actually defying her husband.

As we rounded the side of the House through a narrow walkway—the side lots had already been sold, squeezing Phineas House into the truncated yard I remembered from my childhood—I saw a familiar gig parked by the front gate. Shooting Star turned her head to watch Chantal pass, but Chantal gave no sign of noticing either horse or carriage.

I wondered why I had not seen Chantal and the infant Colette in my previous vision. I decided that it had to do with my focus then being on Colette and the circumstances of her disappearance—extraneous elements had not been shown. Or maybe even then Phineas House had been extending its protection to its residents. I simply didn't know, and it didn't seem important that I know now. What was important was learning whether this time I would be able to cross the threshold and learn what had gone on inside.

I hugged as close as I could to Chantal, all but treading the heels of her shoes as she went up the steps to the front porch. A servant opened the door as she approached, and to my great delight, I passed inside with Chantal.

The entry foyer retained many of the furnishings that were there in my day: the umbrella urn and coatrack were familiar friends, as was a narrow table. This held a tray for cards, a basket for outgoing mail, and an ebullient arrangement of roses. What was missing were the mirrors that the adult Colette had hung everywhere. The only one that remained was set in the middle of the coatrack.

Chantal automatically checked her reflection as she came in. She was a good-looking woman who was probably very pretty when she made the effort, an effort she had not made merely to take the baby out into the house's private garden.

"Beatrice," Chantal said to the serving woman who had opened the door, a short, dumpy woman who was definitely *not* one of the silent women. "Would you take off my shawl for me? Little Colette has fallen asleep and I don't want to wake her."

"Yes, ma'am," Beatrice replied, moving immediately to do so.

Chantal's accents were colored with her native France, but Beatrice spoke with a flat American accent that for all its almost monotone respectfulness managed to sound vaguely disapproving.

"I'm going to take the baby up to the nursery," Chantal went on. "If Felicity is in the kitchen, have her come up immediately."

"Yes, ma'am." Beatrice sounded even more unhappy, and I guessed that she and this Felicity—probably the nursemaid—must not get along.

But this exchange was of passing interest to me. I had been looking side to side, moving as far from Chantal and the infant as my invisible tether would permit me. Nowhere did I spot the adult Colette. Had the kaleidoscope misunderstood me and taken me to see my infant mother, not realizing that the actions of the adult Colette were what interested me?

I gave an internal sigh. Never mind. If there was a mistake, I had allowed enough time for me to rest from this ordeal and try again before midnight. I'd succeed in confirming that Sunday's kaleidoscope would let me view past events, and that alone meant this was not a wasted venture.

Chantal went up the main stair, and I shivered just a little when I remembered that her husband would fall to his death some nine years later, a death caused, if the gossip of a ghost was to be believed, by the baby girl who now drowsed with such contentment in her mother's arms.

I was drawn after Chantal into the nursery, and immediately felt a spark of triumph. The adult Colette was waiting there, sitting in a comfortable chair by a window that overlooked the garden. The room was furnished with a crib for the baby, various dressers and wardrobes, and a bed in which, doubtless, the nursemaid, Felicity, slept. The doors to the connecting rooms were closed, but I guessed that the room that would someday serve as my playroom had already been furnished for the amusement of a child too young even to roll over, much less to play with toys.

The adult Colette watched the entrance of her mother and infant self with cool calculation. A moment later, a buxom, broad-hipped woman came in, a little boy clinging with one hand to her skirts, with his other to a battered toy. The woman was Felicity, no doubt, nursemaid and, quite possibly, wet nurse as well.

Chantal handed over her child with trusting ease. "I think she's wet, Felicity. See if you can change the diaper without waking her."

"Yes, ma'am," Felicity replied with competent calm, accepting the transfer of the infant to her arms. "I'll do as you say."

Chantal left after bestowing a kiss on her baby's brow. The little boy had detached himself from Felicity's skirts and now crouched by the bed, murmuring to himself as he played with his toy. Felicity gave him a brief smile, then moved to check the infant's diaper, unwrapping layer after layer of lacy blanket to do so.

Adult Colette rose from her seat and watched intently as the nursemaid tended to the drowsy baby. Colette looked distinctly displeased when, after the diaper was changed and the baby clean, Felicity moved as if to put the baby in her crib. Colette's tension ebbed when the baby began to fuss and Felicity gave up all attempts to put her in her crib. Instead, Felicity began to walk around the room with a measured tread meant to lull little Colette back to sleep.

Adult Colette was less pleased when Felicity opened her dress and set the baby to her nipple. I was standing near my mother now, but all I could make out of her mutterings was something that sounded like ". . . don't need your tit."

Time passed as Felicity nursed the drowsy infant, continuing her pacing as she did so, humming a lullaby under her breath. Colette paced with her, her motions that of a stalking predator, her gaze alert, her mood shifting with Felicity's every motion.

Eventually, I discerned a pattern in adult Colette's reactions. Whenever Felicity's pacing took her near the room's one mirror—a large one, mounted in a free-standing frame—Colette grew tensely excited. Whenever Felicity drew away, especially when it looked like the nurse might put the baby in her crib or settle them both into the comfortable chair near the window, Colette grew agitated.

*Whatever she wants has something to do with the mirror, then*, I said, *but I can't for the life of me guess what.*

Eventually, infant Colette stopped nursing and settled into a deep, milky sleep. Felicity, unable to hear the adult Colette's protests, settled in the chair near the window, obviously having decided that this was a better course than risking waking her charge during the transition into the crib.

Adult Colette wasn't thrilled by Felicity's choice, but then, when she moved nearer to the seated nurse and child, her mood brightened noticeably, her expression became calculating. Confident now that I could be seen by none of the participants in this peculiar scene, I moved to stand behind Colette and learn what had so pleased her. As soon as my angle of vision matched Colette's I understood at once.

Felicity and the infant were both reflected in the windowpane. The lighting was just right, so that the reflection gave back not shadowy images, but ones almost as good as what you'd get from a mirror, complete to a wash of pale color.

Colette was plucking her gloves off of her fingers now, tucking them into her skirt-pocket, rubbing her hands together as if to awaken whatever sensitivity the gloves might have removed. Then she leaned forward, hands coming together as if she would lift her infant self from the nursemaid's hold. Instead, to my astonishment, she reached past the living child and her hands went up and into the reflected image on the windowpane.

Colette reached as if to pull the reflected child forth, but though she made contact with the nurse's arm, moving the reflected image just slightly back from the child, so that image no longer matched reality, her fingers slipped through the child Colette's image.

Adult Colette straightened, as if as surprised at this result as I had been at her attempt. Then she folded her hands in front of her waist in an almost prayerful attitude, closed her eyes, and breathed deeply in and out.

*Calming herself*, I thought. *Refocusing*.

After several minutes during which I noticed to my fascination that the living Felicity unconsciously shifted her arm so that it now matched the position of its reflection, adult Colette opened her eyes once more. The intensity of her focus was so acute that I found myself glad her back was to me, for it seemed impossible that she would not see me. Under that intense gaze, the images in the windowpane grew more concrete, colors deepening, depth of field expanding so that the reflection seemed as real as the reflected.

Or rather, part of it did. Felicity's reflection and that of the chair grew more solid, but that of the baby Colette remained as it had been, translucent, only lightly brushed with color. Nonetheless, adult Colette moved as if to lift the baby from Felicity's arms. Once again her hands passed through the reflection, coming away without the baby Colette she so obviously intended to take from its image.

Now I saw Colette's anger building. She paced back and forth across the room, but as was always her way, her anger did not externalize, it focused inward, fueling her thoughts, making her more, not less, calculating.

Eventually, Colette returned to Felicity's side. Again she reached into the reflection, but this time she did not try to take the infant. Instead she gave the nurse's bare forearm a hard pinch, twisting the supple flesh cruelly. A red mark appeared instantly, but only in the reflection. With a startled exclamation, Felicity broke from her meditative silence.

Baby Colette whimpered drowsy protest, and the little boy looked up from his game and said, "What's wrong, Mama?"

Felicity rose from the chair, craning to see her arm, but adult Colette had chosen her spot well. Felicity could not see that portion of her forearm without putting the infant down. With little Colette balancing between going back to sleep and waking into a screaming fit, the nurse wisely chose not to put the child down.

Instead Felicity walked toward the big mirror, saying to her son as she did so, "A horsefly must have bitten me. Watch for one, my boy, but don't make a sound going after it. The baby's fussy and we don't want to wake her."

The little boy dropped his toy and began scouting the room for the horsefly, his eyes gleaming with pleasure at this new game. In front of the mirror, Felicity twisted to see the reflection of her damaged forearm, hunting for the mark her nerves told her should be there. As she made her futile search, adult Colette came up beside her. Confidently, she reached into the mirror, grabbing at the child's reflection, but as within the windowpane, her fingers slipped through.

After several attempts, adult Colette seemed to acknowledge she could not succeed at whatever she was attempting. Coldly furious, she gave Felicity's reflection another pinch, taking care not to pinch hard enough that the nurse would unsettle her infant charge. Felicity yelped again.

"Go to the kitchen, Tommy," Felicity said to her son, "and ask the cook nicely if you might have a baking soda paste on a cloth. We've found no flies in here, so I must be getting a rash, and that will soothe it."

Tommy scampered away, and adult Colette followed him out the open door. I found myself drawn after her as she went down the stairs and out the front door, drawing her gloves on as she went. When Colette opened the front door, the vision began to fade, and soon I was back among the fantastical garden of gold and crimson flowers, feeling oddly apprehensive, and more puzzled than before.

When I awoke from my post-scrying nap, I was alone in my bedroom. What I was now thinking of as the usual headache and bone-penetrating weariness were gone, but I made no move to get up. A glass of water rested on a coaster on the bedside table. I propped myself up to drink, and thought about what I had seen.

Colette had gone at great risk into her own past, apparently to steal her own reflection. It didn't make sense. I thought about everything I had read about reflections, about how some primitive peoples believed reflections and shadows contained the essence of a person, that person's soul.

Why would Colette try to steal her own soul? What good would that do her? Try as I could, I simply couldn't make sense of what I had learned. My bladder was protesting the additional water I had drunk, and so I found my robe and went into the bathroom.

A long shower to rinse the cobwebs from my thoughts seemed like a good idea, though I felt rather guilty about a second shower in one day. The summer monsoons had never come, and mandatory water restrictions were in place in Santa Fe. Las Vegas hadn't gone quite that far, but people were being asked to conserve water whenever possible.

"Another rainless year," I thought, settling for giving myself a cold rinse with a sponge. "Like the year in which I was born, the year my mother carried me."

One of the silent women was waiting for me in my bedroom.

"The gentlemen are out in the yard, talking. Shall I summon them to you?"

"Thank you," I replied, "but no. I'd like to go outside. It looks like a lovely afternoon."

"Very good," the silent woman said. "We're pleased you are feeling stronger."

She exited the room by the door, but I had a feeling that if I were to hurry and peek out, she wouldn't be there. It was disquieting in a way, but even more disquieting was the fact that I was coming to take such things for granted.

## 28

I am all the daughters of my father's house,
And all the brothers too.
—William Shakespeare,
*Twelfth Night*

### INSIDE THE LINES

Mikey and Domingo turned as one when I emerged from the kitchen door into the garden. Blanco, stick in his mouth, came bounding across to greet me. I bent and tossed the stick toward my friends, then followed it.

"Feeling better?" Mikey asked. "You look it."

"Thank you," I said, dipping a shallow curtsey that wasn't quite mocking. "I appreciate hearing that."

There was an almost full pitcher of hand-squeezed lemonade on the garden table. Two of the glasses on the accompanying tray showed use, but a third sitting rim down was clean. I noticed that the glassware wasn't anything I recognized and looked at Domingo.

"Is the lemonade your handiwork?"

He nodded. "Please, help yourself. Are you hungry? I can get something for you to eat."

After pouring a glass of the lemonade, I settled myself in my usual chair.

"No thanks. I grabbed a cheese sandwich on my way out. That's filled the crevices. Amazing how using those kaleidoscopes burns everything right out of me. I'd make a fortune if I could market this as a diet plan."

Mikey patted his own ample girth. "I fear using liminal space is not always a weight-loss plan, my dear. As I have said before, I think something is blocking you, making this harder than it should be."

I shrugged. "I have no idea what that could be, but I do have a bit more information. I know what Colette went back in time for, and why she got angry enough that she lost her way home. What I don't know is why she did what she did."

I told them then, and though Mikey had a few questions, mostly they listened in intent silence.

When I finished, Mikey said, "What immediately comes to mind is what you overheard Colette saying in yesterday's vision. How did it go exactly?"

I recited, " 'I suppose I'll need to return the one before I can have another. What a bother! I've made the trip twice now, and hoped never to risk a third.' "

We stared at each other, then Domingo spoke very slowly, very carefully, as if he feared to give offense.

"You said it seemed Colette was trying to steal not the baby, but the baby's reflection."

I nodded.

"And from what you overheard," Domingo continued, "it sounds as if she had been successful before."

"You mean that she had already stolen the baby's reflection," I said, feeling very strange. "And that she intended to do so again, but that for some reason she couldn't."

"Not for some reason," Mikey said firmly, "for the precise reason that she had already done so. You said the baby's image looked paler than the nurse's. It seems that on this last trip Colette discovered she could not take away the baby's image because she had already done so—and that she planned to return the first image in order to steal it afresh."

"That doesn't make sense!" I protested, though somewhere in my gut it did. "Why steal what she already had? Why take the risk again?"

"Why," Mikey said reasonably, "do we ever redo an action? One reason is because we enjoyed it the first time. Another is because we hoped to better our first attempt—like when people keep running the same marathon or playing the same golf course. Another reason is because we made some mistake the first time and want to rectify that error."

"Or," I said, with the insight of an artist, "you're just fascinated with a particular technique or view or whatever and can't help doing it again."

"I think," Mikey replied, "that we can leave out the last. Colette did say that this was something she had hoped not to need to do again—presumably, she didn't want to make the second trip either."

"Okay," I said, feeling oddly grumpy. "We'll discount that last. I think we can reject her doing it again because she enjoyed it. That also makes it unlikely she was trying to better some past attempt—unless there's some prize offered for what she did."

"Not that I've ever heard," Mikey said.

"Then that leaves trying to rectify some error—apparently some error in her own infancy," I said. "Do you think Colette was responsible for tuning her infant self to Phineas House? It's always been something of a mystery why it bypassed Nikolai for his daughter."

Domingo said in the same deliberate tones as before, "You are forgetting, Mira. Colette spoke of having to return the one before she could take the other. Take, not tune or tend. Take."

"So maybe she took the image so she could work her tricks on it elsewhere," I said stubbornly. "Maybe she took the image, messed up, figured she could do a correction on the original, then discovered she had to basically reset the experiment in full before she could make it right."

"I think it was something like that," Domingo said, "but I think that also we have no idea what her experiment was. Maybe it is, as you say, something like attunement to Phineas House. Maybe something else. How will we know unless we ask her?"

"There may be something in her papers," Mikey said. "There have been times when you've been asleep, Mira, that I've been tempted to go through them more thoroughly, but I didn't want to invade your privacy."

"Thank you," I said, my voice icy. "I appreciate that."

Mikey looked rather surprised at my hostility. "I told you I didn't look."

"I'm sorry," I relented. "I think the strain is getting to me. Let's go back to what Domingo just said. We're not going to find out unless we can ask Colette herself. I've been thinking about how we might do that."

"Oh? Another attempt with the kaleidoscopes?" Mikey asked.

"No," I said. "The kaleidoscopes show, sometimes in exquisite detail, but they don't seem to allow any interaction. I need to be able to talk to her, ask her questions."

Mikey's eyebrows raised. "Are you thinking of trying to duplicate Colette's trick—go back in time?"

I bit my lip. "Not in time. I don't think that's necessary. I think she's still alive, at least in a way, suspended out there in probability. I think that's the source of this block you sense. I think Phineas House doesn't know whether Colette or I am its proper—I hate the term 'master.' Not only is it sexist, but it makes it sound like Phineas House is a slave."

"Operator?" Domingo suggested. "Since Phineas House was designed as a tool?"

"That'll do," I said, flashing him a quick smile. "Operator. When I just muddle about the house, it's fine, but when I try and use Colette's things, inquire after Colette, the House gets conflicting signals—gets confused."

"I see your point," Mikey said, "so if you don't plan to use the kaleidoscopes how do you intend to find her?"

"By using Phineas House," I said with a decisiveness I didn't feel. "I think it's tuned both to me and to her. What I need to do is find a way to open a channel or pathway between those two points. Can you help me figure out how to do it?"

"I can try," Mikey said, "but, Mira, even if Colette is alive, even if you can reach her, do you realize that you would still be taking an enormous risk? She's been roaming the edges of probability for over forty years now. That's going to have stirred up all sorts of forces. It's also quite likely that after forty years in exile she's not completely sane."

"If she ever was." I shrugged. "It's either try or give up. I'm all for trying."

"But not today," Mikey said sternly. "Maybe not tomorrow either. You need to build up your reserves."

I met his gaze squarely. "I should think you would want me to hurry. After all, I'm keeping you away from your home."

Mikey shrugged. "I've taken business trips all my adult life. This isn't much different, and it's a lot easier than in the days when a long-distance phone call cost a king's ransom."

I didn't ask why he hadn't just used liminal space to commute home. Not only did I now have a realistic idea of the risks and costs involved, I could imagine the purely mundane complications of not being where you should be when some client came calling.

Mikey went on. "Let me have a day or two to tutor you. I'd like to promise that I could go with you, but frankly, this close to Phineas House the currents . . ."

He shrugged. I nodded understanding. Even if the trustees did benefit somewhat from Phineas House's abilities, the House was not a reliable tool—and if my guess that Colette was in some way alive was correct, that reliability was going to be even more in question.

"I can't see how taking some lessons would hurt," I said. "As long as you don't mind being kept away from home . . ."

"I can manage," Mikey said.

Domingo had sat silently listening to this rather esoteric discussion. Now he cleared his throat. "Not to change the subject, but I have something that might amuse Mira."

Something in the tone of his voice made me wonder if "amuse" might not be the best word to describe what Domingo meant.

"What?" I replied guardedly.

"I did some more family research," he said. "Your friend Chilton O'Reilly, the reporter, was a help to me with this."

"Research?"

Domingo indicated a large manila envelope resting on the table. "I thought you might like to see pictures of your family—my family, too, which is why I was curious. Like Mikey, I didn't wish to go through your library, and the one thing Phineas House seems to lack is the usual solemn portraits of ancestors gone by. Then I thought that such a prominent family in Las Vegas's history might well have appeared in the newspapers. Chilton was a great deal of help in finding what I wanted. I think he now dreams of doing a story . . ."

I thought of how the reporter kept spinning new story ideas from prior ones and laughed. "That sounds like Chilton. So you two dug up some old pictures?"

"A fair number," Domingo said, his face lighting in response to my laughter. "Take a look."

The envelope was filled with photocopied news-clippings. Where the captions did not make clear who was pictured, identification had been written at the bottom.

"So that's Aldo Pincas," I said, looking at the first. "He's a determined-looking fellow—severe."

"Part of that may have been the photography of the time," Mikey said, looking over my shoulder with interest. "Fast films like we have today weren't known, and photographers usually asked their victims to hold a pose or expression."

"This the only picture you've seen of old Aldo?" I asked.

"Not the first," Mikey said. "I think I've even seen this one. I do have to admit, he never looks much friendlier."

As I methodically worked my way through the stack, I noted that Domingo had included collateral members as well as the main line. He'd even found one of his line's founder, Aldo's son, Fernando. Few of the photos were candid, but members of Aldo Pincas's family seemed well-represented in various civic organizations, charitable institutions, and benevolent clubs. I wondered if they'd really been so public spirited, or if this was merely a way for a family with an odd reputation and peculiar habits to stay in good with the community in which it lived.

I was shuffling through the stack, enjoying myself greatly, when in the midst of a crowd scene I spotted a familiar face. The caption at the bottom noted that the men in the photo had been the organizing committee for a fund-raiser to benefit the local fire department. In blue ballpoint pen was written below: Nikolai Bogatyr, middle row, third from right.

I counted. That was the familiar face. I stared, disbelieving.

"Mira?" Mikey said.

When I'd started going through the pictures, he'd taken a seat on the chair to my right and I'd been sliding each copy over to him as I finished. I'd held on to this one, and was looking at the next one, my heart beating so fast I thought I'd choke. It was a solo shot of the same man, the same face depicted even more clearly. This time the newspaper's own caption identified him as Nikolai Bogatyr.

"Mira?" Mikey said. "What's wrong?"

I ignored him, looking directly at Domingo.

"This man, this photo," I said, pointing to the group shot, "how did you identify him?"

"The text of the article did so, quite plainly," Domingo said. "I suppose there were too many names to put in a caption."

I sagged, confusion replacing that heart-thumping moment of panic and fear.

"Mira," Mikey said, pulling the pictures out of my hand. "What's wrong? This is Nikolai Bogatyr, Colette's father, your grandfather."

"You don't understand," I said, my voice coming out choked and hoarse.

"That's the face of the man the kaleidoscope showed me when I asked who my father was. I think that second picture is even one of the same pictures. How could my father be Nikolai Bogatyr?"

Mikey looked as astonished as I felt, but Domingo only looked troubled—and sad.

"I have been wondering," Domingo said slowly, "ever since you told us that the man in the picture was dressed in old-fashioned clothing, and that the images seemed to only last nine or ten years. I kept thinking about how Colette's father died when she was nine or so . . . It seemed a great coincidence that your father, too, would die that many years after his daughter's birth. I asked Mikey questions about how long family members tended to live, about size of families, number of children . . ."

"And here I thought you were just interested in your own genetic heritage," Mikey chuckled, though his shock was still visible.

"You forget," Domingo said. "I know my family for many generations, but I could see why you did not wonder about my questions, and that suited me."

"Beware innocent questions," Mikey said. "They may hide devious purpose."

"Who said that?" Domingo asked.

"I did," Mikey said. "Doesn't make it less true, does it?"

I listened with half an ear, aware that the men had prolonged their banter to give me a chance to recover from my shock. I stared down at the pictures of Nikolai Bogatyr, found several more below the first two in the pile. There was no doubt. The man who the kaleidoscope had shown me was Nikolai Bogatyr. As much as I wanted to believe the instrument had been in error, that it had shown me my grandfather, not my father, I knew this was not so. There was a simpler explanation—and it wasn't incest.

"I'm her?" I said. "I'm really her?"

It was too much like my childhood nightmares to be believed easily, yet ironically, that earlier suspicion was at heart the truth.

"You're not Colette," Mikey said. "You're her reflection, her reverse, not her."

Domingo reached out and touched my hand. "Mira, however you started, you have lived your own life, had your own experiences. You are not your mother—no matter what your origin."

"But why?" I whispered. "Why did she do this? Is it because Phineas House demands continuity?"

Mikey's comment seemed a non sequitur. "It would be very interesting to know Colette's medical history. I wonder if she ever had an abortion."

I shook my head and looked at him. "What?"

"It is well-known that Colette had many lovers, but as far as we know, you are her only child. I wonder what her medical records might show."

"But an abortion?"

"Colette's adventures took place before there was reliable birth control," Mikey explained. "The likelihood that she would have become pregnant is high, but you are her only child."

I nodded, understanding, now. "You're wondering if Colette might have been sterile, aren't you?"

"That's right," Mikey said. "It is far from impossible. She was her parent's only child. We've speculated that Phineas House might have indulged in some special selection, but the answer might be easier—inherited low fertility."

"Or she might have suffered an illness or injury," Domingo said. "My Tia Maria had a high fever when she was a young woman, and after that . . ."

He shrugged, too polite to go further into such personal detail. I looked back and forth between the two men.

"I suppose," I said slowly, "I might ask at the State Hospital to see if Colette's records are still on file. They might tell something. There might be copies of her medical records somewhere in the files in the House, too, but does it matter? We know what she did—or at least we can guess."

Mikey heaved himself out of his chair. "It will matter to you, Mira. Let's go look inside. If we fail to find anything, then we'll try the hospital."

I didn't have the energy to protest. Mikey was right. I needed to know—or rather, I wanted to know. I wanted to know anything that would help me understand the enigma that was my mother—although, as with everything else about Phineas House, it seemed the more I knew, the less I understood.

But that isn't true, is it, Mira? I asked myself. Finally, you are beginning to understand how the jigsaw puzzle fits together. The truth is, you don't like what you are learning, so you pretend to still be confused.

The three of us went inside, but though we methodically searched through files, desk drawers, books, and even a few boxes we found at the back of a closet, we found nothing related to Colette Bogatyr's medical history.

"Shall we call the hospital then?" Mikey asked, his hand half-reaching for the phone book.

I shook my head. "No. In the end, it doesn't matter—and we'd only be guessing anyhow."

"It doesn't matter?" Mikey asked. "I think it does."

I shook my head again. "I've been thinking about it all this time. It doesn't really matter whether or not Colette had a medical reason she couldn't bear a child. If she wanted to solidify her claim to Phineas House and the heritage of Aldo Pincas, there were other ways. She knew her relatives, remember. It wasn't like with me. She knew them—had reason to be grateful to them, especially to her trustees. She could have adopted a child, maybe had a series of children come through and see how Phineas House reacted to each one. You've said that the talent happens outside of the family, occurs even at random. Colette had lots of options, both within and without the Pincas bloodline—but she chose this."

I waved my hands In front of myself, as you might to draw attention to a new outfit.

"She chose this," I repeated. "We can guess why, but only she knows for certain why she did it."

Domingo looked from where he stood, a dusty file folder he was restoring to its place still in his hands.

"So, you are still going to try to find her, are you?"

I nodded. "Now more than ever I need to resolve this. Did I ever tell either of you that when I was a very small child I thought I was my mother's reflection? I thought that if anything happened to her, I would vanish away? It took me years to overcome that belief, and I think it haunted my nightmares long after I thought I had forgotten. I have to find her, to see her, to make sure I'm . . . well . . . real."

The two men listened, each perfectly still, as if they were the images, not me. I went on, hearing myself articulate thoughts as they took shape in my mind.

"Don't you remember what Colette said? That bit about having to put the one back before she could draw out another? Something went wrong with her experiment, something severe enough that she risked another trip into her past in an attempt to fix it. I'm what went wrong. I want to know what went wrong."

Mikey frowned. "Mira, no child ever is what their parent imagines they will be. Sometimes they achieve more, sometimes less, sometimes merely different things. Have you forgotten that your mother was insane?"

I rose from my chair and brushed dust off my skirt. "I'm waited on by women who don't exist. I talk to my house and let it pick its own colors. I expect there are psychiatrists who would happily write me a prescription for something to 'calm my nerves.' Colette may have been no more insane than you or I, just less fortunate."

"Mira . . ."

I shook my head, interrupting whatever reasoned argument Mikey wanted to offer. "I've made my mind up. The only thing left is for you to make up your own."

"Make up my mind?" Mikey replied, his expression blank and confused.

"Are you going to help me?" I asked. "Or not?"

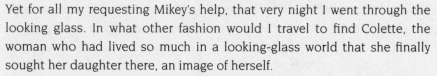

Yet for all my requesting Mikey's help, that very night I went through the looking glass. In what other fashion would I travel to find Colette, the woman who had lived so much in a looking-glass world that she finally sought her daughter there, an image of herself.

I went alone through that looking glass, with no waving of wands or reciting of spells, nor even a prince's favor tucked in my sleeve. I left that same night, leaving Mikey, my good teacher, asleep in his bed, and Domingo Navidad alone with his dreams. If he dreamed of me, I don't know, but I do know I thought of him as I left.

*Let Domingo be my heir should I fail to return*, I said to the House that surrounded me. *He loves you and has cared for you all his life. He will do well by you—and unlike me, he is not too old to sire an heir to carry the tradition onward.*

Why did I leave with such certainty I would not return that I made this bequest? Why didn't I wait and study under Mikey's beneficent guidance a few days longer? After all, forty-some years had passed since Colette had vanished. What would a few more days matter?

Waiting was my intention when I went up to the room I had made my own, and slept in the bed in which I sincerely doubted any of Colette's lovers had ever passed a night, for all the room had been "theirs." I had washed and slipped naked between the clean, lavender-scented sheets, listening to the night sounds outside the partially open window. Sleep, for all I was tired to the bone, would not come.

Eventually, I rose, put on loose trousers and a tee shirt, slid my slippers onto my feet, all with the intention of going down to the kitchen and making myself a cup of mint tea with plenty of honey. Mikey was sleeping in one of the other guest rooms. When I saw light from under the door of Colette's room, I thought he had violated my hospitality and gone snooping.

I strode across the landing, at first with purpose, but then my footsteps began to falter. The light coming out from under the door was the wrong color. It was neither the glaring gleam of electric lighting, nor the dimmer, warmer flickering glow of candlelight. Nor did it have the furtive, shadow-producing quality of a flashlight.

This light had a cool, bluish glow. For a moment, I thought someone had turned on a television in there, but dismissed that immediately. There were no televisions in Phineas House, certainly not in Colette's private room. I thought then of a computer monitor. Had Mikey carried a laptop with him?

Again, that didn't seem right. In the end, I stopped puzzling, kept moving, and put my hand on the doorknob. It turned easily, startling me, for I knew perfectly well that I had made a practice of keeping both Colette's room and the upstairs parlor locked. I turned the knob, though, and went inside, still half-expecting to surprise Mikey, already framing responses to his probable excuse that he had been doing it all for my own good.

But when I opened the door and crossed the threshold, I found the room empty. The bluish light held touches of purple and red, oddly coloring the white and gold with which Colette had decorated her boudoir. Its source was neither lamp nor lantern nor candle, but the three mirrored panels that framed my mother's vanity.

The light thrust forth at an angle, refuting those rules that say light must always move in a straight line. A straight line would have touched one of the few walls on which a mirror did not hang. I suppose Colette did not like to see her back reflected when she sat at the vanity.

This light extended for about a yard, then turned at an acute angle so that it illuminated the full-length portrait of Colette. I turned to look, and saw the picture had changed. No longer was it Colette in her archaic finery. Instead it showed the scene I had viewed repeatedly in both nightmare and kaleido-scope vision: Colette and her elegant gig, patient Shooting Star between the shafts, trotting forward along a road that twisted and fragmented, hardly a road any longer, but rather the potential of many roads, all evident, all manifest, each fragmenting the traveller as she sought to make her way home.

I stood staring at the painting for a timeless stretch of time, viewing every detail. Then I turned toward the threefold mirrors. I knew enough now not to be deceived. The painting might seem to be the image, but I knew this was not the case. The image was the reality, the painting a reflection of a reflection.

My hand dipped down into the drawer where the teleidoscopes were stored, moving as if it had undone the secret compartment hundreds of times, rather than a half-dozen or so. I fished one of the smooth wooden cases out at random, trusting that I would not choose wrongly. Then I centered myself in the light and walked forward, directly into whatever it is that lies behind the looking glass.

29

It is said that the sunlight reflecting off their armor as they [the Valkyries] ride on the gods' errands causes the shimmering colors of the Northern Lights.
—Jeannine Davis-Kimball, Ph.D., with Mona Behan,
*Warrior Women*

## INSIDE THE LINES

I found myself in a realm of translucent silver and frosted chucks of broken crystal, interconnected by a fine network of spiderweb cracks.

The piece of crystal on which I stood bobbed slightly beneath my weight, as if I stood upon an iceberg, but when I knelt ever so carefully to see what the crystal floated upon, I found no break between it and the next piece. Silver and crystal were one flexible entity.

I looked side to side, up and down, and back behind me, but I saw no change in the landscape that surrounded me. Nor was there any sign of Colette and her horse-drawn gig.

"Now what?" I said aloud, and the sound of my voice flattened out as sounds do in vast areas where there is nothing for them to reverberate from.

Then I remembered the teleidoscope I held in my hand. I raised it to my eye and gasped at the transformation.

I had expected the translucent landscape to be duplicated and reduplicated, perhaps into snowflake patterns. I had not taken into account the color I myself would bring to the landscape. The string trousers I had pulled on were pale yellow, my loose tee shirt eggplant purple, my slippers sheepskin brown, trimmed with wool. Then there were the colors of my skin, my hair, even my eyes and lips. These intermingled with the silver and crystal, seeming to bleed in between the cracks, giving dimension to the patterns formed by the inner mirror chamber, transforming cool ice into a richly glittering garden.

Did I walk through that garden? Over it? Beneath it? I really cannot describe what happened next. I know I moved, but the form of my locomotion was like nothing I had known before. It was something like the flitting of a butterfly from blossom to brightly colored blossom, something like the manner in which a prism splits light.

I was everywhere at once and yet there was no sense of dissolution or division. I was one as the rainbow is one and yet seven. I arched through the sky and yet was firmly rooted in the earth. The bobbing beneath my feet was no longer unsettling. I felt as if the surface on which I stood danced with me, sharing my delight.

Eventually, I lowered the teleidoscope, but to my immense delight the colors remained with me. I continued my exploration, chuckling as purple split into blue and red, as yellow blended with the blue and sparked forth stars of pale green, as red and yellow gave forth laughing orange that fountained up like jets from a roman candle, and came down again touched with violet and crimson teardrops.

In time I became aware of a thread that held within its twisted strands gold and white, black and bloodred, warm brown and shining chrome. I followed that thread for no reason at all but that it was different from anything else around me.

My movements as I followed it were sinuous. I lacked bone or body, swam on currents that were warm and welcoming, unfamiliar yet unfrightening. For the first time in my life I felt both graceful and beautiful, my blood humming within my veins, a song with music but no words coming from my lips.

The thread moved among my colors, tightly twisted, giving nothing to the panorama of marvels that shifted and surrounded me, encompassing me and making me a part of it without ever robbing me of a sense of self. The colors in the thread remained undiluted, yet they did not gain in vividness from this lack of dilution. Instead they were flat, dull in their solidity, enervated in their perfect containment.

Where at first I had followed the thread from curiosity, I continued out of a growing awareness that it would lead me to what I sought.

In my joy in joining with the dance of color the teleidoscope had revealed to me, I had temporarily forgotten that I had any purpose for being here. Indeed, I think I had forgotten that there was anything other than this place.

Now I remembered, but fear or hesitation did not come with that remembering. Confident as I had never been before, I paced though the tangle, tracing the thread. Green-eyed wildcats paced with me, darting in and out, pouncing the bending fronds of the multicolored jungle and the tips of each other's tails.

The thread met with another of its type, neither growing thicker or thinner at the juncture point, but fanning out from that point to continue wherever it was they went. I followed one at random, saw it touch another, then bounce away, touch another and go on. I wondered where these many threads went, and with the desire my perspective altered and I was looking out in all directions, up and down and to all sides. Now I saw the thread was not a thread at all, but warp and woof alike of a chaotic web, a network of roadways that might have been spun by a spider on LSD.

And in that moment I knew that I looked upon the wheel tracks cut through the space between space by Colette's forty year journey through trackless wilderness, a journey that left a road behind it, because she insisted there must be a road, and so trapped herself in the maze of her own confusion and conceit.

And here, too, I saw the dangers that Mikey Hart had warned me were there for those who treated too lightly with the thresholds between possibility, probability, and reality. These were not monsters or terrors—nothing so concrete. Rather they recalled sinkholes, mires, thick quicksand, sucking mud, drugged sleep, and fanatic fantasies.

These were the points where desire had become so strong that it bogged down the traveller, drawing her into dreams, swallowing her ability to perceive the difference between reality and phantasm. Here, then, was how Colette had lost her way. In her fury at being thwarted, she had set forth, thinking not of where she was going, but where she wished to be. The road she took led her there, giving her satisfaction but robbing her of direction until she was irretrievably lost.

I reached out and touched the web, running my finger along various strands until I found one that vibrated with regular motion. I led myself by those vibrations, an Ariadne in a labyrinth without walls, a labyrinth no less binding to the one who ran ceaseless through its confines.

I travelled only as long as my own needs demanded, gathering up my courage for a confrontation I dreaded nearly as much as I longed for it. Had I been less determined, I might have vanished into an infinity of indecision as Colette had done into an infinity of rage and indignation. But I was determined.

Colette's daughter I might be—even her reflection—but I was also the daughter of Maybelle Fenn. Aunt May had taught me to press on, to slide through the cracks between expectation and ability. I slid through the cracks now, emerging at last beside a dirt road where a beautiful woman with long black hair drove a horse-drawn gig toward some unseen goal. Her plum-colored dress was as fresh as the day she had donned it, her jewels sparkled as brightly, her skin was fresh and supple, but for all Colette externally seemed unwearied by her long drive, the eyes that met mine as I stepped out of my jungle onto her road were branded with each of the thousand thousand roads she had travelled.

Colette did not rein up the carriage, and her gaze passed through me as if I were not there. Shooting Star shied as she had not during my other encounters with them. By this sign I knew I was somehow present, that this was no vision, but the confrontation I had sought.

"Colette!" I called. "Colette Bogatyr. Stop a while. I would like to talk with you."

Her imperious gaze now rested on me, but I was of no importance to her, therefore, she did not register my existence. So it had been when I was a child and she was infuriated with me, so that she denied me. I felt a renewed pang of that child's fear, but I was not that child any longer. Moreover, I recognized that here there was no wish to personally reject me. Colette was being Colette, and anyone she did not have a use for was unimportant, unessential. It was only when she saw someone in relation to herself that this person became real—and then, as lovers, friends, and bosom companions had learned to their pain, when she no longer had need for them, they simply ceased to exist.

As a child I had never been angered by this behavior. It was simply the nature of my mother as it is the nature of the sun to be hot or of water to be wet. But I was no longer that child. Now I saw the persistent egocentrism of that pose. Fury I had not known was mine to feel raged within me. The air around me flashed hot and orange, heat lightning veined with thin green that I knew for envy and pale blue I knew for shame.

"Colette!" I snapped in a voice perfected in dozens upon dozens of class-rooms, a voice that could command attention from middle-schoolers who viewed art period as free time, not a privilege. "Colette Bogatyr! I want to speak with you!"

Colette turned her face in my direction, but she did not slow. I would have had to run to keep pace with the horse. I did not wish to allow her to subject me to that indignity, but I also recognized Colette would not slow her endless journey even to speak with the one person to demand her at-tention in all these years of wandering.

I leapt astride a green-eyed lion and steadied myself with hands wound in the great cat's thick black mane. The lion easily paced the carriage, even when Shooting Star broke into a faster trot. Now that I could look Colette in the eye and speak without gasping for breath, I found I was at a loss for words. Then I glimpsed my reflection in the mirrored locket she wore pinned to her bodice and words came without bidding.

"Don't you know me, Colette?" I asked, and I fear my tone was mocking. "Don't you see yourself in me?"

"Why should I?" she said, drawing herself up straight and folding her gloved hands over the reins a bit more tightly. "I have never seen you before in all my life."

"But you have, Colette," I said, and the mocking was gone, replaced with sorrow and a touch of fear. "I am Mira, Mira Bogatyr, your daughter."

"Mira," she said, but there was no recognition in the word. "My daugh-ter."

She said the last phrase over again slowly, repeated it a few times as if trying its taste in her mouth. Then she shook her head.

"I have no daughter."

"True," I said. "You had no daughter in the usual sense, but there was someone who for nine years you called your daughter. I am she."

Colette looked at me, and I saw no recognition in her eyes.

"You cannot be that Mira. You're too old."

"Even children grow up, Colette."

She shook her head. "No. There was that Mira, but I put her back. She could not have grown up."

I had felt the web. I had seen where the tightly twisted thread ran, and I knew this for one of the junctures where the thread had met and split, running on in two directions.

"No, Colette." I couldn't make myself call her "Mother." "No. You may have dreamed that you did this, but you did not. You went into the past intending to draw forth your reflection once again, but you found you could not."

She looked at me blankly for a moment, then nodded as if only now remembering. "That is so. I hadn't realized a reflection couldn't be harvested more than once. Perhaps it was because the baby was so young. Still, I needed the baby to be young, otherwise there would be questions. I put the other back and drew a new one forth."

I shook my head. "No. That is a dream. You never made it back to Phineas House. The one was not put back, a new one was not drawn forth. You have been lost for forty years."

"Why have you come here?" Colette said.

"To ask you why you would have put me away," I answered honestly. Then with equal honesty I said what I had never voiced before, even to myself, "and to bring you home again."

She looked at me quizzically, and I saw my reflection again in her mirrored locket and did not wonder that Colette did not see her pale, colorless child in the half-century old woman who rode a lion alongside her carriage. I might have the hair and eyes of that child, but I was far from colorless. There was a brilliance to my gaze, a flush to my cheek, a lift to my head that gave dimension to my pale hues.

"I had to put the first one back to draw forth the new one," Colette said.

I recognized a bartering note in her voice. She had not admitted it aloud, but she knew she was trapped in this place between places, and she wanted very much to find the true road back.

"What was wrong with the first one," I asked, carefully not reminding her of my identity with that child, "that you needed to replace it?"

"I would have kept it," Colette said in a conciliatory tone, so that I knew she had not forgotten my claim to be Mira, "but I could not draw the second one forth without returning the first."

"So why did you need the second one?" I asked. I kept my tone level, clinical, though my heart screamed "Why didn't you need me? Why wasn't I good enough?"

"The first one was difficult to teach," Colette said, "and by the time I had learned how the teaching must be handled, she had learned things that she should not have. I wanted to begin again, afresh, so that everything would be right for her."

"Right for her," I repeated numbly, but what I thought was *Right for you, you mean.*

"That's right," Colette said, and her tone was bossy now, the one she used for ordering the silent women about. I think she was beginning to forget who I was, so that I was one of the many phantasms who must have appeared to her on this long road of rationalizations. "She had learned to play with color, and that would make her useless. Color is not to be externalized, but internalized. She was wasting a valuable ability. I wished to start over and make sure she was taught aright."

"Internalized?" I managed to ask, but I knew what she meant. I had sensed it on that day long, long ago.

"The first one," Colette said, "was already gone into drawing, to externalizing. That attenuates color because the world around you holds color and competes with your own. The real power of color is internalized—it is the glow that makes you the sun in every gathering, the fire that warms . . . or burns. I wanted my child, my heir, to have the power of color as I do. This first one would not, therefore, I must have another."

She said this as reasonably as I would discuss the need to change socks or sharpen a pencil. Replace one with the other, that's all. That's how it's done.

I didn't like to think what might have happened to little Mira if Colette had managed to draw forth another image and the House had maintained its bond with the first child. Doubtless, Colette would have disposed of a nine- or ten-year-old child as coolly as she had her father. Would she have felt more or less regret because that child was in some way herself? I didn't know, and I certainly wasn't going to ask.

As these thoughts went through my mind I felt a thickness in the air, a heaviness. My lion leapt with less power, the surrounding colors dimmed, just a trifle. I recognized what was happening in time to shake myself from my thoughts and concentrate on where I was. Too nearly had I fallen into the same trap as Colette had done. I had begun to live in might-have-beens rather than what was, to let my imagination build fantasies that could replace reality so thoroughly that I would never know when exactly I had been lost.

If Colette had seen the ripple in my personal reality, she did not comment. She continued to drive the carriage along the twisting dirt road, facing me as if we were chatting over tea and shortbread in the formal living room at Phineas House.

"Do you wish to come back?" I asked.

"Of course," she replied with a scornful laugh. "Isn't that why I'm driving this cursed nag along?"

"Things will have changed," I said. "More than forty years have passed since you rode out last from Phineas House."

"Forty years? Surely not!" She smiled a thin, contemptuous smile. "But then I forget. You claim to be my daughter grown old."

"I am," I said steadily. "Believe as you will, I am Mira, whom you called your daughter. What must I do to prove it to you? Shall I tell you things only an inhabitant of that house would know?"

Colette said nothing, but neither did she turn away. I began telling her. I told her things about herself, for she would not have noticed anything else. I described her private rooms, some of her favorite gowns, how she twisted her hair up and secured it with pins of amethyst and pearl. She listened as a cat is petted, luxuriating in the detail, knowing herself a worthy center of attention. She liked hearing what I said, but I could tell I was not convincing her.

So I switched the cadence of my tale, telling her instead some of Phineas House's secrets. I told her about the silent women and where they dwelled. I told her of the family tree in the Bible, and of the additions made to it in her own hand. Lastly, I told her of the kaleidoscopes and teleidoscopes: where they were hidden, and some of their powers. For final emphasis, I lifted my hand and showed her the teleidoscope I carried, cousin to the one she still held in one hand.

Now indeed did I have Colette's attention, and her gaze sharpened as she looked at me. I felt that now she saw me for the first time, and that her gaze was sorting through appearances, looking for correspondences between the child she remembered and the woman who rode alongside her carriage on a green-eyed, black-maned lion.

When she spoke, her tones were coaxing, but beneath the coaxing note was one of command. This was the voice she had used when she had some use for me, when she might trot me out like a warm-blooded doll to impress some caller with her maternal achievement.

"Come back with me, then, Mira, for I see now that you are indeed my daughter—my sweet reflection. Come back with me to the Phineas House of old, and we will make everything right again."

I looked at her, and am shamed to admit that I was tempted, though I knew what she was offering me was dissolution. Still, would that be so bad? I could forget everything that had gone before, and there would be a fresh start, a new beginning in a world where I would not live for decades with the vague sense that I had failed my mother.

"Come with me," Colette said soothingly. "In and out again we will go, then drive to a time when we can start afresh. The old world will vanish, a lesser probability, and we will make everything right."

I rose then on the lion's back, moving perhaps to join Colette in her carriage, in her mad dream, but I glimpsed my reflection in the mirror on her locket and saw myself. Vitality was draining from me, color fading. The vibrant woman of fifty was become a dull thing I hardly recognized as me.

Shooting Star shied. Colette grabbed the reins, and I looked around to see what had disturbed the placid bay. Wildcats were emerging from the dusty fringes of the road: spotted leopards and jaguars; tigers with erratic, zigzagging stripes; lions maned in night; lynxes with tufted ears; pumas with gold plush fur; cheetahs weeping dark tears. All of them had green eyes, eyes that glittered like emeralds and peridots, eyes like nothing in nature.

With them came memories. Balancing on a ladder, brush in hand, paint stippling the back of my hand as I shared a joke with Enrico. Standing beside Domingo, hearing the scratch of his pencil on paper as he made notes as to what colors we should next bring to the carousel brilliance that now adorned Phineas House's deep green sides. Sitting in the walled garden, looking at climbing roses that may have been old in my grandmother's day. The taste of coffee and a sweet roll heavy with pecans and mesquite honey.

Laughter in Domingo's eyes as we shared some joke. The gentle pedantry in his voice as he told me something of the confusing history of this bifurcated town he loved so much. The calm command as he set his little band of painters about their varied tasks. The respect he engendered, the trust. In them. In me.

I saw now that the green-eyed wildcats were in some way Domingo's gift to me. He had encouraged me to be the artist I had hidden from, hidden from, I thought because I feared who might find me through that talent, find me and make me go away as someone had made Colette go away.

Now I saw differently. I hadn't been hiding from an anonymous someone. I had been hiding from the same person all my life. I had been hiding from Colette, Colette who loved me best as an extension of herself. I didn't want to hide any longer.

With that realization Colette's hold over me dissolved as does sugar in a glass of boiling water.

"Color is the great magic," I said aloud. "You taught me that years and years and years ago as you sat before your mirror."

Colette looked frightened now, and slapped the reins across Shooting Star's back. The already terrified mare bolted, fleeing as she had fled for over forty years. My lion loped alongside, easily pacing the carriage. The flood of wildcats joined us, rippling fur in shades of golden brown, toasted tan, honey warm, and the fluffy white of clouds. The dusty road was beaten to oblivion under this host of velvet paws, and I welcomed relief from the drought stricken landscape.

"Child of a rainless year," I said aloud. "That's what you called me. I never understood why the rains didn't fall, not until now. Shall I tell you?"

Colette tensed, and said nothing, but I knew she listened.

"Rain washes away artificial color. Water, too, was the first mirror, the first thing in which any living being glimpsed its reflection. You have an affinity for mirrors, for reflections, don't you? So in learning of them, you learned also of water.

"But water is unpredictable; water washes away what you would keep. Standing water gives back the sky, but the falling droplets make the rainbow, splitting white light into color. You wanted the mirror. The rainbow you feared. Some say there's a pot of gold at the rainbow's end, but it's also a bridge by which gods come to earth—a guide to unimaginable riches, but full of unpredictable power.

"You don't like anything that's unpredictable, as living things are, and when you drew forth a child from the mirror, you sought to make it predictable—a child without water, child of a rainless year."

I knew I spoke nonsense, but I knew also that what I said was right in a fashion that had nothing to do with logic.

"You lock things within your mirrors. I can set them free. Ever since I knew the manner of my birth I have feared that I am you. I'm not, am I? I'm your reflection, your opposite. Therefore, if you bind the color, I exist to set it free."

I gripped the lion between my knees, feeling myself balancing upon his broad back with perfect ease. I shaped a brush out of air and desire, and used Colette as a palette. With the red of her lips I drew roses and poppies along the roadside. From the folds of her skirt I pulled the colors I needed to adorn a drought-seared tree with the clusters of purple blossoms, transforming it into a lilac bush alive with spring glory. A jeweled ring upon her finger gave me sapphire blue, but there was nothing I could use for yellow or green.

Then with a joyful laugh I realized I was trying too hard. The shining black of Colette's hair, like the shine of a raven's wing, held every color in its iridescence. Here was green, here yellow, here a hint of shining indigo. I chose my hues with abandon rather than care, painted as I had wished to paint, painted as I had denied myself since those years when fear rather than delight was what I associated with my art.

All around us my brush brought forth a jungle garden that Rousseau might have rejoiced to paint. Shooting Star had ceased running to graze on the verdure, and the great cats were lazing or yawning or climbing up trees to chase the violently colored birds and sleek brown monkeys. I set the unpredictable rainbow across the sky as my signature, and returned my attention to Colette.

She sat as she had sat, bolt upright in her carriage, her hands upon the reins, but those hands were still, and the reins slid limp to puddle at her feet. She was transformed, and for the first time I saw a likeness between us.

At my soft word, the lion knelt. I dismounted. Then I dipped my hands into a pond, holding them up dripping, keeping the liquid within motionless, so that it would give back a reflection.

"Will you look in the mirror now, Mother?" I asked. "Will you see yourself free of illusions? I can even take you home—but to the Phineas House of my day, my time. I have a life of my own, now. There is no returning me to the mirror and drawing forth another."

Colette moved her head stiffly, side to side, viewing the jungle that surrounded her. Vines surged up, embracing the carriage, bringing forth blossoms like giant morning glories, adorned in dewdrops that gave back sparks of shattered light.

"I see that," she said. "You are no longer my Mira."

"Look in the mirror," I urged. "Accept what is . . . It isn't bad at all."

Colette bent her head, unable to a resist a mirror, though I could tell she dreaded what she would see. She gazed at her reflection, seeing a Colette whose hair was pale, whose lips were pastel pink—not bloodred, and not nearly as full as she had always drawn them. She saw a Colette whose skin was unadorned with shading and shaping, so that the lines of her features were recognizable as the same—though I'll admit slimmer—than my own.

Colette drew in her breath in indignation.

"This isn't me."

"Colette, it is. It's you. You know it. You may have viewed this face as the blank canvas on which you did your art, but it's not. It's the reality. The other is the illusion. Look at me if you won't believe it. I'm your reflection. Your mirror."

She looked up from the water then, and deep into my eyes. I'd never realized that she, too, had those heat-haze eyes, grey with just a hint of blue. The cosmetics with which she had adorned them had brought out the blue, as well as giving them a far more exotic shape and dimension.

"No . . ." she hissed. "That's not me."

With a sudden jerking motion, Colette reached into the rainbow I had left as my signature on the sky, grasping as if she could take the color back into herself.

The rainbow wriggled in protest, opening a mouth like a viper's, complete with curving fangs that dropped venom that caught the light, splitting into an infinitude of other rainbows. But the rainbow did not pierce her with those fangs. Instead its mouth stretched wider and wider, sucking Colette up and in, absorbing her into its colors as she had once absorbed its colors into herself. I watched until I could no longer sort Colette from the colored droplets of mist. I watched for a long time after, then I turned away.

I don't know where Colette went after the rainbow swallowed her, whether she dissolved into the rainbow, or was carried across some bridge to a realm of the gods where she might be appreciated in the fashion she felt she should be. I don't remember how I got home again either.

All I remember is staggering back to my bedroom to the sound of rain beating against the roof. When I woke the next morning, I rose and went to look outside. The ground was still wet. A bay mare was browsing on the side lawn, and the wildcats had returned to the window frames.

## 30

There is something in the air of New Mexico that makes
the blood red, the heart beat high and the eyes look upward. Folks don't come here to die—they come to live
and they get what they come for.
> —Marian Russell,
> *Land of Enchantment: Memoirs of Marian Russell*
> *Along the Santa Fe Trail*

### INSIDE THE LINES

You don't adjust to something like that all at once, at least I certainly
didn't. I told Mikey and Domingo my story, and they listened without asking questions or scolding me for my impulsiveness. Mikey did a few things
that involved teleidoscopes and phone calls. After that, perhaps seeing
something in my eyes that I did not, Mikey packed his bags and went home.
He left several phone numbers and an e-mail address. I won't need a kaleidoscope to find him again.

Domingo found Phineas House's neighborhood wasn't zoned for a horse
any longer, so we placed Shooting Star in a local stable. I'll probably keep
her, though I can't ride. I can always learn, and if I'm no good at it, well, that
mare deserves a retirement. The carriage and Colette's teleidoscope seem
gone for good.

I went down to the Plaza and found Paula Angel. We went to a bar that doesn't exist and drank beer. She listened as I told her what had happened to Colette. Then she said something strange.

"I thought something big had happened. Everything feels different. It's like there's been more than that rainstorm. Something was hanging over the city. Now it's gone. Can't you tell?"

I didn't try to pretend I didn't understand. "Somehow I broke whatever made Phineas House divert liminality. It doesn't work in the fashion Aldo Pincas intended anymore. It's still an unpredictable place—any house with that many thresholds is going to be—but the hold Aldo Pincas established is gone—for good if I have my way."

"And you will, *amiga*," Paula said. "One thing that you have in common with Colette. You're both stubborn as mules."

"I have a lot more than that in common with Colette," I said, but I didn't clarify. I was still coming to terms with the peculiar circumstances of my . . . you can't really call it birth, since I was never born, and creation doesn't fit either, since Colette didn't create me, just stole a copy of her favorite thing. Herself.

Whatever. I was. Even though Colette was now gone I was still here. I'd decided to stay in New Mexico. Despite the changes, the silent women are still active in Phineas House. There's a lot more there to discover.

And, lest I fool myself far worse than Colette ever did, I should be honest. Domingo is also one of the reasons I'm staying. He's done a lot for me these last couple of weeks while I've been wandering around in something like shock. He's the one who suggested to me I write this down, get my thoughts in order, at least for myself. When I told him I wasn't much of a writer, he said it didn't matter.

So I started writing, and it came a lot easier when I started thinking of it not as a journal or an account, but as if I was telling Aunt May what had happened, just like I would when I'd come home from school and she'd look up from her housekeeping or the book she'd been reading and make time to listen. She always did.

Domingo's good at listening, too, and I find myself wanting to learn that skill, so he can have someone to listen when he needs an ear. Domingo's been alone a long time. I know what that's like. When I remember that first kiss, I think we're both going to be learning what it's like not to be alone.

I'm looking forward to it.

I had to do one thing before I could get settled in this strange new life. I waited almost a year to do it though, and it's not like I put things on hold while I did. Domingo doesn't stay in the carriage house anymore, for one, for another I'm teaching a few classes at the local high school: art for kids who are at risk. It feels good. This year when I go to the State Fair, I'll be looking at my student's work in the school show. I'm riding Shooting Star in a beginner's event, too.

A year to the day that Aunt May and Uncle Stan died, I stole away from Domingo's side in the bed we share in that front room. I went across the landing to Colette's suite. It's still furnished pretty much the same as she left it, but only because Domingo and I are still working out the details of how we'd like the suite to look when we take it over. Every time we think we've made up our mind, we find something new in some room or box or chest. I think Phineas House is playing with us. I really don't mind.

I sat at the vanity and opened the drawer where the kaleidoscopes are kept and pulled out Saturn's leaden one, the one meant to reveal secrets and hidden objects. I concentrated, thinking back to this day a year ago, hoping for a revelation. Even in my new happiness, I had remained haunted by the possibility that Phineas House might somehow have engineered Aunt May's and Uncle Stan's deaths to get me to Las Vegas. I had to know the truth.

The mandalas cleared quickly, easily, pulling back to show a clearing vision among a surrounding cloud of pale yellow stars. Then I was among the vision, above it, part of it, through it.

A familiar sedan drove down a quiet road I knew very well. I'd been there many times before the crash, but only once after. My heart hurt with raw grief as I looked with longing at Uncle Stan at the wheel, Aunt May at his side. She was talking. Her hand rested on his knee.

All at once a large cottontail rabbit ran out from the underbrush on the side of the road, right out in front of the car. Uncle Stan twisted the wheel in an attempt to avoid the rabbit. He did, but overcompensated. The car went out of control, hitting a tree. Both passengers were flung forward.

Tears flooded my eyes, blurring the details, even before the vision ended. I didn't need to see more. An accident. That was all. Just an accident. I wept with renewed sorrow, but with relief as well. They hadn't died because of me. It had just been one of those things.

I heard soft footsteps, looked up, tears making rainbows of the light from the hallway. Domingo touched my shoulder, took the kaleidoscope from me and set it safely away. He didn't ask why I was crying. I think he knew.

"Come back to bed, Mira, or maybe we could go downstairs. It will be morning soon."

We went downstairs where coffee was waiting along with sweet rolls. Holding hands, we rejoiced in the colors of the sunrise.

## OUTSIDE THE LINES

So, Aunt May, you kept a journal for me. I've been writing this account for you. You'll never read it—or maybe you will. Maybe you've been reading it all the while, looking over my shoulder as I type these words into my computer. Never mind. What's important is that I've tried to tell you. I've found the answers. That all they led to are a whole lot more questions is fine with me.

You gave me a way to accept such things once long ago, back when you were on your oriental religions kick. Remember that opening verse from the *Tao Te Ching*? I think I understand at last.

"The Way that can be known is not the eternal Way." That's because every Way we understand opens up a host of new possibilities. We all live in liminal space. I'm just lucky enough to see the lines.